DARK DEEDS
DOWN UNDER

EDITED BY
CRAIG SISTERSON
& LINDY CAMERON

Clan Destine
PRESS

First published by Clan Destine Press in 2022

PO Box 121,
Bittern Victoria 3918
Australia

Anthology Copyright © Clan Destine Press 2022

Story Copyright © Individual Authors 2022

All rights reserved. No part of this book may be reproduced or transmitted in any form or by any means, including internet search engines and retailers, electronic or mechanical, photocopying (except under the provisions of the Australian Copyright Act 1968), recording or by any information storage and retrieval system, without prior permission in writing from the publisher.

National Library of Australia Cataloguing-In-Publication data:

Editors: Craig Sisterson & Lindy Cameron

DARK DEEDS DOWN UNDER

ISBNs: 978-0-6453167-9-7 (hardback)
978-0-6453167-8-0 (paperback)
978-0-6453168-0-3 (eBook)

Illustrations:

Kiwi by Māori artist Māhina Bennett

Platypus by Noongar artist Seantelle Walsh

Cover design by Willsin Rowe

Design & Typesetting by Clan Destine Press

Cover image: Church of the Good Shepherd in Tekapo, South Canterbury, located in the Aoraki-Mackenzie international Dark Sky reserve.

For Peter George Sisterson
Teacher, parent, sportsman, mystery lover
A lifelong example: the best man I know
Aroha nui ahau ki a koe

Contents

Craig Sisterson   7
Introduction

Alan Carter   11
Takin' Out the Trash

Aoife Clifford   25
Summer of the Seventeen Poll

David Whish-Wilson   37
The Cook

Dinuka McKenzie   55
Skin Deep

Fiona Sussman   69
Hiding Something

Garry Disher   81
Sinner Man

Narrelle M. Harris   97
Observations on a Tragedy, Act One: Incitement

Helen Vivienne Fletcher   101
He Who Laughs Last

Katherine Kovacic   113
Water Damage

Kerry Greenwood   131
The Rooming House

Dan Rabarts & Lee Murray   141
Rock-a-bye Baby

Lisa Fuller   161
The Falls

Narrelle M. Harris   175
Observations on a Tragedy, Act Two: Complications

Nikki Crutchley   179
Save Me

Renée   191
Certain Kinds of Light

R.W.R. McDonald   201
Nancys Undercover

Shane Maloney   217
The Lost Murray Whelan

Stephen Ross   227
Mister Pig

Narrelle M. Harris   241
Observations on a Tragedy, Act Three: Denouement

Sulari Gentill   247
The Company of Rats

Vanda Symon   257
Top Dog

The Authors   271

Our Artwork/Acknowledgements   279

Introduction

Ahakoa he iti he pounamu.
Although it is small, it is greenstone.

Kia ora and g'day. Welcome to *Dark Deeds Down Under*, a special anthology of crime and thriller short stories from a diverse array of fantastic Australian and New Zealand storytellers.

Like many of you reading this, I'm a long-time fan of fictional tales of mystery, murder, and mayhem. I grew up in the top of the South Island of New Zealand trying to unmask villains and killers alongside the Hardy Boys, Hercule Poirot, Sherlock Holmes and Agaton Sax.

In the decades since I've enjoyed thousands of crime novels from many hundreds of authors all over the globe. Just over 14 years ago, I became an accidental book reviewer for a magazine (a late article meant a hole needed filling, right on deadline, and my editor asked if I'd 'read any good books lately'), then an intentional one for several others, in several countries. Author interviews, book awards judging, festival chairing and founding followed, in Australia and New Zealand, North America, UK, and beyond.

My love for the crime and thriller genre has grown since I was that sports-loving book nerd of a kid. This rich and wonderful form of storytelling delivers page-whirring puzzles and thrills while delving into some of the most important real-life issues of our time. And it comes bundled with evocative settings and fascinating characters who you want to follow not just through one book, but as many as possible.

The quality of modern crime fiction slays any wrongheaded notion that the genre is solely about plots or can't be great literature. In many ways, crime leads the way.

As global readers have discovered, today's Aussie and Kiwi crime writers are at the forefront, crafting cracking tales in vivid settings, with unforgettable characters in standalones and ongoing series.

So, I was absolutely thrilled when Clan Destine Press publisher,

Lindy Cameron, made me an offer I couldn't refuse: to collaborate on an anthology of Aussie and Kiwi crime tales.

Volume One of *Dark Deeds Down Under* is the result: 19 new stories from some of our finest legendary, established and new novelists.

'Ahakoa he iti he pounamu' is one of my favourite whakataukī, or Māori proverbs. It means 'although it is small, it is greenstone' – which is fitting. It's often used to signify the presentation of something precious and valuable, a small gift that's a treasure from the heart. Much like the short stories in our anthology.

Short stories are a wonderful form in of themselves. I still remember the thrill, more than 25 years later, of reading Richard Connell's 'The Most Dangerous Game' in high school English. And the jackhammer impact of Shirley Jackson's 'The Lottery'.

Dark Deeds Down Under will take you across a variety of antipodean landscapes, urban and rural and into the past, present, and future. It's a stunning smorgasbord of stories, styles, and settings.

Kerry Greenwood's baker-sleuth Corinna Chapman brings the pavlova. Kerry's fellow Ned Kelly Lifetime Achievement Award honouree Garry Disher gifts readers a new tale of South Australian constable Paul 'Hirsch' Hirschhausen.

Vanda Symon, a Pasifika queen of crime whose books have been shortlisted for major writing prizes on three continents, delivers a new Detective Sam Shephard crime involving a disappearance at a Dunedin animal shelter.

From Dan Rabarts and Lee Murray's award-winning Paths of Ra supernatural crime noir series come sibling investigators Penny and Matiu Yee. R.W.R. McDonald's raucous trio Tippy Chan, Uncle Pike, and Devon – aka 'the Nancys' – delight in a new addition to his Ngaio Marsh Award-winning series.

Katherine Kovacic's brings us Melbourne art dealer and amateur sleuth Alex Clayton, from her Ned Kelly Award-shortlisted series. The great Sulari Gentill gives long-time fans a prequel tale, featuring her beloved protagonist, artist and gentleman detective Rowland Sinclair.

Alan Carter, Ned Kelly and Ngaio Marsh Award-winning author – and Pom turned Kiwi turned Aussie – gives us a Sergeant Nick Chester story. Dinuka McKenzie, one of the freshest and most exciting new voices in Australian crime fiction, delivers a prequel to her Banjo Prize-winning debut *The Torrent*, featuring biracial Detective Sergeant Kate Miles.

The other half of *Dark Deeds Down Under* is made up of some superb standalone stories. Award-winners West Australian author David Whish-Wilson brings us meth, family, and revenge at a remote mineshaft; and Melbourne's Aoife Clifford goes more upscale with political fixers and vengeful families.

Nikki Crutchley immerses us in secrets by the beach, and award-winning Wuilli Wuilli storyteller Lisa Fuller delivers traditional justice. Narrelle M. Harris pulls the curtain back at a deadly play. Helen Vivienne Fletcher shows laughter may not be the best medicine. Fiona Sussman takes us on a chilling ride through the Southern Alps, and Stephen Ross spins a terrific wartime yarn about a young farm girl and a pig.

'Hang on, that's just 18 stories,' say the eagle-eyed among you. 'You promised us 19, Craig'.

Indeed. How do you feel about the first appearance in more than a decade of slightly shambolic political functionary Murray Whelan, who in six witty novels from 1994-2007 couldn't escape personal and political intrigue. Whelan earned his creator, Shane Maloney, a place among Australia's most popular novelists, and a Ned Kelly Lifetime Achievement Award. Howzat umpire? Good enough to get the nod?

Stories are not the only creative treasures herein. Keep an eye out for the platypus and kiwi that indicate where each author comes from.

These wonderful artworks were created especially for us by young First Nations artists Seantelle Walsh, a Noongar artist born and raised in Whadjuk country (Perth), and Māhina Rose Holland Bennett, a Māori artist (Te Arawa, Ngāti Pikiao, Ngāti Whakaue), based in Tāmaki Makaurau (Auckland).

So, like our platypus and kiwi, which use bills or beaks to uncover the tastiest treats, I hope you'll dig into *Dark Deeds Down Under* and find plenty to enjoy. Thanks for reading. More treasures to come.

Craig Sisterson

TAKIN' OUT THE TRASH

ALAN CARTER

'Anything else missing?'

Thomas Hemi shakes his head irritably. 'Just the hunting rifle and the box of shells.'

His is the fourth place in the valley to have been burgled this week, and it's still only Tuesday. The house is the last one at the end of the Wakamarina Valley; we're talking 15 ks from the main road here. It's a long way to drive, cycle, or walk to piss off a man like Thomas Hemi.

'You checked the campsite, Nick?'

'I did, on my way here.' Butchers Flat, a few hundred metres away, was empty. Unusually so for such a balmy beginning to summer. 'And you only noticed the stuff gone since this morning?'

'Been out pig hunting for a couple of days. Just got back last night. The one they took was my spare. Sighting's a bit off, not so accurate.'

'Maybe it's your eyes, mate. We're all getting older.'

There was a time he might have run with the joke, shot one back. Not these days. Not since Ruth left, taking their only surviving son.

His landline rings. By nature, Thomas isn't usually the type to let himself be interrupted by the outside world. But maybe he holds out hope of Ruth being at the end of the line. He takes the call. Some murmuring. Looks my way. 'It's Latifa, for you.'

'Sarge? We've got a situation down at the Trout.'

A situation at the *Trout Hotel* at the bottom end of the valley. Dispute over the meat raffle, maybe. A nudged pool cue on the black. Chips too cold, Speights too warm. 'What kind?'

'A hostage situation.'

Of course. Tuesday. Hostage-taking day and schnitzel special. I check my watch. Nearly lunchtime. The place can't have been open much more than half an hour. 'Armed Offenders on their way?'

'A squad driving up from Blenheim and another being choppered over from Nelson. We should all be in place by the time you get here.'

'See you soon.'

'Armed Offenders?' says Thomas as I close the call.

'Never a dull moment. We'll continue our enquiries about the burglaries. Be in touch.'

'Yeah.'

'Stay well, Thomas. Look after yourself.'

'Yeah.'

Driving back down the winding valley road past my old house, half-rebuilt now after being razed to the ground. Some empty-nesters from Christchurch bought the property but apart from the odd tradie I've seen little sign of movement there for weeks. Maybe once we're on the other side of this pandemic. There's a metallic clang as I drive across the new Deep Creek bridge; the old stone one is a hundred metres below, gathering moss courtesy of Thomas Hemi's handiwork with a few sticks of gelignite a few months ago. Some of the hills are green once again after being shaved of their pine crop. Others look braced for their turn at decimation. Through it all the Wakamarina flows, today a summery trickle but there's rain forecast at the end of the week and the river will roar once again. I miss the place, despite everything.

Halfway down the valley my mobile comes alive with a signal and I see two messages from Vanessa. The first tells me she'll pick up Paulie from school, the second instructs me to get some milk and bread before I come home. It's easier now we live in town and Havelock is blessed with the best little Four Square in the Top of the South. Cold storage room notwithstanding. At the Trout, all the gang is here. The sun shines, the sky is blue, and SH6 is down to one lane of traffic as police marshalls keep it flowing to deter gawpers. The *Trout Hotel* bathes in the early summer sunlight. Picture postcard perfect.

'Nice day for it.' District Commander Keegan flattens down the Velcro on her body armour and adjusts her headset. Must be a quiet day at Nelson HQ.

'I didn't anticipate you being so hands-on.'

'I'm a fully-trained hostage negotiator, Nick. And the usual bloke is on mental health leave.'

Constable Latifa Rapata is in the background pulling one of her funny faces but I'm not playing today. 'What do we know?'

'Five people inside: the new owners, Rob and Sharon. Welcome to Canvastown, eh? An old regular, Lawrie Owen. That's his abandoned coffee cart outside and his ATV is round back. Some other bloke, that's his Suzuki Vitara parked out front. We've run the rego plates and, if that's him inside, his name is Geoff Gates, a real estate agent from over Motueka way. Lastly, the perpetrator, as yet unidentified.'

'No communication from inside?'

'Some shouting and swearing but nothing of consequence so far.'

The Armed Offenders Squad have taken up positions. Keegan goes to confer with the leader, to check the communication set-up, and sneak a last ciggie before battle stations.

Latifa sidles up and hands me a Kevlar vest. 'You'll be needing one of these.' Hers is left unstrapped at the bottom. The baby bulge is beginning to show; no time wasted after her October nuptials.

'Who called it in?'

She nods towards a woman in lycra and bike helmet, seated at the picnic table beside the rusty old mining equipment which serves as a monument to the valley's history. The gold deposit they recently discovered behind the pub is still in situ; the Canadian company who found it was refused resource consent to dig it up. Three cheers. I introduce myself to the cyclist, interrupting her screen time on the mobile. 'Care to run me through what you saw?'

'Again?' Her name is Roz and she's irritated. This life and death hostage situation has upset her exercise routine and is no doubt playing havoc with her Strava targets. 'I was going to use the hotel toilets. The public one over there is locked – vandals or something. I was about to go through the door when I heard a shot and some shouting. Looked through the window and saw a guy waving a rifle around. I didn't hang about. Did a leak behind the tree and called you lot.'

So, shots had already been fired.

'Any idea when I can be on my way?' Roz tries out a winning smile on me but I'm not sure she's genuine. I know I'm just an obstacle between her and a PB.

'Give your contact details to my colleague over there.' I thumb towards Latifa. 'You live locally, don't you?'

'Pelorus Bridge.'

'You'll have to change your mountain-biking plans today. The Waka road's closed.'

'Bugger. All because of that bloody kid.'

'Kid?'

She nods. 'He looked scared even though he was the one holding the gun. Hardly looked older than my Oliver.'

'How old is Oliver?'

'Fourteen.'

'And you've mentioned this age thing to other officers already?'

'Yeah, of course.'

'You know what happened last time we put the AOS up against a kid with a gun.' Spoiler alert. He died.

'We can't be constrained by previous mistakes, Nick.' DC Keegan is ready to roll.

'But we can try to learn from them.'

'That's rich, coming from you. Here.' She hands me a spare set of headphones, Bluetooth-ed into the comms. 'Two minds are better than one. Sometimes.' She gives the tech woman a thumbs up and we hear the landline ringing inside. Given the patchy mobile signal in these parts, that seems wise.

'What?' Yep, that's a scared, teenage voice alright. His vocal cords searching for their register.

'My name's Marianne,' says DC Keegan in a voice designed to encourage adolescent boys to nestle into her bosom and suck their thumbs. 'What's yours?'

'Fuck off.' The line goes dead.

'Try again,' she says. 'Maybe I'll lay a bit more matron on him.'

Ring, ring. 'I told youse to fuck off!'

'Hey, kid. You want to live to see tomorrow, you better pin your ears back. Got it?'

'Suck my dick.' The phone dies again.

'When was the last time you did hostage negotiations?'

'Bit rusty, but I'm sure he'll come round eventually. He doesn't really have the choice, does he?'

'Hello?' The kid is back.

'See?' says Keegan, mike muted. 'Told you.'

'That bloke with you.'

'Which bloke is that? And mate, give us a name to work with.'

'Jarrod. You got a bloke there...' phone muffling, some talk in the background. 'Chester. Nick Chester.'

'What about him, Jarrod?'

'Send him in. I'll speak to him.'

'Give us a moment, will you, Jarrod?' She closes the call and gives me one of her looks. 'Explain yourself.'

'Haven't a clue, boss. But I suspect one of the hostages has recommended me. Lawrie the coffee guy would be my bet.'

'What do you think?'

'It's a breakthrough, of sorts. And we've already learned something.'

'What's that?'

'His accent. The way he says "Nick Chester". All those vowel sounds in the right place. No way he's a Kiwi.'

'You don't have to do this, you know.' The unspoken: in your condition, after what you've been through, the cancer, and all that.

'I'm fine. Really.' I am too. Six months clear. And counting.

Latifa checks the straps on my Kevlar vest. 'Make sure you come back out of there. I've got you down as godfather to Arlo.'

'Arlo?'

She rubs her belly. 'Ultrasound confirmed it yesterday.'

A brief congratulatory hug. 'You're counting on me to offer guidance and set a moral example to him?'

'Yep. So don't fuck it up.'

No pressure. One more check with Tess the techie that my headset and mike work, and it's thumbs up all round. Then I start the long, lonely walk to the door of the *Trout Hotel*. About twenty metres to my right, the Wakamarina River bubbles by, shimmering in the sunlight. A soft breeze tugs at the trees on the far bank. At the edge of my field of vision the AOS are making last minute adjustments either to their sniper sights or their angle of approach. Some have already scaled the walls of the two-storey building and wait patiently on its second-floor balcony, others at the side and, no doubt, the back. Meanwhile Jarrod and his hostages await me in the downstairs bar.

'Arms out from your side,' he shouts through an open window, shielded by my mate Lawrie.

I do as I'm told.

'Chuck your headphones away as well.'

Okay.

I hear the landline go inside. Probably Keegan telling Jarrod she wants me to keep the headset and Jarrod giving his usual reply. He's at the doorway now, blocked by Lawrie, waving me forward.

'Hurry up.'

Is it my imagination or did the air just grow colder? A cloud scuds across the sun. Ah, that explains it. He gets Lawrie to pat me down for hidden weapons. Finds my mobile. Throws it outside onto the gravel. Inside it's dingy. The Trout always was, I suppose, that's part of its charm. Some curtains have been drawn to minimise sight lines from outside. The tang of last night's beer hangs in the atmosphere. Rob and Sharon are face down on the sticky pine floorboards, perhaps wondering if they can quickly sell up and move on when this is over. Maybe that's why Geoff the Realtor is here.

'Face down,' says Jarrod. 'Hands out wide. Both of you.'

'I told you about my back, mate,' says Lawrie. 'It's murder.'

'Do it.'

We take up position. The blackboard menu hasn't changed, I notice, despite being under new management. The treasured collection of beer tankards still hangs along the bar. I guess the semi-pornographic poster of Anna Kournikova playing tennis still haunts the Gents' too. I catch the eye of the realtor. He gives a half-smile. Playing cool? Each to his own.

'I'm Nick. You'd be Geoff, that right?'

'Shut it,' says Jarrod. 'No talking.'

'You invited me in, mate. We're not going to get very far if we can't talk.'

'I make the rules around here.' His voice cracks as he says it.

'Jarrod, tell me what I can do to help.' He squats a few metres from me, silhouetted by the glare from an uncurtained window. I wonder if he's in the laser sights of an AOS sniper. A flickering dot on the back of his head and bingo, we can all go home. But you know what? He doesn't look like he deserves it. His face and eyes tell the story of a shitty life that just got shittier. His rifle, I see in close up, is the same make as the one missing from Thomas Hemi's home. I'm guessing Jarrod is our one-man Wakamarina crime spree. But how did he get all the way up to the Hemi property? He hardly looks old enough to have a licence.

'Jarrod?'

'What's that accent? You a Pom?' he asks.

'Don't hold it against him,' says Lawrie. 'Nick has been known to be useful on the pool table sometimes.'

By Lawrie's standards that's a compliment. I'll treasure it. 'Yep, mate. You don't sound local either. That doesn't sound like a "fush and chups" accent. Aussie?'

'S'pose.'

'Not sure?'

Jarrod sits cross-legged. Lines the rifle up on my face. Squints down the sight.

'Cops,' he spits. 'Fucken hate 'em.'

'He's different,' says Lawrie. 'Give him a chance.'

Am I different? I don't feel it. If this kid gets taken out by a sniper, I'll still sleep tonight. Probably. 'How old are you, Jarrod?'

'What's it to you?'

'It's just that you don't seem like a hardened criminal, and it'd be a shame if those ninjas out there treated you as if you were. Those guys don't mess about.'

'Such is life.'

Ned Kelly has a lot to answer for with today's bogan youth. 'Fourteen, fifteen? What?'

'Seventeen next week.'

'Happy birthday, Ned.' It's Geoff in the corner. 'Chk, chk, boom!'

'Shut it!' Jarrod and I chorus.

'Mate,' says Lawrie. 'You're not helping.'

'Staying around here, Jarrod?' I roll my neck to ease the stiffness. 'Moved into the area recently?'

A bitter snort. 'You could say that, yeah.'

'He's been living in our shed this past week,' says Lawrie. 'Helping out around the place. Setting the wasp baits. My back, I can't reach these days.'

That explains the fragile bond they've formed. And perhaps how Jarrod was able to move up and down the valley, maybe using Lawrie's ATV. 'And before that?'

Silence. An exchange of looks between Lawrie and the kid.

Take a punt. 'Trouble at home, Jarrod?'

'Home?' he says, eyes filling. 'What's that?'

'Can I tell him, mate?' Lawrie winces, his back must be giving him grief. 'Set the ball rolling? That way you get to concentrate on what those cops are doing out there.'

Thanks Lawrie.

'Yeah. You tell him.' Jarrod pulls over a chair. 'And sit on that if your back's hurting.'

'Good lad.' Lawrie climbs up into it. 'That feels better.'

'Stockholm Syndrome,' says Geoff the Realtor. 'It's a thing.'

'I'd strongly advise you to zip it, pal.' This joker is set to get us all killed. 'Stage is yours, Lawrie.'

Rob the proprietor isn't faring too good. Face pale. Thousand-yard stare. Low stress threshold, I'm guessing.

'You feeling okay, Rob?'

'He's on heart medication,' says Sharon. 'This shit doesn't help.'

But Jarrod doesn't look like ceding, so I guess the more we know of his story, the better. 'Lawrie?'

'Jarrod got dropped off here by bus, middle of last week. He looked a bit lost and sorry for himself so I gave him a coffee.' Lawrie shifts in the chair, trying to find a sweet spot for his aching back. 'I recognised him straight away. Mirror image of his dad and grandad.'

It turns out Jarrod is in fact a Kiwi. His family used to live in the Wakamarina but left a good 15 years ago. The boy was just a tacker at the time. They ended up in Brisbane, and later the Gold Coast. Over time Jarrod got in with the wrong crowd. Drugs, street gangs, violence – a melee and a stabbing. Low-level stuff, relatively speaking, but yep, he made some poor choices in his life. That might not have been so bad if his folks had got him naturalised in Australia. But they never got around to it.

About a month ago he got deported back to his country of birth.

'At sixteen?' And during an unfinished pandemic at that. I shake my head.

'Takin' out the trash,' says Geoff. 'Not my words, the Aussies. But I can see their point.'

Really? The Aussies seem perfectly capable of breeding and exporting their own trash. Look at that guy who came to Christchurch with his guns. I give Geoff the Death Stare but he seems unfazed.

Back to Jarrod. 'Your folks?' Surely the Aussies didn't send him off alone.

'Dad's dead, some cancer. Mum's with a new bloke who hates me guts. It's mutual like.' A shrug. 'They can't go anywhere, even if they wanted to, unless the borders open up again.'

'Nobody from social services at this end to help out?'

'First few days, yeah, but I'm not a priority. No hostel places available. I phoned Mum and she told me to come here. Try Lawrie.'

'Very moving,' says Geoff. 'Can we go home now?'

I've had enough. 'Last warning, Geoff. If you can't say anything helpful, then keep it shut.'

'Or what?'

Thing is, he has a point. I'm in no position to shut him up.

The landline goes. Jarrod answers it. 'Yeah? What?' Some static and nods. He turns to us. 'They're offering food and drink. Anybody want any?'

'That'd be nice,' says Lawrie.

'Me too,' says Geoff.

Sharon is too busy tending to her husband.

'Tell you what,' says Jarrod back into the phone. 'Get fucked.'

Keegan is no doubt trying to get an idea of how things are going. By now the AOS guys up on the balcony should have been able to insert mikes or even cameras through the spider's web of fissures in the ceiling. Those cracks the result of constant mini-earthquakes, the nearby highway, and years of neglect.

'What do you want from this situation, Jarrod? How's it meant to end?'

He shrugs. 'Like the guy says, I'm trash. No future, no hope, no point. Oz is all I know. My mates, my life, shit as it was.' Flicks a hand towards the outside world. 'I don't recognise this country. Trees, rivers, bitey fucken flies. Why would ya?' He lifts the rifle stock and studies it absent-mindedly. 'Maybe I should just go down in a blaze of glory. Be famous.'

'Where do we figure in that?'

'Statistics, I guess.'

The landline goes again. He snatches it. 'What?'

Firm measured tones from the other end. Keegan laying down an ultimatum. God knows how she passed that hostage negotiation course; patience is not her strong suit today.

'I'm the one with the hostages,' he says. 'I decide what happens and when.'

The lights go out behind the bar and the poker machine dies before us. They've cut the power. Luckily the landline is one of those independent of power source; you need that with all the earthquakes.

'How about I start my own countdown?' says Jarrod before slamming the phone down. He cradles the gun in one arm and with the other he retrieves a 10 litre container from behind the bar, unscrews the cap and starts sloshing petrol on us.

From his vantage point in the chair, Lawrie is the only one in a position to try to take quick defensive action. He makes a move towards Jarrod and is clubbed with the rifle butt for his efforts. He drops like a stone, blood oozing from a gash above his eye. Breathing shallow. Skin turning grey before our eyes. The rifle is trained back on us and Jarrod has taken a cigarette lighter out of his pocket, set it on the table beside him.

Take him out, you bastards, I'm thinking. Just end it.

'What triggered this, Jarrod?'

'Hmmm?' He seems to be in a daze, gone somewhere and can't find his way back.

'It's been a month. Things are tough, yeah, but you've got a roof over your head and somebody looking out for you.' I nod towards Lawrie. 'It was a start. Something to build on, Jarrod. Still is.'

'Nah.' He shakes his head. 'All over, isn't it?'

'Doesn't have to be. Lawrie's a very forgiving fella. It's not too late to save the day.'

'A week ago, my Mum messaged me. She's not going to follow me here. She's got pregnant again with this new… this, ah, he's just a fucken dog.' Eyes brimming. 'Moving to Perth, he's got a job over there. I'm on my own, she says. But we can always fucken Skype.'

He toys with the lighter. Click. Flame. Click. Flame.

'Fuck this,' says Geoff. He stands up, walks over to Jarrod, pulls the gun out of his hands. 'You're a shit psycho, mate. Like a bad film.' He smashes the butt into the kid's face and pushes him to the floor. 'I'll show you how it's done.'

Not your average Tuesday. Maybe there's something in the water.

The landline goes.

'That'll be for me.' Geoff picks up. 'Who am I speaking to?' A pause. 'Hi Marianne. Um, Jarrod? No, he's indisposed. I'm looking after things now.'

Jarrod looks like he's got a broken nose and might need some bridge work on his top teeth. His face is a mess of blood. He's crying; pain, humiliation, despair – maybe all of the above. Lawrie has come to and is tending to Jarrod's injuries, oblivious to his own. Meanwhile mein host Rob seems to be hyperventilating. Jesus.

'Geoff, mate. How about we stop this and all go home? You get to walk out of here a hero. Good result.'

'Mate, now, is it?' He mimics my nice new soft voice. 'I'm up to here with people telling me to shut my mouth. Be a good boy.'

Geoff tears the phone out of its socket and casually flings it across the room. 'Where did it get me? Work your arse off for 20 years and who gets offered the partnership in the firm? Not me. No. Some jumped up little madam half my age with nice tits and a diploma, that's who.'

Here we go.

The usual rant follows. Women. Minorities, blah blah. Maori. Woke lefties and greenies. Things aren't the way they used to be. Things aren't the way they should be. It's tough being a middle-class middle-aged white man. Cut and paste from a Murdoch press editorial. At this rate it'll be musical hostages and I'll take the fucking gun off him next. Have a whinge about how Sunderland keep losing and really belong in the Premier League or else everybody dies.

'Finished?' He looks at me. Clearly, I'm first in line for whatever he has in mind. 'Okay. New story ending. What do you want out of this, Geoff?'

'Everybody to remember my name and what I stood for.'

Fuck's sake.

Can they see or hear this outside? Have the techs slotted a camera or mike through the ceiling rose yet? The last phone call would surely tip them off that the game has changed but what to make of it?

They'll be looking closer at Geoff Gates. How near is he to the edge? Does he have a history of violence? And biggest question of all: how long to wait before sending the ninjas in? Usually, patience is the thing. Sit it out, wear them down, keep things calm. Only go in as a last resort, if things look like turning ugly. They look pretty ugly now and patience was never DC Keegan's forte. Or was it? Usually, I'm the impetuous one and it's her reining me in. Maybe I need to give her credit where it's due. But not too patient, please. This guy is a different kettle of fish to poor little Jarrod.

'You make me sick.'

Sharon.

'Who asked you, love? Pipe down.' Geoff is taking the spirit bottles from behind the bar. Emptying them around the place, adding to the flammability.

Sharon's not finished. 'How much blood needs to be spilled to make you feel better?'

'We'll all find out soon enough.'

'Pathetic.' She's on a roll. 'No wonder Sophie left you.'

'What did you say?'

'I know you, Geoffrey Gates. I know you're a controlling, lazy, entitled pig of a man and that you're shit between the sheets. Sophie couldn't wait to be shot of you.'

Please, ninjas. Come now.

In three strides he's standing over her. Gun poised. Directs his attention to Rob. 'You need to control your wife, mate. No wonder, though. Look at you, weak as fucking piss.'

He tips a bottle of vodka over the two of them. Chucks the empty away and fumbles in his pocket for the lighter he confiscated from Jarrod. One single focus now – Sharon will pay for her insolence.

Seize the day.

I suppose if I'd been brought up in NZ, I might have done a more elegant rugby tackle, but it works after a fashion. The rifle is out of his hands. But the lighter isn't. He's clicking away like a lovesick tui and we're rolling around in a heady mix of petrol and grog. If it goes up, it isn't going to be pleasant.

Geoff is stronger than I expected of a real estate agent. Maybe he hits the gym in Motueka. Works off some of that impotent rage on the weights. He's on top of me, straddling. Raining blows down on my poor head which is still recovering from the cancer op. I'm weaker than I realised. Losing it. Losing again.

Losing.

He holds the lighter up triumphantly. 'Watch this.'

'No, mate.' Jarrod has the rifle barrel at the back of Geoff's head. 'Watch this.'

Jesus. It's amateur night at the *Havelock Playhouse*. Who'll come rushing onstage next? The sly butler? The giddy aunt?

'Don't,' I say. 'He's not worth it.'

'Think so? Be my pleasure. Really.' Jarrod wipes his still bleeding mouth. 'We're both going to jail anyway.'

After the usual chorus of banging and shouting, the AOS are in the room. 'Put the gun down,' one of them says.

'Jarrod,' pleads Lawrie.

Another shouted order. 'Gun down, face down. Do it.'

'Suicide by cop,' says Geoff. 'What you always wanted, kid. Your fucken Ned Kelly moment.'

'Ignore him, Jarrod. Do as they say.' I can see his finger tightening. He's seconds away from dying.

He lets the gun fall and the ninjas rush him.

A chopper has taken Rob to Nelson Hospital. He has chest pains that don't bode well. Sharon has gone along for the ride but not before landing the realtor a kick in the ribs while he was being held down. Geoff is in custody. He'll be joined soon by Jarrod. He and Lawrie have been ambulanced to Blenheim to check their head and facial injuries; Jarrod with his own police minder.

Me? Felt nowt. Bit of mopping with a hankie and betadine, some steri-strips, and it's no worse than that time I got smacked with a pool cue one Friday night in Sunderland.

'Where did the can of petrol come from?' Keegan wonders aloud.

'Probably the back of Lawrie's ATV. Intended for a wasp nest maybe.'

'You country bumpkins. Full of little tricks.'

'Tell me about Geoff. No doubt you ran him deeper through the system after things kicked off.'

A tearing of Velcro as she sheds the Kevlar. 'Red flag. Entitled kinda guy but they're a dime-a-dozen these days, aren't they? Restraining order, domestic violence. Family life in tatters. Drink problem. Career on the downward trajectory.'

'That explains the Vitara. Real estate agents normally drive something more expensive.'

'Big time loser.' Retrieves her ciggie packet. 'I mean you'd have to work at being a failure in this property market. Prices through the roof. Like the pandemic never happened.'

'Where to for Jarrod?'

'We can't deport him back to Oz. He'll be lucky to escape a custodial sentence, even if he was a hero in the end.' She sees the expression on my face. 'He put lives in danger, Nick. Assaulted Lawrie.' Lights up and blows out a blue plume. 'You can't save them all. He made some bad decisions and will stand or fall by them.'

'S'pose so.' She's right. Jarrod will have to make his own way. Nobody's child, Australia specialises in them. Strange place, Oz: a strident but brittle sense of national identity; ruthless and unforgiving to those who don't fit its tight confines.

'Get home to your family, Nick.'

Still broad daylight. It feels like darkness should have fallen but it's only mid-afternoon. A cow moos somewhere. The river runs out into Pelorus Sound. The traffic once again flows freely on SH6.

'A lift back into town?' Latifa waggles my key fob at me. 'You look like you need a chauffeur.'

We pull away from the gravel in front of the Trout and hit the highway with Latifa's customary speedy aplomb. I make a quick call to Thomas Hemi to tell him we've found his rifle. Thanks, he says, but his heart's not in it. The hills are green as ever and Pelorus Sound shimmers in the afternoon sun. Boats on the water. Birds in the sky.

'Arlo, huh?'

Latifa drops down to seventy for the tight bend. 'Like it?'

'Like the folk singer, right?'

'Who?'

'Never mind.'

Summer of the Seventeen Poll

Aoife Clifford

'SUMMER OF THE SEVENTEEN POLL' was the headline. The usual sub-editor was on a beach, and a stand-up comedian was moonlighting. A 17 per cent primary vote means not even the Premier's mother was prepared to vote for him anymore. We were reduced to the candidates themselves and idiots who didn't understand the question. The numbers weren't surprising considering it had been the Twelve Days of Political Nightmares leading up to Christmas, starting with 12 pollies boozing and moving to five front-page leaks; four harassment suits; three resignations; two apologies; and a Premier spending January expecting to get knifed. Anyone working for a political party with those numbers should start the New Year looking for a new job, but I wasn't clicking on the classifieds just yet. My problem wasn't being unpopular. Quite the opposite.

My name is Callan Valient and I'm a 'smokejumper'. I get the first phone call from the powers that be, even before they press 's' for spin. To be able to spin, you need to know the truth. I find that out and then it's someone else's job to ensure the public never does. When there's a fire, a catastrophe, or a complete cock up, I'm the first one in.

Actually, to be correct, I'm the second one in.

First is my boss – Roland Gesink – known as 'Stainless' because he's the Man of Steel, despite looking like an overgrown chipmunk with alopecia. He is an incorruptible political genius, and I don't need to tell you that is highly unusual in our circles. I am a mere grasshopper of metal alloy by comparison.

However, the world was on holidays and could not care less about my problems. Stainless was having a well-deserved break and in one more day so was I, heading for the coast to swelter in 40-degree heat waves or alternatively brave hailstones the size of golf balls. January weather in Victoria could be as brutal as the average swinging voter.

I woke early on Friday morning, so early it was still Thursday night. As I picked up a buzzing mobile, I saw it was Stainless.

'Aren't you on holidays?' I croaked.

'Not anymore, and yours have just been cancelled.'

'But I won the lottery this year, I'm going to be camping at the Prom.'

'Just be ready in fifteen minutes.'

I drove because Stainless had lost his licence again. As he sucked on Kool Mints, he told me that a dead girl had been found in a holiday home at Rye. The police guessed early teens, but it was quite a guess because she had been dead for at least three months. As a rule, I try to avoid corpses, so I wondered aloud about our involvement.

'The house belongs to our Glorious Leader, the Right Honourable Jack Prendergast,' Stainless explained.

Premier Prendergast might be a pig, but he was our pig, and it was part of our job description to continually get him out of the shit. Keeping him out of it in the first place had proven to be impossible.

We pulled up in front of a dilapidated California bungalow. Stainless got out of the car and started chatting to the policeman guarding the crime scene tape surrounding the property. Remembering how much I really hated dead bodies, I began deep breathing, focusing on the 'I Hunt, I Vote' sticker peeling off the back of the battered white Holden Barina in front of us. It wasn't quite 'warm blue ocean' but beggars can't be choosers. I was interrupted by Stainless who banged on the window.

Reluctantly I got out of the car. 'No media yet, thank goodness.'

Stainless just grunted.

A heavy-set guy in a cheap suit and surgical gloves stopped us before we opened the front door. 'Hope you didn't speed Stainless, because we've got more cameras on that freeway than your party has legitimate members.'

'Murphy, this is my offsider, Ms Callan Valient.'

Murphy ignored me. 'Can't have you disturbing the crime scene, but she's been bagged. You can take a look when they bring her out.'

Stainless declined and I decided I could get through the morning without vomiting.

'How long has she been here for?' asked Stainless.

'At a guess, since October 12th.'

'You a cadaver whisperer these days?'

'She had a receipt in her pocket, from a shop near Frankston station.'

'Frankston station,' repeated Stainless slowly.

'I know,' said Murphy, wisecracks forgotten. 'Takes you back.'

Stainless gazed thoughtfully into the middle distance before asking 'Anything else?'

'Nothing so far. Toxicology will take at least a fortnight. The house is as clean as a whistle, and we found her neatly tucked up in a bed like Goldilocks so we're putting out an APB on three bears.' With a sense of humour like that he could be a sub-editor. 'The real estate agent who discovered the body is sitting over there on the nature strip.'

Stainless nodded at me and I slipped past.

Drawing on a cigarette like it was an asthma inhaler, was a woman in a velour tracksuit and makeup as thick as a kabuki mask. An older lady in her dressing gown was being violently ill into a shrub.

'She alright?'

'Patsy? She'll be fine in a minute.'

Patsy turned and squinted in my direction.

'Want me to get a water, Pats?' Kabuki asked.

'I think I'll go lie down,' she gasped.

I watched Patsy shuffle quickly in the gate of a nearby fibro bungalow.

'Dead bodies make me feel ill,' I said.

'Wasn't the body.' Kabuki hoovered in a lungful of tar. 'Memories can make you as sick as a dog.'

'Mind if I ask you a few questions?' I asked.

'You a cop?'

'An interested party.'

She shrugged. 'Ask away.'

'What were you doing here?'

'Got a call yesterday that the owners wanted to sell. If I didn't move quickly that stuck up bitch Alison Dickey over at Murray Real Estate would be onto this like a shot. Money for jam this close to the beach. Came here to have a quick squiz and recognised that smell when I opened the door.' There was an odd note of pride. 'Mobile reception is patchy here, so I ran down to Patsy Wakelin's house to phone the police. She's our company's cleaner. Does all our rentals and the Air BnBs in the area.' She gestured towards the house the lady had scuttled into.

'You find a lot of decomposing bodies?'

'All the bloody time.'

'The owners want to keep this quiet.'

'Guarantee me the sale and I won't breathe a word.'

I nodded my agreement.

'Would a dead body make a difference to the asking price?' I always wanted to live near the beach.

'Almost none at all.' She smiled the smile of sharks and salesmen as my dream disappeared in a cloud of dollar signs and inter-generational mortgages.

Stainless and I got coffees and pies from a servo and drove down to Rye pier, while dawn broke as gently as a politician's promise.

'I've got a bad feeling about this one,' he muttered.

'You don't think the Premier's involved?'

'No, thank Christ. Overseas junket prostituting Victoria until late November, remember.'

The actual slogan had been 'Victoria – open for business'. Some consultants had been paid a fortune to come up with an ad more suitable for an escort agency but perhaps it explained the unexpected spike in single male visitors to Melbourne.

I had forgotten. As far as the trip went it had been a disaster with him being labelled 'PRENDERGHASTLY', having offended people in three different time zones. Still, as far as alibis went it was a winner.

Unfortunately, I was also reminded of a little imbroglio that we had been involved in at the same time. Tony Prendergast, his son, as thick as two planks and therefore a shoo-in for a safe seat in the future, had been caught drink driving opposite Frankston Hotel early on Saturday October 13th. I had spent my birthday successfully bailing out and unsuccessfully sobering up Tony the Human Octopus.

'That dickhead again,' Stainless sighed after I told him. Tony was in the right place at exactly the wrong time.

Silence descended as we wrestled with lava-hot meat erupting from slightly frozen pastry cases. Stainless didn't talk until he'd finished spraying crumbs all over the dash.

'And as if this isn't bad enough, it's going to remind everyone of the little Sally Wakelin case from 20 years ago.' Stainless was as depressed as a bloodhound.

That name conjured ancient memories. My mother sobbing into a dishcloth in the kitchen, with the radio saying at last Sally Wakelin's body had been found, murdered by an unknown killer. Standing in the playground chanting 'Wakey-Wakey Wakelin' while a kid lay down pretending to be dead. It was a name repeated by worried parents to a generation of errant school kids. But it also triggered something more recent.

'Any relation to Patsy Wakelin?'

'That's Sally's mother.'

'She cleans that house.'

Stainless gazed through the windscreen out at the bay. Grey clouds covered the horizon giving the impression that the sun had already called in sick. As he turned the key in the ignition, the car coughed and then purred into life. 'You better make sure she doesn't talk to the media.' As I rolled my eyes, he smiled, 'Women handle those things better. The gentler sex and all that.'

Complete rubbish, of course, and demonstrated two days later. You don't become the Police Commissioner of Victoria by being gentle. We received a summons to appear before Ma'am, and you don't ignore a woman who could lock you up for the term of your natural life.

'Mr Gesink and Ms Valient, pleasure as always.' She gestured for us to sit down. It wasn't a command, but it was safer to treat everything she said as one. She was powerful, by which I mean that not only could she order big burly blokes in blue to kneecap you, if she wanted to, she could do it herself. There was a long history between her and Stainless filled with arguments, heinous crimes and traffic infringements.

'Good holiday, Commissioner?' Stainless asked. He was getting his licence back in a couple of weeks and didn't want to lose it again.

'I don't take holidays Mr Gesink. In this job, you can't even have a haircut without it being on the front page.'

She walked around her desk and sat down opposite. 'The fact that the media haven't discovered the link between the Premier and the off-shore trust that technically owns this crime scene, has bought us both time before this particular political tsunami hits.'

'Dedman's off until the end of January,' Stainless answered. 'We need it fixed before then.'

Andy Dedman was the State's senior crime reporter. Our problem was Dedman told tales and knew even more. He'd discover the link before morning tea.

Ma'am nodded her agreement, 'As much as I dislike this, I am suggesting a course of cooperation for mutual benefit.'

'You scratch my back...' Stainless began to wheeze but then thought better of it. The nearest approximation to physical contact he would receive from Ma'am would be her holding a police issued Smith & Wesson at his head and pulling the trigger.

He tried again with, 'What have you got?'

'Casey Siddle was a 14-year-old from a family known to Social Services. Signs of old bruises and fractures on her body, probably from her father. Death due to a drug overdose. We are working on the assumption that it was not self-administered.

'At 11.20pm on October 12th security camera footage has her alone on the platform of Frankston Station but no footage after that. A group of enterprising young locals had smashed several of the external station cameras the day before. She wasn't reported missing for a couple of days by which time she was already dead.'

'Parents involved?' asked Stainless.

She shook her head. 'No great shakes as parents but we can't pin this on them.'

'Is the Premier or his family being investigated?' I interrupted. It was political problem number one.

Ma'am didn't like being interrupted, but the question amused her.

'The Premier might be suffering a political death, but I don't think we can tie him to this one. Nor his lovely wife,' a ghost of a smile crossing her face. Eileen Prendergast had all the charisma of pit bull crossed with an accountant. 'But we'll be talking to Tony.'

Stainless gave me a meaningful look which, from experience, would mean trawling around nightclubs in the shortest skirt I owned, to find a man whose social skills made inebriated footballers seem keen students of *Debrett's Guide for the Modern Gentleman*.

'Now for the cooperation,' she said. 'Any political whispering? Who hates the Premier so much that they'd put a dead girl in his house?'

Stainless wasn't one to lag on a comrade, even in a murder investigation, so he tried a diversion. 'I'd suggest you should look at our opponents,' he ventured hopefully, but in his heart, he knew it wasn't them. Their idea of a sex scandal is being caught getting disciplined by someone called 'Nanny'.

The Commissioner gave a mirthless laugh. 'I don't think we need to look so far afield, not when we have a veritable conga line of possible suspects among the party faithful.'

Stainless tried to look doubtful.

'I expect a phone call if you hear anything.' Ma'am gave Stainless the evil eye.

'Is there any connection to the Wakelin case?' I asked. This was problem number two.

The Commissioner's starched exterior wilted slightly. 'There are some troubling coincidences. Runaway girl with lousy parents last seen alive at Frankston train station, drugged and raped by person unknown and body found months later.'

'Did the investigators have a strong suspect for the Wakelin case?' Stainless asked.

The Commissioner shook her head. 'Her father, Terry was in WA at the time or else I would have put money on him. There was another suspect, but we didn't have enough evidence to press charges, and it can't be him this time.'

'Why not?' I asked.

'He died in jail. We couldn't link him to Sally but there were plenty of others.'

Stainless stared out the window at Ma'am's views. On a clear day you could see the cranes down at Dockland. 'So best case scenario, we're dealing with a copy-cat killer.'

'Best case?' I squeaked, but Ma'am nodded her agreement.

'Otherwise, what has Sally's killer been doing for the last 20 years?'

I found Tony in the fourth nightclub I tried. The music was loud, the lights were dim, and he was both, sitting at the bar, surrounded by empties and mouthing such witticisms as 'Don't you know who my father is?'

'Let me buy you a drink,' I told him.

'I know you,' he slurred, gaping as if I was a shimmering mirage. A minute later he had slipped unconscious onto the floor. I took him home in a taxi and sobered him up as he lay face down on the lawn. Thinking of clouds and silver linings, I pretended the garden hose was a water cannon and aimed for his head.

Much later Tony was conscious, shivering in a blanket. He looked at me with red-rimmed eyes. 'Do you know—'

I interrupted him before he could get started, 'Who your father is? That's the only reason I'm here. We need to talk about last October.'

Most of the interrogation occurred with a bathroom door between us, but eventually I got what I wanted. Tony was supposed to go to the beach house that weekend. He'd even rung the real estate agent to get it ready for him, but then never made it. All night boozing at the Casino had made him an easy target for the police when he drove down the next morning.

The next day I checked this with the Casino, who kindly showed me footage of Tony sexually harassing female croupiers into the wee small hours. I got the impression they had it on high rotation for when they wanted a laugh, or it was time to renegotiate their licence. Still, as far as alibis went it was a winner. A family tradition, I guess. That and being a wanker.

Stainless was relieved when I told him, but it was tempered by the knowledge we were back at square one. There hadn't even been a whisper about it around Spring Street. He stared grumpily at the calendar. Dedman was back from his holidays in a week.

'You go see Patsy Wakelin and make sure no journo has got in touch with her because the minute anyone hears that surname, it will be serial killer on the loose on every Reddit thread, and every underemployed journo will want to make a ten-part podcast about it.'

'First Tony, now grieving mothers,' I complained. 'You should pay me danger money. Besides, what are you doing?'

'I am sullying my reputation by having to go cap in hand to the Military & Naval Club.'

I knew what that meant. Stainless was desperate enough to consult his opposite number. The yin to his yang. A white-haired patrician type who would salute the flag, pay homage to the Queen and speak of sacrifice for the country, all while ensuring he never paid a cent in taxes. It was the code of the 'smokejumpers' to 'fess up if requested.

Patsy was getting out of the 'I Hunt, I Vote' Barina as I pulled up. Small and brittle, she resembled a broken bird and stared nervously at me, 'You're the girl from that night.'

'I hope you're feeling better.'

She made a dismissive gesture.

'Can we talk? I won't take long.'

Succumbing to my naked desperation, she took me into her house. Faded carpet, shabby lino, peeling paint on cupboards and sideboards. It felt like it had been stuck in a time warp for 20 years.

'Don't get many visitors,' she said.

'Any journalists been in touch?' I asked, trying to sound off hand.

'What would they want with me?' She was jumpy.

'I just thought, with your daughter...' I couldn't finish the sentence, ashamed I was trampling over raw wounds for a Premier who scarcely deserved it.

'Wouldn't talk to those vultures even if they did. Police have been, didn't stay long. They asked if I wanted counselling. Didn't have that 20 years ago. They couldn't wait to leave, just like everyone else.'

She was giving me an open invitation to disappear and part of me wanted to grab it with both hands but instead I found myself trying to prove that I was different, that I really cared, so I asked to see a picture of Sally.

'People told us not to keep pictures of her around. Got to think of the future, they kept saying. But they didn't care about us, they just wanted to forget what had happened. Doesn't matter to me. She's the first thing I see when I wake up and the last thing I see when I shut my eyes.'

I remembered what the Commissioner had said about them being bad parents, but bad parents still love and grieve.

'Terry got rid of the photos, but I know he still thinks about her every day, just the same. Twenty years and he still spends all hours sitting at the station, hoping he'll see her get off a train.'

There are some statements that sever time into two, a before and an after. Before she spoke of Terry, I was feeling the uncomfortable intruder, blundering over a tragedy, afterwards was something else entirely.

'Frankston Station?'

The words hung there between us as Patsy began to tremble.

'Casey went missing from Frankston Station.'

Patsy blinked and flinched as if I was shining a light into her face.

'He took Casey, didn't he?' I said softly, and her head nodded. 'Did he do the same to Sally?'

'He never killed Sally, he loved her like he never loved anyone else.' Patsy's head shook violently from side-to-side it was as if I was smacking her.

It sounded like a politician's idea of the truth, technically correct but actually misleading.

'Tell me what happened to Casey.'

Patsy's face changed to a more ambiguous expression. It was a long time before she spoke.

'When I opened the boot of the car and saw her, I couldn't keep pretending any more. I decided if someone asked me, I'd tell them what happened.'

She told me about a last-minute cleaning job and not being able to find her vacuum and how eventually she went into the garage to find it, the garage where Terry had told her she was never to go, and then hearing banging coming from the boot of his car.

'Before I didn't care. Let their parents suffer as I suffered. But when I saw her, so young just like my Sally. I got her away. She was in bad shape. I took her to that Prendergast house. No one saw us. I tried to make it nice for her, told her she was safe. I didn't know what else to do, so I just did the cleaning. But he must have given her something, and when I came back, she was dead.'

'You didn't get help? Call the police? An ambulance?'

'I just shut down, went home and put the vacuum back where Terry had it. He never guessed I was involved. In the end, I couldn't save her, just like I couldn't save my Sally.'

'What do you mean?'

'Terry had been… interfering with her. Sally told me that once he had left to go to WA. I threw her out of the house and didn't ring the police until it was too late. She had nowhere to go, there was no one looking after her. It was my fault she was killed.'

Slowly, very slowly Patsy slid to the floor and huddled into a tight ball, as if trying to ward off the grief and the guilt that had broken her. She didn't speak another word to me.

I phoned the police.

Not strictly smokejumping procedure, but Stainless overlooked it in the circumstances and the police weren't far behind me anyway. They'd discovered video footage of Terry sitting in Frankston Station's carpark the day before Casey disappeared, pointing out the security cameras to a couple of skateboarding hoodies.

In politics, a win's a win, no matter how you get it, but I tried my best to forget all about the Wakelins and their grief. Grief that had detached Patsy from humanity so that she could stand by as a dumb witness to terrible crimes whereas Terry's grief had fed his internal demons and darkness so that he re-enacted his own daughter's murder over and over again.

Work kept me busy. Despite our best efforts, the Premier was a lost cause and retired soon afterwards to 'spend more time with his family', which was immediately undermined when Elaine filed for divorce and Tony got the nod for his seat. To no one's surprise we lost the next election in a landslide. At least it ended the Prendergast dynasty before it had even begun.

But sometimes in the middle of the night, my thoughts turn to Sally, Casey and all the rest. Girls running from one horror only to find themselves somewhere much worse. Ma'am informed us that holes were being dug all over the State, trying to find more of Terry's victims.

The latest count is seventeen.

THE COOK

DAVID WHISH-WILSON

A FATHER IS GOD TO HIS SON.

My father said that before I killed him, but he wasn't talking about us. His own father. His father's father. His fathers father's father, perhaps.

Today I leave Casuarina Prison after five years – no step-down into minimum.

But not because of what I've done – what I know.

My history as a speed cook, forced to stay in the SHU, with the psychos, peds and catamites, to keep me away from my suitors. There are five bikie mobs in Perth and they all want to own me, despite my history with the needle. I've avoided them because that part of my life, it's over. They aren't the kind to take no for an answer, but I'm not complaining. I haven't done the time hard, not like my earlier stretches. Not when even the screws have watched all four seasons of *Breaking Bad* – the same screws who call me Heisenberg with a mocking respect, although I was always more Jesse Pinkman than Walter White.

Their respect isn't for me, the waster, but for the science of the thing. The working with explosive materials in confined spaces. The alchemy, what I see as chemistry, following a recipe. The mystical transubstantiation of base materials into the manna of heaven, as another old crim described it.

I make no such claims myself. Starting with sulphate back in the eighties; bog-standard crank, learnt from a smuggled copy of Uncle Fester's cookbook, whose recipes I have adapted, improved over the years. The ice I made was sought after by the criminal and social elite who could afford it.

I didn't come cheap, but that is simply the price of blood. I hear stories now and then. Like a gun manufacturer will hear stories. Like the brother of a cellmate of mine who after a three-day binge injected his cock and lost both legs to gangrene. Stories of psychosis and ruin. Violence and poverty visited upon innocents. You get the picture, and why I've had enough.

The only man I confided my decision to is the prison psych. Nothing to do with going straight or walking the line. I told him that the very worst things I have done were done with the best of intentions.

Isn't that punishment enough?

My second son, Danny. The only person in the world I want to see. Waiting for me outside the prison gates, sun shearing off the bonnet of his Valiant Charger.

This is a good sign. On the prison wireless I've heard Danny's running wild, working as a deckie for Gary Warner, although everyone knows what that means. Warner is the only non-bikie crim who, because of his Calabrian connections, gets to make speed and ice and ecstasy, distributed through the insulated Italian smack networks.

Warner is the same bloke who most pundits think offed my first son, Kevin, those five years back, after he ripped him off for a kilo of pure.

That Danny still has the Valiant means something. It was my gift, once he got his licence, to celebrate his coming out of foster care, and it means that he hasn't gone too far off the rails.

Danny was 13 the last time I went inside. Keep your friends close, and enemies closer. The kind of Machiavellian dictum that a 13-year-old needs to understand. Last thing I said to him. Danny never visited me in jail because I wouldn't allow it.

If he had, I wouldn't have told him any different. Play it smart, but don't let them stand over you. Once you're down, life will keep kicking.

Danny doesn't get out of the car. He's seen Detective Inspector Brett Ogilvie, smoking a rollie beside his fleet vehicle Falcon, perk of his shift to Federal Police. He's parked, deliberately, behind a black TRG mini-tank, stationed there in case of a riot. Like the US President's wartime speeches, back-dropped by rows and rows of jug-jawed soldiers, a wallpaper of quiet menace.

This whole prison release thing is a movie cliché, but there you have it. The hard-looking kid in a muscle-car, the concerned cop, the sunlight on my pale skin, my squinting eyes.

Danny passes me some Oakley sunglasses, and the world goes feather-soft. Both of us ignore Ogilvie as we cruise down to the main road, but as we turn left towards Fremantle a black Hummer limo enters from the right. I keep my head down but can't avoid Mastic's mutt face framed by panels of tinted glass, in the rear. He simply points at me, as the sergeant-at-arms of The Nongs is given to do, master to his minions. Mastic will have chilled beer in there, the kind that tastes like chemical soup, and some hard-faced prossies with plastic tits.

'Should we go back?' Danny asks. 'I been hearin—'
'That he's been protecting me. I know. It's bullshit.'
'I forgot to ask. You want to drive?'
'No. You drive.'

I saw it in Danny the moment he picked me up, but I hoped I was wrong. Two minutes inside his flat proved me right. Fit-pack on the coffee table, base of an upturned Coke can for a spoon. He worked the powder into the water and drew up a shot, passed it to me. I shook my head, looked at him coldly. Baby blue eyes and ice-cream skin, hair like finely blown toffee. Like his mother.

He looks hurt. All his childish needing to please, there on the surface. Softness, vulnerability, and it catches in my gut.

Because where I've come from, the first instinct is to squash it, in yourself and others. What the psychs call learned behaviour.

And then it comes through, the deeper and stronger, longest held. The moment of his birth.

My quiet, tender child. My second son.

Working the fit into the serpentine vein on the back of his hand, the puff of blood in the glass, driven home.

He smiles and caps the fit, lights a Styvie, slumps in his chair.

I can't take my eyes off him. My youngest boy, grown into a man. I barely notice what my hands are doing, although he watches closely. He is both in the first flush, but long gone, and yet there is time to catch him. After all these years, it's not far to go. To follow my child. That he not be alone.

Wherever he assumes he's going.

Thinking that he knows where I've been.

It's only when his friends arrive that the trouble starts. Two rat-faced morons that are clearly his best mates, kids Kevin's age, early 20s. Juvie boys, the kind that Warner attracts. Strangely androgynous and PVC white, all the usual tatts and prominent labels. Dickhead hip-hop on the speaker. Porn on the laptop. Ice in the pipe. Laughter with a dull edge of malice. Eyes vague and fierce. They repulse me, disappoint me, but not only because I fear their unpredictability. The kind I've been among these past five years. The kind as likely to stick a pencil in a sleeping man's ear, heel of the hand forcing it home, as to suck him off for a cigarette.

They can see what Danny is. Not like Kevin.

'Danny, you ready?'

Danny takes the pipe and sucks it down. The smack was strong, and not because I'm green again. I can hardly lift my head. Danny is just as greedy on the pipe as they are, something I wouldn't have expected.

'Ready for what?'

'Never mind, old man. Stay here an' nod off.'

Danny can't meet my eyes. Starts gathering his shit: ciggies, wallet, knife. The other one is back from the bedroom, lugging a green sports bag heavy with iron.

I shake my head, start to rouse myself.

I have left Danny with his brother's world, a world that Kevin belonged to, mine before him. I feel like stabbing my fit into the kid's eyes. He can sense it, too, and laughs.

'Yo, Danny, your dad is fierce.'

Where I want to go. The only place I've been where my radar doesn't ping, once, twice every minute. Where I can sleep easy. The place where my father lies unburied, at the bottom of a mineshaft. Not a place I ever expected to yearn for.

But there is peace there.

I wait behind the wheel of the stolen Camry sedan while they do the armed robs – three of them. Two servos and a late-night chemist. Not a few ks from where they live.

Such is the life of a moron.

They whoop and rap and smoke the short drive back to the port city, down along the eerily quiet Capo D'Orlando Drive, through gritty sulphur halos and clanking marinas and the smell of diesel and antifoul and rotting seaweed. We park before the long line of Warner's crayboats and trawlers, strung with red and green halogen caps, decks awash in hard fluorescent light.

Danny and his friends divvy up the 800 cash and transfer the weapons from the stolen car to a nearby Falcon ute, the rush of the thieving gone now they're at work.

Prison's full of kids like this. There because they want to be, the stupid ones to prove themselves to others, the smarter for themselves.

But Danny's not prison material, and his friends aren't the kind to stand by him, should he be marked out for special attention.

I hadn't allowed Danny to talk about what he was doing for Warner, either in the car or at his flat. Ogilvie would certainly have bugged the car, perhaps the flat. But I let the others in the Camry bray how they worked the presses for Warner, who'd been importing high-end E from Amsterdam, cutting it down by 50% and re-pressing his own pills with his own logo: Jagger lips.

The kids worked the presses all night, another shift worked days, cray season nearly over. Warner's fleet could easily get out into international water, to trawl up submersible barrels tagged with homing devices, his MO now for close to two decades.

Danny and the kids expect me to take the Camry and leave, but when I don't, there is anticipation in their eyes. Mastic has offered to knock Warner for me, but because I've always refused, it's assumed that I intend to do him myself.

Warner has never denied killing my son, Kevin.

Warner strides down the dock towards me, while gumboots stained with fish-guts and scale, black boardies and skin-tight bluey, bunched forearms and hairy hunched shoulders, the body of a worker.

Danny stays beside, but the other kids draw back.

Warner right in my face, stale sweat and ashtray mouth, flecks of fish blood on his cheek, eyes yellow beneath the sulphur light, moths batting around our heads.

Ogilvie will be watching from nearby.

He knows our history, was a beat copper when Warner and I ran plantations for Joe Italiano in the Gascoyne. Warner married into the family, took on the fishing licences as both a cover and a going concern, has done well, never gone to jail.

I've gone the way of most. Habit. Jail. Habit. Jail.

But along the way I've taken on the trade, become the best at what I do. A good cook is excused things that put others in shallow graves.

Except for one thing.

Warner puts out his hand, but he's so close it's more like a jab to the stomach.

Ogilvie will be watching, long-lens camera at his eyeball.

But Ogilvie is not the only one watching. Danny flinches when I take Warner's hand, something that is noticed by Warner. 'You got work to do?'

Danny's face is unreadable, until he meets my eye. Disappointment. Disbelief. A flash of something else.

I have chosen Warner.

Had in fact chosen him years earlier, made a promise of sorts, when an emissary of Warner's was transferred into the SHU. A wiry old Noongar crim, with blurred tattoos and oiled rockabilly hair, large fighter's hands. He told me about Danny, his message not couched in threat. Said Warner thought I'd like to know. Because of that unspoken history of ours. Fathers both dockworkers, did time together at Freo jail, drifted into the only union that would have them, the Painters & Dockers, before my dad went bush. Did he want me to hire Danny, or fuck him off?

Warner could see that Danny was no hard nut, had his father's weakness for the powder, but missed his father's luck. I say luck, because like most junkies my age, it's always the people around me who die, people like Danny's mother, so many others. I survive, like a curse.

But not Danny. He was headed one of two ways – neither good.

Hire him, I'd said. Then nothing else. No news. No threats, or further importuning. I'd appreciated that. And I had my own reasons for wanting to be close to Warner.

I go back to Danny's flat and have a shot, drift quietly in my body, seated slumber, nodding bringing me round. Hours pass like the years have passed, my whole fucking life, sleepless but asleep, the old anaesthetic.

The deal is good. Warner's set-up is good. I'll be making MDMA at nights on a customised trawler, out on the Sound, when it's still. Plenty of ventilation, all the newest kit. The precursors there, dropped off in the shipping lanes, direct from India.

Ogilvie can't get to Warner, not with his connections. Warner has men in the Ports Authority, the local drug squad. The Federal coppers would work alone for this reason, but they would need boats and choppers to get to the floating lab, and Warner would hear.

Warner is also safe from The Nongs and the others, because of his father-in-law, even if I'm not. Mastic has boasted widely that if I don't work for him, then I won't work for anybody. Has put it about that I owe him, for his protection inside, and now he'll have to demonstrate that he isn't full of shit. His signature demonstration involves a ball pein hammer.

I'll live on another boat, nearby the lab, safe as long as I don't leave the port. I've told Warner that I'll work for a year, pocket the money, take Danny and head elsewhere, up North, or New Zealand, start again.

He doesn't trust me, but that's no surprise. It's still worth his while.

I'll be close to him, and I'm a patient man.

The explosion at the port rocks the apartment, sets clarions in the street to wailing. From the kitchen I see flames down on Capo D'Orlando, fizzing white, incendiary secondary detonations, oil black streaks over the watercolour night sky.

The moment I think of Danny my legs weaken, and then I see him limp into the street. Vomit into a gutter. Limp towards the Charger, pop the boot, drop in a canvas bag, lean his weight on the closed trunk.

I understand. Feel a surge of panic. Start grabbing stuff, hearing Danny's key in the lock.

Turn, stand to face him. 'Warner's dead. Danny? Warner.'

His face tells the truth. He's burned on his neck, suppurating red blisters, what looks like a broken wrist wedged into his armpit, pupils dilated, in shock.

Eyes already on the coffee table, the fit-pack and powder.

I sit him down and fix him, watch his pupils screw inward, take the Charger keys from his hand and help him to his feet.

Dawn finds us out in the mallee scrub, beyond the wheat-belt and into cattle country, headed north. The dirt reddens and the heat falls hard and granite mesas rise out of the plains and dry gullies. Beneath the gnarled trunks of the mallee and currajong and corkwood the horizon fills with a floating carpet of pink and white everlastings, surreal.

Danny is in a bad way, and I fix him twice in cutaways beneath the feathery shade of beefwood and quandong, but then the packet is done. I'd stopped at a 24-hour chemist on the way out of Bassendean, had bought downers, painkillers, burn-salves, bandages, whatever they had. The blankets from the beds in the flat. Stuff from the cache of stolen property in the bedroom cupboards, to trade perhaps: some cameras, binoculars and a telescope, a fucking leaf-blower, some mobiles and laptops, miscellaneous tools.

That was before I looked inside the bag in the boot. Saw the cash, banded and loose, range of colours, no time to count it – and a handgun, a .38 S&W snubnose, no bullets.

I pay for petrol with cash at Payne's Find roadhouse, buy food for a few days, put us back on the highway north. The vintage two-door Charger is a distinctive ride, but eats the road between the towns, a few more hours we're in Cue. I take a dirt road before we hit the main street, buildings like a stage-set in a Hollywood mirage, then head west towards the Rock, parachute of dust curling over the floodplain of poverty bush and salt-grass, the abandoned gold diggings of Big Bell on the horizon north.

We get to Walga Rock when the sun is overhead, Danny still dazed and mute, angry because I'd chosen Warner, but afraid of what he'd done. The Rock slopes high and red beside the road, granite dome filling the sky, plated like a half-buried turtle, a lone wedge-tail circling in the higher thermals. I drive the opposite direction over the graded lip of red gravel and twenty yards into the bush. From here on there are no roads. I return to the lip and build it up again, sweep over our tracks with a mistletoe switch. It's slow going, lost in the low scrub, every now and then getting out to climb a beefwood, trying to catch a glimpse of the blue-grey monolith to the east, no name beyond what my father and his father called it: home.

It takes four hours to drive the 20 ks, at walking speed. Danny is too sick to get out and guide, and not wanting to stake a tyre, I circle round the fallen acacia and dry gullies over plains of purple mulla mulla and flannel bush and everlastings, knee-deep dry grass, plovers and bushquail sailing off in brief clucking parabolas, waves of locusts rising like a parting sea. It's hot on the vinyl seats, but the setting sun to the west is the best compass I have. Working slowly through a clump of fruiting quandong, hundreds of green and red budgerigar chirruping above us, I see the sparrowhawk and know we're close. It glides above us, taking a good close look through unblinking eyes, circling before rising off the scrubline in an effortless arc. I remember that the sparrowhawk feeds on the swallows at the rock, and follow it. Soon the broad red flank of the granite monolith looms before us, a couple of hundred metres high, unlikely as always in the broad flat plain, the red dirt around it as trackless as I'd hoped. We circle round to the eastern side, into the shade, looking for my father's camp, marked by a screen of casuarina and the quandong planted by my grandfather, its seeds buried beside jam wattle saplings, to feed off its roots.

I drive the Charger into the cleft of rock that curls beneath an overhang, invisible from the air, and turn off the ignition. Immediately the eerie silence settles over us, just the ticking of the overworked engine.

I help Danny climb out of his seat and sit him against the smooth trunk of a leaning redgum. Light him a cigarette and set off to get firewood, dragging the dry mallee boughs caked in dirt, a few sticks of sandalwood. I set a fire in the cave, in the ancient fireplace used for so many thousands of years that the rock has melted into a scoop, ochre handprint of a Wadjari child on the smooth wall above. When I leave the cave Danny's still slumped against the tree, but has lifted his sunnies, watching a young male bowerbird perform for him, flacking its wings in a fan dance, hopping on its thin legs.

The anger that made Danny do to Warner what I wouldn't is gone now. He won't meet my eye.

'What's that?' he asks.

'Bowerbird. Young male. No pink on its back. He's trying out his moves on you.'

'So I shouldn't laugh.'

'How's your neck? Your arm?'

'Flies are bad.'

'Wipe your arse with your shirttails, keeps the flies away from your face.'

'Really?'

'No.'

I lift the collar of his shirt and pull back the gauze on his burn, still angry red but the blisters have stopped weeping. Important to keep the flies off, so I set about applying the salve over the dry powder I'd caked it with earlier; lay down some new gauze.

'That one of your dad's sayings?' he asks.

'Good guess.'

'Don't piss on my back and tell me it's raining.'

'You remember that?'

'Sure. He's tighter than a stocking on a chicken's lip. Face like a pox-doctor's clerk.'

Image of my father, face red with drink, propped up at the Fremantle Workers Club, the idiom of his generation bustling in the air, laughter.

Before he went mad, wouldn't leave his room, pissed off out here with his rifle and a single bag of clothes.

'I ever tell you about this place?'

'No.'

'You need water?'

'I need hammer.'

'None left.'

Danny's face goes ugly for a moment, brought back to normal with a strained effort. 'S'alright. My fault. All this.'

'Wait here. Watch the show.'

The bowerbird, who's been silent and watching while we talk, resumes his dance as I leave the camp, zebra finches techno-thrumming in the mistletoe by the cave. I walk up onto the rock and climb through the fading light onto a ledge that looks over the desert, mallee scrub to the horizon in every direction, a mob of kangaroo grazing near the soak. The gnamma holes on the rock still hold fetid water, tadpoles squirming in the shallows; poor man's caviar, my dad used to call them, swallowed them live and whole, as his father had taught him. Beneath a slab of red granite streaked with long quartz veins I pull out the oilcloth and sports bag, shovel and pick, ammo box filled with Dad's cutlery, ledgers, tools.

It takes two trips, but I get the lot down to camp, leave it near the old fireplace, coals glowing. Unwrap the .303 from its oilcloth. Grease is clean and golden. No sign of rust. Not enough moisture in the dry desert air. Bullets dull brass in their cardboard cartridges, couple dozen of them. I load one into the breech and sight on the mob of goats that have come down the rock to observe, the billy goat coughing, staring at me down the sight, never seen a human before. I sight on the smallest kid, take in his colours, for later, when the food runs out. My father lived out here on goat and grass seed Johnny cakes for months at a time. Quandong in season. Tadpoles. Frogs. Bush turkey. His father before him. Famous among local prospectors. Had been so confident he'd found El Dorado he'd traded a ten-ounce nugget for a crate of sherry, before the hole went dry. It was when Grandpa died that my father followed him out here, worked the hole deeper into the granite and greenstone bands, gelignite and pick and shovel, mercury and cyanide extracted, right through summer. Dug out enough to pay for his smokes and bullets, but not much else. Everything listed in a shivery hand in his ledgers.

I take the rifle and the shovel and go and dig out the soak, hefting the dry sand that becomes damper, the rifle laid over a rock beside me.

The soak begins to fill with muddy water, and I keep digging. I had a lot of time to think on the drive up. We could live out here, make furtive trips into town, pay with cash. This is somebody's land, part of a cattle station the size of Victoria, no reason the owners would ever find us. My father and his father had never cared whose land it was, had always kept the .303 handy. This wasn't the kind of country you walked up on someone unannounced, even if you were the owner. Hunters out here. Prospectors. Fugitives.

But Warner is still alive, and Warner knows my father's diggings were near Cue. The logical place for a city-boy to run, with Danny.

Warner knew that I was going to have a crack at him. Most likely, he would have offed me after a couple of good batches. But he wouldn't have expected it from Danny.

Cue was 80 k to the east. Lot of country between us. We would probably be safe here.

Not a lot of other options.

It's a feudal world, the drug trade. My only other choice is to go to Mastic, bow and scrape, swear undying loyalty. Hope he can protect us.

Or go dog for Ogilvie and hope for the same.

But no legs in either option. Once I'm no use, they'll burn me to trade up, part of the game.

The sun has nearly gone and the light softens in the warm shade. Tiny tree frogs begin their migration from the gnamma holes to the grass and nearest scrub. A babbler singing on the rock. The sparrowhawk flies over for another look.

I watch the water drain into the soak clear and sweet, lob the shovel into the grass and carry the rifle over to the camp. Danny's still leaning against the gum, staring up at the rock, at the fat retreating tail of a giant bungarra, belly scraping rhythmically on the rock, flicking tongue tasting the air.

'It walked right past me. Wasn't scared at all.'

'Top of the food chain. Probably the same lizard I used to see here, 20 years ago. Dad used to shoot goat for it. The odd feral cat. Lives in a cleft of rock up there. A good sign. Keeps the snakes away.'

'Talkin like a bushie already. What's the plan? Stay here for the night? I'm gettin real sick.'

'Don't be an arse. If you'd killed Warner, we might go back, one day. Years from now.'

'A hospital. Morphine, for my bust wrist.'

'Not a chance. We're here until I figure it out. I've got some pills.' Danny's face turns ugly again, and I know the look.

'Can you walk?'

'Sure. But I need some pills.'

'One pill, every few hours.'

Danny's first time coming off. I've done it a hundred times, maybe more, and it will be hard to watch him suffer.

He thinks it's bad already.

Before it starts, I want to show him the mine. We walk through 50 yards of scrub, ancient trees evenly spaced, has the feel of an orchard planted by a careful hand, everything radiant in the last warm light, to the edge of the mineshaft.

'Careful.'

My hand across Danny's chest. Just a big hole in the ground, vertical, my grandfather's hand-sawed boughs framing the edges, perfectly square, dug out with a pick and shovel.

'Why here?'

I shake my head. 'I've always wondered that. Don't think my dad knew either. Just that it produced a bit, for his dad. Between them, they worked it for close to 20 years.'

'He died out here, didn't he?'

I ignore the question, looking down into the hole. 'We'll have a better look tomorrow. But first, what my father told me when I was your age. Don't wander. At first, all the trees look the same. It's easy to get lost, and hard to get found. In this heat, you'll last two days without water; three at the most.'

'But the rock.'

'You can be 50 metres from the rock in this scrub, not see it. Just do as I say. Don't wander off.'

'Ok.'

We're nearly back to the rock when I hear the chopper. It's gone dark enough for the searchlights to stand out against the red horizon, the clear twin beams of white light sweeping towards us.

We make it to the cave before the police chopper sights us, turning slowly around the edge of the rock, looking for our camp, but the searchlights make one thing clear.

Either Warner has a mate in the local coppers, out doing his bidding, perhaps even up there with a rifle, or else the fire at the wharf got too big for Warner to control. Meaning there's a general manhunt out for us. Meaning every copper in the state is on our tail.

If it's Warner pulling the strings, and they find us, we're dead.

Warner's name is on the line, and he will never give up. Plenty that went up in smoke, not covered by insurance.

Beyond forgiveness now, or recompense. Even for a prized cook.

I dose Danny with three pills at once, bed him down in a nest of blankets, leave him a pot of water, the rest of the food, scratch crude directions into the cave floor, should I never return.

Walk out into the night, rifle over my shoulder, the full moon rising over the eastern horizon, enough light to drive by.

It takes me five hours to make the road, following our earlier tracks, another hour to get into the Cue town site, make the roadhouse just before it closes. Fill up the Charger, pay using Danny's credit card, make sure my picture on the servo surveillance video is clear. Do the same at the bottle shop. Hope to Christ the coppers don't get me in town. I'll have to go down shooting. The strong possibility that one of them is owned by Warner. Don't want to be beaten to death in the Cue cells. Don't want to give up Danny's location. Don't want to not give it up, under torture – leave him out there alone, helpless.

I make small-talk with the bottle-shop owner, mention I'm camping at Walga Rock, take my half-carton and leave. Watch from my car to see if he runs to the phone.

He doesn't, which is not a good sign. Coppers are looking, but not asking.

I return along the dusty track beneath the risen moon and make camp not far from Walga Rock. A big fire, within plain sight of the road, near the car. Pile a few bags under the last two blankets, on the ground by the fire, two sleeping scarecrows, then walk back to the road with the leaf-blower, use it to blow away the car-tracks into the first 50 metres of bush the other side. When I've built up the graded lip again and I'm sure that our track is covered, I retreat back to the nearest flank of Walga Rock with the rifle, spend a night shivering and watching the road, herd of goats using the wallaby path behind me, coughing and snorting, my smell like an odd dream among them. I leave the rock only to keep the fire at the camp going, the urge to lie down and sleep strong.

Back in my stone eyrie I keep myself occupied cleaning the .303 by moonlight, with screwdriver and strips of my shirt, hope to hell the sight is still good. Count the stars coming out as the moon sinks to the horizon, as the inky darkness settles for an hour before the first flushes of dawn, there behind the distant lights of Cue.

I hear the chopper just before the sun spills red over the horizon, high up in the dark sky, just the distant syncopation among the winking stars, one of them moving slowly around the rock. I crawl beneath the nearest wedge of granite, to mask me from their infra-red, and settle down to wait. I'd placed the two swags as near the fire as possible, the whole camp glowing white on their screen.

It's working as I hoped. One of Warner's copper stooges in Perth, alerting him to the time and place of Danny's credit card use, last night. The chopper sent out to confirm the campsite. Warner likely on a light plane these past hours, Perth to Meekatharra, the short drive from there to Cue.

He'll be coming armed, in company. He'll want his money back, but this isn't about money.

An execution. An example. Done himself.

The chopper circles for a while then heads back to the town, dropping in altitude. I hunker down on the cold granite ledge and draw a bead over the plain, looking for plumes of dust.

The thought of Danny, probably awake now, shivering and sick. The certain knowledge that if I die, he dies too.

The last of us. The only good one.

I'm trying, but it doesn't feel real. The .303 heavy in my hands, the rifle my father taught me to use, when I was Danny's age.

And always the question I've been asking myself, ever since I decided to follow Danny – to never leave him, until he's safe from my world, from me, my good intentions.

At what point did I pass from being The Son, to The Father? It wasn't at the boys' birth, or even during their childhood. I was no real parent. Kevin always a pain in the arse. But Danny, never far from my mind. Knowing that until I find a place for him somewhere safe, I will not be able to die in peace.

Because my father did not die in peace.

The moment of his death the answer to my question. The moment I pulled the trigger, his eyes on mine, but grateful, I passed from being the son to the father. A father in a fatherless world. The godless world that he had lived in, when his father had died. What my father meant.

My father had been out here, dying, alone, when I found him.

The cancer, right through him by the time I arrived, just out on remand, come to collect something I'd left, the only bloke I could trust. He hadn't told anyone he was dying. He didn't have any meds. No transport to get into town. Too weak to walk the 20 k to the track, to hitch a ride.

It was already too late. The depth of his suffering. The sounds he made, like a flayed animal. The cancer in his brain. Helpless in his agony.

I broke parole and stayed with him. Couldn't leave him to go to town, for help, too far gone. Made him broth that he couldn't swallow.

Fed him my own pills, useless.

Then the moment came. He was ready. Eyes became clear for a moment, drawn out of his delirium by the pain. Lost. Confused. Understood where he was. What was happening. His last act of will. Told me to do it. His own hands, no good.

Told me that I could do it.

I knelt before him on the cave floor, the .303 barrel in his mouth, his eyes on mine, watering, afraid. A paste of snot and blood, mixed with the red dirt, in his hair, his eyes, his mouth, in his bedding, all over his skin.

He said it then. 'A father is God to his son.'

I hear the Hilux engine before I see it, the plume of red dust rising out of the riverbed, settling over the red gum and casuarina grove, the car parked there amid the cover. One vehicle. No chopper. Cops keeping it at arm's length. Warner and one other, a Maori bloke I know, Morgan, who knows me, a good bloke who's come to do me in. Both armed with shining new shotties, a Sunday stroll, walk in the park, hunting the junkie and his junkie son, their navy-blue jumpsuits like coppers' or miners' uniforms, black boots and caps, should there be any witnesses.

No witnesses out here.

I wait until they're in a sparse patch of cynic grass framed by a field of white everlastings, no cover beyond a few crumbling termite nests, shoot Morgan first, the crosshairs on his chest true, swing the bead onto Warner, who's pitched into the dirt, put a bullet into his shoulders, load another, put two more into each of them, watch their skulls burst like puffballs, red spores settling over the dirt, then start running, down the flank of the covering rock, towards the dried riverbed, to get in behind their vehicle, in case there's a driver.

There isn't. The Hilux is parked on a carpet of casuarina needles, the tracks of emu and roo and goat in the dried mud around. Windows down, passenger seat reclined, Warner having snoozed on the drive in, the bastard.

Doesn't look like a rental. Or a copper's car, on loan. In the glovebox I find the rego – a company car, Styx Gold Ltd, from a nearby mine, an Italiano family company.

Iced coffee cartons on the floorpan, some bacon egg roll wrappers, breath mints, Warner's cigarettes.

On the back seat, an overnight bag, two new sleeping bags, dunny paper, some cash in a bum-bag, wank mags, a blue tarp and two shovels, a jerry-can of fuel.

Warner no mug.

He'd make me dig our grave, mine and Danny's, pile on wood then pour on the fuel. Burn us into ashes and bone rubble, cover us over.

Gone forever.

I park the Hilux 50 metres into the bush, walk back over our track, build up the graded lip of gravel road and use the leaf-blower to cover our trail. The Valiant is waiting hidden in the riverbed; its rego plates in the tray of the Hilux.

Warner sits beside me on the drive to the rock, buckled in, reclined, the other bloke in the tray, wrapped in the tarp. Both of them bled out already, into the dirt.

I want to keep this car, for later. An Italiano company vehicle, unlikely they'll claim it as missing.

Would raise too many questions.

No sign of the chopper either. Same reason. The slightest sniff of something gone wrong, Warner's stooges will abandon him, start covering their tracks, deleting searches from computers, wiping the flight logs of choppers, until his body is found.

But it will never be found.

Danny takes one look at what's inside the Toyota and says, 'Oh, what a feeling.'

Late afternoon. All day driving and walking. Parking the Hilux in the cave, before I walk back to Walga Rock to collect the Charger.

Now Warner and Morgan are in the front seat of the Valiant, strapped in, sightless eyes staring over the bonnet, beginning to smell bad. Danny stands aside and smokes, says nothing as I roll the Valiant, slowly, carefully, over the lip of the mineshaft, wanting it to slide, which it does, crashing once or twice on the way down.

I have no idea how deep the shaft is, and I will never know. Danny helps me drag the lighter firewood and tip it in. I put whole dried boughs down, mallee, beefwood, sandalwood, whatever is at hand. Pour over the fuel, follow it with a burning torch of poverty bush, stand back as the whump of heat rises in a vertical column of shimmering clear.

Keep feeding the fire, the compressed explosion of the Charger's tank, the sound of crumbling rock, superheated, the support boughs burning through.

The work of generations, collapsing in on itself, spume of red dust rising out of the shaft.

An end to it.

I am tired and covered in blood, dirt, charcoal. Haven't slept for close to 60 hours. We retreat to the cave. No words are necessary. We'll camp here, a week or two, perhaps a month. I'll hunt and cook. Danny will get clean.

Then we'll move. Enough cash to last a year, if we're careful.

A new start. New Zealand. Different line of work. Set Danny up with some kind of trade. Sit back and give him a chance.

The light in the cave is soft and red, like a child's crayon drawing. There's nothing to do now but sleep, rest, live my father's hermit life for a while, walk the rock, feed the bungarra, watch the light over the desert change as the gnamma holes dry up, as the birds fly to the coast.

I feel it for the first time in a long while, my eyes upon my son, feeding the fire: my father's presence in the cave with us, and it's not the violence of our last moments which haunts me, but the feeling that he is looking over us, perhaps, and then I am asleep.

SKIN DEEP

DINUKA MCKENZIE

Kate hesitated on the front porch, her discomfort making her nervous. She was certain they would be able to see though her spiel; intuit the real reason she had been sent. Constable Kathryn Aneesha Grayling, a nice brown face to calm everything down. Keep them all on side. Make them understand that the police had everything under control.

A shard of light from the setting sun caught her eyes and she blinked, her shadow climbing the yellow brick exterior of the house. Blood orange rays on egg-yolk yellow. Cooking smells spilled from the home, the scents mingling with the musk of fallen Jacaranda blooms that littered the street like purple crepe-paper. Jacaranda and curry leaves. She felt the traitorous beads of sweat prickle across the bridge of her nose as her skin absorbed the aroma of spice and chillies. Rubbing her face furiously, she pressed the doorbell.

A quietly spoken, South Asian man met her at the door. Middle-aged, pressed jeans, polo shirt and thongs; a neat side-parting divided his thinning hair into opposing teams. He smelled of cigarettes and fried food. For a moment she mistook him for Mr Gunathilake, before she realised her mistake. He wasn't the right height. His carriage not as pillar straight and forceful. Probably a brother or a close cousin.

The man ushered Kate into the house and through a living room stuffy with knickknacks, dominated by a black leather lounge suite and flat screen TV. The room buzzed with people of all ages. An extended family of *aunties* and *uncles* and their kids. The community coming together. Faces glanced up at her as she passed. Some with curiosity, some with open hostility. Others too dulled by sorrow to care. She felt the heavily kohled eyes of a young woman dressed entirely in black shadow her as she followed her guide around the corner.

Kate was shown into a bedroom heavy with incense and grief. The man motioned her in, forcing her to squeeze past him to enter.

Inside, a twentysomething woman sat on a queen-size bed attending to her mother who was curled in a mound under the covers. Kate caught a glimpse of Mrs Gunathilake's crumpled face, her dark hair threaded with grey fanning across the pillows in disarray. The sound of whimpering, like a child in pain. The daughter coolly competent in her professional garb – charcoal grey suit, pencil skirt, low sensible heels and sparse makeup – bent over her mother, alternately stroking her face and exhorting her to eat something. A platter of food sat untouched by the bedside.

Kate recognised the short-eats from her childhood: crumbed tuna and potato croquettes and empanada-like pastries filled with spiced minced meat. *Cutlets* and *patties* – a world away from Aussie lamb cutlets and hamburger patties.

At the back of the room, she clocked Mr Gunathilake moulded to a chair by the window, his larger-than-life frame collapsed in on itself.

She cleared her throat and the young woman looked up. Kate recognised her face from TV: the jutting chin and glowering eyes, coal black and hardened by grief. Her name came back to her: Kavita; meaning 'poem'. Her eyes assessed Kate now, just as they had done the interviewer on the news program two nights ago. *Are you here to help or offer platitudes?*

Kate suddenly felt very young, stripped bare by the gaze of this woman, who knew her place in her world and her community.

'Mr and Mrs Gunathilake, the coroner has released your son's body. It means you can go ahead now with his funeral arrangements.'

A wail rose from the mother. Mr Gunathilake remained entirely still, as if by remaining motionless he could stop the effect of Kate's words.

'On behalf of the New South Wales Police, I want to once again extend our deepest sympathies for your loss. A family liaison officer can be made available if you need anything.'

Anil Gunathilake – a 23-year-old, working towards his real estate license while earning money as a food delivery driver for a local Indian restaurant in his spare time. He had been bashed senseless after delivering a Saturday night takeaway – vindaloo, lamb biriyani and three cheese naans – to a house down-river. The two meatheads who had answered the door had insisted that the food was cold and the delivery late; that a refund was in order. Anil had disagreed. Words were exchanged and things had escalated. The entire incident had been witnessed by neighbours who had rung 000. Anil had been unresponsive by the time the paramedics had arrived, and had been pronounced dead in Grafton Hospital.

Kate stumbled over her words. Keenly aware of their inadequacy. Feeling the trespass. The hollowness of the gesture.

Kavita snorted, a strangled sound.

She waved Kate out of the room, dismissing her.

Chastened and embarrassed, Kate left the house, impatient to get away.

'Hey.'

A figure peeled away from the darkened garden, just as she had reached her patrol car.

'You're that coconut cop, yeah?'

From the porch light, Kate could make out the girl with the heavy eye makeup. The young woman blew out a delicate curl of cigarette smoke.

'That's what Kavita calls you. Brown on the outside, white on the inside.' She laughed, a mocking cackle before stamping out the cigarette and heading back to the house.

A heaving mass of protesters. A sea of brown, mostly male, mostly young, shouting into the faces of an all-white police force in riot gear. The saffron, white, and green of the Indian flag rose against the sky. Signs punctured the air: *Racism Down Under. Stop Asian Hate. We Are Not Safe.* A young man caught in the moment, his face contorted with rage, spat at the feet of the police and was tackled to the ground. Bodies swarmed in to help, falling and being pulled into the melee.

The news footage cut to further images of protests followed by shots of serious-faced politicians fronting a press conference. The banner at the bottom of the news screen read: *Protests escalate in Sydney and Melbourne as the Prime Minister calls for calm.*

Kate pointed the remote and switched off the TV. She needed a break from the story that seemed to be dominating every second of print and television media. A wave of bashings in the capital cities which appeared to be targeting South Asians. And now with Anil's death, the story had struck home. Their town in the Clarence Valley, seven hours drive north of Sydney, had become ensnared in the national narrative of racially motivated crimes. Whether or not Anil's death was part of that was beside the point.

The ethnicity of the victim made it so.

Her sergeant's words rang in her mind. 'They come here wanting to be Australian. God, forbid you notice their skin colour or ask where they came from. But the minute something happens, watch how quickly they pull out the race card.' He had been looking straight at her when he had said the words, daring her to disagree.

She still felt the shame of his words. For not reacting. For toeing the line and not making waves. For being the good little police officer, she was.

'That poor family. I still can't believe what happened. Has the man been caught yet?'

Kate started out of her thoughts and shook her head, briefly. It wasn't something she wanted to get into with her mother.

Of the two men involved in Anil's bashing, one had fled the scene and was still to be apprehended, four days on. It was a sore point at the station. His mate had been arrested on the night, found cowering in a neighbour's yard. Kate had been at the station when the young man was brought in: all bravado gone, shocked into silence. A death on his conscience before he was out of his teens. The result of a stupid testosterone-fuelled fever. Two mates egging each other on into bloodshed and brutality.

Kate pulled her mind back to her meal. She was seated at her kitchen counter, an array of freshly prepared Sri Lankan curries laid out in front of her. Her mother hovering waiting for her verdict.

'Try the mallung. Aunty Lucky's daughter who works at the Asian shop found some gotu kola for me. Lovely girl. Too much makeup, but lovely figure. Nice and slim.'

Her mother nudged the dish of closer and Kate obliged by accepting another helping of the lightly stir-fried greens, laced with red onion, shredded coconut, dried ground bonito flakes and seasoned with chilli flakes, turmeric, and lime. She swallowed and smiled, making a thumbs-up sign.

It was one of the handful of Sri Lankan dishes that Kate remembered from her childhood, though her mum had resorted to the more readily available flat leaf parsley. Dishes that her mother would only prepare when the mood struck her. When she would cook up everything she had learnt from her own mother in one frenzied rush of cooking. The house would swell with the scent of spices, ground and dry-roasted from scratch as if her mother was trying to drown out any memory of their everyday fare: meat and three veg, roasts, and sausages on the barbeque.

Kate's younger brother had taken to the spices more easily than her. She recalled her mother's laughter, gently mocking as she'd tackled the rice and curry, eyes watering from the chilli and sweat pouring from her face, gulping iced water between each bite whilst her brother calmly inhaled his plate with not a hair out of place. It had been the family joke. Luke who took after their father, complete with his fair skin and freckles and outwardly for all the world a true-blue Australian, could handle his spice like a pro. Meanwhile, Kate who had inherited all of her mother's South Asian features – dark hair and skin – could barely look at a chilli without breaking into a sweat.

Kate pushed her plate away now, feeling overfull and uncomfortable. She still wasn't used to her mother's presence in her apartment; the home-cooked curries every night and the obligation to make conversation when all she wanted to do was collapse in front of the couch with a beer.

Her mother's visit, which was only meant to last a few days, had stretched out over a week. Kate's work in Grafton was her haven away from her parents and her childhood home in Esserton in the Northern Rivers hinterland south of Murwillumbah. Her means of creating her own identity, away from the claustrophobic shadow of her father, the Police Chief of Esserton Station. She burped, feeling the burn of spice scorch its way up her throat.

'Did you visit the family today? Lucky told me the father has gone to pieces. What a thing to happen.' Her mother shook her head in disbelief.

Kate didn't reply. She had no intention of discussing the details of the case with her mother. Not that it made any difference. Her mother appeared to be entirely plugged into what was going on without the need for Kate's input.

She wondered at her mother's sudden and complete absorption into the Northern Rivers South Asian community. It was a new development. Growing up, Kate couldn't remember her mother showing any specific interest, seemingly content with the life she had chosen. Apart from the occasional spice-laden culinary foray, Kate and her brother had grown up entirely immersed in their father's world: the regional, middle-class Australian life they had been born into.

Watching her mother now, Kate wondered when she had lost her confidence, her sense of self. In recent years, she seemed to be only interested in spouting the second-hand views she had absorbed from her friends on Oz-SL.net, an online community of expat Sri Lankans, and its Northern Rivers chapter. Suddenly all that mattered was what the community thought. To Kate's annoyance, her mother's lens seemed to have switched to Kate's own life. Her choice of dress, the friends she kept, and in particular her choice of relationships. *I met a lovely family the other day. Their son's a dentist with a practice in Byron Bay. Very successful.* Kate had not told her mother of her most recent date, an architect from town, definitely not Sri Lankan.

She looked up catching the concern in her mother's eyes.

'Kate, you need to be careful, especially now. The uniform's not going to protect you.'

'Mum, I'm fine. Stop worrying.' She headed to the fridge for a beer to wash away the reality of her mother's words.

Shattered fragments crunched under Kate's boots as she took in the remains of the glass frontage of the physiotherapy practice. She could just make out the wording of the original signage: *De Silva Sports Physiotherapy*. Mucous trails of egg yolk and bits of shell were smashed across the walls. The eggy remains would soon start to turn in the sun.

A crowd had gathered. A contingent of the local press had already sniffed out the story and were framing their cameras for tonight's headlines. Overnight, the business had been egged and its shopfront smashed in with a brick. On any other day it would have attracted little media attention. But the business was owned and operated by a person of South Asian heritage: Kumar De Silva. So here they all were. Another day. Another hate crime.

Mr De Silva was at the station making a statement and Kate had been dispatched to collect the CCTV from the premises.

She was ushered inside through the back entrance by a woman who introduced herself as Lakshmi De Silva, co-owner of the business and wife of the physiotherapist whose name had until recently adorned the front of the building. Lakshmi's face was marked with worry, a smudge of hastily applied lipstick streaked her front teeth and her thick hair was pulled into a messy ponytail.

'I can't believe it. What a mess! What have we done to deserve this? First that poor boy and now this. Why are they targeting us?'

Kate remained silent, allowing her to vent. She had no assurances to offer that would make any difference anyway.

She followed the woman into a cluttered office: a study and shelves installed with the usual printer and modem, trays of stationery, stacked files and framed qualifications on the wall. A family photo sat slightly ajar on top of a filing cabinet. Kumar De Silva posing with his wife and grown-up daughter: clean shaven and smiling, looking distinguished and debonair in a suit and tie and moussed raked-back hair.

Mrs De Silva motioned towards desktop computer set up at the back of the room.

'Have you had a look at the footage?' Kate asked.

Mrs De Silva shrugged. 'It's someone wearing dark clothes and a cap. Who can tell who it is?'

As Kate downloaded the files, she could feel the woman's eyes on her. 'You're Aneesha's daughter, aren't you?'

Kate looked up, curious, taking in Mrs De Silva's features. Lakshmi as in 'Aunty Lucky'; her mother's friend. She felt the narrowing of her personal space.

'You look just like your mother. She talks about you all the time.' Mrs De Silva's face broke into a smile. 'That's a relief at least. You understand us. I feel better knowing you'll be the one taking care of this.'

Explaining her status within the station hierarchy; her lack of authority to take care of anything but follow orders, fell mute on Kate's lips. Somehow saying the words out loud felt like a betrayal of her mother in this woman's eyes.

Kate returned a cramped smile, feeling the binds of obligation tighten.

Lakshmi De Silva's prediction had proven correct. The CCTV that Kate had retrieved from the vandalised shop and its neighbouring businesses had revealed nothing obvious in terms of the assailant's identity. The black-and-white images only showed a slight figure, dressed in dark pants and a long-sleeved top, their face obscured by a plain baseball cap pulled low. The perpetrator had arrived on foot just after 2am, carrying the brick and eggs they were intending on throwing. The footage showed the figure walking calmly away after the incident, even though the security alarm would have been blaring at full volume in the background.

It felt odd to Kate. She had assumed the attack would be the work of drunken teenagers out for a lark. But this felt far more deliberate. Planned, even.

'So, Grayling. Cracked the case, have we? Found the white bastard who smashed your friend's place?'

Kate turned to face Sergeant Cromer, his too-close eyes and bloated face marked by too many years in the sun and too many nights at the pub. He manoeuvred himself beside her to watch the footage, standing just close enough to make her uncomfortable. She could smell the sourness of his breath mingled with the tang of aftershave. Halitosis and pine. He had always treated her with disdain, but since her elevation to a pseudo-community liaison role at the behest of Northern Region Command following the furore with the South Asian community, his dislike of her had multiplied. In his eyes she was the poster girl for special treatment, to be pulled back and cut down to size at every opportunity.

He grunted as the footage ended. 'Looks like someone's got it in for your mates.'

'He's not my mate.' The words were out before she could stop herself. She wanted to assert her impartiality but the words had come out wrong. Disloyal. It sounded like she wanted to ingratiate herself with him.

He regarded her, a sneer playing on his lips. 'Yamba just called. They got a walk-in. The kid's been brought in by his uncle. Admitted to the bashing.' He winked at her. 'But don't you get up, princess. I'll go and bring him in. I know you'll be busy with all that cultural liaison.'

He smirked and stalked away. She gritted her teeth, swallowing down the bile, hating herself that he always managed to get a rise out of her. It was times like this that the temptation to transfer home rose within her. The mirage of an easier path, working under the protection of her father in Esserton. She closed her eyes and the fantasy crumbled. She would only be replacing one set of complications with another.

Kate waited by the river. The wide, calm expanse of the Clarence River spread before her, the occasional patch of reed beds and scrubby vegetation fringing its flat grass-lined banks. The water shone green-grey in the late afternoon sun; a hint of breeze cooling her skin with the breath of brine and mangroves from up-river.

She checked her watch and made her way up the street. She had timed it well. The Asian grocer was in the process of closing for the day. She waited for the young woman at the tills to finish and call out her goodbyes, before falling into step with her.

'Hi Yasmin, do you have a few moments to speak?'

'You. What do you want?'

Kate regarded her: the girl with the heavily made-up eyes who had stopped her in the front yard of the Gunathilake's. She wasn't wearing any makeup today. Just like she hadn't been in the photograph in her parent's office at De Silva Physiotherapy. She still retained her preferred uniform of black: t-shirt, jeans and Doc Martens. Upon seeing Kate, her face took up the sneer Kate recalled from the previous night.

'I'd like to chat to you about what happened to your dad's office last night.'

Yasmine shrugged, losing interest. 'Shouldn't you be speaking to my mum?' she asked, pulling out a packet of Wrigley's from her backpack and popping a tab in her mouth. She chewed in silence, her jaw mechanically working the gum.

'I met with your mum this morning but I wanted to speak with you as well, see if you had any thoughts.'

'Yeah right. So no leads then. What a surprise.'

Kate glanced at the girl, taking in the scornful turn of her lips and stubborn tilt of her chin. According to Kate's mother, Yasmine was a straight-A student, a school prefect and in the debating team. Her bad-girl act felt forced, like an ill-fitting jacket she was trying on for size.

'You're in the middle of Year 12 exams, aren't you?'

Yasmin inclined her head, without bothering to reply.

'It's a stressful time. You must be under a lot of pressure.'

'Whatever, I can handle it.'

'Do you know what you want to do after school?'

'Psych at UNSW.'

Kate nodded impressed. 'You're travelling to Sydney? You don't want to study closer to home?'

'The further I can get from this dump, the better.' There was venom and conviction in the statement. She turned to Kate, 'Look, what do you want? Aren't you meant to be investigating or something? We're being targeted and all you can do is ask me about school.'

They had reached a square of green space, a dog park, dotted with date palms and Eucalypts and a scattering of benches. Kate turned in. 'Sit with me.'

Yasmin scowled, making no move to follow her.

'It's just an informal chat, Yasmin. You're free to leave at any time.' She gestured to the bench seat and the girl flounced beside her with a huff.

'Well?'

Kate's voice was gentle. 'I know it was you who threw that brick, Yasmin. I thought I'd give you the chance to explain, before I speak to your parents.'

'What? What are you talking about? I was home, asleep. This is bullshit. You're meant to be finding the rednecks who did this. Not trying to pin this on me!'

'I recognised your Doc Martens, Yasmin, in the security footage. Plus the person caught on CCTV has the same height and build as you. They also seemed to know exactly where the security cameras at your dad's store are positioned, to make sure they kept their face down.' Kate didn't miss Yasmin's flinch, the quick calculation in her eyes.

'If I recognised you, other people will too, Yasmin. Your family or school friends. Or maybe one of your parent's friends.'

That arrow landed; Kate could see the realisation set in. The fear of recognition and of bringing shame to the family, so entrenched and pervasive, a virtue which had been drummed into her since birth.

'We could publicly release the footage to test the theory, or you can just tell me why you did it.' Kate waited as Yasmin remained silent.

'You also forgot to clean the egg yolk from your shoes.'

She jerked her boots in front of her. 'What? No, I didn't. I mean. Shit!' Yasmin clamped her feet back, furious at herself for walking into the trap.

'So, what's going to happen now?'

'Not too much from our end. Your dad will probably find it hard to claim insurance on the damage, but that's about it.'

Yasmin squeezed her hands into fists, emotion sparking in her eyes. 'So in other words, business as usual for him.'

'Is this something to do with your dad, Yasmin? Were you mad at him about something?'

Yasmine shook her head, clearly not trusting herself to speak. She glanced at Kate and looked away.

'That place, it's not a good place.' Her voice was strained like the words were being wrenched from her. 'I just wanted to break his stupid face, smash that shit-eating grin. I know it was dumb. I wasn't thinking.'

Kate recalled the shattered glass frontage that had once featured the smiling decal of Kumar de Silva, head physiotherapist. Something slithered and coiled inside her chest.

'Tell me about your dad, Yasmin.'

Yasmin shivered, an involuntary reaction to a memory; the silence stretching like a rubber band waiting to snap. 'He's been doing rehab on my shoulder after hours. I hurt it during netball training, over a year ago.'

'That seems like a long time to be under treatment. Sounds like it was a serious injury.'

Yasmin screwed up her face, flexing and stretching her left shoulder, as if to prove its fitness.

Kate paused searching for the right words, aware of her own inexperience. 'Does your dad... Does he do anything during the treatments? Anything to make you uncomfortable?'

Yasmin, laughed, a sound of pain. 'He massages me. That's his thing. I have to remove all my clothes so he can, you know, do whatever.'

She grimaced and turned away embarrassed, her words barely above a whisper. 'Not every time. We can go weeks when it's completely normal and then it'll start back again.'

Kate reached for the girl's hand but stopped short as Yasmin flinched.

'Have you spoken to anyone about this, Yasmin?' she asked.

Yasmin shut her eyes and spoke through gritted teeth. 'No one's going to believe me. Not my mum. Not any one. Everyone loves him. It'll just be my word against his.' She whipped around to face Kate. 'And everyone will know. I'll be the one they'll all be talking about and pointing and whispering about.'

'You're right, Yasmin. It's not going to be easy. In fact, it'll probably be a shitfight. But what your father's been doing, it's not right.' Kate held Yasmin's gaze until she looked away. 'You're his daughter. He shouldn't be doing this.'

A silence fell between them. Kate watched a young couple playing fetch with their Jack Russell. The ball sailing through the air as the dog tore across the grass after it.

'It's only for a few more months.' Yasmin's voice was ragged, stumbling over her words. 'He promised me. Once I get into Uni, it'll be over. He's going to pay my fees, so I can live in Sydney. That's what he said. That's our agreement.'

The man had negotiated terms with his daughter. Kate swallowed her fury and pressed on, doing her best to keep her voice even. 'What if he doesn't keep his promise, Yasmin? What then?'

'It won't matter. School will be finished and I'll just leave. There are people in Sydney who'll help me.' Her voice trembled, her age slipping through. 'He won't be able to stop me. I'll be shot of him and the whole lot of them.'

'But what about your father? He would have gotten away with it. He'll be free to do this to someone else.'

She sprang to her feet and stared Kate down, her expression swerving from desperation to defiance. 'Don't do that. That's not on me. This is not my responsibility. What he does to anyone else, it's on him. I've got to look after me.' She jabbed a fierce finger at her chest.

'Yasmin—'

'Do what you want. I don't care.'

Before Kate could stop her, she had run off, pounding across the grass and disappearing behind the trees.

'You'll be coming up for Christmas?'

'I will Mum, I told you. I've already put in for leave.'

'Good.' Her mother sounded relieved. She fussed with her handbag and checked her mobile.

Kate stood in the terminal, her mother's luggage at her side. The coach to Esserton was due just after 7am; a five-hour trip with a changeover in Lismore. After 10 days in Grafton, her mother had decided it was time to go home. Kate knew that she would have stayed longer if Kate had asked.

They waited together, her mother tying and retying her scarf against the morning chill. The skies were overcast, the ground still clammy from overnight rains. A lone whipbird made its distinctive laser-like dart sound somewhere in the trees.

'Do you want me to grab you a coffee for the bus? The bakery will be open. Or a muffin or something. You hardly ate any breakfast.'

'I'm okay. I've got some muesli bars.' Her mother patted her bag and pulled out her mobile once more.

'Expecting a call?'

'No. It's Aunty Lucky. I texted her a few times to tell her I'm going home and to invite her over if they're visiting our way, but she hasn't replied.'

Kate looked away. She wasn't surprised that Mrs De Silva had cut her mother off. Kate had followed up her conversation with Yasmin with a visit to her parents and a referral to Family Services. Kate's standing with the family had turned to dust. The De Silvas had closed ranks, and so far Yasmin had refused to speak out against her father or confirm the matters she had disclosed to Kate. But she hadn't given up on the girl. Not yet.

'I hope nothing else happens to them, at least. They are such a nice family. They don't deserve all this terrible violence.'

Kate nodded, a non-committal gesture. It was a conversation for another day.

The coach lumbered into the terminal and she kissed her mother goodbye.

'Love to Dad. Text me when you get home.'

'Okay, and remember to give that boy a call. The dentist. I've left his number on your fridge.'

Kate smiled and waved.

The skies opened as she reached her car. She brushed the rain from her face as best she could, reaching for her mobile as she heard the familiar beep of an incoming message.

Fancy a drink tonight? Walkers @8?

A text from Geoff Miles, her architect date from a few nights back.

She grinned, her fingers tapping out a reply. *You read my mind.*

HIDING SOMETHING
FIONA SUSSMAN

Evan did not usually pick up hitchhikers. It had nothing to do with fear. It was more about not having the energy to invest in another person's needs. That some stranger's day might be made easier with a free ride from A to B was not his concern. He didn't care.

Why then he stopped to pick up the man at the bottom of the Crown Range was a mystery, even to him. Predestiny? Fate? The pull of some power beyond his understanding? Evan didn't believe in any of that.

When Sky was small, maybe five or six years old, he used to pretend he had the power to change traffic lights.

'Go green,' he'd say, tapping the steering wheel three times. Sometimes, it had to be four or five times.

Sky bought into the magic wholeheartedly, her belief-disbelief unshakeable.

'Do it again, Daddy! Do it again!'

She was like a Labrador puppy that never grew slow and grumpy.

Even at 18 she still had a breathless excitement about her. Just like her mum. It's what had first attracted him to Debra.

The man was standing beside the STOP sign at the intersection of Golf Course Road and Cardrona Valley Road. He looked to be in his early 30s, dressed as he was in a pair of ripped jeans, black puffer jacket, and a rust-orange beanie pulled low. His stained canvas rucksack was propped up against the signpost pole.

A brazen place for a hitchhiker to stand, thought Evan. Right beside a STOP sign. It didn't really allow for driver discretion. You were obliged to stop and then had to make the uncomfortable decision to drive away again. It felt a bit like being bullied into having your windscreen washed at a red light.

Evan had overseen the windscreen-washing fundraiser at Sky's school when she was in her second-to-last year there. They'd raised a heap of cash for the November ball just by positioning the kids at a major traffic intersection. Every two minutes the lights turned red, trapping a queue of cars behind the solid white line. It was next to impossible for a commuter to avoid eye contact with the troop of beaming teenagers standing at the ready, squeegees and buckets of suds in hand.

To be honest, the kids would have raised good money even if the lights had remained green all day; they just had that infectious energy about them.

Evan still thought of them as kids, though really, when he reflected back, they were already young adults on the brink of adventure, love, and freedom from the school bell.

As he lowered the passenger window, a bone-hollowing chill blew into the car – a reminder that the cocoon of heat was only a temporary escape from what was really out there.

'Where you headed?'

'Queenstown,' the man said, his almost-grin skewed in an unsuccessful bid to hide his broken front tooth.

Immediately Evan regretted his decision. There was something about a broken front tooth. Front teeth were important. The first introduction.

'I'm going over the range, but only as far as Frankton.'

The man yanked open the door, as if sensing Evan's ambivalence, and climbed in. He pulled the door shut with a thud. A grubby mustiness smothered the ute's standard smell of apples and damp dog hair.

'You can throw that in the back.'

'I'm alright,' the man said, hugging his cumbersome rucksack like a window-dresser grappling with a dismembered mannequin.

There were traces of Birmingham in his accent and his *I'm alright* turned the key on a cellarful of memories.

Evan and Debra had honeymooned in Britain. Their first and only trip outside of New Zealand. They'd been a bit cheeky, or maybe just ahead of the times, when they'd asked wedding guests to contribute to a holiday fund instead of some vase or casserole dish from a wedding registry.

Fifty-four guests helped them celebrate, yet despite people's generosity, the contributions still came up short. So, Evan withdrew the small sum he'd saved in his sharemilking days, paid a penalty for breaking the term deposit, and booked their flights. Auckland. Sydney. London. It felt good to be the provider. Good to begin married life ahead of his father-in-law's expectations.

The UK was like nothing either of them had experienced before, and the memories on replay in his head were as sharp and intense as they'd been in the moment 25 years earlier. Sharing a pint of Guinness and a plate of smoked trout on the banks of the Norfolk Broads. Precipice-steep escalators diving into warren of platforms and tunnels and tubes. Kissing in Regent's Park, surrounded by a sea of grass and an English summer. Demolishing a whole bag of Russian fudge while waiting in line for the cheap seats to *Phantom of the Opera*. (He couldn't look at fudge now without feeling nauseous.) The awe and inadequacy he felt as Debra commented on artworks hanging in the huge galleries and museums and public places. Lying in bed together in some grotty hostel, planning when to start a family.

The man cleared his throat. 'You from around here?'

'Yup,' Evan said, reluctant to encourage conversation. Small talk was like a horsefly imprisoned in a small space. Annoying. He preferred the numb silence he was used to when driving over the range.

He wanted to say, Sit back. Relax. No pressure to chat. But instead, found himself saying, 'And you? Where you from?'

'The UK.'

No kidding!

'It's a big place.'

The man flicked his head back in a sort of nervous tic. 'Was born in Birmingham, but I've moved around some since.'

Everything about the man looked tense — his cheeks flushed with tight circles of pink, his fists clenched.

Sky used to clench her fists when she didn't want them to see that she'd been biting her nails. It was something she'd done from way back, gnawing her fingernails right down to the bulgy bits. Debra tried everything to discourage the habit — bitter lacquer from the pharmacy, star charts, the promise of presents — but nothing worked. A typical pose of Sky was her sitting, head folded forward, thumb nail wedged between her teeth. Deb called her the modern-day Rodin's Thinker.

Evan wondered whether his passenger's clenched fists were hiding something.

As they started to climb, Evan changed down gears. He was relieved, if surprised, to see that the orange Chains Compulsory sign had been covered up, considering the forecast.

It would be a slow ascent nevertheless, and an even more cautious descent what with patches of road still trapped in shadow. Black ice conditions, for sure.

'Pretty country,' the man said, almost begrudgingly.

Evan looked out of the window. It had been a long time since he'd seen the scenery. It was just there, like a wire fence. Invisible.

Was it pretty? The huge cones of snow interrupted by dirty patches of tussock. The gritted asphalt that wound up, around, and down. The low, grey sky.

'You here on holiday?'

The man shifted in his seat. He did not look comfortable sitting there with his arms wrapped around his rucksack, as if ready to jump from the vehicle at a moment's notice.

'Sort of. It's a long story.'

There was something about his caginess that annoyed Evan. Funny how only moments earlier it had been the man's attempt at small talk that Evan found irksome.

Do you even know what you want, anymore, Evan? You're being otherwise just for the sake of it.

That would have been Debra's summation. And she'd be right, of course. She always was.

'Sort of a holiday?' he prompted.

In the early years, he and Debra had often talked about taking Sky on a proper family holiday. Fiji. Rarotonga. Even Auckland, at a push.

But there never seemed to be any leeway in their finances. Not on her teacher's salary, supplemented by his sporadic gardening jobs.

As soon as school was out each term, Debra would take Sky to stay with her dad in Clyde. The old man rarely returned the visit, which was just as well; their house in Arrowtown was too small for a father-in-law so set in his ways. Anyway, the Clyde arrangement suited Evan fine. It meant he could take on some extra shifts shuttling skiers or mountain-bikers, depending on the season, up the mountain.

The man shrugged. 'More of a pilgrimage, I spose.'

Evan looked over at his passenger. The guy was staring straight ahead, his beanie and tight black beard making up most of his silhouette, with little room left for the expression of skin in between. He was still clenching his fists.

'I guess you Kiwis would call it an OE,' the man said, after another long pause.

Evan sucked his teeth. He didn't like the guy's dismissive manner. 'It's not an OE in someone your age.'

The ensuing silence felt less comfortable than Evan had hoped it would.

As they approached the top of the range, the cloud lifted, as if the sky had just breathed in. Then the light took on a yellowish hue. Evan had seen this often enough to know what it meant. And sure enough, not long afterwards, the sky breathed out, dumping its icy cargo. It was not a light dusting. More like the white-out you get after turning a snow dome on its head.

In a matter of minutes, visibility had dropped to a few metres and the windscreen wipers were labouring under their load. MetService had warned a blizzard was coming. Evan had hoped he'd be well over the range before it hit.

He pulled over and put on the car's hazard lights. 'Going to get chains on while I can. There aren't many places to stop further down.'

He knew the road like the back of his hand, though that didn't diminish his respect for it. He did not want to be negotiating the steep, tight switchbacks without the claw of metal on his tires.

Living close to the mountains meant Sky had pretty much grown up on skis, and by the time she was 12, could match her mum or dad on any slope. In speed that is. When it came to grace and style, she'd long surpassed them.

'We can fit in one more,' she'd call over her shoulder, as she made for the ski lifts, just minutes before the mountain was due to close.

Sometimes he and Debra retreated to the café, exhausted, while Sky kept going. The pride they felt watching her ski down the mountain never palled; she moved like music.

It sometimes worried them though, that she was fearless, but her confidence was contagious, and eventually they succumbed to it.

Evan blamed himself. By not worrying about her, he had invited misfortune. As if the act of worrying in itself offered some sort of protection.

He could still remember the August evening 10 years back as if it were yesterday. Debra's face contorting as she lowered the phone. 'It's Sky. She's had an accident.'

Bits of her right leg bone were sticking out.

That day felt like a death sentence. But what did they really know? So, their little family had skimmed close to the edge.

And by the next winter Sky was back on the slopes, a titanium rod and screws unable to cramp her style.

Years later, Evan would wonder if the accident on the mountain had been designed to prepare them. Give them a glimpse of what was to come.

'Can you give me a hand?' he said, opening his car door. The wind grabbed it, swinging it wide and almost ripping it off its hinges.

'Jeez, it's wild out!' he said, tucking his chin into his chest and headbutting his way through the weather.

His passenger climbed out gingerly and stood hunched over, awaiting instructions.

'Ever put on chains before?' Evan shouted, as he sheltered under the roof of the ute's hatchback.

The man shook his head, his eyes dark and sunken into his curd-pale skin. Evan held out a pile of chains. 'Here, lie these like a ladder alongside the left back tire.'

'Like a what?'.

'A ladder!'

The guy nodded, reaching for them with open hands.

'You got gloves?'

The man shook his head.

Great! The guy was going to be about as useful as tits on a bull.

'It's fine,' the man said, picking up on Evan's exasperation and lugging the chains round to the left of the car.

He hadn't made much progress by the time Evan was finished fitting the right rear.

'No! No!' Evan said, crouching down. 'These need to be facing upwards.'

The man fumbled with them.

Evan stopped. Squinted. Tilted his head as he tried to make out what was inked across the guy's fingers.

A – T – O – N

His name? A lover's, perhaps? Or maybe some dead relative?

'I'll finish this,' Evan said, flipping the chains over. 'You may as well get back in the car.'

'I can help.'

'Your fingers look like they're about to fall off, mate.'

But the guy insisted, and almost 40 minutes after they'd first pulled over, the job was finally done.

Evan started the car and turned the heat dial to high. 'Put these on,' he said, taking off his gloves.

The man hesitated.

'Go on! Your hands will be blocks of ice by now.'

The man took the gloves and slid his hands into the still-warm wool, his expression thawing. 'Cheers.'

'Might be worth your buying a pair sometime.'

'I've got gloves. They're at the bottom of my bag.'

Evan noticed that the rucksack was now on the back seat.

'Ah well, at least they're keeping your bag warm.'

The man turned, his mouth twitching into an almost smile.

Evan extended his hand. 'I'm Evan, by the way.'

'Nat,' the man said, swinging over a limp left hand.

'And here I thought you were called Anton.'

The man's eyebrows dived below the rim of his beanie.

'You know. From the tattoos on your hand.'

The guy shook his head but offered no explanation. Then, almost as a second thought, pulled off the left glove and spread his hand wide.

A-T-O-N-E, not Anton, ran across the tops of his fingers.

Atone. That was an interesting one. Evan wondered if the guy was super religious. Or perhaps it was more some counterculture statement.

He put the glove back on.

Evan realised that he had absolutely no sense of who this man was, despite their having spent going on an hour together.

'Better get a move on,' he said briskly, pulling out into the road, 'or the road will soon be impassable.' His fog lights were just managing to melt small circles in the whiteout.

The sensible thing to do would have been to turn around and head back to the *Cardrona Hotel*. Wait it out in the pub. But the thought of more people, more forced conversation, and more of this odd character for company... Furthermore, the blizzard wasn't likely to be a two-hour thing, and Jesse, his border collie, would be waiting at the shed door for her evening feed.

Suddenly, without any warning, red taillights were coming at them through the fog, like bullets.

Ewan pumped the brakes frantically; brought the ute to a controlled crawl.

'What do you do if you have to stop suddenly on a wet or icy road?' he asked Sky, as she sat hunched over the steering wheel.

'Brake?'

'Yup. But gently. On off. On off. That way you prevent the wheels from locking and the car doesn't go into a skid.'

He and Debra had shared the responsibility of teaching her to drive, though he'd landed up doing most of it, Sky growing 'too stroppy' for her mother.

'Dad does it differently.'

Debra and Sky were going through a rough patch even before parallel parking was added to the mix. Apparently, a fiery mum-and-daughter dynamic was not uncommon, especially when a daughter was preparing to leave the nest.

He felt for Debra. She and Sky parted on good terms, but Deb's memories of those final battles would smother the years of closeness she and Sky had enjoyed. Not even a counsellor could help reframe that. As far as Deb was concerned, she'd been a bad mother.

Evan glanced over at his passenger, who was still braced against the dashboard in anticipation of a collision.

'Bloody awful visibility,' Evan said, by way of an apology.

The guy looked spooked.

Despite the near miss, Evan felt oddly comforted knowing that there was another car on the road.

'What you planning to do while you're in New Zealand?' he asked, trying to ease the atmosphere.

Another long pause followed. There was something about the silences that expanded around the closed doors of this musty-smelling man.

'I lost someone some time back,' the guy said, just as Evan was about to give up on getting an answer. 'She came from around here. I'm sort of trying to fill in the gaps, if you know what I mean.'

In an instant, the nine years Evan had bricked himself in with, fell away. Yes, he knew exactly what the man meant.

'I'm sorry.'

The guy shrugged. 'Nobody's fault but my own.'

Evan could relate to that too. The only reason Sky had been able to afford to go overseas was because he'd put money away for her. Every year since the day she was born.

'It's the best present ever!' she squealed on her 18th birthday. 'You guys are the best!'

In truth, it had all been Evan's doing – a secret that upset Debra when she learnt of it. And she was right; he shouldn't have hidden it from her. But he didn't want a whole bunch of sensible reasons why they couldn't afford to do it. What's more, he only ever took the money from what he earned.

'I just wanted to give her what we had, Deb. It's a gift from both of us. A once in a lifetime sort of thing.'

A once in a lifetime sort of thing. Debra never forgave him that.

GO TO GATE fluoresced in Evan's memory.

How tightly he hugged his daughter.

'Evan, she's going to miss her flight.'

He held Sky out at arm's length and looked her in the eye. 'Have a Guinness on me,' he said, then quickly, 'but don't ever let your drink out of your sight in a bar. Not for one second. You hear me!'

She laughed.

'No skydiving. No drugs. No hitchhiking, either.'

'I know! I know, Dad! Stop worrying. I wasn't born yesterday.'

The sliding doors were closing. Debra was crying. Sky was walking backwards.

'And no tattoos!' Evan called out.

Then the doors closed, and Sky was gone, and he and Deb were left holding hands in the Departure Hall like a broken chain of paper-dolls.

'You got any other tattoos?' Evan asked, trying to change the conversation in the car.

The guy sniggered. 'You could say. Not many clean skins in prison.'

Evan's gums prickled.

'So, you've spent some time inside?' he said, trying to sound casual.

'Eight years.'

Evan's mouth went dry. A man did not get eight years for some parking misdemeanour.

'It was meant to be a longer lag, but I pleaded guilty. No trial. It saves you some.'

Now he wanted to talk!

'I killed someone. A girl.'

Evan's eyes remained fixed ahead of him.

In 50 minutes, weather permitting, he'd be able to drop this man off on the side of the road and never see him again.

He glanced at his phone in its hands-free holder. There were no bars in the righthand corner. No reception this side of the range.

Suddenly didn't want the man's hands inside his gloves.

'You warm enough yet?'

The guy took the cue, pulling them off, finger by finger. 'Cheers.'

'You can put them in the glovebox.'

Glovebox! Ha! A box for gloves. Funny that, how something so obvious could go unrecognised for so long.

As the man stuffed the gloves away, Evan stared. At the man's right hand. At the number '4' tattooed on his thumb. And the letters S - K- Y inked across the tops of his last three digits.

4 SKY

On his left hand, ATONE. On his right, 4 SKY.

ATONE 4 SKY.

A car horn broke the spell.

Evan swerved in time to miss a truck coming up the hill towards them.

'Jesus! That was close,' the guy said, his voice robbed of its terseness.

Evan did not apologise.

'Nat short for anything?' he asked, turning to look at the guy again.

'I don't want to distract you with chatter, mister,' the guy said.

'What? Nathaniel, Nathan, Nate?'

'Uh, yeah. Nathan. But I haven't been called that in a long time.'

A shot of stomach acid pooled at the back of Evan's mouth.

He cleared his throat. 'Nathan,' he said, nodding slowly.

They took the first switchback at 30km/hour.

'How long you reckon it'll take to get to Frankton,' the man asked, his words tripping into each other.

'In this weather, anybody's guess.'

He wondered how his passenger liked the vagueness of his answer.

The two of them were quiet for a while, the only sound that of the windscreen wipers grating against the glass.

Out of the corner of his eye, Evan could see the guy's posture tense and ease with each bend. Every second switchback put the comfort of the mountain on the car's left, every other, and it was just a flimsy barrier between the car and the steep drop-off.

'How did you kill the girl?'

The guy pulled off his beanie.

'Too hot for you?'

He nodded.

Evan did not adjust the dial.

'You were saying?'

'Drink-driving,' the man said dryly. 'She was a pedestrian. I didn't see her.'

Evan took the next bend at 40 km/hour, then overcorrected.

'Careful!' the man blurted. 'I– This road is pretty treacherous.'

'Eight years. That's getting off lightly for taking a life, don't you think?'

A life. It hadn't been real until Sky arrived home. Before that, the truth was only what people said it was. Long distance phone calls offered nothing except static and words gone as soon as they were spoken. But a casket wheeled across the runway... That was real. The hard wooden lid, chilled from having travelled in a hold alongside other people's belongings. That was real too. And seeing her, despite the caution from police. A mangled body and so much mortician's makeup. That was real.

As for finding her story embedded on the internet.

Name suppression has been lifted on the man who drove into a pedestrian on Upton Road, killing her instantly. Nathan Roderick

> Powell, 22, had three times the legal limit of alcohol in his blood when he ploughed into New Zealander, Sky Amelia Walker, 18, at a pedestrian crossing. Walker, who had been in the Britain only three weeks, was on a one-year working visa.

As they came around the next bend, the red taillights were there again.

Evan pulled out to avoid a collision, but then, last-minute, decided to overtake. It was a gamble. For all he knew, there could have been a car coming in the opposite direction.

The ute was much higher than the small blue hatchback with square little windows.

As they passed it, the occupants looked up – disbelief in their fright-wide eyes.

Evan pulled sharply in front of them, just in time for the next switchback.

The driver behind blasted his horn.

'Slow down some!' his passenger shouted, gripping the handle above his door 'You're gonna kill us.'

How can you kill someone who's already dead, mused Evan?

He braked hard.

There was no mountain cushioning them on this sweep of the road. Just thick white air.

The car went into a skid, thrusting Evan and his passenger against the restraint of their seatbelts. Then Evan floored it.

The ute slammed into the barrier at an angle and flipped over the band of metal into freefall.

Someone looking from below might have glimpsed what looked like a toy car somersaulting down the vast white slope.

Nathan Roderick Powell's screams echoed around the cab, but by the time the ute had bounced twice, he was dead quiet.

As the car kept tumbling, Evan held onto the thought that Debra would now be able to finally forgive him.

And just before everything went black, he remembered Jesse. He hoped someone found her soon; she'd be waiting at the shed door for her feed.

SINNER MAN

GARRY DISHER

Hirsch's nominated best song of all time, so far that week, was *Badge*. God knows how his girlfriend's 13-year-old daughter had sourced that old Cream number when she'd collated an Old Fart's Compilation CD for his 37th birthday, but it was apt in the circumstances. There was always a badge somewhere in his life: on his uniform, on the doors of the SA Police Toyota, on the legions of disapproving senior officers in his life.

But right now – Eric Clapton filling the cab of the Hilux – there was not a sergeant or an inspector in sight, for he was on a remote back road east of Tiverton, in rain-shadow country halfway between Adelaide and the Flinders Ranges. He'd seen the dust of one far-off vehicle and a minibus of tourists photographing the spring wildflowers, but otherwise he was alone out there, in that mostly droughty red dirt and saltbush country, distant blue-grey hills on the other side of the mallee scrub, under a vast, cloudless sky.

He was out there because his sergeant, down in Redruth, wanted him to follow up a stolen-caravan post on the WTF Mid-North Facebook page. What the Fuck was happening in the mid-north rarely amounted to much – a stolen ride-on mower; missing sheepdogs; a haystack fire – so Hirsch wasn't expecting to run into a Mafia hitman, but he was mildly intrigued.

Rose Llewellyn, a watercolourist from a property south of Mischance Creek, had posted the theft of her 17-foot Jayco caravan from outside the Peterborough Art Gallery the previous day, imploring people to 'share the hell out of this post'. And she hadn't twiddled her thumbs in the meantime: 'I have obtained CCTV footage of my van being towed away by a bright red tradie ute, possibly a Ford Ranger Maxi Cab with a silver tray and silver tradie boxes on the back'. Heading south along the Barrier Highway at high speed – too fast to read the numberplate – at 3.15pm on Friday 3 September.

Two things struck Hirsch: according to general store and pub CCTV he himself had obtained, the ute and caravan had passed through Tiverton but not Penhale, further south, meaning it was still in the area. And the heartache in Rosa's claim: 'My whole life is in that van'.

'Clothing,' she informed him, half an hour later, 'a laptop, high-end camera, paints and easels, an iPad, photos going back years, and 30 watercolours for my next exhibition.'

A stringy, sundried woman of 60, she barked a laugh, a distressed yelp. 'I was inside the gallery, talking to the owner. Another five minutes and I would've been outside, unloading my paintings. A year's work down the drain.'

Hirsch, making a mental note to check her insurance history and question the gallery staff, looked about Llewellyn's sitting room. She lived in the renovated overseer's house on a long-abandoned sheep station homestead. He could see, through an archway, a studio, full of light. The place was homely, but her real home, her real studio, was the caravan. She travelled for several months a year throughout the mid-north, the Flinders Ranges and central Australia, painting blue-grey ranges, massive silvery gums, stone farmhouse ruins, Ngadjuri rock art along dry creek beds. The paintings sold well, she told Hirsch, but Covid restrictions had hit the Adelaide gallery scene, so she'd started exhibiting in country towns.

She showed him the Peterborough CCTV footage on her mobile

phone. Hirsch peered: there was the red ute, the grey-white caravan, tearing out of town. Looking at Rosa, he said, 'We think it turned off somewhere between Tiverton and Penhale.'

'Can't you just check for Ford Rangers registered in that area?'

'Worth a shot,' Hirsch said.

If it was a Ford Ranger. If it was registered locally.

An hour later he was back in Tiverton, unpinning his mobile phone number from the main door of the police station – aka the front room of a little brick house on the highway, opposite the primary school and a short walk from the general store – when his friend Bob Muir pulled up in his Tiverton Electrics ute.

'Got a minute?'

'Sure.'

'Marj Woodrow,' Muir said. 'Something's not right.'

Bob's job took him all over the district: replacing a farm widow's carport fluorescent tube, rewiring a generator for the town's lucerne seed business, fixing the electronics on a computerised irrigation rig. A burly, slow-moving man, he was often underestimated by those who didn't know him. Hirsch did, and if Bob said something wasn't right, it wasn't right. 'In what way?'

'I've been installing spotlights on the silos the past few days.'

Hirsch nodded. Tourists flocked to see the silo art: a huge merino ram head, a sheepdog, a kid on a horse. 'And?'

'This morning there was rubbish everywhere, as if Marj had parked there last night and cleaned out her glovebox. Sunglasses, tissues, a torch and a Honda owner's manual with her name in it.'

Hirsch recalled the Honda. New, shiny blue, it showed the dust of the red-soil plains – as Marjorie herself had ruefully pointed out when he'd knocked on her door back in March, following up on a stalking complaint.

'Have you called her?' he asked Muir now. 'Checked her place?'

Muir nodded. 'Yes and yes. No one home. Only the dog, and it was in a bad way. Hungry, thirsty.'

'The car?'

'Not there.'

'Rolf?'

'Not there. Halfway through his shift, I think.'

Rolf Woodrow, Marjorie's husband, was a two-weeks-on, two-weeks-off geophysics fieldhand at the Roxby Downs uranium mine, five hours north.

'If I pin a Corn Flakes badge to your shirt,' Hirsch said, 'and deputise you as a special law enforcement officer, would you come with me for another look?'

Muir looked at him. 'Do I get to shoot someone?'

A general Hirsch mantra, police mantra, was: Don't involve civilians. But Hirsch worked alone in that country, and this might not be a crime, just an everyday tragedy. And Bob Muir knew everyone and everything and was full of useful handyman skills, so Hirsch thought: fuck it.

They took the Toyota, Hirsch switching off *Gimme Shelter* – another ranking song, if he was any judge. 'The dog?'

'I gave it food and water.'

'Did you go inside?'

'Locked.'

'Windows?'

'Couldn't see anything.'

They knew each other; had entire conversations like that, interspersed with wordless passages. Muir added now: 'That problem earlier in the year.'

That problem earlier in the year was a man named Gregor Haliburton, who, Marjorie Woodrow had informed Hirsch, had been her boyfriend 20 years earlier. 'He appeared out the blue last month,' she'd said, 'wanting to reconnect with me. His wife died, and he thinks he and I can, you know, take up where we left off. Twenty years ago! I've been married for 15!'

Haliburton had very quickly become a pest. Emails, phone calls, letters, knocks on the door, chance encounters in the Tiverton general store or on the main street of Redruth. 'As if he knows when Rolf's away up north,' she told Hirsch.

'Where does he live?'

'Adelaide Hills somewhere.'

If he's been bothering her for a month, he's staying locally, Hirsch had reasoned, and he'd tracked Haliburton down to *The Woolman* pub in Redruth and put the fear of God in him. Or so he'd thought at the time.

The Woodrows lived in a transportable home on the outskirts of Penhale, halfway between Tiverton and Redruth. The sign on the gate – *MW Hair and Beauty* – had struck Hirsch as sad in March and did again now. You scouted around for any way to earn a living in hardscrabble country, where kids headed for the city as soon as they left school, family farms were bought up by Chinese agri companies, and your hair and your beauty were ravaged by the sun.

They got out, Hirsch knuckling the skull of the kelpie, which reacted with painful gratitude. He knocked on the door of the low, crouching house, Bob staying back with the dog. No answer. He circled the place, peering through windows: shadowy furniture in shadowy rooms.

'I'm going in,' he said, ready to boot the door.

Bob pointed. 'Under there.'

A garden stone, daubed thickly in white paint, beside the front steps. Under it was a key. 'Good thinking.'

They entered. The air was shut-in, smelling faintly pungent. Hirsch found the source: congealed spaghetti Bolognese in a pan on the stove. He also found an overturned kitchen chair, a smashed bowl, and some blood spatter. No one had died here – but maybe someone had been snatched.

Hirsch conferred with his sergeant, who said she'd inform Port Pirie CID detectives, request a crime-scene unit and issue an alert for the Honda. Meanwhile, she said, why didn't Hirsch check on the whereabouts and movements of Haliburton and the husband.

He called Haliburton first, landline and mobile. No answer, so he checked with *The Woolman*. Zilch – but there were plenty of pubs in the mid-north. Finally the police station in Mount Barker. They called back late afternoon: Haliburton's house was shut up, car shed empty, and the neighbours hadn't seen him all week.

Meanwhile, Marjorie's husband. According to the mine's office manager, Rolf Woodrow had attended the head mechanic's birthday party Friday night and right now was out in the field, an hour from the office.

Hirsch attended to emails and memos and the erosion of his soul and finally Woodrow called, sounding tense. 'I was running a geophysics line. Just got back. Can I ask what this is about? Is it my wife?'

A reasonable question, given that his wife had been a stalking victim. 'I'm afraid so,' Hirsch said, going on to give him the bare bones.

'Missing?' Woodrow said, his voice crackling tensely in Hirsch's landline handset. 'It's that prick Haliburton. Why you lot didn't lock him up early in the year, I don't know.'

'When did you last see Marjorie?'

'Me? A week ago, the end of my two weeks off.'

'Did she mention Haliburton at all?'

Woodrow gulped his words out. 'I definitely got the feeling something was going on; she was pretty subdued. But nothing specific. She gets sad every time I leave for the mine again; I'm actually thinking of jacking it in.'

'Any strange cars, phone calls, people bothering her?'

Hirsch heard panting now, as if Woodrow were having a panic attack. 'No. Look, I need to come back, I need to look for her.'

Hirsch couldn't stop the guy – but didn't want him getting in the way, either. Or having an accident. 'Can someone drive you down?'

But the line was dead.

Rolf Woodrow knocked on the police station door at 7pm, just as Hirsch was knocking off. Maybe Marjorie Woodrow likes tall, gruff, barrel-chested men, he thought, noting the resemblance between her husband and her old boyfriend. Different natures, though. Where Haliburton had displayed a sleepy-eyed, scoffing slyness when Hirsch booted him out of town, as if to say that rules didn't apply to him, Woodrow was a bundle of nerves, helpless, dithery, brittle with tension and fear.

'I don't know what to do first,' he said, in Hirsch's sitting room.

Hirsch, in the kitchen nook pouring him a mug of tea, said, 'It'll soon be dark out. Maybe join one of the search parties tomorrow. Meanwhile, ring around all the friends and family you can think of.'

Woodrow shivered. 'I can't go home. It would spook me out.'

'A friend?'

Woodrow gnawed his bottom lip. 'I've got a sister in Redruth.'

'Go there,' Hirsch said. 'We'll speak in the morning.'

He watched Woodrow's taillights disappear down the highway, pinned his mobile number to the door of the police station and drove to Wendy's. Weeknight sleepovers were trickier – police work, Katie's homework,

Wendy's marking and lesson plans – so Saturday nights were pretty sacred. Tonight it was roast chicken and amiable insults at the table, then chocolate in front of the TV, the usual.

Sunday morning he asked Katie about *Badge* and *Gimme Shelter*, telling her they were songs from his parents' generation, not his. 'They are the old farts,' he said, 'not me.'

'Oldish,' she said. 'Fartish.'

'I'm pretty sure that's not a proper word,' he began – and was interrupted by his phone.

His sergeant, playing him a triple-zero call that had just come in. Female, young, scared. 'There's a burnt car on the other side of Wildongoleechie Reserve.'

Wildongoleechie Reserve was a small forest of huge old eucalypts that had escaped the settlers' axes in the 1870s. Situated a kilometre off the highway, on the road to Morgan, a town on the River Murray, it boasted a parking area with a toilet block, picnic tables, and sheltered coin barbecues. But Hirsch was on the rutted, little-used dirt track that ran behind the reserve, gloomily eyeing the remains of Marjorie Woodrow's Honda. A stinking, blackened husk, sitting on its rims. The stench of burnt rubber, upholstery, and petrochemicals. The stench of burnt flesh.

Human flesh: the clenched, charred remains of an adult were in the passenger seat. Male, female, killed by the fire, killed before the fire, no way for Hirsch to know until a pathologist examined the remains.

He peered at the ground. There had been rain late week, but he saw only the tyre tracks of the Honda. How had the killer left the scene? The place was remote, and not enough passing traffic to hitch out – and you'd be mad to hitch anyway, risk some passing motorist tying you to a murder scene. Hirsch sighed: they'd have to search up and down the track and in the little reserve itself; there could be another body.

He walked back towards the highway, scanning the dirt and, a few hundred metres later, found bicycle tracks. A clever guy, he thought. Brought the bike with him, unloaded it, torched the car, then carried the bike a long distance before mounting it and riding off into the sunset.

Sunset. Ask the crime-scene techs when they thought the fire had been lit.

He was walking back to the Hilux when a cavalcade overtook him: his sergeant, a carload of detectives, a crime-scene unit, the first outside broadcast van.

He watched it on the news that evening. *Channel 9* had sent a drone over the Honda and its skirt of scorched spring grasses – a scene that managed to look bleak and lonely despite the proximity of police vehicles and men and women in forensic gear. Then a head filled the screen, a police spokesperson asking for witnesses to come forward.

'Particularly anyone in the vicinity of the roads on either side of Wildongoleechie Reserve. If you have dashcam footage, or saw any person or vehicle that seemed out of place, please call Crimestoppers.'

There goes my Monday, Hirsch thought – following up phone calls, some genuine, most useless, many made from mischief, boredom, or loneliness.

But his Monday started with a call from his sergeant. According to forensics the victim was Marjorie Woodrow, her hyoid was broken, and her car had probably been torched on Friday evening, not Saturday.

Then a walk-in, Vikki Bastian, the primary school teacher. Leaning on the counter that separated Hirsch's desk and computer from humankind, she said, 'Sorry to bother you, Paul.'

Hirsch swung away from pecking at his keyboard. 'Saving me, in fact.'

Bastian looked agitatedly at her watch. A glossy blonde when not at work, prim and buttoned down when she was, she said, 'This will have to be quick, school starts in a minute.'

'Okay.'

'It's just, I saw a car at the reserve, Friday evening.'

'Where? On the back road?'

She seemed to think he was an idiot. 'What back road? No. No, me and Den were driving to Morgan for the weekend.'

'Den's your boyfriend?'

'Yes. About six o'clock, just getting dark, and we saw a car parked at the picnic area. The barbecues.'

'A blue Honda?'

A little frown. 'What? No. Mr Krauth's car. Alan Krauth's.'

There was good reason why she'd recognise that car: it was a 1968 Mk 2 Jaguar, British Racing Green, chrome wire wheels. But Hirsch said, 'You're certain?'

'Just parked there, a car you can't miss, gotta go, bye,' she said, and was gone.

Hirsch didn't know how Krauth was connected to Marjorie Woodrow, but he might have seen something, so it was worth following up. He recalled what he knew about the guy as he drove north through farmland. Mid-40s, a slim, handsome bloke who liked to shake hands, clap you on the back, show a set of big, friendly teeth. He'd arrived in the district with his wife and their teenage sons a year earlier, after buying and renovating an old church on a hill near Willalo. A wool-buyer; his wife a nurse at the Redruth hospital; the kids attended Redruth High. That was the sum of Hirsch's knowledge.

He was pleased to see the Jag in the driveway. He got out and took a moment to enjoy his surroundings. This church – they might have placed it on top of a hill to bring worshippers closer to God, but now it appealed to a baser emotion, vanity. The building itself was a graceful marvel of local stone, stained wood and glossy paint, and the view, of bright yellow canola crops and vivid spring grasses threaded together by scribbling dirt road that stretched to the horizon, uplifted Hirsch's soul.

'Lovely, isn't it?'

Hirsch turned. Krauth was limping across the gravel towards him in chinos, an untucked linen shirt and R. M. Williams boots. Tidily built; a man with a lean, clever look.

'Al Krauth,' he said, shaking hands with Hirsch. 'Pleased to meet you at last, Constable Hirschhausen.'

'Hirsch will do. Shorter, for a start.'

'Hirsch,' Krauth said, trying out the word. 'Can I help you with something?'

Trying not to stare at Krauth's ear – swollen, a tiny band aid stuck to the lobe – Hirsch said, 'I can't tell you why just now, but would you mind telling me where you were Friday afternoon and early evening?'

A look not of guilt but of calculation. Doesn't mean anything, Hirsch thought. He sometimes had to stop and think about his very recent movements.

'I spent the afternoon checking out a Bristol someone's selling down in Gawler. Beautiful car – but way overpriced.'

Gawler was two hours south. A four-hour round trip with an hour of tyre-kicking and test driving. 'After that?'

But Krauth said, 'Look, is this about that burnt car, that woman from Penhale?'

Hirsch deliberated. Eventually he said, 'Yes.'

'Someone saw my car near where it happened, am I right?'

'You are.'

'I was driving back and needed the loo and when I saw the Morgan turnoff, I remembered there's a toilet block at the reserve.'

'Fair enough.'

'I was there maybe five minutes,' Krauth said, 'but didn't see anything, not that I can recall. No other vehicles were parked there, anyway. I could smell smoke though. Acrid.'

'What time was this?'

'About six.'

Hirsch couldn't think of any other questions, so he thanked Krauth and climbed behind the wheel of the Toyota; watched Krauth return to the house as he drove out. The guy was walking stiffly, his spine tight – as if to show displeasure with Hirsch's intrusion. Or maybe it was related to his damaged ear.

Hirsch spent the rest of the day making his regular long-distance, back-country Monday patrol. His job was as much counsellor and welfare officer as policeman, so he called in on a farming widow with a schizophrenic son, a single mother with an ice-addict daughter, an elderly shearer who cared for his wheelchair-bound wife.

Finding himself within 15 minutes of Mischance Creek, he called in on Rosa Llewellyn, who had something to show him.

'It just popped up.'

An anonymous Facebook message: *Your caravans at Tiverton Agricultural Supplies.*

Tiverton Agricultural was a depressed one-hectare lot on the Barrier Highway a kilometre south of the town. Rusting tractors, harvesters, harrows, augers, trucks, and farm utes sat in collars of grass facing the highway and some were even sold from time to time. Sheds full of hay and fertiliser. Drums of weed spray. Coils of fencing wire.

A nasty old drunk named Murtagh ran the place: all whiskers, doughy nose, greasy overalls and rolls of $100 bills in his pockets. He patted the police Toyota and said comically, 'I can give you a good deal on a Falcon ute with 300 ks on the clock.'

'Tempting,' Hirsch said, 'but I'm more interested in that caravan parked behind the shed.' It was the Jayco and wore a coat of poorly applied pale blue paint.

'And,' he added, 'that red Ford ute.'

'Sorry, it's me nephew's,' Murtagh said. 'Not sellin.'

The nephew was at the front window of the shack marked 'Office'. Catching Hirsch's eye, he ducked.

'I'll just ask him, shall I?' Hirsch said, beginning to run as the door opened and a figure streaked across the yard towards the ute. Young, muscular, mullet hair, jeans, work boots and an old Sex Pistols T-shirt, he was lunging for the driver's door when Hirsch grabbed him.

A street fighter, he immediately squatted, pulling Hirsch down with him, then uncoiled, drew back his right foot and kicked. Hirsch let it happen, taking the metal toecap on his ear, but grabbed the heavy boot while the kid was still off-balance, twisted the ankle, put him down.

All of Rosa's paintings and other belongings were intact, but the caravan was a mess: the botched paint job, a scrape – swiped a gatepost? – and beer cans, vomit and a methamphetamine fug. As for the ute, it had been stolen in Whyalla a week earlier.

'Quite a crime spree, Justin,' Hirsch said.

Justin Gouger, handcuffed inside the Hilux's prisoner transport compartment while they waited for police from Redruth to collect him, used his hollow cheeks and ice-rotted teeth to say, 'Lawyer.'

Hirsch laughed. 'Good one.'

Gouger looked past Hirsch to his uncle, who sat on the steps of the office. 'Don't fucking sit there, get me a lawyer.'

'See what I can do, son,' Murtagh said, getting to his feet.

But just as he turned, Murtagh gave Hirsch the ghost of a wink and a smile. He sent Rose the text, Hirsch thought.

He resumed cataloguing the high-end gadgets he'd recovered from inside the ute. GPS and dashcam units, binoculars, an iPad, a hunting rifle – 'Were you going to shoot me, Justin?' – and two mobile phones.

One phone – scuffed, the screen cracked – was Gouger's, according to a driver's licence and a credit card in the flip case pockets. The other was a new-looking iPhone 12, locked. Not expecting much, but hoping it would lead him to the phone's owner, Hirsch entered the district postcode, 5417.

He was in, the home screen a shot of a smiling, vaguely familiar woman in a black one-piece swimsuit on a sunlounge beside a swimming pool. He tapped the home button twice to see if any screens were still open.

Facebook, G-mail, the camera, photos.

Nude photos of a girl who looked, to Hirsch, older than 12 but younger than 16. In one shot she was topless, grinning at the camera, holding out the skirts of a Redruth High School uniform.

He shoved the screen in Gouger's face. 'Your doing?'

Gouger recoiled. 'Fuck no. What do you take me for?'

'Who, then? Who is she? Where did you get the phone?'

'Found it.'

Hirsch shook his head, fed up, scrolled back through the photos, looking for background detail. There were no older shots, as if the photographer regularly deleted them as he went along or uploaded them to the cloud, but there was something about the topless shot.

The girl was standing, and she was outdoors. And, behind her left shoulder, a familiar toilet block and picnic tables. He checked the other shots: all closeups but, blurry in the background, red leather seats and an old-style walnut dashboard.

Alan Krauth's bandaged earlobe, he thought.

He gave Gouger one of his slow, empty smiles. 'The car was just parked there, right? No one around, easy pickings. But the driver wouldn't hand over his phone, you had to use force?'

'Dunno what you're talking about.'

'Okay,' sighed Hirsch. 'Justin Gouger, in addition to theft, resist arrest and assault police, I am further charging you with possession of child pornography. You–'

'Fuck! No! Okay, okay, wasn't me took them pictures. Fucking pervert. She could have been his daughter.'

'You knew him? Or you were just passing and thought you'd have a go.'

'Never seen him before. Gimme a lawyer.'

'Did you hit the girl, too?'

Justin Gouger was outraged. 'What do you take me for? I never hit a kid or a sheila in me life.'

Some crims – many crims – had standards. It keeps them going, thought Hirsch. 'Do you know who she is?'

'Not a clue. She run off into the trees, last I saw of her.'

After Redruth police had carted Justin to their lockup, Hirsch secured the caravan, gave Rose the good news, shook hands with Murtagh – who winked – and texted an enlargement of the girl's head-and-shoulders to Wendy with the words: *Do you know her?*

She called half an hour later. 'Sorry, I was in the middle of a Year 12 maths class. Her name's Janine Galloway. Year 9.'

'She at school today?'

'Yes.'

Hirsch could read curiosity and concern in Wendy's voice. He generally told her most things but now said, 'I'll know more tonight.'

A relaxation. 'I understand.'

Hirsch said goodbye. He knew that life was subject to chance and coincidence, but all he could see just now were two separate stories. The first was messy, involving as it did a 14-year-old's welfare and ongoing family life, and the bringing of serious charges against a pillar of the community old enough to be her father. It was above his paygrade: all he could do was pass it up the line.

The other story – Marjorie Woodrow's murder – was also above his paygrade, but if Janine Galloway had crossed to the other side of Wildongoleechie Reserve and seen something, if she had been the triple zero caller, then he needed to act immediately, before she was caught up in South Australia's unwieldy and inadequate family welfare apparatus.

Just after four o'clock now and Hirsch thought long and hard about this next stage. The only Galloways in the district were Eric, the Penhale dentist, Mary, his nurse, Janine, their only child. The Redruth High bus would have dropped off the Penhale kids by now and Janine was more likely to be at home than at the surgery.

He didn't want to go in hard – she'd have a taste of that later, when sex crimes detectives, bureaucrats and her parents got involved – so he changed into plain clothes. And he left the police Hilux parked outside the Woodrow house, where it was unlikely to excite local interest, and walked two streets south, to the Galloways.

Janine answered his knock and he said, immediately: 'I'm Constable Paul Hirschhausen and I'm here to talk about what you saw at Wildongoleechie Reserve on Friday evening, your anonymous triple zero call, and your relationship with Alan Krauth.'

She closed her eyes, swayed, recovered and stood aside to let him in. 'Kitchen.'

The kitchen was a sunny expanse of marble benchtops, copper-bottomed pans on hooks and whispering white drawers. She stood on the business side of the main bench, as if to barrier herself, and he perched on the stool opposite her.

'You may have an adult present,' he said. 'Your parents.'

A vigorous headshake. 'How did you find me?'

Hirsch was blunt. 'You were identified from nude photos found on a mobile phone.'

She went pink, then stubborn, almost proud. 'So?'

He showed her Gouger's photo. 'The phone was in the possession of this man – who is in custody, so you have nothing to fear. Do you recognise him?'

'Yes. We were, you know, parked at the reserve and he just drove in and attacked us.'

'Towing a caravan?'

'No.'

Dumped the van, headed out again on his spree, thought Hirsch.

'Did he hurt you?'

She shook her head. 'Alan. Wouldn't give up his phone. But I thought he was going to rape me, so I ran.'

'Into the reserve?'

'Yes.' She paused. 'If I tell you something, can you forget about the photos?'

'I'm sorry, but no.'

'We're in love.'

'I understand, but I can't ignore it.'

She searched his face. 'It was mutual. He didn't force me. He didn't sweet-talk me.'

'I understand. But right now I need to know what you saw when you reached the other side of the reserve.'

She cocked her head, watched him tensely. 'Can you protect me?'

Hirsch watched her back curiously – and the answer came to him. 'You saw someone you recognised.'

'Yes.' She seemed to shrink. She looked past Hirsch reflexively, as if towards the edge of the town. 'Mr Woodrow.'

Hirsch took a long breath. 'Did he see you?'

'Almost. I was running and stopped in time and hid behind a tree.'

'Describe what you saw.'

'He splashed petrol everywhere and set the car on fire.'

'What else?'

Janine clasped herself protectively. 'I think Mrs Woodrow was in the car.'

'Alive?'

She hunched further. 'Don't know.'

'What happened next?'

'He had a bike and walked off carrying it.'

'What did you do?'

She leaned both hands on the bench in an attitude of ease, but Hirsch saw the tension in her. 'I ran back. Alan was still there, and he drove me home.'

Hirsch touched the back of her hand reassuringly. 'That's all for now. But to be on the safe side, grab your homework and I'll walk you around to the surgery.'

He watched her close and open her eyes, then turn solemn, alert. She's got grit, he thought. She's planning how she'll talk to her parents.

He drove back to Tiverton, recasting Rolf Woodrow's Friday alibi. He must have told everyone he'd be spending the day out in the field, working solo, and might even have done that for a while, but he spent the afternoon driving south to Penhale and snatching and killing his wife. Then back to the mine in time to show his face at the birthday party.

Meanwhile, Haliburton – missing for a week. Bumped him off, too, back during his two weeks at home?

Hirsch needed to speak to the Woodrows' friends and family again, asking hard questions: Was Rolf a tyrant? The jealous kind? Paranoid?

Hirsch finished the trip making a mental list of actions and calling his sergeant, CID and sex crimes. Just as he was entering Tiverton, briefly plunged into darkness as the main silo blotted the sunlight from the sky, Mount Barker police called him.

'That bloke you want to talk to, Haliburton. His car's been found, the *Calvary* in North Adelaide. He's a patient there. Cancer.'

Hirsch said thanks, crossed another item off his list, slotted Katie's CD in the slot.

Nina Simone filled the cab: *Sinnerman*.

Now that's a song, he thought.

OBSERVATIONS ON A TRAGEDY
ACT ONE: INCITEMENT

NARRELLE M. HARRIS

THE PHRASE WAS 'BREAK A LEG', THE ONLY WAY TO SAY GOOD LUCK WITHOUT inviting disaster from the fickle gods of theatre. Brady Templar must have committed spectacular hubris to tempt those bastards into revenge, because his leg was only one of many broken bones, and not even the important one. Templar's broken skull was definitely the last word in bad luck.

With nowhere else safe to look, Tee focused on Brady Templar's outflung hand while she waited for the 000 summons to deliver a Responsible Authority. The elegant curl of his fingers remained untouched by the violence of his evident fall. Short nails, clean of the blue polish he often wore on his right-hand ring finger. Tanned skin, pale palm cupped like an offering to take her hand in his. The only blemish here was a circular scorch mark on the cuff of his white cotton shirt.

> *Brady Templar's death embodied his career to the last detail. Reflecting his body of work, this young actor at the threshold of greatness died in a*

way that was unexpected, out-of-the-ordinary, shockingly graceful, and heartbreakingly vulnerable.

Too soon?

Too soon.

The blessing and the curse of a writer, and a theatre critic in particular, thought Tee, was the tendency to render real life into more manageable narratives. Storifying Brady Templar as she sat beside his cooling body was infinitely easier than looking at his ruins and wondering how his mother and sister would feel once they knew.

Tee made herself look away from Brady's hand, heartbreakingly vulnerable, and up.

Up. Up.

Brady had certainly fallen from the roof of the theatre, where countless cast and crew had hidden for smoko, away from paparazzi eyes. Tee had been there herself, once or twice, and observed the younger ones, the more daring ones, sitting on the wall that overlooked the alley, feet dangling over the edge, dropping ash into the wind.

Had Brady, skylarking around after three standing ovations and the knowledge of next week's film premiere, slipped on the precipice of The Big Time and Icarused his way to dusty death?

Too many metaphors. Tee very much wished she'd had a lot more to drink at the free bar.

Tee had loitered on the periphery of the afterparty and heard when cast, crew, media, sponsors, other critics, the whole ragbag of Melbourne Theatre Elite, began to wonder to whence their star had vanished.

Tee, curious, had nipped off to find out if she could perhaps snag an exclusive chat, or an appointment for one. A selfie at least. Even critics weren't above a little fame-whoring for social media.

Well, she had an exclusive now.

Brady hadn't been in the alley leading to the secluded first floor bar. He hadn't been in Russell Street surrounded by fans from the evening soapie he'd starred in three years ago, who'd made the play as much a commercial success as it had been a critical one. He hadn't been at the front door or the stage door, or at the roller door that would open to allow larger sets to be wheeled in or out.

Puzzled and slightly annoyed, Tee had been about to give up, go home, when the shape in the narrow alley beside the theatre had taken her by the curiosity and led her to Templar's final performance.

The inevitable questions crept into Tee's head, swirled around it, settled on her tongue, where attempts to answer led only to more questions.

Why had Brady been alone? *Had* he been alone? If someone had been with him, they'd have raised the alarm when he fell. Unless he didn't fall. Jumped? Alarms stage left, right and centre would have followed that, too. Alone, then. Or… pushed?

Who would push the golden boy from the rooftop?

Well, apart from the two people Tee could name immediately.

A torch shone on her, and over Brady's body, making the blood that was black under the alley's low light stand out red on the cobblestones, and projecting her own shadow-silhouette on the wall of the theatre.

What a striking poster that would make.

Too soon.

'Ms Mahoney? I'm Officer Pallas–'

'Like the theatre?'

'Wh-?'

'No, that'd be Palace.'

'Let me through, officer.' A gentle voice. A paramedic, Tee saw. They probably thought she was in shock.

'I think I'm in shock,' she said.

The next few minutes were curiously staccato. A performance in strobe lighting. Tee told Officer Pallas (not Palace) about the party; about leaving; about looking; about finding.

In between, or after, or before, the paramedic asked questions and took readings. At one point, after maybe, Tee pointed up and told Pallas (or someone else; she never did remember their names, later) that Brady Templar didn't smoke. Then explained why that was important. He wouldn't have been up there for smoko. Too much light pollution for stargazing. Notorious non-drinker, they'd ordered non-alcoholic champagne in for the party especially. He was a straight-edge superstar, should've been flying high, not…

Not...

Not whatever this was.

A DBO, maybe. The sudden, instant killing of all the theatre lights. Brady Templar, halted mid-performance with a dead blackout.

HE WHO LAUGHS LAST
HELEN VIVIENNE FLETCHER

THE FIRST WAS AN ACCIDENT – A JOKE GONE WRONG, AS THEY SAY. Or perhaps a joke gone really right, depending on how you look at it. The second was mostly an accident – maybe an experiment if we're being completely honest. I didn't think I could kill someone twice, but I had to try, you know? To see if that first one had been a fluke.

After that, I can't claim innocence. There was intent. There was motive. And the bodies began piling up.

There was a power to it. People didn't normally see me as powerful, and there was something seductive about that. I was used to feeling small – being treated like a child. Funny how not being able to walk makes people see you as little. If you've ever tried to manoeuvre a wheelchair in a bathroom stall, you'd realise how much space I actually take up.

It wasn't just about the power, though. I picked my victims carefully. I'm not saying they deserved to die. All I'm saying is they pissed me off, and sometimes that's the same thing. Of course, with methods like mine, I had to choose my moments carefully, too. Certain medical predispositions helped, but I could make it work without. All it took was favourable – or unfavourable depending on your perspective – atmospheric conditions, the right type of food in front of them, and the element of surprise. Surprise was easy. Most people didn't expect me to be funny. They also didn't believe "died laughing" could be literal.

I wheeled into the bar, negotiating the tight doorway. The wind slammed it shut behind me, drawing more attention than I would have liked. I'd had to change locations a lot, to keep from being detected, so I'd got used to navigating all sorts of barely accessible spaces. It had been a good excuse to travel, but the last few months I'd enjoyed being back in my hometown, even with the Wellington wind adding its own special brand of propulsion to everything I did. I'd be sad when it came time to move on.

All going to plan, today would be my eleventh victim. I already had him picked out – "Gazza" as he insisted everyone call him. He was outside, having a cigarette right now. That gave me a good 20 minutes. When we'd worked together, his smoke breaks had expanded like his ego. Anyone unlucky enough to take theirs at the same time would be caught in a self-serving spiral of bragging anecdotes, as he chain-smoked any cigarette he could get hold of, whether or not it came from his own pack.

I went to the counter and scanned the ever-expanding list of craft beers, picking out the ones I would try on another night. In Wellington, you had to be a connoisseur of either beer or flat whites to fit in. Tonight, I'd be drinking neither. I needed a clear head, and neither alcohol nor coffee-jitters would help me there.

I ordered a plate of extra spicy hot wings, and a large bowl of potato wedges. In my experience, peanut butter sandwiches were the best thing to get someone to choke – they didn't even need to have a peanut allergy. I tried to avoid people with allergies as a general rule; it didn't feel like as much of an achievement to bring them down. Of course, ordering a peanut butter sandwich in a bar would be a sure-fire way to draw attention to myself, so wedges and spice would have to do.

I hadn't wanted to do too much research. If things ever came to light, a search history of "foods that increase the likelihood of heart attacks" or "choking hazards in adults" wouldn't do me any favours. But I felt safe in assuming solid lumps of potato were among the riskier foods to consume.

I set myself up at a table and waited. Gazza was the easy type of victim. I wouldn't have to persuade him to join me. If I had food in front of me, he would feel entitled to it – entitled to my time and air space too. That's why he'd ended up on my list. He was a bully, and he deserved a good laugh.

I wouldn't have much trouble in that department either. He'd been laughing at me for years.

My food came. The server – Sophie – smiled at me. She placed a bottle of water and a glass on the table beside the food. 'You here by yourself tonight, Charlie?' she asked. She'd recently gifted me with her name, and I felt a surge of warmth every time she used mine.

'For now,' I said. 'I always make friends here.'

She smiled again, her face filling with sunshine. 'Good on you, Charlie.'

I frowned. Good on you, Charlie? Patronising? So many people were, sometimes it was hard not to read it into every sentence spoken.

'All else fails, I'll just pick someone up,' I said. 'They'll have to be my friend if I'm wheeling them away at speed.'

Sophie gave a surprised laugh, a delightful hiccupping sound. Her cheeks turned the prettiest shade of pink, and her eyes sparkled. 'You're so naughty, Charlie.'

I grinned, my own cheeks warming. 'Or I could run over their toes. That's a great meet cute.'

She let out a whoop. Some of the other customers glanced our way, and Sophie's laugh spluttered into a cough. The pink in her cheeks turned to red, and liquid filled her eyes. My grin fell. I reached for her, handing her the water she had given me just moments before.

She waved it away, still coughing. 'Thanks, I'm all good.' She cleared her throat, then touched my arm gently, turning back to work.

I watched her carefully as she moved to chat with another customer, her smile warm and easy as she cleared their plates. Kindness filled every movement she made; genuine kindness, not the fake type so often thrown in my direction.

Once upon a time, I would have loved making her laugh. Now something clawed at my stomach, and I wanted to clap a protective hand over her mouth to make her stop. She hadn't been eating, I reminded myself. A laugh could just be a laugh; she wasn't going to choke. Unlike Gazza.

The bar filled, the after-work throng filing in. This was good. The chaos of a crowd helped take the focus off me. I resisted the urge to stuff one of the wedges in my mouth. Steam spilled from them, and I preferred my tongue unburnt. Though now that I thought about it, a munted tongue and a lisp might add something to my jokes. I'd have to try it out sometime, but tonight was not the night for untested material. Besides, the food had to look appealing when Gazza got inside. I wanted him reaching over to grab a handful, rather than picking at limp leftovers.

The chair beside me scraped back. I looked up, startled, not quite ready for Gazza to join me, but the man beside me was a stranger.

'Hello?' I said.

He gestured to the chair. 'Do you mind?'

'No, you can take it.' Not ideal, as I had assumed Gazza would sit there, but there was still a chair to my left. Funny how things like that can throw you. It shouldn't matter whether he sat on my left or my right, but once I'd pictured it one way, it felt wrong to adjust.

The man took off his coat, placing it over the back of the chair, then sat down.

Well. Now this really threw things. I'd thought he wanted to take the chair away, not to sit next to me. I couldn't kill Gazza with a stranger watching on. Or could I? It would be the ultimate test of my abilities. My methods had gone undetected until now, but I'd never tried under such close scrutiny. Could I even get two at once? A double-hitter kill would be quite the achievement.

There was a comfortable rumpledness to the man in front of me, that made me think he might be a father. The untucked end of his shirt drooped down on one side, hinting his waist had expanded since purchasing those pants, and his hair needed a cut. Grey-streaked strands fell across his face in a way that spoke of disorganisation rather than style.

Sophie returned to the table, raising her eyebrows to ask the man's order.

'Just a coke, thanks.'

Pleasant enough to thank her – a point in his favour.

'No worries, mate.' Sophie smiled at me again, as she left, but it didn't have the same warmth from earlier. Her hand snuck to her temple, rubbing it gently, before she turned to another customer.

An image of her crying flashed through my mind. Maybe I should have waited until a night she wasn't working. She'd be the type to blame herself, you know? Even if she thought it was an accident. Another flash followed – her head on my shoulder, the tears falling on my neck. My arms wrapping around to comfort her.

I dropped my gaze to my food as she caught me staring.

'I've seen you before.'

I turned back to the man. Often, that sort of statement had a question mark at the end – not really a query in and of itself, but an invitation to conversation.

'I come here a lot,' I said. I kept my voice flat, invitation declined.

'Good on you.' The man stared at me, a slight smile teasing the corners of his mouth, as if we were sharing a joke.

I didn't return it. I'd given Sophie the benefit of the doubt, but the words were definitely patronising from his lips – a congratulations for being capable of frequenting a bar. I got comments of a similar nature a lot. Leaving the house is apparently noteworthy when using a wheelchair.

Sophie returned with his coke, and he thanked her.

My wedges had cooled, and I picked one up, admiring the solid cut and greasy coating. Under different circumstances, I would have turned up my nose, but these were perfect for my purposes.

The man watched me eat it, with far more interest than was warranted. His lip quirked into another smile as I swallowed. Clearly, leaving the house wasn't the only thing he was surprised I could do independently. I waited for him to congratulate me on ingesting food without choking.

I pushed the plate towards him. "Would you like some?"

He hesitated. Something flicked across his face, and for a moment, I could swear he was afraid. Then it was gone, replaced by the familiar smile.

'Thanks, friend,' he said. He took a napkin from the metal pail in the centre of the table, laying it in front of him, then he grabbed a wedge and broke it in two before eating. Sensible. Smaller pieces certainly reduced the choking hazard. I allowed myself to feel a touch of disappointment.

He held out his hand. 'You can call me Mike.'

'Charlie.'

His smile widened at that, and I couldn't help thinking I should have given a fake name. Not that anyone would find anything suspicious about Gazza's death, but anonymity couldn't hurt.

'You here alone tonight?' he asked.

'Yeah, alone, I said. Without thinking, my gaze travelled toward Sophie. I forced it back, but his attention had followed mine.

'But I saw someone I used to work with outside,' I said quickly. 'He might join me.'

What was I doing? Why had I told him I used to work with Gazza? Not smart, Charlie. Not smart at all.

'I've never been here before.' Mike glanced at something over my shoulder. I didn't turn to look, but I knew it would be Sophie. His smile stretched into a leer. 'I might just have to become a regular.'

A roiling wave of heat rose inside me, and my ears pulsed. Don't look at her like that! I wanted to yell, but I had no claim to the moral high ground. Just moments ago, I'd been fantasising about comforting her over Gazza's literal dead body.

I shook my head to clear it. Choosing Sophie's bar had been a risk, but maybe not for the reason I'd thought. I couldn't think straight when she was around.

Where was Gazza? His exorbitantly long cigarette breaks weren't unfamiliar, especially if he'd found someone to indulge his storytelling, but this one had dragged out even for him.

I glanced back at Mike. He stared at me, his gaze intent; expectant even. I picked up one of the spicy wings, to give myself something to do. Mike leaned forward, watching.

I fumbled under the scrutiny, the slimy barbeque sauce slipping between my fingers. The corners of Mike's lips curled again, the smile unnerving. The wing finally reached my mouth, but my appetite dissolved. I nibbled on the chicken before setting it down.

'Would you like one?' I asked Mike.

His smile turned into a baring-of-teeth grin. 'Yeah, nah, I'll pass thank you. Never been a fan of spice.' He reached for another wedge, breaking it into pieces once again.

I couldn't say I was a fan of the spice either. I didn't need to see my face to know the intricate pattern of blood vessels under my skin had flushed crimson. Sometimes I fell victim to my own methods.

'You're here a lot, Charlie.'

I frowned. Mike said my name like we knew each other. I studied his face, but there was nothing familiar there. He stared back just as intently, then he turned to look at Sophie. 'Won a heart there, have you?'

I let out a breath, and a new wave of heat painted my skin. 'I... I'm a regular.'

Mike chuckled. 'A regular. That's a good term for it.'

I frowned. Why was that funny? His tone was amiable, but something cold glinted in his eyes. Whatever the joke, I wished he would let me in on it.

I edged my chair back. People filled the room, but at least three tables stood empty around the other end of the bar. Why had he chosen to sit with me? He leaned forward, closing the gap I'd created between us. His stare locked me in, making it impossible to look away.

'You said you'd seen me,' I said.

'I have.'

'But you've never been here before.' My throat felt raw, and not just from the spice.

Mike's smile turned sly. He took a slug of his coke as if he was downing a shot of whiskey. 'I have. I've been watching you for a while.'

I blinked, wondering if I'd misheard him. 'Excuse me?'

His rumpledness didn't look so comfortable anymore. Hard edges seemed to form on his features as I watched. I looked for Sophie, but another customer held her attention.

Mike followed my gaze once again. 'Sweet girl. Let's not involve her in this.'

'What is this?' Sweat dampened my temples and my shirt. You can call me Mike. Odd wording – a fake name, for sure.

He grabbed another wedge, placing it on the napkin in front of him, then took a knife from the pail. He cut the potato in half, examining the pieces, but he didn't eat them. I had the distinct impression it had simply been an excuse to pick up a weapon.

'You know how many people I've seen die, Charlie?'

'What?' I could barely force the word out.

Sophie crossed the bar. Her movements seemed to crawl, but somehow, she was still getting further away from me. I wanted to yell for her. I wanted her to come and save me.

'Five. Most of them on the job..

Oh god, he was a cop. But how? I'd been so careful. Or had I? I'd been getting complacent lately, sure I was undetectable. But how? How could they link me to the deaths? I'd never touched any of them; I'd just made them laugh. That wasn't a crime.

'So imagine our surprise when we keep hearing about this man in a wheelchair at the scenes of seven deaths around the country in the last year.'

I'd been stupid, so stupid. They hadn't even caught me for all of them, but they would. They would. They would find those other victims, and I'd be done. It was over, it was all over.

'Funny thing is, they were non-suspicious deaths. See, that's even rarer. Most of the people who see a lot of death, it's suspicious as hell.'

I clasped the wheels of my chair. "Mike" reached out snapping on the brake. He carried on as if he hadn't moved.

'No known poisons in their systems, no wounds we can see, eyewitnesses who all say no one touched them. Yet there you were, sitting next to each one of them as they died.'

I reached for the brake, but he caught my hand. I watched Sophie, like a lifeline, but I'd floated too far from her. Would she help me? Would she still smile if she knew what I'd done?

'The thing we still can't work out is how you did it.'

He almost laughed when he said "you". Even now, knowing what I'd done, he still saw me as weak. He looked at me with disgust, but a light sparked in his eyes – eagerness, or maybe a hint of admiration. He wanted to know, not because he was a cop, but because he was jealous.

'I don't know what you're talking about.' I surprised myself with the steady tone of my voice. I sat up straighter, suddenly confident in my safety. Making someone laugh wasn't a crime. He had circumstantial evidence at best.

The slow smile crept over Mike's face again, and my newfound confidence wavered. 'Yes, you do, Charlie. We know you do.'

Out of the corner of my eye, I saw the door to the courtyard open. My heart pounded, matching Gazza's steps as he strode over to me, just as I had hoped he would. Mike's smile turned back into a baring of teeth.

Gazza grinned too when he saw me, a cat spying a small creature he could play with. Light glinted off his forehead, hitting the sheen of sweat he'd built up from the prolonged period of breathing smoke instead of air.

Run, I wanted to yell. Run, Gazza, get away while you can. But I had been going to kill him tonight. He should be running from me, not just from Mike.

He flopped himself down in the chair to my left. 'Got some company tonight, have you Charlie?'

'This is Mike,' I choked out.

Gazza's eye travelled over Mike, assessing and finding to his liking. Someone like Gazza would always prefer to talk to people like Mike – normal people. On another day, they would have been friends, ganging up to make fun of me.

'Kia ora, mate. Call me Gazza.' He held out his right hand, slapping Mike on the shoulder with the other. 'What are you doing with little Charlie here?'

Mike shrugged. 'Charlie's got some interesting talents I'm curious to know more about.'

If I'd been able to see myself, I'm sure I would have been turning green.

'Talents? Charlie?' Gazza let out a guffawing laugh. 'What, are you hiring for a freak show?'

Mike frowned, his distaste for the joke evident. 'Nothing like that. I work in a… specialised line of work.'

'He's a cop,' I blurted out.

A cop? Gazza's laughter turned to wheezing.

If I'd still been trying to kill him, this would have been the perfect moment. Another one-liner, before he could catch his breath, and he'd be gasping his way to the floor. Nausea and the rasping pain of spice burns battled it out in my throat, neither leaving room for jokes.

Gazza shook his head. 'You're barking up the wrong tree, mate. Charlie's a right crack up – wouldn't think it to look at him – but he ain't going to help you with police work.'

Mike's lips turned thin, the smile forced, as he glanced between the two of us. 'You'd be surprised what Charlie can do.' There it was again – that hint of admiration in his voice.

'I'm telling you, mate. Little Charlie's useless. Look at the kid!'

Gazza and I were the same age, not that you could tell by looking at us. Indulgence had aged him, but he fooled himself into thinking I was the one who looked young.

Mike regarded Gazza coolly. He took a pen from his pocket, doodling on the napkin he'd used earlier. 'I just came to get a feel for Charlie's skill. I'm sure you're right – nothing to brag about.'

Mike tossed the napkin down, as if over the whole thing, but I knew that tone of voice. It was the one we'd all used in the office to placate Gazza into silence.

Gazza picked up one of my hot wings. Mike leaned forward, sudden energy filling his face. His eyes flicked to the greasy chicken, following Gazza's hand as he lifted it to his lips.

Gazza tore the meat from the bone with his teeth. 'Now, me–' he said, his mouth full, 'I'd make a great cop.'

Mike's gaze slid back to me, a question in his eyes. He thought I'd used poison. That's why he'd refused the wings. We both watched Gazza take another bite, Mike waiting for a death, me for an opportunity to escape. Gazza tossed the stripped bone onto the plate.

Mike sat back in his chair, his face crinkling into a frown. I wondered at the fact he hadn't intervened. Did he actually want me to kill Gazza? I shook my head. Not today, Mikey. I wasn't that stupid. He'd as good as admitted they had no case against me. If I killed Gazza now, circumstantial would turn to actual evidence. If I played this right, I'd be home free.

'You're quiet, Charlie-boy,' Gazza said. 'No jokes tonight?'

Mike's fingers drummed an irritated rhythm on the tabletop. He picked up the napkin, tapping it against the table in an expansion of his personal percussion. The sheen of sweat on Gazza's face had turned to a flood with the spice. He rubbed his chest, as if the hot wing had given him instant heartburn.

'I–' My eye fell on the napkin in Mike's hand. He'd folded it into a point, which now aimed at Gazza, and he'd scrawled our names on the end of it. Charlie Mike. That meant something, didn't it? Some military term?

They both stared at me, friendly expectation filling Gazza's face, but something darker and more urgent crossing Mike's.

'No jokes tonight,' I repeated.

Charlie Mike – C. M.

Mike looked from me to Gazza, then pointedly down at the food.

C. M. – Continue… mission?

Suddenly, I saw it all through Mike's eyes – unexplained deaths, no hint of harm or cause. He wasn't trying to catch me; he thought I was an expert in chemicals or weapons; something he could learn from.

I just came to get a feel for Charlie's skill. Maybe he really did want me to kill Gazza. I should do it. Make them all laugh, and watch Gazza drop dead of the heart attack he'd been threatening for months.

Gazza reached for a wedge, again with both Mike's and my eyes trailing his movements. He popped the whole thing between his teeth. I opened my mouth, but nothing came out. No jokes, no quippy comments, not even a non-sequitur odd enough to prompt a surprised laugh.

I picked up a wedge of my own. The idea of eating churned my stomach, but I put it in my mouth anyway, chewing over all I knew about "Mike" as the food rolled across my tongue.

What would he make of my methods? He came here looking for an assassin; what would he do when he found a comedian instead? I'm sorry, sir. I don't know how to use a gun, but would you like to hear a knock-knock joke?

I started to laugh, a big bubble of it building from my chest. Gazza joined me, so ready for my humour he didn't even need to hear the joke. I gasped. The irony. He didn't know how funny his death would have been. I leaned forward, tears streaming from my eyes.

'So good you can't even get the punchline out, eh?'

I nodded, cackling in just how good it would have been. I opened my mouth to tell them, and the half-eaten wedge slipped back into my throat.

I spluttered, a sound I had heard from all of my victims, as my jokes lodged food in their windpipes.

Gazza chuckled. 'You right, little man?'

I clasped my throat, the sign for choking, which I had pretended not to see so many times.

Mike slowly shook his head, something close to admiration growing on his face. He thought I'd done this on purpose.

Underneath the sweat, Gazza's skin paled, turning a waxy grey. 'Sophie,' he yelled. 'Call 111!'

I gurgled, saliva pooling in my mouth. Sophie met my eye across the bar, her face paling too. She grabbed the phone and ran towards me, her thumb punching the three numbers without looking. And then someone was pulling me from my chair, slapping me on the back, but it was too late. The stodge of potato had expanded to fill my spice-swollen throat.

Mike stood, putting his jacket back on. He stretched, then turned towards the door, his pace casual. I'd made similar exits myself, slipping away as the crowd tried to save my victim.

Sophie fumbled with the phone, and a customer took it from her. Black spots peppered my vision, blocking out her face.

'Ambulance, hurry!' the woman said.

Wait, I wanted to call after Mike. Wait, it wasn't me! I didn't do anything. I just made them laugh.

He looked back at me, and suddenly the dishevelled father had returned, smiling kindly at me. He almost seemed sad.

A tear rolled down my cheek. Moisture filled Sophie's eyes too. It was so close to how I had planned it. Her tears, falling on Gazza's neck as she leaned her head on his shoulder. His arms, wrapping around to comfort her.

I blinked, darkness crowding in. Charlie died doing what he loved – laughing, my eulogy would say, and everyone at the funeral would laugh too, with tears in their eyes. Maybe one of them would even keel over, the two of us the final victims for my list.

WATER DAMAGE

KATHERINE KOVACIC

I'VE KNOWN KEL FOR YEARS, HE'S OLD SCHOOL, WITH AN INHERENT DISTRUST of technology, so it's a surprise to hear his raspy voice on my answering machine.

'Alex sweetheart. I hate these things! Are you there? I need to talk to you. I've got a bit of a problem. Call please. Or better yet, come over and bring that dog of yours.'

I sigh, twirling the car keys on their Georg Jensen fob. I've only just walked in the door at the end of what has been a long and disappointing afternoon – the owner of the painting I wanted to buy is asking way too much – and all I want to do is take Hogarth for a walk then eat something hot involving a lot of carbs. But Kel is a crusty bugger, and back in the day I'm sure he swung his fair share of punches. So if Kel left a message, his bit of a problem is probably not so little.

'Dude,' I say. 'How about a road trip?'

The wolfhound is standing beside me and he lets loose with a full-body shake that leaves the tail still quivering long after his head has stopped moving.

'I'll take that as a yes, shall I?'

Less than 15 minutes later we're in the Citroen heading for the West Gate Bridge and it's not long before we're turning off towards Williamstown and the small, un-renovated, yet highly desirable cottage Kel calls home. As I swing into his street, another car pulls out, and for a moment we're side by side. I register a battered old station wagon – once blue, now faded and rusty – seemingly held together by a series of equally ancient Painters and Dockers' Union stickers. And behind the wheel, a grey and grizzled countenance beneath a Bulldogs football beanie.

I park directly in front of the trim little weatherboard and as I'm getting Hogarth out of the car I notice the neighbour's curtains twitch. Kel has mentioned the lady next door, a widow in her 70s. He provides her with produce from his tiny garden which she turns into preserves and hot meals, servings of which are passed across the low fence between their properties. I've never met her, but today I do what I always do when I see the chintz flicker, which is smile and wave. And I get the same response, which is nothing.

Undeterred, I open the front gate and Hogarth and I make our way down the narrow concrete path to the front door, where I twist a tiny handle, causing the doorbell to ring with an importance far greater than either the house or our presence requires. We stand there as the echoes fade, Hogarth waving his tail gently, no doubt in anticipation of the treats Kel always has on hand for our visits.

There is no answering shout, no sound of footsteps on the creaky floorboards. Only silence.

'Kel?' I call, knocking on the door at the same time. 'It's Alex and Hogarth!'

Still nothing.

'Maybe he's round the back,' I say to Hogarth.

I lead the way off the porch and along the side of Kel's house. The path ends abruptly at the edge of the veggie patch: neat rows of corn, tomatoes and carrots with potato and pumpkin plants sprawling in the background. But no Kel.

'Should have called,' I mutter.

As we make our way back to the front, Hogarth stops beneath a window. It's open slightly but the blind is down, making it impossible for me to see in. The hound raises his snout and scents the air, then whines softly. I glance between window and wolfhound and fear sluices through my system.

'Kel!' I shout.

I turn and sprint for the back yard, Hogarth close on my heels. This time we keep going, trampling plants as we cut across to the back door.

It's hanging open.

'Kel!'

I listen, hoping for a groan or sound of some sort, anything.

The back door opens directly into the kitchen, somewhere I've been many times before, and even as I'm hurrying through, I register the mess: cupboards open, things strewn about, flour and sugar spilled across the floor, crunching under my feet. Kel has always been a stickler for neatness. I pull out my mobile phone, ready to dial triple zero.

The narrow hallway is empty. All the doors are shut but light streams in from the leadlight panels around the front door. This space, with its picture gallery, is also familiar to me, but two of the four closed doors represent Kel's private domain, spaces he has always guarded firmly but without rancour. I don't hesitate, throwing open the nearest door. Beyond is the room with the open window. There are pictures on the wall, a double bed with a faded but trim green chenille bedspread and, sticking out from behind that, a pair of feet shod in old work boots.

My thumb is pressing the screen of my mobile even as I dive around the bed.

'Police, fire, or ambulance?' the operator asks.

I stare. I was expecting a stroke or heart attack, not–

'Police, fire or ambulance?' The pitch of voice has risen.

'Ambulance,' I say. 'And police, please.'

'Putting you through.'

'Ambulance, is the patient breathing?'

Somehow, I'm already kneeling on the floor next to Kel. I switch the phone to speaker and throw it on the bed.

'I don't– Head injury, there's lots of blood.' I give Kel's address without waiting for them to ask. 'Hurry.'

I feel for a pulse, registering the cool waxiness of his skin, and start CPR. From my phone comes the calm voice of the operator, counting me through the compressions, occasionally telling me that help is on the way, help is close, help has arrived.

But I know all along there is no help for Kel.

I stop to let the ambos in, and after showing them the room, I slump to the floor in the tiny hall, head hanging between my bent knees. Exhausted, disbelieving. It's too early for grief. Hogarth sits next to me; a steady presence amid the chaos. I answer the paramedics' questions, nod when they formally deliver the news, ask if the police are coming, dig my fingers into the hound's fur.

'Alex.' The gruff voice breaks through my mental fog and I look up.

'Detective Daikos? What are you doing here?'

The police detective and I have crossed paths on a number of occasions in the past. I think I annoy him, but to his credit it never seems to get in the way of the job.

He shrugs. 'The locals were on their way to your triple-oh, then a neighbour phoned in talking about a woman in an old green car with a large grey dog running around shouting. As soon as I heard that I figured it would save everyone time if I came.'

He pauses and runs a hand over his jaw. 'Then we got another call from the ambos about what they'd encountered here, but by that stage I was already on the way. SOCO should be arriving shortly, so perhaps you'd like to come outside and fill me in on exactly what happened and why you're here.'

We go out the front door but end up around the side of the house, away from the small crowd that's gathering in the street, but also out of what I already know is a crime scene.

'So.' Daikos regards me with slightly narrowed eyes. 'Let's start with who the old gent is and how you know him.'

I take a deep breath, willing myself not to think about what I just saw. 'Kel Evans. Not sure of his exact age but 70-something. I've sold pieces of art for him for years. Today—'

But Daikos stops me with a hand, his expression incredulous. 'You sold art for him? It's not exactly a blue-chip residence! Are you saying he was secretly cashed-up?'

I shake my head. 'Hardly. The things Kel gave me to sell were just minor pieces – a few etchings, woodblock prints, drawings, that sort of thing. Never anything worth more than a couple of thousand bucks.'

'I'm never one to judge, but on first appearance he doesn't strike me as an art collector.'

'Kel was in the navy in World War II, then he became some sort of merchant seaman before getting a job at the naval dockyard here in Williamstown,' I say.

Daikos quirks an eyebrow at me.

'When Kel was sailing he'd visit galleries and selling exhibitions wherever his ship docked, buying cheap pictures that took his fancy. His version of souvenirs, I guess.'

I rub my hands across my eyes, feeling the tightness of unshed tears.

'Why did you ask for the police straight away?' Daikos's tone is gently curious.

'Because the kitchen is a mess and Kel liked things shipshape and Bristol fashion. Plus he was very fit for his age, not the sort to lose his balance.'

I study Daikos's face. For a moment there's nothing but then he relents and nods.

'Well, you were right.' He doesn't elaborate. He doesn't need to: someone hit an old man over the head.

'Why?' The word is strangled in my throat.

He twists his mouth and tips his head to the side, as though his neck is suddenly painful. 'Don't know yet, but looks like an ag-burg that went too far. A couple of other rooms have been turned over. No pictures missing though.'

'Kel's pictures wouldn't…' I trail off as memory tickles a corner of my brain.

'Wouldn't what?' Daikos is watching me closely.

I shake my head, trying to flick the thought loose. 'I was going to say, the average burglar couldn't sell the things Kel had on his walls but there's something else, something I saw.' I close my eyes, picturing the scene in the kitchen, then in the bedroom. My attention had been on Kel, but even so—

'The picture over the bed, Kel's bed,' I say. Now I can see it clearly in my mind.

'What about it?'

'It was slightly crooked, but more importantly, it wasn't Kel's taste and the shadow on the wall was larger: a different picture must have been hanging there for years.'

'Seriously?'

'It's my job.' I shrug. 'The thing on the wall was a cheap, photographic print. Kel is – was an art man.'

A uniformed officer appears at the end of the path and catches Daikos's eye.

'Wait here,' he says.

I watch as the two have a short conversation before being joined by another person, this one in a white disposable jumpsuit that marks her out as scene-of-the-crime. Hogarth leans against my thighs and tips his head to stare up at me, pulling my attention, offering comfort until Daikos is back.

'They'll check the picture but it already looks like there's cash and other valuables missing,' he says. 'I'm sorry about your mate. Sorry there are scum who'd do this to an old bloke for a few bucks.'

For a moment his mask slips, and Daikos looks as though he's aged 50 years. 'Go home Alex. I'll be in touch about a statement or if anything else comes up.'

He reaches down and gives Hogarth a gentle scratch behind the ear then hurries away, back inside, back to trying to make sense out of a senseless death.

Out in the now-crowded street, I keep my head down as I get the hound buckled up in the back of the Citroen and slip behind the wheel. I'm just about to turn the key when a sharp rap on the window makes me jump. An elderly woman is peering in, hugging a thin cardigan around bony shoulders. For a fleeting moment I consider just driving away, but she's going to hear about Kel sooner or later and perhaps it's better coming from me rather than the six o'clock news or a uniformed officer. I wind down the window.

'Kel,' she says, making his name a question loaded with significance.

'I'm sorry,' I reply.

She nods sharply, but her eyes are watery behind her thick glasses. 'Heart?' Then her mouth twists. 'No, not with the plods here. I'm Mrs Bauer from next door. You're Alex. Kel told me about you, and I've seen you of course, you and your dog.'

Hogarth has stuck his head out of the rear window and her gaze slides sideways to regard his hairy visage.

'Yes, I'm Alex. You're the wonderful cook,' I say, aware of how weird this conversation is.

She smiles, a smile that instantly twists and quivers, acknowledging the originator of the compliment. Suddenly Mrs Bauer unfolds her arms and thrusts an envelope through the open window.

'Kel was worried. He said if anything happened I should give you this and you'd know.'

'Know what?' I frown.

Impatiently, she flaps it at me. It's a business-size envelope, overstuffed and bulging. I take it, bewildered.

'What?' I repeat.

But Mrs Bauer has already withdrawn. I watch as she bustles back onto her own property and takes up position behind the gate, watching the unfolding drama at Kel's place. A moment later she looks across at me and makes a shooing gesture. There's no reason not to oblige, so I fire up the Citroen and point it towards Melbourne Road, wondering about the envelope, hearing Kel's answering-machine message in my head; *I've got a bit of a problem.*

Once we're home, I deliberately delay looking in the envelope, messing about with Hogarth's dinner, making myself a toasted cheese sandwich that I don't eat, putting on a load of washing and generally stuffing about until I can't put it off any more.

I pour myself a whiskey from the good bottle and settle at the kitchen table. Ripping open Kel's envelope, I let the contents spill across the Laminex surface. Photographs. Most of them are black and white, their dimensions and some discolouration indicating their age, but there are splashes of colour in the pile. I pick up a couple at random, then drop them and snatch up more.

There must be at least 50 photos here and every one shows a different painting. The lighting and angles aren't great, and in some you can clearly see the painting is propped on the floor, not hung on a wall, but if these paintings are genuine, it's a staggeringly good collection of French modernism from the first part of the 20th century. I recognise Picasso, Dufy, Solange, and a number of other artists. There's even a work that I think must be by Vieira da Silva, although I'm not familiar enough with her oeuvre to be certain.

Finally I pull out the colour photos. There are only two – one of a painting by Matisse, the other a Chagall – and I stare at them for a long time, because in both of these snaps I can see something else: the top edge of a bed covered in green chenille. Whether these are real or fake, both have hung in Kel's bedroom.

I put them down and pick up the one remaining item that fell from the envelope: a key, attached to a paper label marked Praetorian F29/4982.

After a while I get up and make myself a coffee, then return to my contemplation of Kel's pictures. Something about them resonates, something about the collection as a whole rather than the individual paintings, but I can't remember what it is. And the feeling of not-knowing-what-I-know grows more and more irritating.

I phone John.

'Can I ask you something?' I say the moment the call connects.

'Does it relate to why I'm up at this late, late hour? Because actually, I wasn't.'

I look at the oven clock: it's after midnight. 'Shit, sorry John. I lost track of time.'

'It's okay Alex. I was awake and I always like hearing your voice.'

'Thanks.'

'So what is it? Do you have an artwork in need of emergency after-hours repair?'

As well as being my best friend, John is one of the top conservators in the country.

'No but it is an art problem worthy of your vast knowledge.'

'Okay hit me.'

'I have a series of photographs of French Modernist paintings. The photos were probably taken in the 1950s or 60s. For some reason I feel like I know about this collection of art, but I can't figure out why, so if I give you a list of artists' names, will you tell me what you think?'

'Sort of like Jeopardy, only with art?'

'Sure, whatever.' I flip through the photos in front of me, reeling off names as I go. When I get to the end John is quiet. I wait.

'Basically every art movement from that period is there, abstract, surrealism,' he says before falling silent again.

'The thing is, I can't recall ever seeing one of these paintings,' I say. 'It's like the whole group is hidden or lost.'

'Wait, what? What did you just say?' John is suddenly alert.

I repeat myself.

'Lost! Hang on!' I hear John's phone fall then muffled speech and a bit of crashing in the distance, then he's back. 'New Year's Eve 1953, French Painting Now, MV Cheviot.'

'No!' I say.

'Oh yes,' John replies.

'Uh oh.'

'What?'

'Let me just clarify,' I say. 'I'm assuming you've pulled a copy of the original 1953 exhibition catalogue for *French Painting Now*, and my list of artists corresponds with the paintings in that show.'

'Correct.' John sounds very pleased with himself.

'First of all, thank you for solving that part of the problem.'

'My pleasure, but what do you mean part of the problem?'

'That exhibition was sensational for all the wrong reasons. It never happened in Melbourne because the ship, *MV Cheviot*, that was transporting the paintings down from Sydney ran aground near the Heads on New Year's Eve, 1953, and sank with its cargo.'

'Right.'

'Except I have photos of all the paintings, and what I didn't mention was that a couple of the pictures were taken quite recently.'

'Where did these photos come from again? I mean, could the whole thing be some elaborate hoax or a series of fakes?'

I shake my head slowly, even though John can't see me. 'That's what I thought at first. The thing is, the photos came from an old guy who used to be a sailor before he became a dock worker.'

'So ask him.'

'Yeah, no. He was killed today. Murdered. And I'm starting to think that it might be more than a simple burglary gone wrong.'

John inhales with a sharp hiss. 'You think–'

'I think maybe not all the paintings went down with the ship in 1953, and that for some reason, after half a century, it's become a problem.'

After only a few hours' sleep, Hogarth and I head out in the strange pre-dawn half-light for a long walk. No matter the weather, this is always an enchanted time, and for me a time for thinking or rather putting aside thought and letting my subconscious throw ideas into the brightening day.

My eyes water as we stride along. I tell myself it's not sadness for Kel but the cold southerly whipping my face: I don't do crying. My talk with John had ended with me promising to call Detective Daikos and tell him everything, but now I'm not so sure. The idea seems so far-fetched. The sinking of the *MV Cheviot* with its priceless cargo had been front page news. Surely someone would have noticed if the art was saved? And if it was smuggled off, wouldn't the secret have unravelled before now?

We break into a gentle jog and I think of the key marked Praetorian.

'Praetorian guards,' I say. Hogarth quirks an ear in my direction. 'Sounds like a storage company to me.'

Back home, after a shower and breakfast, I pull out the Yellow Pages and there they are, Praetorian Self-Storage with an address in Newport, just one suburb over from Kel. I figure there's no harm in checking it out before I talk to Daikos. I mean, I don't want to waste his time or make myself look like an idiot if there's nothing there but a bunch of photo albums and an out-of-tune banjo.

We cross the West Gate and take the same exit, but this time I pull off Melbourne Road almost immediately, taking us into a blasted industrial landscape of oil refineries, marine storage and, oddly, a wonderful science museum housed in an old sewage pumping station. In a street notable for a lack of features other than fences of cyclone, barbed, and razor wire, I drive past Praetorian, not seeing the discrete sign until it's too late. I'm mid U-turn when a tanker truck rumbles past at the bottom of the road. As my head swivels in that direction, I catch a glimpse of a faded blue station wagon. Seconds later they're both gone. I complete my turn with a feeling of unease, glad of Hogarth's presence.

There's a keypad glowing next to Praetorian's heavy metal gate, and the eyes of several security cameras are currently trained on the Citroen. Trying to look confident, I roll down the window, lean out and key in 4982. Instantly the gate clicks and begins to roll to one side. I nose the Citroen through then wait while the gate closes again, suddenly paranoid that someone will try to follow us. An impregnable barrier offers no security if the bad shit is on the same side as you.

I park the car next to the only building here: a windowless concrete cube with a door and a loading dock, both closed. The slamming of our doors echoes and a stiff breeze sends a KFC bucket tumbling across the otherwise-empty property, the combined effects creating a bizarre post-apocalyptic version of a western movie showdown scene. I check my mobile and thumb through contacts until Daikos's number is ready to dial with a single button press. Hardly a six-shooter, but it makes me feel better.

The four-digit code gets us through the door and Hogarth's claws click loudly as we make our way down corridors of locked doors. Fluorescent lights snap to life as we advance, reminding me this place is likely loaded with cameras as well as sensors. Finally we find a corridor marked 'F' and seconds later I'm standing in front of number 29 with Kel's key in my hand. The padlock is old and large, its hasp almost too thick to fit through the bolt, but it's well-oiled and the key turns smoothly. Typical Kel. I pull the padlock free, lift the hasp and swing the door open.

A cord hangs at head height and I tug it sharply. The small space is immediately bathed in harsh light, and for a second or two, my spirits sink, because all I see is junk: a bar fridge and a lawn mower blocking access to some wooden chairs, a couple of sagging, over-filled boxes and a standard lamp with a plastic-covered shade. Hogarth sniffs the dusty air then sits down to have a good scratch, clearly deciding there is not even a rodent to make this place interesting.

But then I think of the envelope, of Mrs Bauer's insistence and of Kel. I know he liked a laugh down the pub, but a practical joke of this magnitude was not his style, even if he'd been here to see my face.

I drag the mower forward and shove boxes until, with a few minor gymnastics, I can see the back wall of the locker: several blanket-wrapped rectangular objects are propped in a corner. A sigh escapes my lips and I clamber over the remaining detritus until I can lay my hands on the topmost bundle and strip the blankets away.

It's a crap copy of Van Gogh's *Sunflowers*.

'Shit,' I mutter.

The next one isn't even an oil painting, it's just a cheap print of a Monet. I'm starting to feel really stupid, but also very glad I didn't bother Daikos with this.

Then I unwrap the penultimate picture and a thrill races through me, coiling from my gut to my heart. A Matisse of Cap d'Antibes, and even though this is outside my area of artistic expertise, the bold colours and uncontrived simplicity of this exquisite painting tell me it's the real deal. I half-open the final painting, just enough to see that it's the Chagall gouache photographed in Kel's bedroom – and it also looks genuine – before rewrapping it and putting everything back where I found it: the paintings have clearly been safe here so far.

Then I turn and see Hogarth. He's standing at the entrance to the storage locker, looking down the corridor to his left, ears up, body stiff. He begins to growl. I scrabble back through the junk and grab hold of his collar.

'It's okay dude,' I say. 'Other people are allowed to be in here.'

I stick my head out into the corridor ready to offer reassurance, but there's no-one there. Somewhere, a shoe squeaks on concrete and a door closes. The hairs on the back of my neck rise to match the hackles on Hogarth's back. In an instant the hound's unease has changed my mind: the paintings are coming with us.

Fortunately they're small enough to carry easily and after locking things up, the hound and I make our cautious way back to the exit, Hogarth scouting a few steps in advance. We emerge into the same desolate parking area, the Citroen apparently its sole occupant. But as I stow the paintings in the boot and hook up the hound's car harness, I keep looking over my shoulder at the corner of the building, wondering what – or who – might be back there.

'Let's go home and call the nice detective,' I say to the hound as we drive towards the gate.

Once we're amongst a bit of traffic, I start to relax. We're waiting for a green arrow to turn onto the Bridge when I catch sight of something in my rearview mirror. A couple of cars back is a driver in a Bulldogs beanie, and a check in the side mirror shows me enough faded blue duco to be sure. Twice is coincidence, three times means the bastard is following us. On the plus side, his car is as distinctive as mine, making it easy to monitor as we merge onto the Bridge and head for the south-eastern suburbs.

I get off the freeway a couple of exits early and manage to lose him in the back streets of Albert Park, but the experience has shaken me and rather than heading home, I drive to my local police station. A quick call and Daikos is there within 45 minutes, glowering at me as I explain about Praetorian, what I found, and the car that was following us.

'Correct me if I'm wrong, but haven't I told you in the past not to mess around in my investigations?'

'I'm not. I didn't want to waste your time if it turned out to be nothing. Besides, if you had gone to the storage locker you would have ended up calling me for an opinion anyway, wouldn't you?'

For a moment his mouth twists, presumably as he swallows the words he really wants to say, then Daikos sighs. 'Show me the paintings then.'

I unwrap the bundles and explain what he's looking at, then hand him the photographs. 'Do you think whoever murdered Kel was after the paintings?' I ask.

Daikos is flipping through the photos and doesn't bother to look up. 'What I think is none of your concern. How many paintings were on this ship when it went down?'

'Sixty.'

He holds out a hand. 'Key to the storage locker.'

I drop it in his palm.

'I'll get these paintings secured and yes,' he raises his voice in response to the look on my face, 'I will be certain to record your interest and possible claim to them, should that become relevant.'

'Thank you.' I smile sweetly.

'Now go home. Stay out of it and call me immediately if you see that car or there's anything amiss.'

I consider pointing out that staying out of it and calling him immediately is a bit of a paradox, but Daikos is still radiating tension so I head out, collecting Hogarth from a group of admiring coppers as I go.

A week passes with no word from Daikos. I call the detective a couple of times and leave messages, but either they go unanswered, or some anonymous officer tries to fob me off with enquiries are continuing or something about ongoing investigations.

Thursday afternoon rolls around and I'm at a loose end: clients sorted, deals in progress, a weekend auction looming but nothing to keep me occupied. Usually when this happens and the sun is out – as it is on this balmy Melbourne day – I take Hogarth for an extra-long and rambling walk.

'Fancy a stroll around Williamstown, dude?' I ask, reversing the car into the street.

We haven't had a walk along the water in Willy for ages and now seems as good a time as any. I tell the hound it's just a walk, nothing to do with Kel or missing paintings, but I don't think he's buying it and by the time I park on Nelson Place, I've stopped trying to fool myself.

We walk from Gem Pier towards the timeball tower, past the shipyards where Kel worked back in the day, and around to Point Gellibrand. I stand there for a while, wrestling with my own thoughts and breathing the sea air while Hogarth splashes through mini whitecaps. On the way back, we stop outside the *Crown & Anchor*. It's the pub nearest the shipyards and despite the gentrification of Williamstown, clearly still a working man's establishment, right down to the Eureka flag fluttering above the entrance. The afternoon shift will still be in full swing at the shipyard, so I push through the door, Hogarth close on my heels, and stop, momentarily blinded by the transition from bright sun to dim interior. The smell of beer is almost overwhelming, only tempered slightly by a top note of fish, presumably the star of today's special, which, according to the chalk board outside, is beer-battered flake and chips.

'Help you, love?' The bartender continues the blue-collar theme with his flannel shirt, sleeves ripped out to display arms covered in tattoos.

'Hope so,' I say, trying for a breezy tone.

Hogarth steps out from the shadows behind me and I lay a hand on his shoulder. There are a few men scattered around the room and as I hoped, they are all past retirement age, drawn to the *Crown & Anchor* by old mates and the habits of a lifetime. I give them a quick once-over. Most are looking back – some with undisguised curiosity, some with mild alarm – but one group is making a point of ignoring me, hunching their shoulders and turning away as they mutter under their breath. I take a couple of steps towards the bar.

'I was wondering if Kel Evans drank here, and if there are any mates of his I could talk to?'

The publican's eyes involuntarily flicker towards the unwelcoming group, but all he says is, 'And you are?'

'My name's Alex.' I focus my attention on that one group. There are five of them, all grey haired, all broad shouldered and thick-set, although there's age evident in the curve of a spine, and the way one man's leg is stretched out to the side, his gnarled hand rubbing the knee.

'Can't help you love, sorry.' The publican shrugs and turns away.

There's a tension crackling through the air that wasn't there before I dropped Kel's name. I swallow and take another step forward, Hogarth pressed against my thigh.

'Here's the thing,' I say. 'Someone murdered Kel Evans. I'm sure you've heard that, even if you didn't know him personally. Well, I think he was killed because of a couple of paintings he owned.'

In my target group shoulders stiffen, the bull neck reddens, and the hand on the knee clenches into a gnarled fist.

'I reckon Kel got those paintings from a certain ship back in 1953 and I doubt he did it alone. There were quite a few paintings on the ship, so Kel and his mates probably divvied them up and everyone has kept quiet about it ever since. But just before Kel was murdered, he got worried enough to hide his paintings. So I think after 50 years either someone found out about it – in which case everyone who still has a painting is at risk – or more likely, someone got greedy.'

The room is silent, except for the faint sound of a race caller's voice, spilling from a small TV at one end of the bar, and for a moment everyone seems frozen in place. Then someone in the group of five slams his glass down on the table, the sound echoing like a gunshot.

'I think you should leave.' It's a harsh, smoker's voice and it emanates from that corner of the room, but the speaker remains anonymous.

'I know where the paintings are,' I say quietly.

I hear a hiss, a sharp intake of breath, from the same table. The publican looks across then back at me and jerks his chin towards the door.

I nod and the hound and I turn away.

'What are you, some sort of copper?' The question is hurled at our retreating figures with utmost contempt.

I look back over my shoulder: every one of those five men is looking back. 'Better,' I say. 'I'm an art dealer.'

Before we leave Williamstown, I decide to call on Mrs Bauer and see how she is. Her neighbour was murdered in his bedroom, she's an elderly woman living on her own and besides, Mrs Bauer was Kel's friend. Parking spaces are scarce, but I find a spot for the Citroen a bit further down the street and Hogarth and I walk back.

The door opens while we're still coming up the path.

'I hoped you'd come back,' she says. 'Kettle's just boiled.'

We follow her through a house similar to Kel's in layout but lightyears away in decor. It's clear that as well as cooking, Mrs Bauer has a thing for crochet and needlework - there are throw rugs, cushions and doilies everywhere. In the spotless kitchen, a plate of scones sits in the middle of the table, next to a steaming teapot, snug beneath its rainbow-coloured cosy. She bustles about organising a bowl of water for Hogarth and checks to see if he can have a scone of his own before carefully quartering it and serving it up on a china saucer.

Even before tea is poured and I've slathered butter and jam – 'from Kel's plum tree, dear' – on a scone, Mrs Bauer starts talking about Kel with the urgency of a woman desperate for a friendly ear. I let her go, putting in the occasional encouraging noise, eating far too much as she absent-mindedly adds things to my plate every time it's empty. Hogarth scores a few things I discreetly drop to the floor, but Mrs B seems oblivious.

The afternoon slips away and the kitchen dims, forcing Mrs B to get up and turn on the light, shaking her out of her memories.

'Was the envelope important, dear?' She asks, raising the cosy and touching the back of her hand to the teapot.

The question comes so suddenly it takes me a moment to catch up with the conversational shift.

'Yes it was,' I reply.

She nods, satisfied. 'The police had a lot of questions, and I gather from the general drift, that the attack on Kel wasn't random.'

'No.' I hesitate. 'Were you able to tell the police anything?'

'I don't think so, nothing important anyway. They kept asking if I'd seen anything out of the ordinary about the time Kel was… Any cars or people who didn't belong, but there was nothing like that. I would have noticed.'

Something about her words bothers me and I study her face thinking about what she just said.

'So you told them you didn't see anything different.'

'That's right. More tea?'

'No thanks, I really should– But did you see something? Something normal? That struck you as perfectly ordinary?'

'Well yes, dear. But the police aren't interested in normal things.' She stands and begins to move plates and cutlery to the sink and I automatically follow suit, passing her the pot and plates, accepting the Wettex to wipe down the table.

'What did you see?' I manage to keep my voice neutral and matter-of-fact.

'Oh just Mick Johnston as usual.' She turns on the tap and squirts dishwashing liquid into the sink.

'Mick Johnston?' I brush crumbs into my hand.

'One of the men Kel used to work with at the shipyard. Drives a terrible car, mad football supporter. He and Kel were thick as thieves for years and Mick was around almost every other day.' She dons a rubber glove.

'I think I might have seen Mick,' I say. 'Blue car covered in union stickers and wears a Bulldogs beanie?'

'That's Mick.'

I wrap things up as quickly as possible, promising to come again soon and politely declining her offer to crochet a coat for Hogarth. She watches us go out the gate and I only hear the door close when we have passed out of her line of sight.

Unlocking the Citroen, I reach in to retrieve Hogarth's harness. My back is to the street when Hogarth suddenly presses up against my legs and starts barking. I turn and grab his collar, unsure of the emergency but knowing from his furious tone that this is serious.

A bull-necked man in a red, white, and blue beanie is standing a few metres away, and the look on his face as he glances between me and Hogarth makes my blood run cold. I try to put the hound behind me, but he's having none of it: as far as Hogarth is concerned, security is his job. He reduces the barking to a menacing growl, eyes glued to the figure in front of us.

'Mick Johnston,' I say, pleased my voice doesn't crack.

'Nosy bitch,' he says, by way of greeting.

'I assume you wanted Kel's paintings, but why? Didn't you get a couple of your own when the ship went down?'

He nods. 'Sold 'em back then on the Q-T for bugger-all. We all did, except Kel. Stuck 'em on his wall, silly old bastard. Fifty years! Now they're worth a bloody fortune.'

'So you wanted the money.'

He shrugs nonchalantly, and that's when I notice the knife in his hand. He sees me looking.

'It's for filleting and gutting,' he says, shifting his weight slightly.

I'd like to think I can outrun a man in his 70s, but Mick looks fit and I have the hound to think about. In the time it would take me to convince Hogarth to turn away from a threat, Mick would be on us.

Just as I'm weighing up my options a police car turns into the far end of the street and screeches to a stop 50 metres behind Mick. He doesn't flinch, but the knife shifts slightly in his hand. I try to read his face, vaguely aware of a familiar figure leaping from the cop car.

'Drop the knife!' Daikos shouts. 'Drop it!'

Mick's lip twists as he raises the knife. Hogarth snarls and tries to leap forward but I have him by the collar and I pull back, hard. The momentum spins us around and I cringe, waiting to feel the knife between my shoulder blades.

Then I hear the clatter of metal on concrete and pounding feet.

'On the ground! Hands where I can see them!'

I turn.

Mick is lying face-down, being dealt with by two uniformed officers while Daikos stands to one side, his gun trained on the killer. The detective shoots me a look then returns his attention to the job.

I move out of the way and sit on the kerb, holding Hogarth close, burying my face in his grey fur, only looking up a few minutes later when the hound's tail begins to wag and a shadow blocks the sun.

'Alex bloody Clayton,' Daikos is staring down at me, shaking his head. 'What did I tell you?'

I reach out a hand and he pulls me to my feet. 'I was about to call you, detective. I've become aware that something's amiss.'

THE ROOMING HOUSE

KERRY GREENWOOD

IN CASE YOU HAVEN'T MET ME BEFORE, MY NAME IS CORINNA CHAPMAN. I am a plus-sized baker, and I don't care. Anxious friends used to tell me about their favourite diets in an attempt to make me lose weight. I have a new set of friends now who appreciate me for what I am. My bakery is called *Earthly Delights*; and while starting work at 4am is not exactly fun, I have to say that 1pm on a weekday is one of the best parts of my week.

On this particular day my assistant Kylie had been despatched to the bank with the cash proceeds for the day; Gossamer had gone off to yet another casting call for the beautiful and anorexic; my apprentice Jason had retired to spend quality time with Bruce the bunny, and normally I would be free to spend my afternoon cuddling my cat Horatio, or (on red-letter days) relax with my beloved Daniel. He was interstate on a hush-hush Mission Improbable, so – in the general run of things, I would have free time.

Not today, however. I ascended the stairs to my apartment (Hebe), stroked Horatio, offered him Kitty Dins, and lay down on my bed to gather my thoughts. Which were in a state of chaos. And why? Because my ex-husband James had turned up in my life again. I ran over in my memory the salient points of our phone conversation. Somehow I could remember all of it. I must have been radiating high-tension stress, because Horatio joined me on my bed and gave me a good purring. This is what had happened.

'Hello, Corinna?'

'Hello, who is this?'

'James.'

'James who?'

'James your ex-husband. I need your help, if you're free tomorrow.'

'Oh, that James. If you'll forgive the question, what's in it for me? I don't wish you ill; but I'd love to know why I should get myself embroiled in your escapades. Again.'

There had been a prolonged and awkward silence at that.

It wasn't long ago that I had read in the news that a Robert Strahan had been remanded in custody over the seizure of one point four tonnes of date-rape drugs, imported by Zymosis P/L hidden inside a container from Indonesia, which according to its lading bills contained only automotive parts.

Strahan's fellow-director James Beard had been interviewed by the police, and had been released without charge. It was not suggested that Mr Beard had any knowledge of the smuggling plot. He had had some explaining to do; but back then I had given him the phone number of Rachel Swarc – a much-feared criminal lawyer with whom I had been at university – and she had extricated him by convincing the police that James really was just a gullible idiot.

The problem was that this had only encouraged him to regard me as his personal crisis intervention team. Our conversation today had continued as follows:

'Not trouble with the law this time. But you used to be a top-quality accountant, I recall. And I need your advice about a joint venture. I'm meeting them tomorrow and I'd love it if you could come along.'

'Planet Earth to James? Yes, I'm sure you would like me to come and hold your hand. But why on earth should I? Come on. I'll give you 30 seconds to convince me, and then I'm hanging up.'

'I've made a lot of money, Corinna. Honestly. I sold that Camberwell house – you know? The one we used to live in?'

'I'm trying to forget that house, but go on. Your clock is ticking down.'

'And I built a rooming house for the poor and homeless.'

'You did WHAT?'

'I'm charging them only nominal rent. It's brand new; everyone gets a proper unit with a door that locks; there's security on call 24/7; and everyone there seems to be happy.'

'So, what's the problem?'

'Some guys at my church are really impressed and want me to join in a consortium to make this whole thing really big. They're putting in 20 million!'

'I'm sorry, James, this must be a terrible line. For a moment I thought you'd just said something about your church!'

'I did. I'm going to church these days. Didn't I tell you?'

And that was the moment I pretty much lost it. I gibbered for a moment. I may even have raved. But it was absolutely true, apparently. James Beard, a man I could have sworn worshipped only money and rolled-steel joists, had joined the Happy-Clappies.

This particular brand were called the Intercostals. They did a lot of heavy breathing, shouting Hallelujah and the like. Well, if James wanted to join a bunch of psychic belly-dancers it was no business of mine. But this mob had connections in high places. Cabinet Ministers were numbered among their flock.

What they wanted with James was more than I could imagine.

I said yes. I don't really know why, but I did. Reader, I married him, and how I wished I hadn't. And so in less than an hour I would be meeting with The Dodgy Brothers. I wanted my best accountant's garb, I considered. I arrayed myself in my white cotton shirt with rococo frills down the front, a severe black jacket, corporate black trousers and my best square-toed black leather shoes. I walked down the stairs to keep my appointment with destiny, in whatever form it should manifest itself.

569 Bourke Street turned out to be one of those gigantic office blocks with an atrium which could have hosted a stadium rock concert. You know the sort of thing. A great deal of natural wood colouring, and strange geometrical shapes strewn indiscriminately around the walls and ceiling. The architect had doubtless had a traumatic childhood experience involving building blocks. There was a concierge's desk, where a fussy man in a dark blue uniform looked me in the eye. Before I could say

anything I found James hovering near the lobby like a man trying to hail a taxi. He greeted me and I held his arm in mine as he ferried me into the lift.

'Now, James. Before we go in, have they got anything for you to sign yet?'

'There's a draft Heads of Agreement. They told me I could sign it today if I was satisfied.'

I nailed him with a chilling look. 'You're not going to be satisfied, though, are you, James? You're not in the market for satisfaction this afternoon. If you are, I don't want to know. We're going to take this draft away and look at it thoroughly first. Or rather I am.'

He blinked at me. 'All right, whatever you say. Here's our floor.'

James ushered me past a glamorous but severe PA who was typing away at something. She looked up at me, and just for a moment flashed me an amused grin. The moment disappeared almost instantly, but I filed it away for future reference.

We entered the meeting room. Two moustaches greeted me: a pencil-thin one as worn by spivs and cardsharps the world over, and another caterpillar one. There was a general impression of blue suits, white shirts, and slender red ties, but their faces faded into obscurity as soon as you looked at them. You only remembered the moustaches, which was probably their sole purpose. They were on their feet at once, and both offered me the most untrustworthy handshakes I have ever suffered. The more luxuriant of the moustaches took up the tale. He was apparently Robert Tasker, and he was delighted to see me and tell me all about his amazing plans for my ex-husband.

Today, apparently, we were going to pivot with agility to resiliently improve our strategic outcomes through corporate synergy. My eyes must have been visibly glazing over because my ex-husband actually kicked me under the table. I tuned back into the monologue in time for another onslaught of synergy.

'You see, we really believe in what James is doing, and we'd like to help in every way we can,' concluded Tasker, breaking into English at the uttermost last gasp. 'Going forward,' he added breathlessly, as if unwilling to abandon Managerese entirely even in an outburst of faked sincerity.

'And what will you and your friend bring to this joint venture, Mr Tasker?' I asked.

His right hand brushed lightly across his nose. 'We'll be putting substantial resources into it, Ms Chapman,' he assured me.

'That's good to hear. How much upfront?'

Mr Pencil Mo frowned. I was told his name but it dropped through my short-term memory like groceries through a wet paper bag. I didn't really care. He had Spear Carrier written all over him.

'That will of course depend on our building pipeline,' he assured me. 'It's still blue sky at the moment, but we'll get into specifics once the agreement is signed. We can talk that through at our next meeting.'

'Of course. We will of course need to take copies of the draft Heads of Agreement away to study. That's understood? And I'll need a copy of your last annual report. The version with your balance sheet in it.'

There was an awkward pause. Mr Spear Carrier looked at Mr Tasker, who returned the look. They contrived, for a long, dragging moment, to give me the impression that I had asked for a live octopus with a rat salad as a side dish. I knew this one. They were hinting that I was being excessively forward, and hoping I'd say 'Oh no that won't be necessary'.

I entirely failed to say it. I saw James open his mouth to speak, and returned his kick under the table. Which seemed fair enough under the circumstances.

'Of course,' they chorused, eventually. Mr Tasker strode to the door and summoned Ms PA. He handed her a sheaf of papers, returned to his seat, and gave me the most blatantly confected smile I'd seen in years.

'Well, I'm sure you and Ms Chapman will want to look through the proposed arrangements as soon as possible,' Tasker intoned. 'Shall we say same time same place, next Wednesday?'

'Why, certainly,' I heard James say beside me. 'That would be great.'

Ms PA entered through the open door, leaned over James with a waft of Lanvin and just a hint of creamy breast in front of his eyes, and laid two stapled copies on the table in front of him. She gave him a broad smile which lasted entire milliseconds and swept out of the room. James tucked them into his shiny briefcase. I hooked my arm through his and propelled him towards the door and escape. We endured another round of handshakes and thank you for your times, and I managed to steer my gullible ex-husband into the lift.

'Yes, James, she's very beautiful. A most lissom girl, to be sure.'

He gave me a hurt look. 'Are you saying she's a dumb blonde?'

'James, I suspect she possesses more actual brain-power in her manicured fingernails than both of those crooks rolled together.'

As the lift whooshed to a halt at ground zero James' expression of hurt intensified. 'Corinna, you're being a bit unfair, aren't you? They're putting 20 million into this venture.'

I held out my hand. 'James, if you give me my copy, I will study it at my leisure and we'll see how that stacks up, shall we? And their annual report. And if the balance sheet isn't in it, we are going back to get a copy that has it.'

He handed them both over, gave me a hurt look, and I abandoned him forthwith. Back in my apartment I gave the Hambledon Holdings P/L annual report a good once-over. There are a number of places to hide dead bodies in a balance sheet. The amortisation schedule was suspiciously virginal, which told me that they weren't actually doing anything much other than having meetings.

So, check the Receivables column. Which listed 23 million-odd dollars' worth. Their actual cash at bank was over a million. But not much more than that. Some of the entries in Contingent Liabilities looked a bit suspicious too. I had neither the time nor the willpower to investigate them. Their claimed profit was over five million for the last financial year. But accountants don't take profit-and-loss statements seriously. There were even cash flow projections.

I silently blessed their little cotton socks. Because we know where cash flow projections come from. Accountants pull them out of their backsides. I was so glad I wasn't one of them anymore.

I rang James and told him to hold his horses for now. I had bread to bake, and Zoom calls to my beloved in the early evening. I had some more sheep-dogging to do, but I was blowed if I would interrupt my working week any further on James' behalf. So, I and my staff baked bread, made muffins, and sold bready products all over town. I played with my cat and blew salacious kisses to my beloved over my video camera.

Until Friday afternoon. Daniel was returning home on Sunday; and I was determined to wrap up this case – such as it was – before then. I had two texts from James asking if I had come up with anything, but I ignored them. By mid-afternoon on Friday, after a satisfying gin-and-tonic, I was ready to tackle the mystery of the rooming house.

I had asked Jason to check it out for me on Wednesday. He had returned and pronounced it satisfactory. So at least James wasn't fibbing to me. I would have to take his religious zealotry at face value. But why were his happy-clappy friends so eager to deal themselves in? To hear James talk, they had been inspired by his philanthropy and wanted to help put the purveyors of disgusting hovels for the needy out of business. I tried to match this up with our moustachioed friends and couldn't make the picture fit in my head.

So I began to googling our friend Tasker. All I came up with was his directorship of a few companies, including Hambledon Holdings. Nothing was known about him beyond that. Then I looked up the Intercostals. The top-ranking search result was one which made me sit up straight and pour myself another G & T. And this is what I read, straight from the *Financial Review*:

More Turmoil For The Intercostals

The recent collapse of Jehoshaphat Holdings appears to have caught several prominent members of the Intercostal Church. Readers will recall that Jehoshaphat was being spruiked by the late Tibor Ignatieff, last seen hiding out in his native Kazakhstan.

Church members are tight-lipped about their losses, but given that over $200 million seems to have gone walkies with Ignatieff the bill is likely to be severe.

Interviewed at his Sutherland church door last Sunday, Pastor Bill Fostle concurred that Ignatieff had indeed been a member of his flock.

'Many of our members were persuaded to invest in Jehoshaphat. We don't know where the money went. We trusted him. No, I didn't invest in his company.'

The scam dates back several years. Ignatieff was reported to be a very friendly man and good at salesmanship. Jehoshaphat appears to have been nothing more than a tax avoidance Ponzi scheme.

During the first year, dividends flowed back to investors, but the supply of funds dried up thereafter, though Ignatieff continued to enlist new investors until he abruptly left the country late last year.

Unconfirmed reports from Almaty suggest that Ignatieff died suddenly two weeks ago. The missing money is nowhere to be found. A number of Australian companies are said to have lost heavily in the collapse of Jehoshaphat, including...

And there it was. Not Hambledon Holdings as such, but Fourth Bridge P/L. I looked again at Hambledon's Annual Report, and Fourth Bridge was listed as owing them $2.5 million in the Receivables column. Further cross-checking produced two more companies listed as having lost money to Ignatieff, and they also were listed as debtors to Hambledon.

The 20 million of fictional money they had promised to put in to this alleged joint venture with my ex doubtless represented money owed to them by Jehoshaphat Holdings and its subsidiary debtors. I had no doubt that this debt was to be used as collateral in all manner of hanky-panky. Like persuading a gullible investor like James into merging his entirely solvent company with theirs.

So, what did we now know? James' new friends were trying to swindle him out of his money and his rooming house. Why?

Old-fashioned greed, doubtless. Hambledon's ship was going down with all hands, and they wanted James to throw them a life-belt. Could they get away with this? Surely not? I picked up the Heads of Agreement again and stared at it.

On Saturday morning I summoned James to *Café Pandamus*. I ordered my usual Greek coffee, *metriou*, and baklava, exchanged pleasantries with Del, and waited for my ex-husband to show up. He was a few minutes late, and arrived out of breath, his tie askew, jacket and shirt rumpled, and a fetching shade of puce. He was both thinner and balder than I remembered. I stood up for him. After a while, you can find that you'll stand for anything.

'Hello, James. I have good news, and I have bad news.'

He took a seat and rattled off an order to Del in what sounded, to my utter amazement, like reasonably fluent Greek. He shook my hand and parked himself opposite me. He offered me a weak grin. 'What's the good news, Corinna?'

'I sent a secret agent to check out your rooming house, James. I know it would be nice if I could trust you to be on the level with me; but you'll appreciate my scepticism.'

He tugged at his right earlobe. 'Is that who it was? I heard someone had been to visit. My security team thought he was looking for a room.'

'Well, no he wasn't. He is my midshipman; although fairly soon I'm going to promote him. And you'd be amazed what he found out.'

He gave me a puzzled look. 'What was that?'

'That it really is a model village. On the basis of what he told me, it's very clear to me that you aren't doing this for the money, are you? You'll never get your investment back. So why are you doing this, James?'

He looked embarrassed. 'I told you I'd been going to church, didn't I? And you know what those rooming houses out there are like. They're disgusting. They charge a fortune for rooms you wouldn't put animals in. I want those bastards out of business, Corinna. And I thought Tasker and Hambledon could help me spread the word. Think how many rooming houses I could make with their 20 million!'

Del Pandamus brought coffee and baklava for me, and a Greek salad and a small ouzo for James. I sipped, took a bite out of my honey-flavoured slice of heaven and gave it to him straight.

'And now, the bad news. James, they're bankrupt. They don't have any money. Have a read if you don't believe me. I've circled all the relevant passages.'

Give James credit, he read through all my documents and frowned. 'Oh my. So they've been having me on?'

'I'm afraid so. And it gets worse. Let me show you the Heads of Agreement. Again, you'll find the pointy bits circled in red.'

He stared at them and frowned again. 'Sorry, Corinna, but I don't understand.'

I called upon the celestial powers that be to give me strength.

'James, do you know what a takeunder is? That's what they're offering you. Yes, you get to nominate two voting shareholders of your choice; but so do they. So you'll be outvoted four to three every time and they can take all your money to the Cayman Islands if they want. These people are NOT your friends, James. So right now, I want you to tell me what you intend to do about it.'

'It's going to be a bit awkward at church, isn't it?' he managed.

I drank the rest of my coffee and finished my baklava. Then I took his hand and squeezed it. 'James, are you serious? Are you telling me you're still going to attend this nest of vipers and speak in tongues after what they're doing to you?'

I let go his hand. He stared at me. I stared back.

'James, I'm convinced. You really are doing the Lord's work, aren't you? But these people are Pharisees, or worse. They're whited sepulchres, James. May I remind you that we were married in an Anglican church? If you want to do God's work then why not reconnect with your Anglican past? You could do a lot worse. I know it's none of my business what you do with your soul, but these weirdos are not your friends.'

He stared at his Greek salad for a long while, in obvious torment. 'But they have my mobile number! They're going to call me. What do I do?'

Under stress he seemed to have reverted to the feckless adolescent I remembered only too well. Then I had a brainwave. 'James? Didn't I hear you order your brunch in Greek? When they call you, just answer in Greek! It's a great language for doing grumpy old man impressions. They won't speak it, and you obviously learned some when you were doing business in Athens.'

I saw this was making an impact and pressed the point home. 'Do it, James! I've seen for myself how persuasive Tasker can be. He just drones corporate drivel at you until you'd saw your own legs off just to make him stop. So don't play! Last week I overheard Dion Monk deal with a scammer by reciting Homer's Catalogue of Ships in Ancient Greek until they went away. Just do it. Practise with me. Now!'

And so for the next 10 minutes I pretended I was Tasker and enjoined him to Corporate Synergies Going Forward, and he grunted things like *Dthen Katalaveno*! at me.

Del Pandamus cleared away our plates and grinned at him. 'You sound like Yai-yai!' he commented. 'You want to make bad men leave you alone, Ne? Is good. You talk like that to them, they leave you in peace.'

With that, I left the café. And, wonder of wonders, James paid the bill.

And I wished him all the luck in the world.

Rock-a-Bye Baby

DAN RABARTS & LEE MURRAY

In the shade of the porch, Whaea Marama clutches Penny's knee.

'The waves. Rising,' she whispers. She looks off into the distance, and her pupils darken. 'See? A black tide.' Her grip tightens. 'A taniwha. He's coming to swallow the children!'

Penny rocks the armchair, hoping to settle her aunt by invoking her parasympathetic nervous system in an age-old technique used by mothers everywhere. Poor Marama. Her mental state has never been great – the reason Mum and Dad adopted her son Matiu as a baby – but she's especially agitated today. Even Cerberus has noticed, the big golden retriever Lab padding over to lick her hand.

Her aunt shrinks backwards. 'Tell Matiu, baby girl. He's coming.'

'No one's coming after Matiu,' Penny soothes. 'That's all over now.'

Months ago, in fact. Penny trembles, in spite of herself. Everything is fine now, but then she thinks how close they'd come to losing it all.

Her phone trills. Not wanting to abandon Marama, Penny glances at the caregiver, but the woman is busy with her jigsaw puzzle. Cerberus picks up the vibe in that uncanny way dogs do; he moves forward to drop his doggy head in Marama's lap. Only when her aunt has buried her hands in the hound's fur, does Penny step away to take the call.

'Dr Yee.'

'Officer Clark.' It has to be him. No one else addresses her by her title. 'How can I help?'

'Sorry to interrupt. I'm afraid we need your services again.'

Another homicide. Penny wonders what the body count is now. It's this damned heatwave. Pervasive. Oppressive. Stretching resources and raising everyone's tempers. Although Penny can hardly complain about the city's escalating crime rate, since the constant police contracts are keeping Yee Scientific in the black.

'Detective Inspector Tanner's hoping for a quick-solve on this one.'

'It's your lucky day, Officer Clark; I'm available now.'

'Uhm. I doubt the victim would agree, Dr Yee.'

Penny feels her colour rising. 'Quite right,' she backtracks. 'I meant, I have my sampling satchel with me.'

'I'll text you the address,' Clark says, ringing off.

Penny phones her regular driver.

'Yo.'

'Matiu, got a case. Can you pick me up from Marama's?'

'Not right now, sis. Erica's press-ganged me into picking up Charlotte's sprog from daycare.'

Penny smiles. Despite his choice of words, and the smouldering bad-boy persona Matiu tries to cultivate, her baby brother is head-over-heels for his girlfriend's niece.

'Mia? Is everything okay?' Penny helped deliver the baby; it's fair to say she has a bit of a soft spot for Mia, too.

'She's fine. Charlotte's at counselling and Erica's in meetings, so Uncle Matiu got the short straw.'

If anyone's drawn the short straw, it's Charlotte. Embroiled with a cult since Mia's conception, she's still struggling to rehabilitate, seeing doctor after doctor for treatment, and nothing seems to stick. Brainwashing's a bitch. Re-educating someone to think for themselves is even harder. Penny hopes this time Charlotte has better results.

'No worries,' she says. 'I'll call Clark back and get him to swing by and pick me up on his way to the scene.' She hangs up, fires off the text to Clark, then turns to the caregiver. 'Can you see Marama gets a cup of tea, please?'

When the woman has gone into the kitchen, Penny leans over Cerberus to give her aunt a hug. 'Gotta run, Whaea Marama,' she says, smoothing her aunt's hair. 'Work.'

Leaning back in the rocker, Marama closes her eyes. 'I told you, didn't I? The tides never stop.'

Maybe he's screaming, or is it this endless agony of childbirth? He tastes blood, lightning, rage, and futility. The sky boils, something hungry coiling through the void. There's pain, made worse by the terror, the fractured razor splinters of this recurring nightmare. The writhing shadow of tortured trust, coming for her baby. A tentacle, twisting into his eye.

Matiu jerks awake. He's nodded off again, in the heat and the heavy air, the car windows rolled up nearly all the way because part of him is always looking over his shoulder, wary of who or what might be trying to get to him.

Paranoid, much? If the last couple of years have taught him anything, it's that paranoia is the healthiest state of mind to maintain. That way, when the worst happens, you're ready for it.

2.45pm. Close enough. He steps from the car into the muggy autumn afternoon, and heads for the crèche, glancing at the Cov-42 reader at the entrance. His phone will be shaking hands with the tech right now. Probably knew the moment he drove into the parking lot. He reminds himself it's about keeping the little ones safe while they develop another new vaccine, not about the government monitoring his movements.

'Hi Matiu,' Ava greets him as he enters, her face puzzled. Honestly, he never thought a day would come when he was on a first-name basis with the staff at a daycare, but the world is a truly strange place.

'Hey, just here to collect Mia. Charlotte and Erica are both busy, so I said I'd pick the little tike up. All good?'

Ava's frown deepens. 'Well, I know you're on the list, but didn't anyone tell you? Child Services collected her, about an hour ago. They had all the right paperwork, said they were taking Mia, for her safety.'

Matiu's gut clenches. 'Taking her where?'

Only an irresponsible owner would leave a dog in a car in this heat, so while Clark is consulting with uniformed officers on the driveway, Penny ties Cerberus in the shade of the rear veranda. Then she kits up, snaps on her gloves and, stepping over the yellow police tape, heads through the sliding doors – into the cloying stench of blood.

Pausing a moment, Penny considers the rimu desk, the bookshelves lined with medical texts, and the leather couch. All the trappings of a clinician's office – only the dark stain on the carpet isn't coffee. She moves into the room, and freezes. The victim, a man in his 60s, is supine on the floor, his bloodied eye sockets staring at the ceiling where a single blowfly buzzes near an antiquated fan.

No. This can't be happening. Not again. Penny's knees quiver. *Get a grip, Penny.* Scientists deal in evidence, not emotion. Except the parallels to a previous crime scene are difficult to ignore: the respected doctor-sort, dead in his clinic, eyes gouged out.

What had the detective inspector said the last time? *It's usually symbolic. See no evil.*

There was no doubt this is evil. The dead man had been mutilated then murdered, judging from the glut of blood. Cause of death: a blade tip through the eye socket to the brain, she'd wager. Perhaps the victim put up a struggle? Given the blood everywhere, it's hard to know.

Crouching, Penny uses a small spatula to scrape the cells from under his fingernails. Focused on her work, she doesn't notice Cerberus snarling until she pauses to put the samples in her satchel. On the other side of the window the dog is going berserk, twisting on the lead, his hackles raised, and his eyes rolled back to white.

Cerberus's response freezes Penny's marrow.

Like last time.

Clark appears in the doorway, startling her. 'Dr Yee, your dog is going off his head out here.'

Yes, he's sensitive to blood and evil.

'Shall I get one of the uniforms to take him for walk?'

Penny nods. 'Thanks.'

Clark shouts over his shoulder to his colleagues, a young woman peeling off the group to untie Cerberus and lead him away. That's when Penny spies the dark smear, almost black, on the glass near the top of the sliding door. Too far away from the victim to be spatter? Perhaps it has nothing to do with the murder. Perhaps the doctor cut himself the last time he unlocked the slider? Getting out her sampling tape, Penny climbs on the sofa to take a sample of the smear, tucking the specimen in her bag.

'The victim's name is Stephen Yung,' Clark says. Still hovering in the doorway, he's slipping on his booties. 'A psychiatrist, 58, lived alone in the front house. No sign of forced entry. He was discovered by a patient when she arrived for her 2pm counselling session. She walked in and found him here.'

'That'll be another decade of therapy she'll be needing, then,' Penny says grimly.

'And a new therapist,' Clark adds.

Penny tilts her head towards the computer. 'It's still logged on.'

Clark clucks his tongue. 'Please tell me the doctor was recording the session.'

They navigate their way through the blood to the desk. Penny clicks the mouse. The screen leaps to life. She blinks.

It's a photo of a woman and a baby. The image is grainy, like it's been taken through a voile curtain, but the positioning suggests that the woman is choking the child.

'Is that—' Clark says.

'No,' Penny snaps. It can't be. The woman's in profile. All babies look alike. Auckland has hundreds of counsellors. What are the odds?

Easy enough to find out. Her hands shaking, Penny toggles to the doctor's calendar for the day's appointments. She scrolls down the list.

12pm.

1pm.

Shit.

Penny's heart lurches as she reads the name.

Matiu swipes up his speed-dial options. If the air in the car was heavy before, it's positively suffocating now. The phone rings twice before Scour picks up.

'Yee, what'd I tell you last time you called me?'

'Bro, I've told you before not to rely on my short-term memory. Whatever your problem was, let it go and listen up. Can you crack a Cov-42 active scanner?'

'Those things? They're begging to be hacked. You in range?'

'Yip.'

'Gonna send you a link to open. It'll let me use your phone to crack it. What do you need?' That's the thing about Scour. He can't resist an opportunity to stick a needle in the man, and nothing's more Big Brother than these scanners that record every smart device that comes within a couple hundred metres of them. Matiu's phone pings, and he swipes open Scour's link.

'I need to know who was here about an hour ago.'

Keys click down the line. 'Got a few hits. Been a lot of traffic through this place.'

'Daycare centre. Parents. I'm looking for someone official, what's the chance you can cross-reference the phone ID against government DBs? Child Services, specifically.'

Matiu can almost feel Scour's excitement. 'What mess've you got yourself in now, bro?'

'Mate, it's not me in trouble this time. Think of me as the Guardian Fucking Angel.'

'OK, I've got a hit. How's an office address work for you?'

'It'll do, for a start. And a name.'

'It'll cost you.'

'Add it to my bill.'

As the info drops into his message box, Matiu swings onto the street. Dropping the call to Scour, Matiu swipes up Erica's number. The dial tone croons a few too many times for comfort before Erica answers.

'Going into a meeting, can't really talk.' All business, all the way. Matiu still hasn't figured out why this is what he likes about her, but it works for them. Better not to think about it too hard.

'Mia's been kidnapped. By the Government, no less. Any chance you can chase up a name for me?'

Silence. That's a good sign, means he's got her attention. 'Who?'

'Check your inbox in a sec.'

Erica's voice changes, like she's stepped away and is masking her phone with her hand. 'What the hell's going on?'

'Tell you more when I know. Find out everything you can on,' he glances at his screen, 'Aranya Huang. Works for Child Services.'

'You know I can't do that.'

'Yeah, I know you can't, but you will. Get hold of Charlotte, make sure she's OK, will you? Call me back.'

He drops the call, forwards her the message by way of punctuation, and taps open the office address link. Twenty minutes away, practically next door by Auckland standards. He punches the gas.

While Clark's overseeing getting Yung's body into the coroner's van before the corpse parboils in the heat, Penny stands under a tree in the garden, her coveralls rolled down to her waist, and calls Matiu.

'Can't talk now,' Matiu says. 'Got an emergency.'

'Matiu, I don't care if you're covered in poo, you need to put the baby wipes down and listen to me now.'"

'Pen. I–'

'It's Charlotte,' Penny blurts. 'She was the last person to see our victim.'

'What?'

'It gets worse. There's evidence on the doctor's computer that… that–'

'Pen. I've got my own situation here. Use your words.'

'There's a photo on the doctor's screen, and it looks like Charlotte.'

'Looks like, or is?'

'I think it could be her.'

Tyres screech. 'Well, he's her doctor,' Matiu says at last. 'Why shouldn't he have her image on file?'

'The photo. She's been choking Mia.' It comes out in a whoosh.

'No,' Matiu says, and Penny imagines his jaw rippling in anger. 'It isn't her. Charlotte's fucked up, for sure, but she would never harm Mia.'

Penny bites her lip because Matiu hadn't been there, hadn't seen Charlotte on the rim of Maungawhau crater that night, when his sorta-sister-in-law's head was so full of the cult's Kool-Aid, she would've happily killed herself, and little Mia with her. 'Could the Touching the Sun people still be manipulating her?'

Matiu groans. 'Of course, they're still manipulating her! For god's sake, Penny, they're in the poor woman's head. The only way you escape a cult like Touching the Sun is to flip open your skull and scoop out your brains.'

'Close,' Penny whispers.

The tyres squeal, then there's silence, before Matiu comes back on the line. 'Tell me.'

'You know I can't release–'

'And you know you will, so spare me the confidentiality speech.'

'They scooped out the therapist's eyes.'

'No.' There's a thump. And another. Somewhere in the city, her brother is banging his palms on the steering wheel.

'I know it looks bad,' Penny says, 'but it's all circumstance and conjecture right now. We're only just getting the investigation underway: Clark's pulled the GUID from the photo and sent it off to cyber-forensics, so we can find out its provenance, Mather will do his thing down at the coroner's lab, and I've gone over the crime scene with a tea strainer. If the killer has left even the tiniest scrap of DNA, I'll find it. I promise we'll get to the bottom of this.'

'And what am I supposed to tell Erica?'

'Matiu,' Penny says slowly. 'I don't want you to take this the wrong way, but please, you need to keep Mia with you. Whatever you do, don't take her home to Charlotte's. Not yet. Not until the police can ascertain where Charlotte was when her counsellor was killed.'

Matiu laughs. 'Here's the thing, Pen. I can't find her.'

'Can't find who? Charlotte or Mia?'

'Mia,' Matiu croaks. 'Child Services uplifted her from daycare this afternoon. And Charlotte's not answering her phone.'

Matiu glares through the gate at the secure carpark. He's never considered social work dangerous, but then again, he's never experienced the anger of having a child removed from his care, and wanting to break someone for it. Mia's not even his child, but damn, this fire burns fierce in his gut. This Aranya Huang might be doing her job, and the whole suspected-murder-and-abuse scenario might justify snatching a six-month-old baby from a crèche, but how about contacting the whānau first and arranging for the child to be cared for within the family like they're supposed to, before going straight to Defcon-4?

Anyway, he can't just waltz in the front door and get an appointment, so he's lurking near the gate instead. No point starting a scene, not with the amount of CCTV in the building, and no doubt duress and lockdown buttons within easy reach. Playing it calm and cool is not his forté.

The gate whirs and rumbles as a car pulls out and onto the street. With practised ease, Matiu sidles along the wall and slips in through the automatic gate before it closes. Someone will have seen him. He doesn't have much time. He crosses to the line of cars and runs his hands over each driver's-side door handle, until a rush of guilty anxiety sweeps him. This is the one Huang was driving when she collected Mia.

'Can I help you?'

Matiu spins. A young woman wearing a severe grey suit and carrying a leather briefcase has exited the building into the car park. 'Are you Huang?'

'Who are you, and how did you get in here?' Huang asks, finger hovering over a remote duress button on her belt-clip.

'I've come to collect Mia Langley. You picked her up from *Little Tikes* daycare today.'

'Are you family?'

'I'm whānau, yes. Erica Langley's my partner. If there was an issue with Charlotte then Erica should've been the first call, and I would've come down. So, let's just keep it simple and let me take Mia home to Erica.'

Huang gives Matiu a hard look, adjusting her sleeve cuffs. 'Married? De facto? I'm afraid the bar for being considered family is rather specific. There's currently a police investigation underway regarding the child's mother, Charlotte, and the courts have deemed her a danger to her child, so an order was issued to remove Mia from her care, for her safety. No protocols have been breached. I attended the daycare centre to deliver the necessary paperwork, and to accompany the family member who has taken temporary custody of the child while the investigation is underway.'

'Family member? Who?'

'Charlotte's brother.'

Matiu's frown deepens. 'Brother? They don't have a brother.'

Huang pales, rubbing harder at her wrist. 'I can assure you—'

'And I can assure *you*, Charlotte doesn't *have* a brother. Either you've been lied to, or someone's hacked your database to make it look like the truth when it's not. Easier than you might think.' Matiu advances on her, fighting to stay calm. 'Who was it? What was his name?'

'You have no authority in this matter. I'm going to have to respectfully ask you to leave the premises. I'm going to open the gate; please step away before I have to escalate this situation.' She clicks a button on her belt clip and the gate whirs to life.

Matiu narrows his eyes. 'What's wrong with your wrist?'

Huang tugs her sleeve down. 'I'll ask you one more time to leave, before I call for the police.'

But he's seen enough, the redness peeking through against her olive complexion. 'New tattoo? Or maybe you've had one removed?' Her eyes widen, just enough. Enough that he knows he's right. 'All good. I'm leaving.' He holds up his hands in surrender, and heads for the gate, returning to his car and dialling Scour.

'It's after hours, bro.'

'It's 3.15pm. Even teachers haven't finished work yet.'

'What now?'

'Couple things. You said there were multiple hits on the reader. You got a timeline?'

'Yeah, the reader keeps pinging devices as long as they're in range.'

'I need to find the one that arrived and left around about the same time as the first one you sent me.'

Afternoon sunshine streaming though the lab windows, Penny is preparing the Yung scene samples for analysis by her new benchtop Breadmaker™ DNA sequencer. It's the most expensive piece of equipment in the lab, and the second of its kind owned by Yee Scientific – well, the bank mostly – after the last one was destroyed in a field experiment. There will likely be a melting pot of DNA signatures in this lot, representing every client Yung has consulted since the last time his office was deep cleansed with decontaminase – which was probably never.

'Charlotte's DNA will certainly be among these,' Penny tells Cerberus. 'And perhaps the killer's, too. Let's pray they aren't one and the same.'

Sprawled flat out on the floor, cooling himself on the tiles, Cerberus barely flicks his tail.

The fridge hums dubiously.

Ignoring them both, Penny transfers the crime scene samples into cuvettes and pipettes in the reagents – SST proteinase incubation solution, lysis solvent (as recommended by the manufacturer), primer, and polymerase – taking comfort in the routine. When the samples are spinning in the centrifuge, she tidies up her workspace. She's just snapping off her gloves when the phone pings.

'Dr Yee, the GUID results on that photo have come back.'

'That was quick.'

Clark chuckles. 'I had the department throw some money at it.'

'I'll remember that when I send my invoice.'

'Turns out you were right; that photo might not be Charlotte Langley after all. The original image differs from the one on Yung's computer.'

'Thank goodness. That takes the heat off Charlotte, at least.'

'Not entirely,' Clark replies. 'Not if the image provoked her into a crime of passion. Seems she was struggling with her mental wellbeing.'

'Clark. She's seeing a psychiatrist. I think that's a given.'

'Unfortunately, according to Yung's notes, things have been going downhill. Anxiety, paranoia, and, get this, hallucinations of tentacled taniwha-demons.'

Penny's blood runs cold, Marama's ramblings ringing in her ears. A taniwha she'd said. Coming to swallow the children.

'Dr Yee, are you still there?'

'What happened to client confidentiality?' Penny stammers.

'Surely, I don't have to remind you that this is a murder investigation, and the killer is still at large?'

'No, no of course.' It's all Penny can do to keep her voice even. The detective inspector wants a quick-solve, and Charlotte is an easy collar for the murder.

In the background, the fridge hums again. Penny wishes it would change its tune.

Cerberus nudges Penny with his nose. She gives him a pat.

Clark goes on, 'But it's early days yet. I've got a couple of uniforms checking on Charlotte Langley's current whereabouts – CCTV have her car a block away from the doctor's clinic at 12.45pm – and forensics is running an IP history match on that photo. I'll keep you posted.'

The centrifuge has finished its cycle. Penny lifts out the cuvettes. Time to cook up a batch and let the Breadmaker™ reveal who was at the scene. She stops. Lifts one of the cuvettes. Frowns. The spun-down solution is as black as Marmite. It's a phenomena she's seen before, the sample in question taken from a mangled vehicle on Auckland's Harbour Bridge. She checks the labels on the cuvettes. Her hunch was correct; the black sample corresponds to the smear she discovered on the sliding door.

No jumping to conclusions. Rigour is what's required here. She runs through what she knows.

1. Yung was dead, his eyes brutally hacked out.
2. Clark mentioned tentacles.
3. Charlotte and baby Mia are missing.

Penny curses under her breath. She'd be willing to bet her lab and everything in it that Touching the Sun are involved. May as well put her money where her mouth is. Or the bank's money, anyway.

Putting on a ventilator mask, Penny secures her safety glasses and slips the sample in the Breadmaker™, then flips the switch.

Matiu pulls over and takes a deep breath, looking up at the gothic façade across the street. His fingers hover over the list of numbers, trying to decide who to call first, if anyone. This really makes no sense. Why would anyone manipulate a social worker into handing over a baby, and then drive straight to Auckland's most historic prison facility. The same prison whose comforts Matiu had the pleasure of enjoying for some of the darkest days of his former years.

But this *is* where fake-brother Langley drove after parting ways from Huang, and according to Scour the device which pinged the daycare's Cov-42 reader is still in the vicinity.

He hits a number. Erica answers straight away.

'Where are you?'

'Prison.'

'That was quick. Did I miss the trial?'

'Funny. Someone's posing as your brother, used it as a cover to get Huang to hand Mia over to him. But she's compromised anyway, she's got a Touching the Sun tattoo on her wrist.'

'You saw it?'

'Not exactly, but her eyes gave it away. Anyway, whoever took Mia has driven straight to Mt Eden. I'm parked outside now, but I don't know who I'm looking for or why they'd come here. Ever heard of anyone smuggling a baby into a prison?'

'No, but Matiu–'

'Yeah?'

'Axel Weis. He's in Mount Eden.'

A shudder runs through Matiu, despite the heat. Weis was arrested when the cops broke up Touching the Sun's final attempt at a mass suicide event on Maungawhau. A death cult leader with an unhealthy disregard for human life, he was also instrumental in the cult's plan to get Charlotte pregnant, and was there when Mia was born, attempting to offer the newborn up as a sacrifice to a demon.

Penny broke up that little party – hit him in the head with a fire extinguisher – but clearly he's never lost the urge to claim the baby that he clearly thinks belongs to him.

'The kidnapper came here to update Weis, probably using the compromised network switch that's around here somewhere.'

Erica continues. 'I ran down close contacts for Huang, and you're right, she is connected to Touching the Sun. Her partner is Roland Driscoll, who runs a boutique small press out of Orewa called *Helucidate Publications*. Guess who their biggest selling author is?'

'Alex Wise?'

'Bingo. Axel Weis's highly unimaginative *nom de plume*, and his library of new-age occult pseudoscience psychobabble. I'd bet my last paycheck that Huang and Driscoll are about to disappear off the map with Mia, while they work on breaking Weis out of prison.'

'And then it all starts again, with Mia in their clutches and whatever's left of the cult ready to harbour them in any way they can until High Priest Weis gets his hands on her. We have to find Driscoll. I'll call you back.'

'Matiu–'

But he's dropped the call, and Scour's phone is already ringing. 'Hot on the trail, bro?'

'Where's that car at now? Any chance it's heading towards Orewa?'

'Definitely heading north. I'll link you to its Geepee.'

'Dude, you rock. I need another favour. You know that citylink network switch near Mt Eden Prison, the one with the insecure transceiver that allows certain lowlifes a way of getting illicit calls into the inmates without the prison guards knowing about it?'

'Doesn't everyone?'

'Yeah, well, I need to tap that line.'

Twenty minutes later, the fire alarm blares. Green smoke belches from under the lid of the Breadmaker™, the stench so violent that even Penny's mask can't keep it out entirely. Meanwhile, poor Cerberus is going off his head, howling like a hellhound and hurling himself at the machine. His teeth dent the casing. Gobs of drool run down the surface. Whining, Cerberus skitters away.

Before the machine implodes, Penny yanks out the plug. She smacks her palm on the fire alarm, stopping it, then cranks up the fume hoods to purge the laboratory of the sulphurous fog. That done, she gathers the hound into her arms.

'I'm sorry, Cerb,' she whispers into his fur. 'You knew all along, didn't you?'

When he's no longer quivering, when *both of them* are calmer, she sets him aside and checks the results.

Fuck.

Touching the Sun might be a collective of psychopaths with a knack for disappearing into the woodwork, only re-emerging to wreak bloody havoc, but it tends to be the leaders who are the most dangerous. Driscoll and Huang are just puppets, being played like Charlotte was. Weis is the real threat, and apparently even being locked away hasn't curbed his ambitions to summon otherworldly demons in the hopes they'll grant him immortality in return. *Nutter.*

While he waits for Scour to set up his connection, Matiu watches Driscoll's car as it heads north, towards the Harbour Bridge. If he's quick, Matiu should be able to deal with Weis and overtake Driscoll before he gets away.

'Come on, Scour,' he mutters.

'Please stay on the line, your call is important to us,' Scour sing-songs as he works. 'Best I can tell, this Weis guy has a cellphone somewhere not far from his cell – ha, that's funny, a cellphone near his cell – and a wireless earpiece. Or he's got a neural implant tapped straight into the network. Probably paid off a guard or something.'

Or there are guards in there who are in the cult. Matiu considers the implications of that possibility settling in his gut like a sack of dead kittens. *Keeping him comfortable, letting him run his operation from the inside. Planning his escape.* Matiu's phone suddenly chirps with a soft dial tone, ringing into a void.

'Something the matter?' Weis sounds calm, relaxed. Matiu imagines him lying back on his prison bed, soft pillows under his head, staring at the ceiling, watching his plots circle round in the world beyond those stone walls. *He thinks I'm Driscoll.*

'Yeah, bit of an issue.'

'What's wrong with your voice?'

'Bubble tea. The one with the ginseng, always makes my throat weird, but damn it tastes good. Anyway, there's a situation.'

A creak of bedsprings. 'What sort of situation?'

'The baby's mother, she had some sort of episode and attacked her counsellor. Cops are crawling all over this.'

'How is that not what we planned?'

Matiu's throat tightens, the pieces sliding together. Weis is behind not only the kidnapping but the murder as well. Weis orchestrated everything from behind bars, positioning Huang to remove Mia while everyone was busy looking for Charlotte as a killer, giving Driscoll the window he needs to vanish. No wonder Child Services were on the scene so fast. Huang didn't just take an opportunity when it presented itself, the wheels of public service don't work that fast. They were waiting for the signal to act, using Driscoll to remove Mia so Huang could get back to work and not raise any suspicions.

'Who the hell is this?' Weis snarls.

'I'm the guy who put you in there,' Matiu growls back, 'and I'm going to make sure they bury you there.'

'Matiu Yee.' Weis seems to relax. 'What a genuine delight. And so considerate of you to call a lonely old man in prison.'

'Why Mia?' he blurts out. 'What's your obsession with that baby, that makes her worth killing for?'

'The same thing you're valuable for, Matiu Yee, only without all the attitude. Have you not worked that part out yet? You keep thinking about poor Charlotte and her baby, but what about her father? Given what we know about you, I'm surprised you haven't already asked the question long before now, of who Mia's father is and why that makes her so precious.' There's a long, silent ring of laughter behind Weis's words.

Matiu is sinking, drowning in an unseen tide. Weis is trying to fuck with him, to get inside his head. Matiu wants to deny the dawning realisation, the simple truth that makes so much of what has gone before make sense, but the dread that it brings is overwhelming. He swipes the call away, letting the silence ring in his head for a long moment afterwards.

If what Weis says is true, then his own connection to Mia is a hell of a lot closer than he'd ever imagined. And Mia is a whole lot closer to hell.

Penny phones Matiu. *Please, please let him have found them.* 'Did you find them yet?'

'Think I've got Mia in my sights. Charlotte, no idea.'

'Listen Matiu, you need to hurry. I found XNA at the crime scene.'

'What even is that? Rocket fuel?'

She groans. 'Not rocket fuel. I've told you this.'

'Humour me.'

Penny sighs. 'DNA are—'

'You said XNA.'

'I'm getting there. DNA are double helical strands of natural nucleotide sugars, which store and retrieve genetic material, whereas—'

Matiu cuts her off. 'The Spark Notes, Pen. Please.'

'XNA is synthetic DNA. It doesn't occur naturally. It's *unnatural*.'

'Your fancy-schmancy machine blew up,' Matiu says.

Penny beams inwardly. Seems he *had* been listening. 'Not quite,' she says. 'I turned the Breadmaker off before the smoke got too toxic, but only after it spat out the results. Poor Cerberus wasn't too happy though.'

'So Kingi's your killer,' Matiu says.

There was only one Kingi. Simon Kingi: gang leader with a taste for Yee blood. Yung's murder was right in his wheelhouse.

'Very likely,' Penny says. 'Or someone like him.'

'It's him.'

Penny doesn't argue. Matiu has his hunches. She hates them because there's nothing scientific or rigorous or even *rational* about Matiu's creepy-arsed premonitions. Trouble is, he's often right.

'Matiu, you know I can't send these results to the police. They don't have a database of otherworldly villains. If Kingi or his kind did this, we're going to have to find some other way to link them to Yung's death.'

'It's Kingi,' he persists. 'Weis just told me as much.'

'You spoke to Weis? How?'

Matiu shrugs, dropping a gear and accelerating onto the motorway. He's got a lot of ground to make up. 'Prison black market stuff, it's a booming business if you have the contacts to bypass the cellphone jammers. Anyway, he knows more than he should, about me. Kingi's gang were always doing their own thing when Makere was in charge, but with Makere gone, whatever loose arrangement they might've had with Touching the Sun in the past, they've made into some sort of alliance now, and are working together towards the same goal.'

'I don't like how much sense you're making right now.'

'Nor do I. But it fits. They all want Mia because she and I have the same father. You know what that means.'

Penny doesn't reply. Some things are better left unsaid.

'Anyway, we know where Driscoll's going, and he won't be there long. If he slips through our fingers, he's gone and so's Mia. Send Clark the address and let's see who gets to Driscoll first.'

A wave of hot air hits Penny as Clark opens the car door for her. 'Thank you for coming, Dr Yee. A familiar face might help.'

'Not at all.' Her satchel over her shoulder, she follows Clark down the narrow driveway of the semi-detached townhouse. A mirror image of the one next door, the only difference is the gnarly pine shading the tiny yard on Charlotte's side of the fence.

'CCTV and phone records indicate Charlotte arrived home at 1.40pm.'

Clark nods at the uniformed officer stationed at the front door, who knocks and calls for Charlotte. 'We've been trying to raise her, but she won't pick up her phone or answer the door. Given that her doctor isn't currently available to certify her as at risk, I had to get a warrant – and that took time.'

Penny snaps her head up, 'She's been here since 1.40pm?'

'Something wrong?'

She frowns. 'Seems odd, that's all. We're a 20-minute drive from Yung's clinic. Which means her session was 20 minutes, at most.'

'Twenty minutes is plenty enough time for her to have killed the doctor.'

'But not enough time for a counselling session. Charlotte clearly expected it to go longer, or she wouldn't have arranged for Mia to be picked up from daycare.'

'It's her first murder,' Clark muses. 'Maybe she expected it to take longer.'

'But if Charlotte were the killer, why even come home at all? As the doctor's last appointment, she'd have to have known you'd come looking for her, if only to question her.'

The uniformed officer turns. 'No response, sir. We'll have to break it down.'

Clark shakes his head. 'Hang on.' He scans the porch decorations – a potted plant, a hedgehog boot scraper, and a welcome mat – then lifts each one. Nothing. The only other ornament is a windchime made of bell-shaped insulators hanging from a nail to the left of the door. Clark puts his hand inside the lowest 'bell' and pulls out a key. 'That won't be necessary.' He unlocks the door.

Charlotte is prone in the hallway, beside an empty blister pack of tablets.

Penny dashes past Clark, crouching beside her friend.

Her eyes glazed, Charlotte tries to lift her head and fails. 'Penny, help. Please,' she mumbles into the carpet. 'Monsters were here. They want Mia.'

'Calling an ambulance now,' Clark says.

The Harbour Bridge recedes in the rear-view mirror like he's emerging from the throat of some primordial beast. Weaving between buses and freight trucks, Matiu keeps his foot hard to floor, the Commodore growling. Driscoll's not breaking any land-speed records, trying not to draw undue attention, but Matiu doesn't have that luxury. If he picks up a tail with flashing lights, they can just join the party.

Matiu hauls on the wheel, one eye on the gaps in the traffic, one eye on the GPS screen and its blue ping, drawing inexorably closer as he chews up the distance between him and Driscoll. The North Shore sprawls out around him, shadowed now in the settling dusk. He accelerates and skips through the flow, braking and cutting in, like some sort of racing sim, but with much higher stakes. Not only a child's life, but the boundary between this world and a world of monsters lurking just the other side, waiting and hungering to be given a doorway into our sanity.

And there they are, a sudden flash of red and blue. Matiu has company. He spots a gap and floors it. Driscoll is just up ahead. The cops are in pursuit. Mia is in the car, so he has to be careful about this.

A plain white station wagon with a baby seat in the back is revealed as Matiu swings between two trucks, lining up with the GPS ping on his screen. It's now or never. He guns the throttle, cuts out into the traffic, swerving to avoid a taxi-van changing lanes beside him, and catches a glimpse of the driver's face. Driscoll meets his eye, his face falling in sudden panic. The station wagon surges forward, carving away to the left.

Matiu presses down the gas and the Commodore lurches into the gap, angling out and around. He draws alongside the station wagon and begins easing to the left, forcing Driscoll to pull over, matching every speed change until Driscoll's vehicle is dangerously close to the barriers. Horns blare around them as all other traffic is forced to slow down, the whole scene lit up by swirling red and blue lights.

Both cars grind to a stop, Driscoll trapped between the barrier and Matiu's car.

Driscoll scrambles to get out of his seat, as if he can somehow get Mia out the back of the car and escape on foot before Matiu or the cops bring him down. Matiu steps out of the car, ready for how this is going to play out, and preparing what he's going to tell the cops who are walking along the road towards him.

Cerberus bounds up the porch ahead of Penny, launching himself at Matiu's birth mother in a big doggy hug.

'Good boy!' Marama gives a rare smile.

The caregiver sets aside her mammoth jigsaw puzzle and gets to her feet. 'Tea?'

'Thank you. Matiu will be here in just a minute. He's parking the car.'

The woman nods and slips inside.

Penny leans in, touching noses with her aunt, sharing their breath in a hongi, before pulling up a seat next to the rocker.

'The taniwha,' Marama begins.

Penny rocks the chair gently with her foot. 'I don't know how you and Matiu know these things, But you were right,' she whispers. There'll be a scientific reason for their heightened perception; it just hasn't been published yet.

Marama only nods.

'It's OK, though. The baby is safe. See?'

She nods towards the bottom of the path, where Matiu is juggling a wiggling Mia, a car seat, and a baby bag, all while simultaneously trying to unhook the gate.

'You know, Whaea Marama, I can't believe I'm saying this, but I think Matiu's going to make a great whangai daddy. At least, he and Erica can give little Mia some stability and a heap of love while Charlotte is getting some help.'

Best all round, given that Kingi is still on the loose. Penny had identified the gang leader's fingerprints on the blister pack. Fortunately, the police had *those* on their database, allowing Clark to connect him to the murder. A quick solve. Tanner will be thrilled.

The gate swings back, thwacking Matiu on the legs. 'Fuck,' he curses.

'Bad father,' Marama says.

Penny chuckles. 'I agree. He definitely needs to clean up that swearing.'

But Marama grasps Penny's hand, digging her fingernails into Penny's wrist. 'No Penny. Bad *father*,' Marama insists. 'Bad father. The tide never stops.' Her face darkens, her eyes flashing. 'Never.'

'Yo, Marama! We're here!' Matiu calls.

Marama's frown relaxes, and she releases Penny's hand.

Cerberus barks, bouncing off the porch as Matiu and Mia, two children of the underworld, come up the path.

THE FALLS

LISA FULLER

Midday, rural Queensland. Dust, heat, empty. The town will wake up around sunset, when people can tolerate leaving their fans and refrigerated water. A flash SUV with its sparkling white exterior covered in a light sheen of travel dust hums along the Bruce Highway. It crests the hills, flickering through the trees before rolling down into the small town nestled amongst them. Those sorts of cars usually don't stop here. The SUV crosses over the bridge, hanging a right down the main drag with its four shops, scattered houses, and park, following the Bruce.

The old Queenslander is the only house on the main street. It bakes in the sun, it's paint peeling so badly only grayed and cracked wood can be seen. No clue what the colour of the paint once was. Despite the heat, the doors and windows are shut tight. The giant wraparound porch takes up three sides, with white lattice doors blocking off one section. The old Commodore in the drive says someone's likely home. In a town this size it's easy to walk anywhere, but in this kind of heat, it's not worth moving too far.

The car rolls to a stop at the front fence. A white man climbs out, his collared shirt and pants that aren't jeans crushed from a long trip. He moves briskly, lifting a clipboard out, wiping his brow and upper lip as he strides through the screeching metal gate.

The stairs tremble at his stomps, threatening collapse at any moment. He grips the rail but carries right on stamping like an elephant. His hand lifts to the door.

Bang. Bang. Bang.

A bullyman's knock.

No accompanying shout from inside.

Curtains stir in the windows to a non-existent breeze.

Bang. Bang. Bang.

'Who is it?' a woman's irritated voice calls through the door.

'My name is Matt Downs, I'm here to see Ms–', he pauses and checks his paperwork, 'Taryn Wells.'

'Bout what?'

'I just want to hear her side.' A long pause. 'This would be a lot easier face-to-face,' he cajoles.

The door cracks and a small brown woman with large dark eyes stares up at him.

'Why da you care what appened?'

'I'm a private investigator, the Ivers hired–'

The door slams shut.

Bang. Bang. Bang.

'Ms Wells, I'm not taking their side. I'm not on anyone's side. I only want the truth.'

'Piss. Off.'

Matt sighs, rubbing the back of his neck.

'Psst.'

He swings around to the latticed doors to the side. A small round figure stands behind them, her silhouette visible between diamond shapes. One hand is on her hip and a cigarette is cocked in the other. She waves the hand, beckoning him closer. He comes to stand opposite her, getting a look at her wrinkled dark skin, and clouded brown eyes rimmed in blue.

'You want to know the truth?' she whispers.

He bends slightly forward. 'Yes, ma'am I do.'

'My Taryn didn't do nuthin,' she says, in a loud voice. 'What appened to that boy was karma, pure and simple. You take that back to the

Ivers. Everything that appened was his own doing, you can tell em Layla said so.'

She flicks the cigarette, sending sparkling ash falling through the spaces onto his pristine shirt. Turning away, she leaves him standing there, his mouth open in shock. Her voice hadn't held venom, she'd said it like someone'd say the sky is blue.

Matt pulls away, staring after the old lady as she shuffles into the house. She never looks back. He walks down the stairs and climbs into the car. Chucks a uey on the main street, and drives to the only pub in town. The parking at the back has the units for accommodation. He goes inside to check in.

Back inside that old Queenslander, the temperature has become unbearable. Layla stretches, pulling the sash window up as far as it'll go. The swollen wood sticks in places.

'Gran, what're ya doin?' Taryn hisses behind her.

'It's too hot in ere.'

'But–'

'But what? Stop actin like ya got a guilty conscience girl.'

Layla spun on her granddaughter, glaring her down. The younger woman's face crumples.

'I didn't do nuthin.'

Layla reaches out, lifting Taryn's chin. 'I know, granddaughter. But ya gotta start believin it too, or no one else will.'

Tears flow from her brown eyes, as Taryn grips Layla's hand in hers. 'If he hadn't followed me...'

Layla snorts. 'Stop carryin shit that ain't yours. He was a grown-arse man in full control. How's what he did your fault?'

Taryn shakes her head and drops her gaze, her shoulders slumping under a heavy burden. It's clear the women can't agree.

'Somethin arrived in the mail for ya today.' Shuffling over to the side table where an old house phone still sat connected, Layla lifts an envelope, handing it to her granddaughter. The university marking on the outside is clear.

Taryn stares at it, shaking. Her application had been sent in months ago. When she felt so much hope. When she'd finally left for good. She'd almost forgotten. It seemed wrong, to carry on, to live, when Andy never would. Her fault.

'Well, open it bub,' Layla insists.

Taryn looks up, before folding the letter and shoving it deep into her back jeans pocket. 'I'm covered in dirt and cleanin stuff, I'll open it later.' She spins on her heel, heading back to the bathroom.

Layla shakes her head, turning to continue opening the house. It's not like it'll help much, but she does it anyway.

The sun scorches to its highest and most horrifying point. Burning everything foolish enough to be out. Waves of heat rise off the bitumen. The road edge looks wet where the tar bubbles.

The pub's doors open and the new figure in town walks into the bar on the whitefulla's side, this time in shorts and a t-shirt. The carpeted area with the respectable old dining chairs and tables is mostly empty. But the bar on the blackfullas side has a few patrons. Most are sat at the pokies along the walls on both sides, dinging and pressing their souls away under the few corner fans blasting what meagre cooling air is to be had.

Matt takes a seat, greets the barman.

'What can I get ya?'

'A heavy please.'

Beer procured and magic card waved at the machine, the men eye each other.

'Just checked in, ay? Where'd ya blow in from?'

'Brisbane,' he extends a hand. 'Name's Matt.'

They shake while sizing each other up. One with hands calloused and rough, the other's soft but firm.

'Gary. You the one the Ivers hired?'

Matt's eyebrows shoot up. 'No secrets here then?'

Gary throws his head back and laughs, flashing a mouth of teeth. 'Nothing stays quiet here.'

'That right? What're people saying about what happened?'

Gary looks wary. 'That depends who ya talk to. Cops say it was an accident. There's some here thinks it wasn't.'

'Oh?'

Gary looks over his shoulder into the blackfullas side. A few men sit at the bar, drinking beers. Most of them dusty and sweaty, taking a break from the heat of the day before they'd have to head back out into it. The odd glance is thrown their way. Turning back, Gary shrugs. 'The blackfullas say he went to a place he shouldn't. Got punished for it or some shit.'

Matt leans in, all buddy-buddy. 'Come on mate, you really believe that?'

Gary snorts. 'Nah. But I don't see how a little thing like Taryn could've done it either. Accident makes more sense.'

'So, people are saying she's responsible?'

'People talk a lot of crap, mostly outta boredom. And they've had time to cook up some good bullshit. Doesn't change the fact that Andy was over six foot and built. No one could've held him anywhere he didn't want to be unless he was drunk or drugged off his tits. Far as I saw, he was only two beers in that day.'

'You served him?'

Gary nods, his mouth twisting. 'Like you don't already know.'

Matt smiles. 'I've read the statements, but it always helps hearing it from the witnesses. You said he was eating lunch when you went to the back for more stock.'

'When I got back he was gone, his food and drink weren't even finished. No idea why he just took off like that.'

Matt leans forward on his elbows. 'So no one else spoke to him?'

'Look, I've had the Ivers in here demanding all kinds of things. If that's what your here for I'll tell ya right now you're wastin ya time. Recantin my testimony won't change what the cops found in his blood.'

Matt frowns. 'I knew you'd served him. But I didn't know they asked you to do that. Anything else the Ivers have been doing I should know about?'

Gary pulls back. 'That's none of my business,' he states, louder than necessary. 'I told the cops what I saw, and that's all I know.'

Matt's eyebrows shoot up.

'No worries. Is there anyone you reckon I should talk to?'

'Can't help ya, sorry mate,' Gary insists, his eyes flicking behind him to the bar and the blackfullas perched there. Then he walks away to serve one of them.

Clearly the man didn't want to be the one to speak out of turn but thinks someone else might.

Taking the hint, Matt picks up his beer and walks down to a side door into the other half of the pub. He notes the shift from green carpet and comfortable seating to concrete flooring and rusted metal bar stools.

The door behind him bangs open. Matt doesn't turn to look, but everyone else does. A hand claps his shoulder, and he swivels around to face an older couple. They mirror each other from their jeans and button-down short sleeve shirts to their gray-streaked hair and sun-tanned faces.

'Matt Downs? Charles Ivers and this is my wife, Carrie.'

Matt takes the hand offered, murmuring a greeting while noting the deep purple beneath both sets of eyes and the baggy skin of distressed faces.

'Mr and Mrs Ivers, I'm sorry for your loss.' Carrie winces and Charles' features harden even as he nods. 'Can I get you a drink?'

'Carrie'll get it while you and me grab a table outside,' Charles says and stomps off.

Matt follows him out. There's more seating here, as well as a pool table. It's a nice area, full of pot plants and large fans rotating above, giving a hint of relief.

Charles plonks on the table furthest from the doors and gestures for Matt to take a seat, although the man looks like he's trying not to jump up again and start pacing.

'I hear you've been to her house. She say anything to you?'

'Not really. She wasn't that friendly.'

'That'd be right,' he sneers. 'She's barely been out of that house since. She doesn't even go to work.'

Matt takes a sip, smacking his lips at the chill bubbles. 'You seem to know a lot about her movements.'

Charles turns his head away, gazing out the side door to the street beyond. 'Small town. Tell me what you found.'

Carrie arrives and sets a beer down in front of her husband and sits beside him. She keeps her chin tucked, one hand on her coke, the other in her lap.

Matt rubs at the sweat on his glass. 'We found something on his sim card. He got a message right before he left the bar.'

The Ivers jerk like he'd yanked them forwards. 'It was sent through WhatsApp, so we can't trace it. It just said: *She's at the Falls*.'

They both slump back like he's cut their strings.

'Doesn't that prove someone set him up?' Charles asks, the wheels spinning now. 'Tricked him into following her out there?'

Matt shrugs. 'Or one of his mates told him. The report says they were broken up at the time.'

'What's next?' Charles demands.

'I'll chase up the police, go speak to any witnesses who saw them that day. Like I said on the phone, it's already been ruled an accident, so you need to prepare yourself that I might end up agreeing with that.'

Charles smacks his palm on the tabletop, making Carrie flinch.

'Accident my arse! My boy knew how to swim. That bitch knows somethin and I expect you to get it out of her. Otherwise, what am I payin you for? They were always breaking up and getting back together. I told the boy, some women are for fun, others for keepin. He could never tell the difference between thinking with his proper head.'

Matt shifts uncomfortably. 'So, he'd have expected them to get back together?'

'Probably.'

'And she would have too?'

'Who knows. Who cares?'

'I'm just trying to understand why she'd want to hide anything.'

'Are you siding with her?' Charles' face goes bright red as he hisses across the table.

'I'm just asking the question. If they were possibly going to get back together, why would she be upset enough with him to hide what happened that day?'

Carrie looks back down at her lap, her arm muscles bunching in a way that tells Matt she's wringing her hands.

A wave of menace, however, washes from Charles. 'Who's been telling you stories?'

Matt sits back, watching them closely. 'As I said, it's just a question. Is there a story to hear Mrs Ivers?'

'Don't talk to her,' Charles snaps, making his wife flinch. 'Talk to me.'

Matt's eyes meet his calmly. 'Is there, Mr Ivers?'

The silence stretches. Matt's relaxed sprawl gives nothing away.

Charles takes a deep breath, sucking all that rage back into a fake calm. He stands, carefully, picking up his hat and dusting it off. His wife follows his lead.

Charles looks down at Matt. 'Stories spread like wildfire here, most of it's bullshit. Just do your job, find out what happened to my son.' He turns and strides out the door, his wife scurrying to catch up.

Matt releases a long breath. He lifts his beer and knocks back the whole thing, before standing to make his way back to the bar. This time he goes straight for the opposite side where the blackfullas are sitting, aware of the eyes that flick his way.

The coolness on this side rises from the concrete. A firing squad of pokies lines one wall, a long table sits in the middle of the space with a few people around it. He stands for a moment, eyeing the patrons. When one of the men at the bar shifts on his stool Matt moves in.

'Can I buy you a beer mate?'

'Me?' the man looks without making eye contact. He's a smaller, thin man but with wiry strength in his forearms disappearing under a sweat and dust-marked collared shirt. 'Um, yeah, a heavy would be good.'

Matt takes the stool next to him, and waves Gary down. The barman's already heard the order and is pouring. Matt introduces himself before paying, turning back as Gary gives him his drink. Clancy is a local council worker, in for lunch. They spend a few minutes shooting the shit, touching on nothing much, before Matt gets to the point they've both been dancing around.

'Do you know why I'm here?'

The man shrugs.

'The Ivers are convinced Taryn did something. What I can't figure out is why they so sure she'd want to hurt him.'

'Yeah well, the Ivers won't tell ya everythin bout their golden boy,' he mutters back.

'Something I should know?'

Clancy glances around the place, before lifting the glass up, obscuring his lips as he speaks between sips. 'He was floggin er.'

Matt tenses, but he keeps his voice just as a low as he sips his own beer. 'There was nothing about that in the police report. No record.'

The man's lips twist into a grim smile. 'Sound bounces off the hills here, you could hear her screams all over town.'

Matt's knuckles go white. 'No one said anything?'

'People said plenty. Doesn't mean they did anything about it. Old Layla had some choice words for im, but what could she do when Taryn kept goin back? Best to stay out of others' business. Besides if the cops won't lift a finger, what could anyone else do?'

Matt takes a swig of his beer. 'So she did have a reason to want him dead then.'

'Not sure bout that. That was the first time she moved out.'

'Meaning he was the one upset?'

Clancy shrugs.

'I just can't see a reason a young, fit man would drown like that. Not without help.'

Clancy shifts, and eyes him sceptically. 'And what, you think I know somethin?'

Matt shrugs. 'No harm in asking.'

'You wouldn't believe me if I did tell ya. Like the cops didn't believe Taryn when she told em.'

Matt taps his beer. 'I heard a rumour, something about going where he shouldn't. So what, he went onto a sacred site?'

Clancy huffs. 'Nuthin like that. He wouldn't ave gone so peaceful that way.'

Silence stretches. Matt's hope that it will make the other man uncomfortable enough to blurt something out proves fruitless.

'I'm just tryin to find out the truth here mate.'

'The truth?' Clancy laughs into his beer. 'They reckon, back in the 20s, the last big massacre happened out on that property. Surprise attack, no hope. One teenage girl made a run for it. Those men caught up to her at the Falls. That place is hers now, and she only allows women there.'

Matt shakes his head. 'That's it? That's the big secret?'

Clancy eyes him with distaste. 'I tell ya about a tragedy, of a woman, of a group, who still have family in this town, and that's how you take it?'

'I mean no disrespect, but what has that got to do with Andy drowning.'

Clancy sighs, and it's filled with disgust. 'Ask one of the whitefullas why they won't go out there, since none of us blackfullas can be trusted.' He slides from his chair shoving his hat back on his head. 'Gotta get back to work. Thanks for the beer.'

After he leaves, Matt leans on the bar and eyeballs a chuckling Gary. 'Any chance you know the way to the place where they found him?'

'Only the real locals know, I'm just a blow in,' Gary shook his head. 'Not sure I'd take you even if I did.'

'I thought you didn't believe in that stuff.'

Gary laughs. 'I don't. Doesn't mean I'm gonna test the theory.'

'Anyone in here who might?'

'None that will take you, but–' Gary lifts an eyebrow and nods toward the door.

Matt turns on his seat and his eyes meet those of uniformed policeman. The sun-wrinkled man with his graying hair checks out the room before making a beeline straight for Matt.

The sun's journey downwards began the slow easing of the heat. Enough that Taryn decides to venture outside. She stretches out her back under the big Queenslander. The old twin-tub washing machine Gran uses is murder on it and the joints. But that's why she does the washing, so Gran doesn't have to. Years of fruit-picking and cotton chipping has fucked the old girl's knees and back so bad, she moves like she's decades older than her 70 years. Taryn's not all selfless though, she's desperate to keep herself busy. So she can't think about that day, or the weight in her pocket.

Shying from both, Taryn turns back to the twin tub and starts hauling the water-logged clothes over into the spin tub. Reaching the bottom is always a bugger for someone her height. With a little hop she dangles over the rim, trying to grab the last socks and undies. There's a weird scraping sound above. She pauses.

'Gran, that you?' she calls. 'Grab the broom please?'

No answer, so she goes back to straining. Hands at last closing around the little buggers. Triumphant she tosses them in the spin cycle, as another sound echoes behind her.

A thud. An explosion in her head as her jaw clacks against her top teeth.

Darkness.

Taryn tastes blood, her head a throbbing mess that refuses to operate. Parts of her feel rubbed raw.

Forcing her eyes to squint open, the sight leaves her gasping.

The Falls sprawl before her in all its freshwater glory. Reduced to a dark stream at this time of the year, the water is a muddied brown. The sandy banks are breached on one side by huge boulders, rubbed smooth from uncounted millennia of standing vigil. It's a lovely place to sit and warm yourself, after the sun has dipped behind the trees. A beautiful place, filled with happy memories and screams.

'Finally awake,' Charles Ivers spits down at her.

Taryn rears away from his hate, but the movement makes her head explode in painful protest. She's lying in the sand, coated in dirt and blood. There's no easy path to this place, they must've dragged her through the brush.

Carrie stands behind her husband, but it's the rifle in *his* hands has all Taryn's attention. Terror freezes her in place. Tears start to leak from her shaking body.

Charles' bloated red face comes closer, as he kneels. His weapon isn't pointed at her, yet. 'Everyone has bought your bullshit. But not me. You'll tell me what happened here girl, and fast. Or–' his fingers drum the stock of the gun.

A sob escapes Taryn, but she forces her voice to work, 'I did not hurt im.'

'But someone did?'

Silence fills the space between them.

He grabs her chin with a bruising hand. 'Who did it?' he bellows in her face.

'You won't believe me,' she whispers back.

'Tell me now,' he shoves her face away, making her head hit the sand, sending another explosion of pain. She can't stop the grunt that escapes.

He's standing, both hands lifting the rifle to his shoulder, aiming. The muzzle touches her forehead and she whimpers, 'Please don't.'

Carrie's hand appears on her husband's shoulder, her voice hesitant. 'You said we'd just scare her.'

Shrugging her hand away, his finger strokes the trigger guard.

'It was her,' Taryn points to the water. 'He came after me in the water, and she took im.'

'Don't give me that bullshit!' His roar bounces off the cliff walls, and around the gully.

Taryn sobs and Carrie steps forward again, resting her hand on his forearm.

'Charles, please. Don't.'

He turns on his wife, dropping the barrel to raise his fist. In the moment his attention is elsewhere, Taryn struggles to her feet and runs, forcing her wounded body to respond.

The water. She has to reach the water.

Her feet hit the swallows, she's up to mid-calf in a second and the deeper she goes the murkier and more opaque the water gets.

Carrie's cry of pain behind her is the only sound, but she doesn't look back. Diving deep, she hears the plunk and swoosh of cushioned noise. Is he firing? No time. No time.

She goes as deep as she can, kicking hard as the water grows ice cold. Even in the middle of a summer scorcher this place is frosty; it's one of the reasons she always loved it here.

Until last time.

Andy, screaming her name. Over and over.

A disturbance in the water tells her it's been hit by a large force; that this time Charles is coming after her. She can't escape the fear, her body is weakened, her head thumping, her legs flailing.

A hand snatches her hair, yanks her backwards, pulling her to the surface. As he drags her to the shallows Taryn releases her own yell, finally doing the thing she's never done before.

She fights back. Her nails rake his face.

He bellows and raises his fist.

'Charles! STOP!'

It's a man's voice and it stops them both.

Taryn's chest is heaving as she tries to reclaim her breath, her scalp is on fire. But still, her eyes swivel, looking for the voice.

Two men stand on the shore. One with his hands up, in a calming gesture, the other with a pistol raised. Neither gives her comfort, they're more likely to back Charles.

The Sergeant is in his uniform, so maybe he'd respect that. But protection can never be assured from cops. He proves it when he slowly lowers his weapon.

'Come on Charles, we don't need to do this. Just let Taryn go.'

The other man is the private investigator who came to Gran's house this morning. He's standing stock still, but the small figure behind him makes Taryn want to cry again. Gran stays quiet, but the rage on her face is clear.

'She knows something Bryce,' Charles growls. 'She's just about to tell me.'

'Maybe so, mate, but this won't help anyone. It'll only hurt you. It doesn't have to though, we can talk about it.'

The hesitation on his purpled face gives Taryn a second of hope; just a moment when he might choose not to hurt her more. But then he looks at her again, and his hate fans into a blaze again.

Taryn knows that look, had seen it on the younger version, so many times.

Charles lifts his fist again. She shuts her eyes tight, waiting, trying to feel relieved that at least he doesn't have the gun anymore.

Afer all, what was one more beating? She'd survived the others.

A soft stirring of the still water at her waist makes her glance down in fear. The sensation is horribly familiar.

Charles however looks confused.

'What is–'

Whoomp!

Taryn is airborne. Her back smacks the water and she goes straight under. She struggles to the surface, coughing and spluttering.

There's no sign of Charles. All she can see is thrashing, stirring currents. A deep whirling space. White water foaming up.

Strong arms grab Taryn and pull her out of the water. She and the PI stagger up the shore together. Taryn drops into the sand and looks up at her grandmother, but all eyes are on the water.

And everyone can hear the screams.

The PI moves like he's going to dive in after Charles, but Gran reaches out, grabs his elbow, she shakes her head. Their strange little tableau stands and watches.

Just like before.

It took seconds but felt longer.

Another Ivers man is floating in the waterhole.

No one moves.

A dark shape swirls around the body. A thing made of rage and pain; but still a protector. A girl who hadn't been protected herself.

Taryn feels the tears leaking from her eyes; knowing she should be grateful she's still alive. But someone else was dead. How can she be okay with that?

And that dark figure in the water? She was trapped, stuck in the moments of the worst thing to ever happen to her. Only able to act to protect and defend. She was tied to Country, but unable to be with the Ancestors. Could she even remember her happy times?

The Falls flare for a moment, and a face emerges from the droplets. A teenager. A beautiful and serene face. A victim who had become a murderer. Forever stuck.

Taryn finally understands what Gran had been trying to say.

She has a choice. One that young face, decades old now, never had.

But Taryn could let the darkness of her past swallow her future, or forge her own path, shaped by what she wanted.

OBSERVATIONS ON A TRAGEDY
ACT TWO: COMPLICATIONS

NARELLE M. HARRIS

Tee signed her witness statement at the police station, in the light of the following day. Relative to the midnight discovery of a celebrity corpse in a dimly lit alley, the cop shop was prosaic. Or rather, it was a different kind of theatrical. The rhythm of a percussive orchestra, not the wailing note of an oboe (an instrument made for sorrow).

Tee wondered if it was unhealthy, the way she kept framing Brady Templar's death through the prism of her vocation. Theatre criticism was perhaps not the best way to process violent death, unless it was in fact the best. Who knew Shakespeare's high body counts could prepare you for life?

The witness statement itself was no work of art, her words transcribed by the police staff who did the paperwork. Tee burned to correct the misplaced and missing commas, the apostrophe that had no right, the blunt and bludgeoning vocabulary of plain English.

I came. I saw. I called the cops to this, thou bleeding piece of earth.

But sudden death was not the realm of blank verse in the real world.

Tee remembered the contents of the statement the way she remembered old productions she'd reviewed, in highlights and at a remove. When had being an observer of the stage turned her into an observer of her own life?

On the other hand, maybe her observational soul had led her to reviewing. Egg-chicken-egg-chicken in a circle forever.

Two things absent from the statement were the two names that might have wished Brady Templar harm.

Max Vickers, always-the-bridesmaid actor to Brady's bridal waltz through the plum young-white-male-lead roles of the last two years. Three backstage sources claimed Vickers had a heart full of vitriol and a hand-made doll with Brady's cut-out face and a felt belly full of needles.

Gracie Gilbert, whose rising star had been consciously uncoupled from Brady's wagon a week ago. Reading between the tabloid lines, the uncoupling had been both swift and bitter. A betrayal had precipitated the split. Gracie's or Brady's? Every day brought new-minted and wholly unsubstantiated rumour that Tee discounted as sounding too much like the plot of an Italian opera.

Did Tee not tell the police about Max and Gracie? Did she say, and was dismissed?

Tee didn't remember leaving the police station to stand on the street in the summer Melbourne sunshine, but there she was. She wheeled about to return to the desk, right the omission, but too many people were inside now. It was too dark and smelled sourly of anxiety, despair, violence. Tee suspected she'd been ignored, anyway. The police didn't like a critic telling them how to do their job.

Well, they weren't alone in that.

Tee took a breath and strode deliberately away from the station, breathing more easily with every step. Her skin stopped prickling, her heart stopped pounding, she stopped seeing, in strobing flashes, the events of last night.

But it niggled. Max or Gracie? Gracie or Max?

Her skills were hardly meant to help her tell the difference between a killer and the merely obnoxious. She used them mainly to measure the various qualities of fictions, distilled them into informed opinions.

A truly great actor got to the heart of fictions and turned them into truths, at least for the duration. Could the truly great create an offstage performance that would last longer than a few hours and without a supporting cast?

Had Brady Templar been a truly great actor? His audiences loved him. The directors, too, and the critics. He seemed a perfect blend of truth and fiction. Charming, kind, generous.

Tee had wondered, sometimes, whether she'd seen a hint of manipulation under the charm. The world seemed to bend to his whims; the luck seemed always to go his way. He had never been seen at a disadvantage. Even the paparazzi shots of him shopping on the weekend made him look delightfully unkempt, unaffected rather than dowdy. Artfully artless.

Tee's feet took her up the hill, towards the clusters of theatres at the east of the city grid. The buildings and streets she knew so well. She felt more real, there, in the places where observing did not make her alone. Sharing her thoughts on art made her part of instead of apart, made her experiences and that of the performers and the audiences all meet in a Venn diagram of entertainment.

Of course, no-one could ever be just one thing or another. Just observer or just participant. Life and art were not so tidy.

Perhaps it was time to step away from the shield of merely looking. Time to step onto the stage, as it were. Time to act.

Because Tee remembered something else she hadn't told the police.

Brady Templar had fallen from a roof where theatre folk went to smoke in secret. His playful pirate shirt, laced at the neck, flowing hem (red and wet last night in the alley) had been marred with a cigarette burn at the puffy white cuff.

But Brady Templar didn't smoke.

Tee's feet took her towards the *Monarch Theatre*.

SAVE ME

NIKKI CRUTCHLEY

I drag myself out of the nightmare. There is laughing, whispering, pointing – rumours that have grown claws that grab, trying to pull me back. I kick out as I make my way into consciousness, emerging from under my duvet, gasping for breath as if I'm drowning.

I pull myself out of bed, walk into the lounge, looking left and right, trying to ground myself in these new surroundings. The pohutukawa tree's gnarled grey limbs knock and scrape the window as if asking to come in. I open the ranch slider and tiptoe across the deck, avoiding splinters and nails intent on injury. I breathe in the air thick with salt. There is a feeling of lightness, of letting go, and the nightmare is banished. Clark Island's rocky, bush-clad hulk rises out of the ocean, the high tide making it seem closer than it is. I like how this house sits directly in front of it. The island breaks up the never-ending view of the ocean which I often find overwhelming.

A week ago, in a bid for freedom, instead of taking a straight shot down state highway 1, I veered eastward, like I was taking a side door in my urgency to get away. I know I've made the right choice. Whangamatā shouts relaxation, holiday – escape.

Ostentatious million-dollar properties flank me either side; this house being the worst on the best street, but I don't want brand new, squeaky clean, sterile. At least I don't think so. I want comfort. I want anonymity. Distance. A new start.

That night, out on my deck, over the crashing waves, I hear voices, arguing. The house next door has its curtains drawn and the impressive bi-fold doors that have been open all afternoon are closed. I can hardly distinguish between male and female voices through the double glazing. I strain to hear and am greeted by the shattering of glass, a final alarmed yell, then silence. It is none of my business, I tell myself.

The next morning I cover myself head to toe in sunblock. The bottle is pink, made especially for babies and toddlers. It advertises an SPF of 50+, just what my translucent, freckle-ridden skin needs. I ram a wide-brimmed straw hat atop my brown curls and regard myself in the mirror, an act that lasts no more than three seconds. Enough to check for food in my teeth and a clean face, not long enough to focus on premature wrinkles, a double-chin, and a smile that curves down at the edges and doesn't make it to my eyes.

Down on the sand, the woman walking along the beach demands to be looked at. She is tall and lean; a huge sunhat and sunglasses cover her face. I try not to focus on how well she wears her hat, almost identical to mine. A mane of glossy blonde hair falls down her back, apparently impervious to sun, salt and wind. She looks fashionable and mysterious, everything I am not, and instantly I want to know her. She doesn't see me – people generally don't – and I watch as she walks up to the house next to mine. She's my neighbour, one of the shouters from the night before.

There is more fighting that night. I guess it's something I need to get used to. It's him tonight. I hear her say 'No!' once. I can't make out his words, but they're deep and pounding, just like the sea out there, unrelenting. I begin to feel sad for her. I begin to fear for her. But what am I supposed to do?

The next morning I lean against the ranch slider, half hidden by my dusty curtains, watching for her, so I can time the perfect accidental-on-purpose meeting. But she doesn't appear, so I take the rickety steps down onto the beach, a suicide mission every time. Directly in front of my house, a group of teens are playing cricket on the long stretch of sand. I walk in a wide circle around them to get to the water, ducking self-consciously as I hear ball meet bat, scurrying further away like one of the cautious dotterels I see amongst the dunes as a yell of 'Got 'em!' cracks through the sound of the surf and a blonde-headed, shirtless teen holds the caught ball in his hand.

I stand in the water; tepid waves break on my calves. This is what I do. I am not a swimmer, never have been. Large bodies of water frighten me. I don't think there is any repressed memory from my childhood, some hideous almost drowning. It's not even fear of sharks or anything plausible like that. Why come away to the beach then?

Because it's as far away from my old life as possible.

I feel something brush my arm and I startle, ready to dance away from a curious bee. But it's her.

'Hello,' she says, her voice is quiet against the waves, not as confident as I imagined it would be. It doesn't match her hair or her skin, or the way she moves.

'Hello,' I answer back.

This is it. You have once chance to make an impression – a good impression.

Up close she seems frail, fragile, and she hugs herself as if to stay warm. She wears a thin black dress, and the straps of a pale blue bikini lie flat against her collarbone and hug her neck. I wonder what she's hiding under those sleeves. Bruises? The colour of the ocean, dark, almost black where the shallows give way to the unending depth, or older ones, a beige-brown like the damp sand between my toes.

'You've just moved in next door?' She raises her voice to be heard above the waves.

'Yes, I have,' I say.

'Where have you come from?'

I panic, unsure, then reprimand myself, stay calm. 'Auckland,' I say.

'Nice to get away from the city,' she says. 'We used to live there. My husband still travels there for work a few times a week. It's a big day. Tires him out.'

Is she making excuses for him?

'But I think it's worth it to live here.'

I nod in agreement.

All through our stilted conversation she continues to look at the ocean, so I answer questions to her profile, which, to me, is perfect, and I wonder if she was or is a model. But not seeing someone's eyes when

I talk to them disconcerts me. They could be telling me anything and it could all be a lie. I clutch my sunglasses in my hand, hers stay on.

I want to say something to her, about him, the arguments. She radiates sadness. Loneliness.

'If you need help, just come over any time. If there's anything I can do, anything, just ask,' I say, urgent, hoping she realises I know the position she's in, that she sees something in me she can trust.

She nods without looking at me, her lips disappearing, as if in pain, or trying to hold back tears. And then she walks away without saying goodbye. I feel like I've failed – both in trying to make her feel better and trying to win her friendship. Why is it so damned hard to make friends as an adult? Although I don't know who I'm kidding, even as a child that natural socialising in the classroom, in the playground, never came easy to me.

I see him one morning and instantly dislike him. He's leaving for work as I'm collecting brochures from the letterbox. I pull my pink dressing gown around me like some pitiful armour. I know he sees me, but he doesn't acknowledge me, in fact, he lowers his head, turns away from me. I pretend to look through the pile of junk mail while taking him in. He's not as big as I imagined, nor as good looking. I had the image of a muscly guy, ridiculously handsome, his good looks hiding the monster underneath, but he looks – normal.

Her name is Emmeline. It's the perfect name for her. Feminine. Classic. Over the next week we see each other every day. She appears out of nowhere and falls into step next to me. We talk of the mundane: weather, favourite movies and music. We never talk about her sadness, about him. But I come away each time feeling I know her a bit better.

There is no shouting tonight. It's nice. It makes me feel happy for her. And part of me – just a very small part, miniscule – feels disappointed that maybe her life isn't quite as bad as I'd thought, that maybe she doesn't need me after all.

One evening there is a knock on my door. I consider not answering. Who could it be? No one important. But they're insistent. I walk to the ranch slider, trying not to show my shock, trying to act like this is totally normal. She's here. She's at my door, without me doing anything, without my invitation. I grapple with the stiff ranch slider, try and stay calm, wince as it screeches open, and say hello.

'I was wondering if you were free for a drink and a chat?' She stands at the door, seems uncertain.

Her hair is in a loose ponytail, make-up is minimal and her skin glows. Full lips shine with a pale pink gloss. I find myself pursing my lips together, running a hand across my cheek, as if the action will liven up my skin.

'Come in,' I say, stepping back as she walks inside, enveloping me in a fresh floral scent that has me inhaling deeply before I know what I'm doing.

'Sorry about the mess,' I say, waving a hand, encompassing the whole room, the old carpet and dated furniture. The house isn't mine, but I still feel the need to apologise.

'How long are you staying for?' she asks, handing me a bottle of wine.

I stumble over my words. 'For a while, I hope.' I take the wine off her, assume it's expensive. I take my only two wine glasses from the cupboard and bring them into the lounge. 'I've only been here three weeks, but I think I'd like to stay. The owner's offered me a year lease if I want it.'

'I've never asked you what you do,' she says.

I look at her, a quick glance, and then go back to filling the glasses. I hand her one, and she takes a seat on the sofa, perching on the edge. I take the old vinyl armchair opposite her, cross my legs, straighten my back, mirroring her.

'I was a teacher. I am a teacher,' I correct myself and realise it makes me sound stupid, like I'm lying or don't know what I'm talking about. 'I'm looking for work.'

'It might be hard around here,' she says. 'We only have the high school and a primary school.'

'I have my CV at the high school at the moment. They've promised me relieving work for the next couple of months before school finishes up for summer and there's talk there may be an opening in the science department. Maternity leave. Next year.'

'Fantastic,' she says. 'We never know who we're going to get when they rent this house out. People are always coming and going. It stands empty for months and then there's new faces here every week over summer. It's been nice to see the same face for a change.'

I smile, sipping my wine, trying to stay cool. I can't believe how well this is going. She's happy I'm here. She, this beautiful, enchanting woman, is happy I'm here.

For two hours we drink and talk. I only have one glass of wine. I'm not a big drinker. Never have been. It goes to my head, makes me feel unlike myself. Emmeline finishes off the bottle and doesn't seem to be any worse for wear. She smiles a lot but doesn't laugh. I can see that unhappiness and loneliness sitting right below the surface. She skirts around talk of her husband and their relationship, her answers, her demeanour, are telling, even if she doesn't realise it.

'How long have you been married for?'

'Too long.'

'Do you have children?'

'I would've liked to, but he decided early on in our marriage that he didn't want to. I'll be 42 soon. I think it's possible, but probably too late.'

'Does he work a lot?'

'Yes, a lot. A few days a week in Auckland plus he also works from home. His job's very stressful. He drinks to unwind – loses his temper…'

She looks at me, and I don't know what to say to make her feel better. Even though I want her to confide in me I change the subject, making it my mission to cheer her up. We talk about travel, where we've been: her, everywhere; me, a trip down to the South Island and a long weekend in Sydney; and where we want to go.

She looks at her watch and drains her glass. 'I should go.'

I don't want her to, but I stand up as she does.

She hesitates at the door and says, 'Would you walk me home?'

I look over at her house. From the bottom of my external stairs to her front door is less than 20 metres.

'Sorry, that's silly of me.' She shakes her head, eyes downcast.

'No, no,' I say. 'Of course I will.'

The security light clicks on when we cross onto her manicured grass. It's almost nine o'clock. I wonder if he's home. Will I meet him? How will I act? Emmeline needs to know I'm on her side.

She unlocks the door and pushes it wide, so I have a view inside. I gasp, a hand over my mouth. In a crumpled heap at the bottom of the stairs is a body. It's him. The husband.

I look to Emmeline, waiting for a response, reach out a hand where it hovers centimetres from hers. Is she okay? She's not shaking. She's not crying. I look back to the body then back to her. Emmeline's reaction isn't one of despair or horror; every move is calculated, choreographed, her breathing is steady as she skirts the pooling blood and heads for the phone.

Maybe she's in shock.

I listen as she speaks into the phone, asking for an ambulance, telling them she's just arrived home to find her husband at the bottom of the stairs. 'A pulse?' she says, looking at me, eyes wide.

I stand there, staring back at her.

'A pulse?' she says to me, louder, more insistent.

I squeeze my eyes shut tight, then open them. Emmeline needs me. I walk across to the body, crouch down, careful to avoid the blood; the thick dark red against the stark white tile looks black, like tar. I ease two fingers into his collared shirt and press down. Nothing. I look up at Emmeline and shake my head.

'I think he's dead,' Emmeline says. After another minute of nodding and murmuring into the phone she hangs up.

We stand in silence. How did this happen? When did this happen? How long has he been lying here? Was it an accident or–

The metallic smell of blood has eased its way into my nostrils, and I find myself breathing through my mouth, but then I feel like I can taste it. I press my lips together and swallow.

'You said you'd help me,' she says.

I look at her. Nod. 'Of course.'

'I'm sorry to have dragged you into this.'

'It's no bother,' I say, like she's asked me to go to the supermarket for her or collect her mail.

'I'm sorry he's gone. I am. It was an accident. He had the day off today, and he'd started drinking at lunch time. It was always worse when he was drinking. I was just protecting myself. But I don't think they'll believe me – the police will say it was murder. But, he was cruel to me.'

'I know,' I say. I feel her pain.

We both hear the siren as it turns into the street.

'If anyone asks, we were together all afternoon and evening. Is that okay?' Her tone is soft but desperate.

'Of course that's okay.'

'Thank you for doing this. I'm finally free.' She reaches across and squeezes my hand. It sends a jolt of electricity through me, and I feel alive.

With him gone it's like she's been given a new life, and me along with her. I start making more of an effort, and I know it's because of her. I buy a shade of lipstick like the one she wore when we went out for dinner a week after the funeral. I leave the chemist with a rainbow of sample marks over my hand. I settle on *Amethyst Smoke*, and when I put it on I feel mysterious, like strangers would want to know me. I buy a sarong, floaty around my calves which I love, tight on my hips which I ignore.

Emmeline notices the next time I see her on the beach. She praises me and I feel light; I stand up straighter, even though the skin on my face burns at the compliment. I am moving on. Just like Emmeline is doing. We both need to move on from the past. I am aware she has more courage than I'll ever have. But now I feel we're equals. I have helped her, she has helped me, even though she probably doesn't even know it.

His death is ruled an accident. Emmeline tells me there was alcohol in his system plus prescription medication, but that it was the fall that ultimately killed him. She was never a suspect and for that we are both relieved and grateful. I hug our secret close to my chest. I am the only one who knows what really happened; she trusted me to help her. I feel special. Needed.

We meet almost every morning for a walk along the beach, cutting through a beach access and into town. We take turns buying each other a coffee from her favourite cafe. I don't like coffee, never have, too bitter, but when I hear her order a long black the first time, I do the same.

I wait for her on the dunes this morning, occasionally looking up to her house to see if she's moving about. Summer is in the air. It's the start of December and the sky is bigger and bluer, the beach busier, the air warming. A clutch of toetoe to the right rustles next to me, and I reach up, running a hand through the feathery tops. I consider leaving, but I don't want to walk without her. It won't be the same. I tell myself I'll count to one hundred and if she doesn't turn up, I'll go to the cafe and get myself a chocolate milkshake. I count to five hundred and then trudge down toward the main beach, where a man and a woman, lithe and fit, dressed in bright yellow and red, are ramming flags of the same colour into the sand, intent on keeping the public safe. I splash through the shallows, trying to dampen the flare of anger that has developed at having been stood up. I nod hello to an elderly woman. Her walking stick sinks into the wet sand as she struggles along.

'You're Emmeline's other neighbour aren't you?'

I stop and turn.

She doesn't wait for my answer. 'I live on the other side.' She waves her walking stick in the direction of her house. Pale blue, immaculately kept, a glass balustrade winking in the morning sun. 'Horrible thing to have happened to her husband.'

I nod in agreement, and she stares at me. I don't know what I'm supposed to say.

'You know,' she says, shuffling towards me, 'if she hadn't been at your place that day, I would've said she did it.'

'What?' I wonder if the deep flush staining my face is giving me away.

'Terrible relationship they had.'

'Yes, I know.'

She looks around, like she is afraid of eavesdroppers. 'She used to abuse him – verbally and physically.' Her eyes light up, enjoyment in her revelation.

'No, I think you're mistaken,' I manage to say as authoritatively as I can. The ocean rushes in my ears, and I can't hear the words that come out of my own mouth.

'I worked in the doctor's surgery up until last year, and he often used to come in. Used to make up stories of course, fell off a ladder, hit his head on a kitchen cupboard, but I knew. I saw her hit him once. They were out on the deck late at night. Both had had too much to drink. Anyway, just because they had such a rocky relationship doesn't mean she killed him now does it?'

I have nothing to say.

She lets out a high-pitched giggle. 'Listen to me spreading gossip like an old lady with nothing else to do,' she says without any irony. 'And of course she was at your place when it happened.'

'She was,' I say.

'And you both got home and found him at the bottom of the stairs.'

'We did.' She needs to stop digging, she is not going to ruin this for me.

She looks down at her walking stick, drilling it into the sand. 'Good to meet you. Must be off dear, have a good day.'

I go back home, look in the mirror and apply a fresh coat of *Amethyst Smoke*. I don't want to jeopardise our relationship. But I need to know. There is a low hum between my ears. Emmeline isn't who I thought she was, and I don't know how I feel about this. I've helped. I've saved her. But she hasn't been honest.

We're drinking wine on Thursday evening. It's become our evening.

'Did he used to hit you?' I ask.

Her glass stops at her lips, she puts it down. 'I never said he hit me.'

I think back. This is true. I've concocted my own story of Emmeline. Of someone who I wanted her to be. Someone for me to save. Someone who I thought needed me.

'Did you kill him?'

'You know I did.' She finishes her wine.

'Was it an accident?' I grip my wine glass tightly, knowing it's too late to take the question back. Why am I doing this? Why would I ruin what we have for the truth? It doesn't even matter.

'It wasn't an accident.' She pours more wine into her glass, finishing off the bottle. 'I didn't want him in my life any longer. He was weak, needy, suffocating.'

This revelation is like a mask being removed, a disguise revealed or a shedding of skin. She's a whole new person. She seems harder around the edges and her eyes squint, challenging me. I think she expects me to be shocked, horrified, and when she sees that I'm not, that I'll gladly keep her secret, something changes again. She inches closer to me.

'Who are you?' she asks. 'What's your story?'

'I don't have a story. You needed my help, and so I helped you,' I say.

She nods and drains her glass. 'I need to go.'

My stomach drops, and I feel like the contents of half a bottle of wine are going to come back up again. I shouldn't have said anything. I should've just left it. Everything was fine as it was.

Emmeline stands and I'm engulfed in her perfume.

'You don't need to go.' I try not to sound desperate but fail.

'It's okay.' She smiles at me with those perfect teeth, her head tilted to one side. 'I have an appointment at the hair salon tomorrow.' She takes a section of my hair between her fingers. 'You should come with me.'

I nod, exhaling. Everything is okay.

Before bed that night I take the newspaper cuttings from the shoebox I keep at the top of my wardrobe. I've hidden it at the back behind bulky winter jerseys so it's not in view – more for me than for anyone else. I've promised myself not to look at them often, just every now and then. A reminder.

The story was well-covered. The attractive and successful principal of a girls' high school and her untimely, tragic death. The sobering, underlying message of the dangerous impact of drinking and driving. There were two photos they used in the numerous newspaper articles. The professional one that she used for everything school related: a head and shoulders, friendly smile but not too over the top, hair straightened for the occasion, black blazer, nude lipstick. The other one was of her at the beach, that same hair messy and sun bleached, her skin tanned, her mouth open in a laugh. That was the one that pulled the heartstrings. Aged 42. Gone too soon.

She showed interest in me from the start – not in a boss kind of way, it was more than that, like she wanted to be friends. She took an interest in my private life, not that there was much of one, asked about my family often. A lot of the female teachers on staff were married and had kids, and if they weren't they at least had boyfriends or girlfriends. We bonded over the fact we had no one in our lives right now. She told me she broke up with the love of her life two years previously. I told her a similar story.

There was no real plan to start lying, but there was the realisation that if I told her the truth – that there had never been a love of my life, that my mother and father were dead, no siblings, no real family to speak of, she would lose interest. So there was an ex-lover, there was a mother, a father, a sister; there were weekends away with my extended family which included two beautiful nieces. There was even a funeral at the start of the year for my sister who we lost tragically to cancer – she mourned with me, comforted me, even came round with a bottle of wine and a takeaway when I got back from the funeral (which was actually three blissful days off school curled up on the couch watching Netflix).

She cheered me up, and I thought, this is what normal people do. Build relationships, friendships. Support each other. And then I felt her pulling away. I wasn't aware what I'd done. She mentioned once that she loved fresh flowers and missed that part about having a boyfriend. I had told her she didn't need a boyfriend for that kind of thing. 'Buy yourself flowers' I had told her, but she had rolled her eyes. And so I bought her flowers. I left a few things on her desk. The Whittaker's chocolate she told me she loved, the latest *House and Garden* magazine after I'd seen her flicking through year-old copies in the staffroom. And when I felt like I was losing her, I invited her on a girls' weekend away. I'd paid for everything, a small Airbnb on Waiheke Island. She said no, and then pulled away even more.

I walked into her office one day, two other teachers were sitting with her. Their lunches were spread out on her desk. They were laughing, flicking through old copies of *Woman's Day* and *Woman's Weekly*. I stood at the door as they stared at me, and then I turned and walked away. They had been talking about me. I knew it.

That same night, I pulled into the Indian restaurant near the school to pick up my takeaway order, and I saw her and those two other teachers walking into the pub across the road. It was Friday night and they'd abandoned dress pants and flats for skinny jeans and heels. Right then I felt anger and sadness, a bitter taste in my mouth.

I waited for hours in my car, the aroma of chicken korma and garlic naan stifling in my enclosed car. They came out two hours later. She said goodbye to the other women and walked to her car. I wondered how much she'd had to drink. I followed her. I didn't know where she lived. Had never been invited. We got on the motorway heading south and exited quarter of an hour later. I took in the signs: Karaka. Waiau Pa. Clark's Beach. Subdivisions gave way to farmland and empty roads and still I followed. I thought of her and those two other women, their cosy lunches and nights out at the pub and wondered where I figured into any of it.

Flicking my lights onto high beam, I accelerated. I nudged the back of her car and braked as I saw it fish tail. My car idled in the middle of the deserted road as she overcorrected. The scream of tyres broke the silence and then the car flipped and came to a sudden halt as it connected with a concrete power pole.

The newspapers reported she had been over the limit and driving too fast. There was some talk about another car being involved. The rumor chased me out of the city, away from my job, towards a new life.

I gather the newspaper articles, thinking now, maybe, I don't even need them anymore. But I still place them back in the shoebox. It's good to remember.

It will be different this time with Emmeline. I can see it. She saved me, even though she doesn't know it. And I saved her. That's the difference this time around.

We both need each other.

CERTAIN KINDS OF LIGHT

RENÉE

THE WOMAN — TALL, DARK HAIR, THIN, LOOKING A LITTLE LESS NERVOUS NOW that her first breaking-the-ice poem was over — smiled at the audience. Behind her the two guitarists played their four chords calling for silence, then moved sideways, leaving her the centre space again. Poets from all over the Kapiti Coast had come to *The Barn* to share their works. Some were assured performers, who knew rehearsal was mandatory if you wanted to give a good reading even if you felt a fool saying your poems to the bedroom mirror. These poets know their lines, know to step up close to the mic, speak straight out to the audience, while others, who work on the assumption that a miracle will happen once they're on stage, shuffle nervously, make a joke no one laughs at, then mumble their poems to the floor.

Whatever the style of presentation, however, all got a good clap. Porohiwi audiences were a kindly lot. They liked *The Barn*. It was old and large, the seats were comfortable and when the night was chilly like tonight, there was a large open fire kept stoked with wood donated by locals as their way of supporting the arts in the town. As well, all proceeds went to the Women's Refuge so there was the comfortable feeling that they were supporting something good when they bought a ticket to The Barn's Big Poetry Night.

The MC smiled at her, nodded, moved closer to the side mic, said, 'Thank you for your warm reception of Alice's first poem, here's her second, and the last of the evening, *If I call you*. Thanks Alice.'

Alice didn't have a piece of paper or a notebook. She looked straight at the audience. Her voice was rich and deep.

If I call you will you come?
when he holds the knotty stick
makes those shadows on the wall
and I whisper to my phone
will you come?

If I call you will you come?
In the middle of the park
silent footsteps by the stand
when I whisper to my phone
will you come?

If I call you will you come?
when the car slides to a stop
door slides, two get out
and I whisper to my phone
Will you come?

If I walk into the river
water shushing at my shoes
shadows thick around the willows
and I do not have a phone
Will you come?

There was utter silence from the audience as she stepped back from the mic, until, taking a collective breath, the clapping began. A few sat with still faces, remembering something perhaps? A few wondered if reading the poem was a challenge to them, a reminder of what had happened to Alice; was it a year ago? Some wondered if it was quite the thing to expose one's life like this? Weren't these unfortunate events better kept to oneself? Better forgotten? Besides, poetry was about blue skies and daffodils, highwaymen and swans on lakes, it wasn't meant to be, like, about real life was it? But they joined in the clapping.

Alice said 'Kia ora, thank you,' to the audience, walked off stage, and the President of the Porohiwi Players raised a thumb of approval then stepped forward to do her spiel on the Drama Student's forthcoming production of *2brnt2b*, by Sarah Delahunty.

In the hallway the woman on the door said, 'Pat yourself on the back. You did it.'

Alice nodded, breathed out, then smiled.

'One step at a time,' said the woman. 'You got a ride?'

Alice lowered her voice. 'I'll cut around Vogel, over the bridge and through the cemetery.'

'You okay to do that?'

Alice ignored the question, said, 'My Gran used to be the Caretaker. I played there lots when I was young and when I got a little older she persuaded the committee to give me a job after school, picking up rubbish. You'd be surprised how much mess people leave after funerals.'

She looked out the glass windows and up at the full moon. 'A certain kind of light,' she said, 'that's what my Gran called the full moon.'

'You good for helping out with the drama kids? Won't be too bad. A little private coaching here and there is all.'

Alice smiled, moved away and once out on the path, eased into that steady loping stride she'd learned from Gran all those years ago. 'Gets you there just the same,' Gran said, 'speed is okay but steady gets you to the end without puffing.'

She'd been thinking about Gran a lot lately.

She could hear the river as she came around the corner onto Vogel. Ages since she'd been this way. Ages since she'd walked anywhere at night. Last time had been early summer, now it was late winter although yellow lachenalia in people's gardens or pots were giving the message – never mind what the calendar says, we say its Spring.

The river was in a contented mood tonight. It chuckled along the sandy edges and over the bed of stones as it forced its way to the bar where it would smash against its old foe, the sea, in that eternal struggle for supremacy as they both hit their side of the bar.

'You don't have to,' the organiser said when she asked her to do the poetry reading, 'but probably good if you do.'

'You reckon?' she'd said.

'I reckon.'

But last night she'd nearly reneged. Almost. Her hand had gone out to her phone, then she'd remembered Gran, that skinny fierce old woman who, if she'd ever had a resentful thought about having a 10–year–old granddaughter landed on her in her 70s, never showed it. 'You promise you'll do something,' Gran said, 'you do it.'

Alice paused at the top of the steps leading down to River Path. It was done. Her first public reading since last Poetry Day and the first ever public reading of that poem. It had got that utter stillness from the audience as if everyone in *The Barn* had been taken into the world of the poem, some accepting the unspoken pact, some more hesitant, a few uncomfortable. That frozen block inside her had begun to warm as both she and the audience (or most of them) were caught together by the lines. The woman who'd asked her to read had been right. It had been good.

Now, halfway along River Path towards the bridge she still felt the warmth of those moments but when the dark figures stepped out of the shadows into the moonlight, instantly that shaky terror washed through her and all she wanted to do was fall to her knees and sob, 'Please don't, please don't', which she knew didn't work because she'd tried it that other time. She felt herself start to shake. She should have got a ride.

'Well, well,' said the taller one, 'you looking for company again darling?'

'Fuck off,' she said, felt for her phone, looked for the number, but they were coming closer – she shoved the phone in her pocket, turned and ran back the way she'd come.

The two men began running towards her. Long giant strides. They'd be at the bridge before her so she swerved to her left off the path, down the bank and into the river. Her feet scraped on the slippery stones, then as the water got deeper, she began swimming. She swam like one of those eels she and Gran used to catch and which she was sometimes allowed to cook on an open fire if Gran, or one of the gardeners, could be persuaded to provide a match and to stay and supervise. 'Only if an adult is there,' had been the rule.

'Tally ho,' shouted the tall one and he and the stocky short one ran across the bridge that led to the track that wound around the cemetery on the way to town.

She increased her speed, she was that girl of 15 again, winning the Combined–Colleges Champion Overarm, she was Katie Ledecky out to win the Women's freestyle at the Tokyo Olympics. Gasping, Alice clambered up the stony bank on the other side, shedding drops of water as she ran across the paddock and hurled herself up over the stone fence on which was the sign: NO ENTRANCE. KEEP OUT.

She was in the Presbyterian part of the cemetery. The men were now off the bridge and on the path. In a second or two they'd be over the fence.

Her jeans and jacket were heavy and dripping, her track shoes squelched and as she ran spits of water from her sopping hair hit her already wet face. She felt in her pocket, grabbed her phone, looked down briefly. Wet, but worth a try. She pressed the number again but there was no light, the phone had died.

The men left the path and hurtled over the stone fence. The taller one pointed to his left and they cut along the spaces between the graves.

She twisted and turned round the old plots. She'd never worked out why dead people were separated into religious groups – like if a Methodist was put into the Roman Catholic part they would contaminate it or vice versa. When she asked, Gran had said, 'The biggest and most successful Ponzi scheme of them all.' Human beings, especially the religious ones, liked to think they can order the universe into in–groups and out–groups. 'The only problem is they haven't figured out that when Jesus said Love they neighbour as thyself, he meant everyone, even the ones who don't go to the same church, or even to church at all and in any case,' smiled Gran, 'whatever our beliefs or no beliefs, no one lives forever – we all end up here or over the road at the crem.'

Alice twisted around the old shingle-covered paths and made for the large modern area where the graves were covered by lawn and the gravestones mainly flat and less ornate. If she could make the path at the far end, the Duggan Street end, she could knock on a door. She swerved around and suddenly saw it over the way. The moon shining over the black patch. She turned left, increased her pace. The dark figures behind her were puffing now and what they'd seen as fun had become annoying and that damned full moon seemed to be smiling at their angry frustration.

'Fucking cunt,' shouted the tall one, 'need a fucking lesson.'

'A fucking lesson,' echoed the short one.

'Wooo ooo ooo...'

'Jesus, what was that?' The short one stopped and looked around. Nothing moved. The running footsteps ahead of them had stopped.

The taller one strode around the graves and along the grass path to where the noise had come from. 'She's playing silly buggers,' he said.

'Wooo oooo.'

This time the noise was from the other side.

The two men looked around. There were lights on concrete poles spaced around the edges of the cemetery but the middle was lit only by the moon. The tombstones in this old part loomed grey and ghostly. *Safe in the arms of Jesus* was a popular postscript. *I was a writer but nobody's perfect*, Dorothy Parker had directed should be written on her gravestone, but no one, at least in this part, seemed to have a sense of humour. *Loved by all, sadly missed* on Charles Pilson's tombstone was carrying charity a bit far. He was an old tyrant and a scrooge, had bullied his wife and children, and only two of his family, plus his lawyer, had attended the funeral service, so the curate had had to do a last–minute ring around of male members of the parish council to ask for their help carrying the coffin to its final resting place. However, the Food Bank had benefitted from the leftover food which, if George had been alive, would have been thrown out rather than support, as he once put it, an institution that encouraged layabouts to leech off their neighbours.

'Fuck this,' shouted the tall one, 'you better bloody stop or there'll be extra payment.'

Woo ooo ooo.

'Okay you bitch.' He turned and ran between the graves towards the sound. They were on the main pathway along which mourners carried their dead. Not so many these days. Most preferred cremation.

The other one, huffing because he was short and overweight, looked up, gave a little grunt of shock and said shakily, 'Mate.'

But the other head had already come up. He stopped, said sharply, 'What the fuck?'

Alice was standing across from the pathway. 'By the pricking of my thumbs something wicked this way comes,' she chanted.

'Huh?'

'So – I'll do and I'll do and I'll do.'

She cackled in a high–pitched tone then turned and ran.

The tall man swerved, took a sharp left, ran around the Methodist section, tripped, shouted 'Oh Jesus,' as he landed hard on the stone edge of a grave. The stone angels on the gravestone looked down at him impassively. The short man, sweating behind him, tripped, fell over and sprawled on the grave. His face was grazed and bleeding.

'Shit,' he moaned, 'shit.' He was scared. The text on the grave said, *Trust in the Lord and You will be Saved*.

'She's asking for trouble,' said the tall one, 'come on.'

'I'll do and I'll do and I'll do...' the voice floated back. She was moving around the old mass grave which the Porohiwi Town Council had organised for that other epidemic, just after the first World War. The town had suffered badly from that one. Been much better this time although there would be other lockdowns, nothing surer.

'Mate, let's go back. Not keen on this.'

'Let her get away with it? Fuck that.'

The tall one ducked along a line of graves and swerved back into another very old part of the graveyard. Roman Catholics. Angels and Latin epitaphs were everywhere. The short man pushed his hands against the ground, struggled upright and followed. But it was no good. Whichever way they turned, at some stage the woman stood across the path, leaving only one way free for them to go.

'I'll do and I'll do and I'll do.'

'Dunno what the fuck you're playing at,' the tall one yelled as she stopped and stared at the men yet again. Do and do and do…

The tall one put his head down and charged and this time, instead of running away, she stood quite still until two seconds before he reached her, she turned and jumped across the open grave and the tall man, legs freewheeling, yelled as he charged into open space and fell. He landed like a thrown brick into the newly dug grave. He was followed a second later by the other one. The force of the landing knocked the wind out of the first one's lungs and when the short one landed on top of him he gave an agonised whoof of pain, tried to breathe but could only manage hard panicky groans that sounded like someone was having difficulty sawing a hard piece of timber. 'My arm,' he moaned, 'my arm.'

All was quiet. The moon shone on the short man, splayed and moaning, almost sobbing, as he rolled over away and pulled himself to his feet. He stood, shaking his head, trying to work out what had happened.

'My arm,' moaned the tall man, 'my foot.' He put one hand on the ground and pushed himself up against the side. 'Holy shit,' he groaned. One foot dangled as he hopped closer to the side and leaned back against it, muttering, 'Christ, oh Christ.'

The moon was right overhead, light piercing the black space, the heaps of black soil on the side, the woman staring down at them.

'And I'll do and do and do,' she chanted. She held the shovel handle as she dug and threw. Dug. Threw. Dug, Threw. She moved easily, fluidly, like she'd done this before.

Do and do and do echoed around the tombstones.

'Now look,' said the taller one, 'This has gone far enough.' He meant to sound authoritative and in control but it came out more of a whine. It was like he'd stumbled into a game and just realised he didn't know the rules.

She stopped shovelling, stood on the side of the hole, looked down into the shadows in the corners and the fall of light in the middle. Then she turned, grabbed the shovel and pushed it back into the pile of black earth, filled it and with a heave sent more dark mass into the hole. Some of it scattered over the short man but most of it hit the tall one in the face, some spraying into his open mouth. He choked, bent over, made retching noises and out came a mixture of dirt and saliva. He coughed, let more saliva gather in his mouth and spat it out. Some of it hit the other one who jumped back, made a bubbling wet gasp and vomited a spray of dark shiny liquid onto the black earth now halfway up the hole. He leaned his hand against the side and breathed in and out, a high–pitched sound like a chugging train screeching its protest against an uneven line.

'Oh fuck me,' said the taller one as if he'd just realised that size and strength might not be the deal breakers he'd always thought they were.

The shovel dug, lifted, turned, threw. The tall man scrabbled at the side of the grave and tried to get purchase but as soon as he put any weight on his arm it was agony and when he tried to dig his good foot into the side, the soil gave way and he had to hop wildly and clutch the side with hand so he didn't fall.

The silent figure at the top, like a well–trained dancer, dug, lifted, threw, dug, lifted, threw, dug, and great heaves of earth shot into the hole. The grave was now three–quarters full and only the taller man's upper chests, shoulders, arms and face, was exposed while the shorter one was up to his neck. They looked like strange exotic plants in a high wind as they yelled up at the moon, waving their arms, spitting out thin streams of black saliva.

The woman leaned over and dragged a hose towards the grave.

At first the men jumped to avoid the stream of cold water but as the water gurgled into the black soil, gradually it all became mud. Any movement just meant more frustration. There was no way of dealing with the wet mush which allowed little movement and prevented any hope of maintaining balance unless you stood quite still. And standing still was impossible in this cold wet muck. The tall man moaned. His arm and shoulder were hurting.

The woman dragged the hose away, turned off the tap, walked back, looked down at the men.

'What is it? What the hell's up?' The tall one spat out saliva and soil along with the words.

'Do you have anything to say before sentence is passed,' she said.

'Sentence? You're crazy. We haven't done anything.'

'No?'

'It was you. You were looking for a bit of fun – we obliged.'

'Fun?' she said, 'fun?'

'Ugly fat bitch, we did you a favour and you loved it. Then when they found you, you made up some crap to tell the ambos.'

'So, let's review the events of that night,' she said, 'when I came along the path did I smile or say hello?'

'You were looking for fun else why would you be there?'

'I was on my way home. Did I smile? Say hello?'

'Walking along River Path after midnight. Looking for trouble.'

'Its a public path. Open to anyone, any time. Did I smile? Say hello? No? So why?'

'You wanted a bit of fun so we obliged.'

'Did I struggle? Say no?'

'Well yeah, but they all do that.'

'If I was struggling and screaming, why did you continue?'

'Girls like it rough.'

'So if I continue shovelling soil into this grave and you shout and scream no, you don't really mean it?'

'Fuck off, who'd want to be buried alive?'

She looked down at them. She simply could not be bothered asking the obvious question.

'So, I'll say it again – do you have anything to say before sentence is passed?'

'Sentence?'

'You dig a grave? You fill it in.'

'Only if someone's dead.'

'You'll be wishing you were by the time I fill it to the top.' She picked up the shovel, edged it under the pile and chucked the soil in the hole. Some of it went into the tall man's mouth and he choked again.

'Oh,' wailed the short one, 'Oh crap.'

The tall one had just remembered his phone but as he took it from his pocket and brought it to the surface another shovel of soil landed on his chest and he dropped it. Another dollop and it was under the earth. He swept his arm around but could not locate it. The short one started to cry in earnest. Great dirty tears rolled down his face and his nose dripped shiny black globules over his lips and chin. He wiped at them with a hand but only managed to spread the wet ooze over his face.

'Oh mate,' he cried, 'oh mate.'

The woman scraped some more soil into the grave, then put her foot on the shovel and pressed it into the ground, turned to go.

'You can't leave us here,' shouted the tall one, 'we'll die.'

'Only if you go to sleep,' she said, 'the caretaker and his offsiders will be here around eight, you can probably stay awake till then.'

'But we might not, we might go to sleep, sink our face into the mud, go unconscious, die.' The man felt the hot sting of urine and shit running down his legs.

'No such luck,' she said.

'They don't start work till eight, that's hours,' sobbed the short man.

'Give you time,' she said, 'you might want to have a think about life, about the River Path.'

Alice picked up the shovel, turned and walked away. They heard the clink as she leaned the shovel against the wall of the Head Gardener's shed.

'But what'll we say?' The tall one was crying now, black watery liquid ran down his cheeks and down his neck, his shoulder was pumping agony with every second. 'What'll we say? They'll call the cops, we'll be charged for interfering with a grave. And what'll we say?'

She turned back.

'Make something up,' she said, 'you're good at that.'

She walked away along the path, and all was silent except for the short man whimpering, 'Oh please don't, please don't,' as that certain kind of light cast by the full moon was blacked out behind a dark cloud.

You promise you'll do something, you do it.

NANCYS UNDERCOVER
RWR MCDONALD

I

WE SAT ON THE DECK SUNBATHING. IT REMINDED ME OF SUMMER LAST YEAR, except this time we weren't at home but at Uncle Pike and Devon's Riverstone holiday home, Number Eight Ronsdale Place. I got up and leaned over the wooden rails, studying the old hospital through the macrocarpas branches below. I just hoped these holidays my uncle wouldn't fall off the balcony again; this one was way higher than the one at home.

Devon lay on a sun lounger, wearing nothing but coconut oil and a white sock thing over his privates. Melanie Brown, my next-door neighbour, had given him her grandma's stash of suntan lotion and another soap on a rope. Uncle Pike lay beside him, a red facecloth over his head, in floral boardies. His big furry white tummy, and massive tattooed pecs and arms, turning pink in the sun.

'I'm going through withdrawals.' Devon pulled out the beige block of soap and put it to his ear. 'I cut off the rope.'

Uncle Pike raised his facecloth. 'She shouldn't encourage you. But it does make your ear smell nice. And that coconut oil: woof!'

'Thank you.' Devon tapped the soap 'screen' a couple of times then frowned, lifting it up like he was searching for a signal.

Bunny Whiskers sauntered over and plopped down beside me and began licking her tummy, relaxing without Fabulon around. My uncle's dog lived in Sydney now. I missed him.

My uncle sighed. 'And you have got to stop stealing their cat.'

Bunny Whiskers paused mid lick and stared at Uncle Pike.

'What?' he said to the cat and poked his tongue out at it before repositioning his facecloth.

'Can we go see NaiNai after lunch?' I asked.

'Of course, Tippy Chan,' my uncle said, under the cloth. 'Maybe this time she'll give me a smile.'

'Yay,' Devon said. 'Our first time IRL.' NaiNai had only met Devon over video before, and the last time she had seen Uncle Pike had been when Dad died and they had fought about the funeral arrangements, my uncle siding with Mum.

It had been one year since we formed the Nancys. I still couldn't believe how much had changed. NaiNai, my grandma, had moved over from Shanghai and lived in Riverstone now. School had finished for the year and Mum was away on a spa retreat Uncle Pike had booked for her. Lots of massages. Which seemed weird as Mum hated people touching her, especially her face, her neck, her head and definitely her feet.

Mum had gone, reluctantly, and would be back in time for Christmas. So far these holidays we had no mystery to solve. Devon had sunbathed and Uncle Pike had *sampled* his way through their duty-free alcohol. The highlight for all of us being the A & P Show weekend and watching Melanie Brown hand her crown to Jess Chung, this year's new show queen.

I hopped into the back of their rental car, blue to match Nancy Drew's, of course, with Bunny Whiskers banging around in a cardboard box. Devon tapped on his window with his knuckles as we waited for Uncle Pike to lock up.

Devon had on a tight metallic gold T-shirt with a picture of a leopard licking its bits with *Licky* spray painted across it. "Bunny Whiskers inspired me," he had said when he revealed it this morning. His white culottes and sandals topped it off.

Uncle Pike got into the car, dressed like Santa on a gay cruise, in a white singlet, rainbow Hawaiian shirt and red short-shorts. He passed me today's copy of our free local newspaper, *The Riverstone Bulletin*, or the *Bully*, as we called it. 'Thought your grandma might like to read it.'

Devon ran his hand lightly over my uncle's head. 'I totally should have worn my red cape, what if a wolf gets into my basket?'

'Again? Let's video it this time.' Uncle Pike grabbed his hand and held it.

'Inapprops.' I made a gagging sound as Bunny Whiskers let out a low throaty yowl.

River View Rest Home was across the river, on the other side of the golf course at the top of our hill on the way out of town. It had no view of the river. After stopping at home to release the cat into the wild, aka the Browns' front lawn, we drove over to the rest home. Its boring building could easily have been an office, or a funeral parlour, or a hospital. The carpark was nearly empty. Devon pulled up near the entrance. As we entered the foyer we were blasted with heat.

'Good for growing orchids,' Uncle Pike said.

My nose wrinkled, a smell of damp washing and must. It reminded me of the stinky Airbnb we stayed at on Hope Street earlier this year. The reception area was carpeted in a swirling spearmint and purple pattern that almost moved. Staring at it made me check my balance like I was on a rolling ship.

A woman about Mum's age, Raelene, sat behind a small desk with a large brass bell. Her grey curly hair pinned back. I remembered Raelene from my other visits. I liked her bright red lipstick but found her thick black glasses judgey-slash-scary.

'I'm not sure how much of this carpet I can take,' Uncle Pike said to her.

She lowered her glasses. 'Excuse me?'

'I said–'

'Oh hello Tippy,' Raelene said. 'Your Grandma will be so happy to see you.' She frowned at Uncle Pike.

Devon rocked back and forth, staring at a print on the wall. 'I can't see it.'

'It's not a magic eye, honey,' Uncle Pike said.

'Oh, Oh! How clever!'

The receptionist shook her head. 'Down the hall sweetie, you know where to go.'

'And so do you.' My uncle smiled and left Raelene with her mouth open.

We followed the psychedelic carpet down a hallway to NaiNai's room. Devon held his arms out as he lurched, trying to keep his balance. I swayed, following behind him. *This is what being drunk must be like.* We passed several open doors. Elderly patients sat in grey vinyl chairs facing blank walls.

I found NaiNai in her room doing the same. She looked over at us, wiped her huge white square framed glasses, then looked again and gave me a big toothless smile. I ran in and gave her a huge hug. She felt like a little bird that would squash if I squeezed too hard. She kept hold of my arm as I sat beside her, and with her other hand she touched my face.

'Hello!' Uncle Pike said. 'Remember me?'

NaiNai dropped her hand and stared blankly at him, then looked past him as Devon came in the room carrying a chair. I introduced her to Devon.

He held out his hand. 'Very pleased to meet you finally IRL.' Devon glanced at me, and I translated for NaiNai. She watched him and nodded her head. 'Sorry again about your son. I wish I had got the chance to meet Weifang, he must have been an amazing person.' Devon looked at me as he said this and gave my hand a squeeze. I gave him a little smile to say thank you. *Dad. Nineteen months. Love you forever.* NaiNai watched Devon as I translated in Mandarin, NaiNai always wanted me to practice any chance I got.

'Also,' Devon said. 'Please tell her I'm obsessed with her glasses. Pure fashion.'

I translated again and NaiNai replied in Mandarin that he was even more kind and handsome in the flesh. She gave him a big smile. Devon got a little teary and asked if he could give her a hug and she nodded. They had a long hug then Devon gently pulled back, wiping his eyes, and smiled.

NaiNai patted his leg and said something in Mandarin that I couldn't pick up.

'Are they looking after you alright?' Uncle Pike said.

She looked at the floor and nodded.

'Doesn't seem very convincing,' Uncle Pike said to me. 'Tippy, can you please find out what's worrying her?'

I asked NaiNai questions about the meals and the treatment by the staff, stumbling on some words. She shrugged and said it was all good, nothing for me to worry about.

'NaiNai says everything's fine.' I missed her and didn't like seeing her like this – withdrawn, she seemed almost frightened.

'Why do so many old people die in this dump?' Uncle Pike said, reading the *Bully*. 'That's the third one this week.'

'Because they're old?' Devon offered. 'Were their heads cut off?'

'No, it doesn't appear so.' Uncle Pike frowned and shook the paper hard as if to see whether the words would stay on it. 'Who would get old, aye NaiNai?' he yelled.

'Shèng dàn lăo rén,' my Grandma muttered in Mandarin, which translated as 'Christmas Old Man' or Santa. Uncle Pike looked at me for a translation. I shrugged.

Something about the deaths and River View Rest Home felt off. *Could this be a case for the Nancys?*

'Did you know Mrs Gallant?' Uncle Pike asked gently.

She nodded. In that moment she shrank and seemed much older.

I took the *Bully* off my uncle and read the death notice. 'The funeral's on Friday at Barron's Funeral Home, would you like to go?'

My Grandmother nodded. Mr Barron was creepy. He was super pale and super thin and super tall. My best friend, Sam, and I used to wonder if he was a vampire.

Right now, I wanted NaiNai safe with us. 'Maybe if we spend more time with NaiNai we might find out more? Can she stay with us tonight?'

Mum wouldn't have been happy; she and my grandma had a massive falling out over my dad's funeral. But Mum was away, and she didn't need to know.

'Of course,' Devon said. 'NaiNai can stay as long as she likes. Is she allowed out?'

I nodded. She used to be always at home. *We were going to add on a bedroom.* I stopped myself. *She's in Riverstone and that's all that matters.*

'Let's bust her out then,' Devon said. 'This whole place gives me the creeps.'

'Would you like that?' I asked NaiNai who nodded.

'Road trip!' Uncle Pike said. She narrowed her eyes at him.

'Did she just hiss at me?' he said. 'Don't forget her teeth.'

II

Devon flicked the living room lights on and off which made no difference to how bright it was with the afternoon sun streaming in.

'Why are you making that noise?' Uncle Pike said.

One of the light bulbs blew and Devon stopped flicking the switch. He cleared his throat. 'I would like to introduce my latest design.' He held out his arm and in came NaiNai wearing a T-shirt dress with large black writing on it: *The Fun Starts Behind*.

She had on bright red lipstick and large wooden bangles.

'Glasses are model's own,' he said.

I clapped. 'NaiNai you look so cool.'

She walked up and down and did a twirl.

Devon snapped his fingers. 'Work!'

We all stood up and clapped.

'Provocative,' Uncle Pike said. 'Brava. And what a statement on ageism and sexuality. Does she know what it says?'

I nodded my head.

'Tippy helped me explain the concept to her,' Devon said. 'The party starts when she arrives. So she is ahead of the party and it is following her.'

'Oh right!' my uncle said. 'So it's not because she's into back door action?'

Devon frowned. 'She could be into back door action, I haven't asked her though.' He whispered, 'I don't think it'd be appropriate for Tippy to ask.'

My uncle nodded his head. 'Quite right, quite right. Great job on the styling. Also, I love the cut and the placement of the letters, it looks very modern. Well done.'

Devon smiled and gave a slight bow. '*Xièxiè*.'

'*Xièxiè* indeed.'

NaiNai glared at Uncle Pike.

'I swear she hates me,' he said.

She smiled at Devon and patted him on the arm and then made a smoking signal with her hands.

'What a great idea!' Devon leapt off the sofa and bolted to his room and came back with one of his *herbal* cigarettes. 'Come on doll, let's go outside. You should see the town lights at night, so pretty.' He held out his arm which she accepted, and he led her to the balcony. Over his shoulder he called out, 'Say no to drugs, Tippy Chan.'

NaiNai cackled and tried to imitate him.

'Are you going to let them do drugs?' I said to my uncle.

'If that's what they want to do, Tippy.' He poured a large whisky. 'They're adults.'

'Can I have some?' I asked.

Uncle Pike glanced up. 'Whisky? Absolutely not! It's illegal Tippy, how could you ask such a question?' He opened the fridge as I rolled my eyes.

'I can hear that,' he said to me, turning around and waggling a can of lemonade at me.

'Yes, please.'

My uncle came over and gave me the drink. 'Barron's Funeral Home, what do you know about them?'

I shrugged. 'Nothing, Tony Barron took over from his dad about two years ago. He's not married if that's what you mean?'

'I'm not thinking of dating him Tippy, but I do think we should check it out.' He groaned as he sat back down. 'I've got a feeling in my waters—'

'So, the Nancys have a new case?' I tried to act cool and focus on opening my lemonade.

'Maybe,' Uncle Pike clinked his glass with my can. Out the window Devon was talking animatedly. Grandma was beaming, something I hadn't seen her do for a long time.

My phone rang, it was Mum. I got up, but before I answered the call I said to my uncle, 'I think it's time the Nancys went undercover.'

His face lit up. It was on.

III

'Do you hold funerals for pets?' Uncle Pike asked in a high-pitched English accent. He sounded like the Queen. 'My Tulip Berry has gone night-night, and my Twinkles simply cuunt cope!'

The Nancys were undercover as widows in the reception area of Barron's Funeral Home and Tony Barron seemed dazed. He was even more pale faced than I remembered and looked like he hadn't slept for a long time.

'What?' Mr Barron said.

Devon peered at him. 'Do you speak English?' he said, slowly and loudly.

'I fear it's no good.' Uncle Pike burst into hysterical wailing.

I wasn't sure if our first undercover disguises were helpful or just scary. Mr Barron had taken a few steps back when we had arrived for our appointment. We were all dressed in black, designed and made by Devon. My disguise was a black hat with veil, black cape, and a pair of his large Chloé sunglasses. Over my arm was Mum's black Prada bag that Uncle Pike had given her. My uncle wore a large black gown, like a professor, or a nun. Devon had on a black halter neck jump suit and looked like a cross between Action Man and Catwoman. Both had little round hats with a veil like mine.

Devon had asked me to brush some bronzing powder with glitter on to his broad shoulders and muscly arms. 'My widow needs to show the world she isn't afraid,' he had said, in a high, haughty voice. 'Remember–' he dropped his voice and whispered, 'what is your name?'

'Irene Insbruck,' I said, using one of Nancy Drew's aliases.

Devon resumed his character's voice, 'Mrs Emma Peel.' He held out his hand and I kissed it. His widow sounded like she was from England. 'Remember Ms Insbruck, stand tall and proud. Death won't lick us. Hold the urn and stay on course.'

The urn, which held the ashes of our imaginary dead pet, was a brown velvet tissue box cover, with a beige crochet trim that had belonged to Mrs Brown.

Devon completed our disguises by giving us all "smoky eye" makeup. I loved it. 'No one will recognise us now,' my uncle said, lowering his veil.

Now at *Barron's Funeral Home*, Uncle Pike was trying to dab his eyes through the veil while still wailing.

'There, there, Lady Douglas.' Devon stroked Uncle Pike's face with a satin glove he'd also found at the Browns. My uncle had named himself after Nancy Drew's great-grandmother in *The Clue of the Whistling Bagpipes*.

'Ladies right this way.' Tony Barron ushered us into a small waiting room. We were his only customers. 'Please take a seat. I am truly sorry for your loss.'

'Thank you, thank you,' Uncle Pike said.

'Pet funerals are not something we normally undertake.' Mr Barron paused to see if anyone was going to laugh at his pun. We didn't. 'Anyway, in this case since Twinkle Berry–' He looked respectfully at the tissue box.

Devon cleared his throat. 'Is this a joke? It was Captain Sparkles. Tulip Berry was his nickname.'

Uncle Pike rolled his eyes and let out a shriek of grief.

'I couldn't possibly imagine,' Devon said, sniffing.

'Of course,' Mr Barron said, softly. 'We'd be honoured to host Captain Sparkles' funeral here.'

Uncle Pike grabbed Mr Barron's hands and pulled them close to his chest. 'Oh thank you, Mr Barron, thank you!' He blinked his tears away.

'Please, call me Tony.' He smiled, trying to get his hands loose. His white fingers were really long.

'My assistant requires your ablution facilities,' Devon said.

I stood up.

Tony pointed me to the room next door. 'Just out there. You can't miss it, ah Miss?'

'Insbruck,' I said. 'Irene Insbruck.'

'Tell us about your service?' my uncle asked in a soft, hushed voice.

As soon as I was through the door I hunted for his office. It didn't take long to find. I could still hear them talking, though it was muffled. I snuck in. His desk was a mess, covered with bills, a racing guide, bank and credit card statements. I flattened them out and snapped pictures with my phone. He was overdrawn in all the accounts, with regular large deposits then larger withdrawals. At the bottom of the pile, I found a letter from a debt collector and took a picture of that too. I shoved it back to the bottom of the pile when the door opened.

'What are you doing?' Mr Barron said, blocking the door.

'Looking for the toilet,' I said, half turning and shoving the camera back in the urn, hoping he hadn't seen it.

'I don't believe you.'

'How rude.' I went to walk past him, but he didn't move.

'I said, what are you doing in my office?'

'There you are!' Devon said. 'Excuse me darling.' He bowled Tony into the wall, allowing me room to run past. 'Oh, I'm so sorry,' he said. 'Are you okay?'

I found Uncle Pike. 'We need to go. Now,' I hissed.

Back at home as we wiped off our eye makeup in the bathroom, Uncle Pike scrolled through the photos on my phone.

'Looks like Tony is in the toilet,' he said.

'What?' I said.

'Barron's Funeral Home is broke.'

Mrs Gallant's service was held in the chapel at Barron's Funeral Home. Tony Barron greeted people at the door, dressed in a blue suit. 'Well, if it isn't the Captain Sparkles family.'

'Hello darling,' Uncle Pike offered Tony his hand to kiss. 'I almost didn't recognise you without my make up on.'

Devon pretended to be on his soap phone and nodded at Tony as he walked past him inside.

'Please excuse her, fax machine problems.' Uncle Pike tapped his nose.

I put my arm around NaiNai and helped her up the stairs.

'Mrs Chan,' Tony Barron said. Grandma bristled beside me. He gave her a wide fake smile. 'Lovely to see you outside of River View.' His lip curled slightly at me. 'Did you find what you were looking for?'

'Not yet.' I held on to NaiNai tight.

She quoted a Chinese proverb in Mandarin about bad people anywhere will still be bad, human nature never changes.

'What did she say?' he asked.

'Crows everywhere are equally black,' I said.

Mr Barron nodded. 'Such a wise woman, and how fitting for a funeral. Please excuse me.' He moved on to the people behind us.

The service was short and towards the end people got up to pay their respects to Mrs Gallant in her coffin. NaiNai lined up and I stood beside her. When it was her turn, she bowed several times. I put my arm around her then led her back to her seat.

Afterwards Mrs Gallant's daughter came over to her. 'Hello Mrs Chan, thank you for coming. Mum always mentioned how much she enjoyed your company.'

Grandma bowed, and said she was very sorry, that Mrs Gallant was her friend.

'Thank you,' Mrs Gallant's daughter said. 'It's not what we would've chosen but Mum had already paid for everything.'

'That was very organised,' my uncle said.

'Mr Barron has been wonderful, such a help for her in her last month.'

'How do you mean?' he said.

'Regularly visited Mum. Apparently, he helps the folk there plan their funerals. His rates seem high, but it provides them peace of mind.' She clutched her order of service. 'Listen to me, I sound like an advert. Please excuse me.' She left to talk to another guest.

'Sounds like a vulture to me,' Uncle Pike said.

'Or a hyena.' I watched Mr Barron laughing by the door. 'NaiNai, how often is he at *River View?*'

Grandma lifted two fingers. 'Wednesday and Saturday,' she said in Mandarin.

'Does he have a relative there he visits?' I asked.

Grandma shook her head. 'He comes to the dining room when we're having dinner.' She made a sign to ward off evil. 'Too many are dying. My friends–' She pulled out a tissue and lifted her glasses, wiping her eyes.

I put my arm around her. Poor NaiNai. I couldn't imagine my friends dying around me, nearly losing Todd and Sam had been horrible enough.

'Something bad is happening,' I said to Uncle Pike and Devon. 'Lots of her friends have died recently.' I rubbed her arm. 'Mr Barron's there twice a week, in the dining room during dinner. That's weird right?'

'Or just fucking rude.' Uncle Pike turned to NaiNai. 'I'm so sorry, we will get to the bottom of this. Is Barron with anyone else? The owner or a particular nurse?'

NaiNai shook her head. She told me he had visited Mrs Pufferson on Saturday night and again this Wednesday.

'Mrs Pufferson could be next,' I said.

'That receptionist, Raelene, must know something,' my uncle said. 'This whole service feels like the funeral version of a show home.'

Tony Barron caught my eye. He twirled his keys around his finger and gave me a creepy smile. NaiNai noticed and told me it was time to leave. We headed to the door where Mr Barron was farewelling people and handing out business cards.

'We meet again darling.' Uncle Pike took a business card and put his hand over Mr Barron's and leaned in. 'I think we have a connection.' My uncle giggled.

Mr Barron's smile got wider as he tried to pull away.

'Tony!' Devon slapped Mr Barron hard on the arm. 'Get your hands off my kitten.' He turned to me. 'Gotta watch this one.'

Uncle Pike fanned himself with his hand. 'Swoon.'

Mr Barron's eyebrows scrunched together and he rubbed his forehead. 'Thanks for coming?'

Uncle Pike bit his lower lip and wrinkled his nose. 'Laters baby.'

We stepped outside into the bright sun, it felt good to be free of the funeral home.

'What do you think?' Uncle Pike said.

'I think you can go bigger,' Devon said. 'I felt you were holding back.'

'Maybe tongue next time?'

'Perfect, speaking of.' They started to make out on the footpath.

'Awkward,' I said.

NaiNai smiled and sat on a neighbouring concrete block fence. She closed her eyes and tilted her face to the sun. I sat beside her and held her hand. Her skin felt so papery, I leaned into her. I didn't want her to die.

With my other hand I scrolled on my phone the pictures from Mr Barron's office. I stopped when I saw a familiar name on a deposit on his bank statement. I enlarged it – Gallant. I scrolled down and saw Pufferson. I gently let go of NaiNai's hand and sat up. All the large deposit amounts had names. A chill ran through me despite the sun. 'NaiNai?'

She opened her eyes and I showed her and ran all the names past her. All of them were residents at *River View*. My scalp prickled. I waved over Uncle Pike and Devon. The Nancys needed to go undercover, again. And this time we would need Raelene's help.

IV

Saturday dinner at *River View* was pretty bland and NaiNai, in her newly designed crisp white tailored pantsuit, was not impressed. I sat beside her at her table with Raelene and another resident and watched as she stabbed at a carrot stick that kept evading her fork. Around us in the dining room old people, in groups of four, crouched over their meals, their grey and beige clothes blending with the walls and carpet. Tonight, however, there was an exception. In the middle of the dreary vanilla-sea, sat an old woman on her own, in a fluoro-rainbow kaftan, her hot-pink hat the size of the table.

She rapped the table with her heavily jewelled hand. 'Waiter!'

Raelene sighed and pushed herself up, shaking her head as she walked over to the woman's table.

The large pink hat tilted in her direction. 'Are you trying to kill me?' Her voice silenced the room.

Raelene gave the woman a sour look and folded her arms. 'Now, Mrs Locklear, what seems to be the problem?'

'Mr Tony,' she said. 'My dear!'

'I'm not Mr Barron,' Raelene said.

'Nonsense.' She waved her big jewelled sparkly hand. 'You must call me Heather, I insist. Now listen here, Mr Tony here is trying to kill me.'

'What?' Raelene said.

All except the deaf had stopped eating dinner, heads and glasses turned to the show in the middle. A nurse entered, pushing a stainless-steel trolley. A glamazon, with bright red lips and big blonde curls, wearing more makeup than the entire room. Her uniform was a short white PVC dress that strained to cover enormous boobies and just covered her butt, showing off her long muscly legs which ended in shiny red stilettos. She waved to the residents. 'Nothing to see here, I'm Mrs Locklear's private nurse.'

Mrs Locklear appeared not to notice. 'At first,' she said, 'I thought Mrs Gallant died in her sleep, and why not just keep signing people up for pre-paid funerals? Why kill them? But then your balance sheet, Tony. Most residents had already paid up with you, so why would you keep visiting them?' Mrs Locklear said, pointing her thumb at Raelene. 'All confirmed by Nurse Rachet.'

Raelene stamped her foot. 'Stop calling me Ratchet!'

'I'm talking to Tony, dear!' Mrs Locklear's head and hat lifted, revealing Uncle Pike, his silver beard caked in foundation. 'Ugh! My reveal is ruined.' He glanced around the room. 'Where is Tony?'

'On his way,' Raelene snapped. My uncle rolled his eyes and fanned himself with his giant hat. There were gasps and muttering with the tinkling of cutlery on crockery as tea-cup discussions began.

Nurse Devon moved in front of Uncle Pike and nervously hopped from heel to heel in front of him. 'Well?'

'Even with the literal palate of pink and rainbow, Devon, the construction is superb. I felt like both versions of Rose from *Titanic*, except cute and without the smell of paint.'

Raelene pursed her lips.

'And the styling?' Devon asked, suddenly still.

Uncle Pike's expression remained stern. 'You made me wear clogs!'

Devon frowned and bit down on a large red fingernail.

My uncle lifted his leg, swivelling a heavy wooden clogged in a figure eight. 'Love! It tied in with the heaviness of the necklace and the rings and made it a cohesive piece. Brava!'

'Yay!' Devon jumped up and down, his big balloon-breasts not moving.

'She's a man!' A grumpy leather faced man said.

'Quite.' Uncle Pike stood and frisbeed his hat across the room. It sailed in the air before hitting Mrs Pufferson in the eye.

Nurse Devon wrapped himself around Uncle Pike, like he was a pole. 'Honey she's all man, if you know what I mean.' He gave a little yelp then leaned back, whipping his long blond hair from side to side. 'Whee!'

Tony Barron ran into the dining room. 'I got a message–' His mouth dropped open and eyebrows shot up as he took in Uncle Pike and Devon.

'Ah, Tony, a little late,' my uncle said. 'I just used most of my lines with Ratchet.'

Raelene growled, balling her hands into fists. 'I'm calling the police.'

Uncle Pike continued, 'As you can see Mrs Pufferson is very much alive and–'

Mrs Pufferson was slumped over her table, her neighbour on the seat beside her prodded her. She suddenly sat up. I let out a relieved breath.

Tony Barron's eyebrows scrunched together.

Devon waggled a long red fingernail. 'Very bad.'

Uncle Pike patted his hat hair. 'When you took over from your father you had the brilliant idea of signing people up for prepaid funerals. It would've been very profitable, except for one thing.'

'Gambling,' I said, standing up. 'As your gambling debts increased you needed more cash, which was when you began the hard sell, coming here every Wednesday and Saturday.'

Mr Barron snorted. 'I'm an undertaker, death is my business. Prepaid means one thing less for them to worry about.'

'Except you needed more and more customers.' Uncle Pike said. 'So this became your hunting ground.'

Tony Barron gave a high-pitched laugh. 'What?'

Uncle Pike continued, 'You had run out of pre-paid resident-customers. You needed new blood to replace the old at *River View*. Those who wouldn't sign you could always try to convince their families when they were dead.'

Mr Barron crossed his arms like a bat, touching his shoulders. Sam and I were on to something with our vampire theory.

'Mrs Gallant didn't die in her sleep,' I said, moving towards Nurse Devon's stainless-steel trolley.

He turned on me. 'Of course she did.'

I raised my eyebrows. 'Not according to the autopsy report.' I picked up a Manila folder from on top of the trolley and waved it at him. 'It says here she was poisoned.'

Mr Barron froze as gasps escaped from around the room.

I slapped the folder down as hard as I could on the table, hoping it was dramatic. 'That's why you always came at dinner time. To slip the poison into their food.'

Mr Barron licked his lips and squinted. 'I don't know what you are talking about. What autopsy?'

Devon strummed his long red nails on the stainless steel. 'Exhumation.' He turned to Uncle Pike and stage whispered, 'Did I say that right?'

Mr Barron's eyes widened, and he backed away. 'This is crazy.' He looked at Raelene. 'Come on, you know me, this is nuts.'

'Oh my God,' Devon said, adjusting his boobies. 'Who even says nuts?'

'A murderer that's who,' Uncle Pike said.

'How many did you kill?' I asked. 'You know you're a serial killer, right?'

'This is crazy.' Tony laughed. 'The autopsy doesn't say that.'

Devon flicked his blonde hair behind his shoulders. 'Russell Campbell can't help you now.'

'What?' Tony glanced over at the door, moving away.

'Remember, Mr Campbell was arrested last year? There's been a different coroner for a while now.'

'It wasn't my idea,' Tony said, his top lip all sweaty. 'Anyway, it's painless.'

NaiNai moved, blocking his path. 'You killed my friends.' She spat on him.

Mr Barron's expression suddenly changed, his eyes narrowed, and lips pulled back. He raised his fist. I launched myself at him, grabbing his hand. He spun around, throwing me to the floor. I braced myself, covering my head for the blow when out of the corner of my eye came a streaky blur.

Barry, the policeman, rugby tackled Mr Barron. They slammed to the floor, Barry on top of Mr Barron, squashing the air out of him. The residents started clapping and we started whooping. Barry's face flushed as he pushed Mr Barron down as he cuffed him.

'Love you Barry,' Devon and Uncle Pike called out as he dragged a shouting Mr Barron to his feet and out of the room.

Raelene came over to me. 'How did you get an autopsy report?'

'It was a bluff,' I said. Devon applauded me with his palms, careful not to hurt his fake nails.

'Great plan, Tippy Chan,' Uncle Pike said. He turned to NaiNai. 'And you speak English?'

'Of course, you noisy stocking stuffer.'

'Nancys group hug.' Devon pulled in NaiNai and Uncle Pike, who were like two repellent magnets. I ducked under Devon's arm and scrunched in, snaking my arms around them all. Devon squeezed us until his left balloon-breast popped.

'Ow!' I said, laughing, as it burst in my ear.

Nancys undercover, case solved.

THE LOST MURRAY WHELAN

SHANE MALONEY

She lay sprawled in the red dust, her wrists tied behind her with baling twine. Tears, sweat, and snot smeared her face. Her light cotton dress was torn and dirty, runched up around her bare thighs. Her fingernails were broken and bloody. A faint breeze had sprung up, coating her lips and hair with powdery grit. Her eyes were wide with terror.

At first she had screamed, loud and hard. But her cries were futile, swallowed by the vast emptiness of the surrounding desert. Nobody was coming to help her. Nobody even knew she was here. She was alone and utterly defenceless. A length of greasy rope was knotted around her ankles, tethering them to the lowered hook of a battered, rusting tow truck. Her mouth opened and closed but no sound emerged.

With a loud clunk, the truck's winch engaged. Slowly the drum began to turn. The cable tensed and the hook began to rise. Slowly, torturously, the young woman was dragged upward until she hung, inverted, in mid-air. The tips of her hair brushed the ground and her skirt hung downward over her torso, exposing her soiled white underpants.

He liked that, the underpants. He savoured the sight. It excited and aroused him. He ran his tongue over his bottom lip.

She spoke. It was just a whisper. 'No. Bitte.'

He was wearing a sleeveless blue singlet, work-worn Levis and a sweat-stained Texas straw. Fresh scratches ran down one of his cheeks. In one hand, he held an axe. He stepped closer, squared his stance and took a two-handed grip. A savage glee lit is eyes.

The young woman's eyes widened.

He swung the axe. The blade rose, paused for a moment at the top of its trajectory, then fell.

'Cut!' called the director. 'Fine, nice, lovely.'

A fortyish guy in an oversize Hawaiian shirt and pith helmet, he was crouched beneath a beach umbrella, hunkered around the VA monitor with the first AD and the assistant DOP.

I knew that because I'd been watching them work for most of the afternoon, so I was beginning to get an idea of who was who and what they did. I'd worked out, for example, that everybody thought the director was an idiot, but they were letting him think he was running the show. The makeup artist was cold-shouldering the boom guy. The actress playing the victim was a German soapie star and a great little screamer. The male lead, a face I recognised from a television series, *Cops on Boats* or *Doctors on Heat* or something, had tabs on himself and a problem remembering his lines, none of which were longer than five words.

As distinct from my son Redmond, who was prepared, professional, and didn't mug for the camera.

Red was the cowboy with the axe, the supporting male lead, the serial killer's psychotic yokel apprentice. When the director called cut, he'd immediately dropped the axe and grabbed the upside-down girl's knees in a bear-hug, taking her weight while a crew member lowered her onto a crash mat. They'd done this four times already, making a slapstick routine of it, lots of laughter and oops-a-daisies.

I gave him a thumbs up and he ambled over to where I was sitting in the shade of the wardrobe van, picking his way through electrical cables and road cases.

Dingo Run was the name of the movie. A backpacker-slasher, it was being shot at Bookaloo, a fly-speck whistle-stop on the Indian-Pacific railway just west of the Stuart Highway, an hour north of Port Augusta.

The train featured in the plot, apparently, but it didn't run on Mondays, leaving the day free for the slash-and-spatter sequences.

It was Red's first feature, his first film role at all, in fact, since graduating from NIDA two years earlier. He was making a decent fist of it, too, or so it seemed to me. A considered blend of ice and ham. Redmond Whelan, the next Heath Leger.

He could have made worse career choices, I thought, as he swished the flies from his face and squatted beside me, his bare arms flecked with fake blood. At least he wasn't a hedge-fund manager or a real estate agent.

'The clammy close-up,' he said, and chugged at a bottle of water. 'An art form in itself.'

'You make a disturbingly convincing nutcase,' I said. 'Must be your mother's genes.'

He let that one go through to the keeper, screwed the cap back on his water bottle, and heaved a weary sigh. 'At this rate, it'll be another two hours before we finish.'

His gaze drifted back to the tow truck where his on-screen victim was perched on the tray, having her disarray freshened. 'You must be bored out of your brain. You don't have to wait, if you don't want to. I can always go back in the minivan with the others.'

Red lived in Sydney and it was three months since I'd last seen him. Knowing I would be in South Australia over the Easter break, I'd wangled an invitation out of him to visit the set, a rare opportunity to watch him at work. It was the last day of shooting at Bookaloo and I'd driven up from Adelaide in a rented Landcruiser, hoping I'd manage to find the turn-off. The plan was for Red to ride with me back to Adelaide, spend the night with friends, fellow artistes of some sort, then fly to Sydney the next day. It was anyone's guess when I'd next get a chance to spend time with him and I wasn't about to make myself scarce just because he suddenly fancied a slice of strudel.

I leaned back against the side of the van and dug my heels into the dirt. 'Trying to get rid of me?'

'Been trying for years,' said Red. 'Nothing seems to work.'

Strudel and Boat Cop were moving back into position. Continuity, a young woman in khaki shorts and hiking boots with an electronic gizmo on a cord around her neck, waved to Red with an upraised clipboard. The director looked around as if he'd lost something. The plot, I assumed.

'Back to work,' I said. 'Chop, chop.'

Again, Red curled his lip and brandished his axe. Again, Lorelei blubbered for mercy. Again, boat cop muffed his lines. Again, a pause was called while equipment was moved or tweaked, make-up applied, instructions issued, suggestions tendered.

Red wasn't wrong about the shoot being boring. A cluster of caravans, trucks, and temporary awnings centred on a concrete railway platform beside empty tracks in the middle of nowhere. A dozen people buggerising with equipment, gossiping and talking tech-speak with each other between spasmodic bursts of activity. After five hours, it was as interesting as watching paint dry or being a member of the Fabian Society.

Still, they were a welcoming lot and didn't seem to mind a middle-aged man in Country Road casuals wandering around, asking silly questions and trying his best not to get in the way.

I got up off the road case I was using for a seat, wandered over to the car and fiddled with the radio. The Lions were playing the Swans at the SCG, and I was hoping for the half-time score. Yet again I got nothing but static and the intermittent twang of contemporary country. At least there was a signal. Phone reception had gone missing not far north of Port Augusta.

The run from Adelaide had taken just over four hours. There was a steady stream of traffic, but it was all going the other way. Hundreds of activists were heading home after three days of massed solidarity with the inmates of the refugee detention centre at Woomera. Twice I passed police roadblocks, vehicles backed up, the cops checking loads. More than 40 detainees had breached the wire and absconded during the demonstration on Friday, some getting as far south as Port Augusta before being collared. Others were still at large. The Attorney General was threatening to prosecute anyone caught helping them.

The sky was clear and bright, an immense canopy of blue. I tugged down the brim of my cap and scanned the dismal panorama of dust, spinifex and mulga. The great Australian Outback. No better place on earth for homicidal maniacs, nuclear bomb tests, secret American satellite stations, and invisible prison camps.

Woomera was just over the northern horizon, an hour up the road. I'd considered driving up and taking a look, but it was easy to resist the temptation. I knew what these places were like. I'd seen inside Villawood and Altona. Woomera was the biggest and most notorious. Fourteen hundred men, women, and children locked behind razor wire while their fate was decided by an apparatus hostile to their very presence. In despair and frustration, they went on hunger strikes, drank shampoo, sewed their lips together.

Now that the election was over, the party had finally screwed up the courage to call for the joint to be closed down. But even as a futile gesture, it was a futile gesture. After all, we were the ones who'd invented mandatory detention. We were pissing into the wind and trying to wash our hands with the stream.

Rocking up to a demo against refugee detention would be certifiably crazy. If anyone recognised me, I'd be expected to justify Labor policy. The very idea was demoralising. Might the *Dingo Run* catering van run to a stubby of beer, I wondered? Bottled water was fine as far as it went, but mostly it went straight through me. I took a leak behind the car and drifted back to the action. I should have brought something to read.

Eventually, they were done. In a cloud of dust, the tow truck roared and clattered into the distance, tracked by a crane shot. A dummy bumped along behind, another victim of the deadly Outback. Everybody cheered and hooted. Cans of beer were peeled from six-packs and handed around. Equipment was dismantled, cables coiled, stuff packed into cases, trucks loaded.

Psycho Sidekick disappeared into the wardrobe truck and emerged, five minutes later, in cargo shorts, tee-shirt and baseball cap. He ran an acerbic eyeball over the Landcruiser. 'Told them you were going on safari, did you?'

The hire car mob had suckered me good with their off-road recommendations. Turned out I could've got to Bookaloo in a 1982 Camry.

'Kangaroos,' I explained. 'You've got to hit them with something big.'

Red threw his day pack onto the backseat and we headed down the perfectly serviceable road to the highway. 'From a place nobody lives,' he intoned, movie trailer style, 'Comes a story nobody will see.'

'I'm no expert,' I said, 'But I thought you looked great.'

'I'm sure they can fix that in post-production.'

It was almost five years since he'd left our two-man bachelor pad to study acting in Sydney. He'd stayed on, chasing work, an independent man.

'How are you going for money?' I said. 'Pay well, this job?'

'Deferred fee. Mum's been helping me out.'

Wendy and I had separated when Red was eight. A senior corporate head-kicker married to a Point Piper tax lawyer, she could afford to be helpful.

'Good,' I said. Bleed her dry, kid.

Not that I harboured any ill-will. It was simply a matter of equitability. Her other two children, begotten by the lawyer, rode gilded unicorns and supped with silver spoons. Eventually, they would be listed on the stock exchange.

'How's Lanie?' said Red.

Lanie was my squeeze, the woman with whom I had taken up in Red's final year at high school. After years of trying to pimp me out to the unattached mothers of his schoolmates, he'd been amazed and gratified to discover I was capable of pulling a bird without his help.

'Good. She said to say hello.'

A half-hour later, we were barrelling down the Stuart Highway, 20 over the limit. To our left, a line of power poles marked the course of the railway tracks. In the far distance, the worn-down nubs of ancient mountains were a vague smudge. At my right elbow, the sun was on its last legs, a ball of exhausted incandescence melting into the horizon.

Red sat slumped in the passenger seat beside me, rooted from the exertions of the day. Since leaving Bookaloo, he'd briefed me on his immediate work prospects, his accommodation arrangements and next gig, a month-long theatre project in a remote aboriginal community in the Kimberly.

'Shakespeare to the natives?' I said. 'A Midsummer's Night Dreaming?'

'Get fucked,' he said. 'It'll all be done in language. I'll have to learn to communicate in Unggarangi.'

'Unggarangi?'

'Unggarangi.'

'I thought it was all French in those parts.'

'Only for emails,' he said. 'Face-to-face it's strictly Unggarangi.'

'As long as there's no didgeridoo involved. Those things are a one-way ticket to busking in the mall. And anything involving sharp instruments and your genitals, steer away from it.'

'Somebody's going to hear you one day, dad,' he warned, reaching across to the dash and turning on the radio.

'See if you can rustle up the footy results,' I said.

The auto-search hit on a voice, intermittent through the background hiss of static: '… Immigration department… illegal…'

The signal faded, then returned: '…with a top temperature of…'

'Some of us went up there on Friday, had a look,' said Red. 'This country's fucked.'

'Tell me something I don't know.'

He was talking to a man who had spent his entire parliamentary career in opposition, first at state level, then federal. Pushing shit uphill was my profession. Up ahead, at the far end of a long, straight ribbon of asphalt, lights flickered. I eased back on the pedal, the distance dropped away and the flickering resolved itself into a police roadblock. Red craned forward in his seat.

A cop in a high-vis vest stepped onto the roadway and waved us onto the shoulder with a fluoro wand. I steered onto the gravel margin, followed a row of witches hats and joined the end of a line of stationary vehicles. The car in front was a Subaru hatchback with NSW plates and a *Free the Refugees* sticker on the rear bumper. The hatch was up and a pair of cops were checking the rear compartment, watched by a two middle-aged women in baggy cotton pants and trainers. One of them looked our way and gave a weary smile.

I lowered the window on a constable about Red's age. His gaze swept the car's interior. The air smelled of hot tar and petrol fumes.

'Problem, officer?' I said.

'Hope not, sir. Your licence, please.'

Northbound traffic zipped past, slowing slightly in the presence of the police. Two more southbound cars were swept into line behind us and the Subaru waved back onto the highway. Turnover was brisk, the cops not wasting time. The constable took my licence to a prowl car and fed my particulars into the radio.

A sergeant ambled over, a big bloke, ruddy faced, heading for retirement, belly straining against his belt.

'Come far?' he said amiably.

I shook my head. 'Bookaloo. They're shooting a film there.'

'*Dingo Run*,' the sergeant nodded. 'We gave them a hand a few days back, some vehicles and whatnot.' Tilting his head, he displayed his chinny profile. 'I'm still waiting for my cameo.' He shone a torch through the Landcruiser's rear window, checking the space behind the back seat. 'In the movie business, are you?'

'Nothing so glamorous, unfortunately. I'm a federal MP.' The Member for Coolaroo, to be precise. A multi-ethnic electorate in the northern suburbs of Melbourne. About as far from this god-forsaken wasteland as possible. 'Labor,' I added.

The sergeant raised a wry eyebrow.

'My son's the actor.' I jerked my thumb at the passenger seat. Red raised a hand, guilty as charged.

The last of the light was draining from the sky, stars beginning to appear. An emu eyed us from the other side of a wire fence.

'Many still at large?' I asked.

The sergeant shook his head. 'Some. Our main worry is the ones out there in the scrub, lying low. They won't survive long without water, food, or maps.'

'Poor bastards,' I said.

'Yep.'

A sudden flurry of activity drew the sergeant away. Further up the line, a man was being led from the campervan, a towel draped over his head, a cop at each elbow.

A horn honked, then another. Toot, toot, toot. A chorus of disapproval. Or endorsement. People emerged from their cars and stood watching. Offering no resistance, the prisoner was fed into the back of a divisional van.

'Pricks', hissed Red.

The divvy van executed a U-turn and headed south.

'Just doing their jobs,' I said. 'Your taxes at work.'

'What will they do to him?'

'They'll charge him with escaping from legal custody. And he's blown any chance he might ever have had of getting a visa.'

The constable returned and handed back my licence. 'Have a safe trip, Mr Whelan,' he said. 'The limit is 100, by the way.'

I steered back onto the highway, anticipating a resumption of our discussion on the fuckedness of the country, with specific reference to the fuckedness of refugee detention. But Red said nothing, and returned his attention to the search for an audible radio station. He'd never been one for the high horse, I reminded myself, and kept his acting-out for the stage.

Red found classical music station, a little fuzzy but tolerable. One of those iddly-tiddly, iddly-tiddly guys, Bach or somesuch. Good driving music. Red leaned back and closed his eyes. Bathed in the faint green glow of the dashboard display, we rode in companionable silence. Hands on the wheel, headlights on the broken white line, I bored a tunnel into the night. Twenty kilometres from Port Augusta, we entered the network footprint and our phones beeped. Red began thumbing his keyboard, scrolling texts. My Blackberry had a missed-call notification from Lanie.

Floodlit businesses began to appear beside the highway, farm machinery dealerships, building material suppliers. The rich material fabric of rural and regional Australia. We joined the Princes Highway, crossed the bridge over the estuary, the tail-tip of Spencer Gulf, moonlight on the ruffled water, and Red pointed out the low-slung chain motel behind a row of stumpy palm trees where the *Dingo Run* team had slept during the five days of the shoot at Bookaloo. I pulled into the Shell station next door and he went to collect his baggage.

While I stood at the bowser, pumping dollars into the Landcruiser, I returned Lanie's call. Her phone went to message bank and I reported that I'd be back in Adelaide in three hours. The smell of the sea hung in the air, mingled with the hot fat aroma of the roadhouse. Mindful of the need to keep alert during the drive ahead, I picked up some hydrolysed vegetable protein and carbonated fructose when I went inside to pay.

Red was waiting beside the open driver's door. He offered to do the rest of the driving. Problematic insurance issues, I pointed out. He wasn't a specified driver. He was under 25. If he hit a hit a kangaroo, the excess would be astronomical.

'Dead 'roos tell no tales,' he said. 'I've never driven one of these. Garn, be a sport.'

His logic was unimpeachable. He rummaged a couple of CDs out of the bulging sports bag he'd tossed onto the back seat, fed a disc into the player, rappy but tolerable, and kept a steady 5k under the limit.

'Handles well', he said, the motoring expert.

Ten minutes out of town, we passed a rest stop. Red bounced the ball of his hand on the steering wheel, three short horn blasts, then slowed to a halt beside a turn-off sign to somewhere called Wilmington.

'What's wrong?' I said.

A figure in jeans and a hooded sweater darted from the low scrub beside the sign. The left rear door flew open. A figure jumped into the back seat and slammed the door shut. Red floored the pedal and car shot forward.

I swivelled in my seat and found myself facing a stocky man in his 30s with sallow olive skin, receding black hair and thick eyebrows. A man of Middle Eastern appearance. '

Hello, thank you,' he said, buckling his seat belt. 'Pleased to meet you. Adelaide, yes?'

There was lettering on the front of his top.

FCUK, it said.

MR PIG

STEPHEN ROSS

Mrs Brown had been gone for a week, and Mr Brown was grumpy. And he couldn't cook. He sat at the table with narrow eyes. He stared at his plate of cold beans like it was some kind of mathematics problem my teacher would set in school. Mr Brown didn't care much for sums, least of all subtraction.

One week times seven days equals minus seven.

'Mercy, pass me the bread,' Mr Brown said.

I passed him the loaf of bread that sat at the end of the table. He stood the loaf alongside his plate of beans and did nothing. He had something new to stare at. I suppose, any day now, he'd ask me to do the cooking. I hoped he wouldn't. Mrs Brown had never taught me how.

I was 13. I had three dresses (counting Sunday best), two pairs of shoes, a half drawer of under things, and three handkerchiefs. I owned three books; and I used to have a doll, Miss Prudence, but she lay at the bottom of the old well.

Our farm was forty acres of hills and scrub that backed onto the Kaipara River. It was a 30-minute walk into Helensville, our nearest town; it took three minutes if Mr Brown drove his Ford. My schoolroom was in town, and Mr Brown never drove me. He had important things to do on the farm.

Mr Brown slammed his fist down on the table.

He had his mouth shut tight; he almost had no top lip. His face was a coil of creases.

One day, the man would explode.

Miss Prudence had no eyes, and I missed talking to her. She had been my friend, but there was no way I could climb down and get her out of the old well.

Mr Brown stood up.

He inhaled.

Mr Brown's eyes were blue. His hair was black, and he hadn't combed it for a week. He hadn't shaved, either. He wore a singlet, brown trousers, and his black work socks. He went over to the door and put his boots back on. He went outside into the yard at the rear of the house and left the door open. It was the dead of summer; it was good to leave doors and windows open in the slow heat.

I watched Mr Brown through the window.

He picked up his axe from the woodpile and took it into the shed.

The late afternoon sky above the shed was perfectly blue. We hadn't had rain for over a week. Not since Mrs Brown had left. According to what Mr Brown had told Constable Wood, Mrs Brown had gone down to Auckland to see a doctor about her eyes, and she never came back.

I left Mr Brown's dinner on the table. I washed my plate and cutlery in the sink and then dried them with the kitchen towel.

There was a photograph of Mr and Mrs Brown hung on the wall. Black and white. Oval. They were younger. She was sitting; he was standing. She had a head of bird's nest hair and dark eyes. He looked grumpy. His eyes were narrow, and his mouth shut tight.

I could hear a slow slurping sound from the shed – the scraping of a file on a blade. Mr Brown was sharpening his axe.

Mr Brown wanted to kill people, and he was very angry he wasn't allowed to. He had taken the Ford five times down into Auckland to visit the army recruitment office. Five times they had turned him down. I never heard why. Mr and Mrs Brown often had conversations I hadn't been allowed to listen to. They'd send me to my room and talk in quiet voices so I couldn't hear.

I could hear the hens; they were starting to make a fuss. The hen house and run stood next to the shed. They could hear the sharpening as well. I went to my room, lay on my bed, and read Mr Wordsworth. The slow slurping of hard file on blade continued into the night.

I wandered, lonely as a cloud

There was a single cloud in the sky – a puff of white floating on a perfect sea of blue. I lay on my back in the river and stared up at it. I wasn't supposed to swim in the river, but no one was around to tell me not to.

If Mr Wordsworth had been here sitting on the riverbank, I could have asked him why a cloud drifting alone was supposed to be lonely. It looked perfectly content to me. But I think Mr Wordsworth was dead. I think he wrote his poems a long time ago, so he wouldn't be talking much.

And I suppose I shouldn't talk to the dead, either.

I wasn't supposed to talk to Miss Prudence. According to Mrs Brown, talking like that led to the devil, and I wouldn't want to talk to him.

I drifted in the river.

So did the cloud in the sky.

Silence.

A perfect Sunday afternoon.

Pleasure.

Bliss.

And then the cloud separated into two and wasn't lonely anymore.

I swam back to the riverbank and climbed out.

I dried myself with my towel and put my clothes back on.

I made my way back along the dirt trail that led from the river and cut through the farm to the house.

I thought about Miss Prudence and how I missed her. I tried not to think about Mrs Brown dragging me along that same trail. Her hand gripping my wrist. Hurting. Her voice angry. Yelling. Her other hand gripping Miss Prudence's neck.

I wasn't supposed to talk to Miss Prudence.

Mrs Brown had dragged us both to the old well at the back of the farm, and she had thrown Miss Prudence in. She said, if she caught me again talking to things that weren't meant to talk, she'd throw me in, too.

She was always threatening that.

I didn't want to live at the bottom of the well.

I was glad she never came back.

A cow watched me with its big eyes. Its jaw chewed. Side to side.

I kept walking.

I thought of Reverend Salt. An ugly old man staring down from his pulpit with one eye half shut and his dentures slipping about in his mouth.

I didn't talk to cows. I tried once, but they didn't listen.

As I walked along the top of the hill, I saw Mr Brown's red Ford moving along the road in the distance, a cloud of dust swirling up behind it. I began to hear the truck's tyres on the gravel.

The truck slowed and turned into the drive that led up to the house.

I walked down the hill.

The truck was in the yard at the rear of the house. Mr Brown was backing it up to the empty pigsty alongside the hen house.

There was a pig on the truck's back tray. It had a rope around its neck so it wouldn't jump over the side.

Mr Brown parked the truck and climbed out.

He climbed up onto the tray and went down to the end. He unlatched the tray door and let it drop open.

He then untied the pig and booted it along the tray to the rear. The pig then had no option but to jump down into the pigsty. It landed hard in the dry dirt, got back onto its feet, and shook itself.

I walked up and stared at it through the wooden fence.

'Why have you got a towel?' Mr Brown asked, climbing down off the truck.

'I swam in the river.'

'Your mother told you not to do that.'

The pig trotted about making pig noises. The pigsty was 10 feet wide and 20 feet long. A corrugated iron roof covered the far end of it. There was a long wooden food trough behind the fence where I stood. Next to it stood a circular concrete trough full of water.

The pig noticed me watching.

He came over and poked his large pink snout through the fence. The mouth and two nostrils at the end of it looked like a cheerful round face.

Mr Brown turned on the hose and sprayed the pigsty with water. The dry dirt of its floor quickly became mud.

The pig was pleased about this. He wandered about in the mud and got very dirty.

'Does he have a name?' I asked.

Mr Brown shook his head. 'No. It's a pig.'

7 + 18 + 9 - (6 x 3) =

Mrs Wilson wrote a long sum on the blackboard. Two additions, one subtraction, and a times. I wrote down the answer in my exercise book. 16. The others pencilled the equation in their notebooks.

After a minute of silence, Mrs Wilson called for hands.

I sat in the back row. I'd been made to sit there. I had answered too many questions and had been called a 'show off' by the others. I no longer put up my hand.

I didn't like the others. I wasn't friends with any of them. I had been friends with Rosemary, but she had gone down to Wellington when her father got a job with the railways. I used to talk to Rosemary. Rosemary had made me laugh.

Mrs Wilson picked Andrea's hand.

Andrea gave her answer.

Wrong.

Mrs Wilson was old and smelled of dough. Her skin was pale and rubbery like she had yet to be baked, and her spectacles were smudged. She wore a cross around her neck as big as my hand. Another cross hung on the wall, to the right of the blackboard. There was a bible on her desk, and no one was supposed to touch it.

Mrs Wilson picked Jason's hand. Jason had a finger missing.

Wrong.

The girl sitting in front of me turned around and put a piece of paper on my desk. It was a pencil drawing. The girls sitting on either side of her giggled.

The drawing was of a stick figure woman with a head of bird's nest hair. Another stick figure wearing boots was strangling her. A cow stood nearby watching.

Two other girls in another row started giggling. The one with the freckled face like a starry night turned and looked at me.

I stared at her.

She poked out her tongue.

It is a beauteous evening, calm and free

'You will cook the dinners from now on,' Mr Brown said.

'I don't know how to cook,' I answered.

'You're a girl.' He said nothing else.

We sat at the table. In front of us stood plates of stew. I don't know what the stew was supposed to taste like, but it smelled like something in a paddock.

'I can make sandwiches,' I said.

'We can't eat sandwiches for dinner.'

I broke off a piece of bread from the loaf and ate it.

Mr Brown dragged his leather tobacco pouch across the table towards him. He opened it and took out a little slip of white papers. He plucked out a single paper, curled it, and held it in his right hand. His left reached back into the pouch and pulled out a pinch of tobacco.

He rolled himself a cigarette.

I studied his hands.

Mr Brown had big hands and long fingers. They were dark from farm work. There were cuts. The fingernails were dirty.

The hens made a fuss.

Through the open door, I saw the faded navy-blue tunic of a police uniform. It was Constable Wood. He was climbing off his bicycle. He wore that silly police helmet on his big red head; it looked like a blue acorn sitting on top of a tomato.

He leaned his bicycle against the pigsty and walked over to the house. The silver buttons of his uniform shone in the late afternoon sun. 'Can I come in?' he called out.

'Yeah,' Mr Brown answered.

Constable Wood took off his helmet and walked into the kitchen. He took a seat at the table and placed his helmet on the floor.

The two men didn't look at each other.

Constable Wood was fat and had a large red nose. There was an old scar on his cheek.

'Pour the man some coffee,' Mr Brown said to me, lighting his cigarette with a match.

The coffee pot simmered on the range. I poured the policeman a cup. I took it and placed it on the table in front of him.

'Thank you, Mercy,' Constable Wood said.

I sat down again.

The two men sat in silence and stared at their coffee cups. Mr Brown smoked.

After a long time, Constable Wood said, 'I hear our lads are giving Rommel hell.'

'Fucking Hitler,' Mr Brown growled.

Constable Wood nodded his agreement.

Silence.

The policeman took a sip of his coffee. 'I spoke to Auckland today on the telephone. They located the doctor where Victoria had an appointment.'

Mr Brown nodded.

'She didn't turn up.'

Mr Brown nodded.

'If Victoria took the bus down to the city last Monday, as you said—'

'That's what she said.'

'Then no one knows where she went after she got there.'

'She said she was going to get her eyes tested. She said she thought she needed reading spectacles. She said she was taking the bus down to Auckland in the morning.'

'And did she?'

Mr Brown shook his head. 'I wasn't here when she left. I went over to Silverdale to get my truck's spark plugs replaced. I left before daybreak. She wasn't here when I came back.' He looked at Constable Wood. 'What about the bus driver? Where did he drop her off?'

'Chester doesn't remember her getting on.'

'That old coot; he's as dumb as a fencepost.' Mr Brown rubbed his jaw. His fingers bristled on his whiskers.

After a moment, Constable Wood asked, 'What time did you come back?'

'Back from where?'

'Silverdale.'

'Around one o'clock. I had a couple of beers with a mate.'

'If I look under your truck's bonnet, am I going to find new spark plugs?'

The two men stared at each other.

For a long time.

And then back at their coffee cups.

Mr Brown smoked.

The policeman studied Mr Brown's hands; one held his cigarette, the other rested on the table in a tight fist.

Constable Wood drank some more of his coffee. He glanced at the oval photograph on the wall. 'My sister-in-law ran away to Australia,' he remarked. 'Just before the war started. A flash fella from Sydney, over here on business. Gold tie pin, shiny shoes, and an expensive hat.'

Mr Brown's fist tightened. The knuckles were white.

Constable Wood stared at Mr Brown's face.

'My brother took it hard,' he said. 'He did some foolish things.'

The air sat silent.

Constable Wood drank the last mouthful of his coffee. 'Best get home before the daylight burns out.'

Mr Brown said nothing.

Constable Wood reached down and picked up his helmet. He stood up, nodded goodbye to me, and went back outside. He climbed back onto his bicycle and rode away.

The hens made a fuss, and then quietened.

Mr Brown got up from the table. 'Clean the dishes and tidy up.' He stubbed out the remains of his cigarette and went into the sitting room. I expected to hear the gramophone.

I scraped the stew from our two plates into a bucket. I tossed in the apple core that sat by the sink and a piece of bread I broke off the loaf.

I took the bucket outside and across to the pigsty.

I climbed up onto the fence, sat on top, and poured the bucket into the food trough below.

Mister Pig wandered over to investigate.

He seemed happy to see me, and he began to eat the slops.

'I have to learn how to cook,' I told him. 'I will make you some proper food when I can.'

Mister Pig nodded. He went back to eating.

I looked up at the sky and smelled the air. It was a beautiful twilight; breathless tranquillity. One of those summer twilights when everything felt right and in order. I remembered the poem I had read the night before, and I recited it to Mister Pig, as much of it as I could remember.

Mister Pig drank from the water trough and then looked up at me. He listened as I recited.

Mister Pig was cheerful, calm, and free. He had no worries. No mother or father. No belongings. He had nothing but himself. He was content.

'My name is Mercy,' I said. 'I don't have any friends. Rosemary used to be my friend, but she's gone now. Miss Prudence used to be my friend, but she's gone, too. Do you have any friends, Mister Pig?'

Mister Pig shook his head.

'Mercy!' Mr Brown yelled from the doorway. 'I told you to clean the dishes and tidy up, not talk to the damn pig.'

'I'm keeping Mister Pig company.'

'He's a pig. He's not a mister. He's not anything. Stop talking to him and come back inside.'

I climbed down off the fence and took the empty bucket back into the house.

Mr Brown was sitting back at the table. He'd eaten the rest of the bread loaf. Crumbs littered the table. A bottle of beer was open. Another two bottles were waiting.

I ran hot water and washed our dinner plates and knives and forks in the sink.

Mr Brown watched me.

'I wanted a boy,' he said. It wasn't the first time he'd said that. 'What I got was another one of your damn mother.'

He often said things like that to me when Mrs Brown wasn't around.

He finished the bottle.

I left the plates and cutlery to dry. I wiped up the crumbs of bread from the table with a cloth.

Mr Brown stood up and went outside.

I shook out the cloth into the bucket and hung it back on its hook. Then, through the window, I saw Mr Brown raise the Ford's bonnet. He stared inside at the engine.

I looked at the beer bottles on the table.

I went to my room and locked the door. It was best to lock the door when Mr Brown had his beer out.

I lay on my bed and returned to Mr Wordsworth.

Life is just a bowl of cherries

I was happily reading when the gramophone in the sitting room started up. It was loud and scratchy. Mr Brown only liked one tune, and he played it, and he kept playing it, over and over, until the dark of night-time came.

After two hours, the music stopped.

Silence.

Shortly, I became aware of a faint sound. I didn't know what it was; I'd never heard it before.

I closed Mr Wordsworth.

I unlocked my door and stepped out into the hallway. The sound came from Mr and Mrs Brown's room down at the end.

I stepped quietly.

Mr Brown was sitting on the floor in front of Mrs Brown's glory box.

He was staring at it and sobbing.

Mrs Brown's glory box stood at the foot of the bed. It was wooden, five feet long, and tall enough to sit on like a bench. There was a padlock; I had never seen inside it.

I stepped back down the hallway.

Empty bottles lay on the sitting room floor.

There were empty bottles on the table in the kitchen.

I went outside into the moonlight and over to the pigsty. I climbed back up onto the fence.

Mister Pig was still awake; he came over to talk to me.

Pigs didn't cry. They didn't need that type of thing. Pigs stood steady on the ground on four feet.

I told Mister Pig about Mr Brown. He told me not to worry about him. I told Mister Pig about Mrs Brown. He told me not to worry about her.

'Mister Pig,' I said, 'I think you are my only friend.'

He nodded happily.

I made a solemn oath. After I had lost Rosemary and then Miss Prudence, I swore I would never lose another friend again.

MCMXLII

Mrs Wilson wrote a series of Roman numerals on the blackboard, and we had to work out what the number was in English. I knew it already. 1942.

The girl with the freckled face turned around and poked out her tongue at me.

I ignored her.

She turned back to face the blackboard.

Robert thought he knew the number; he never did. He put up his hand.

Mrs Wilson asked him.

Wrong.

Mrs Wilson looked out the window. There was the sound of a tractor outside passing in the street.

The girl with the freckles turned around again and poked out her tongue at me.

I threw my pencil at her face.

Her eyes widened like teacup saucers. She jerked her head, and the pencil missed her. It landed on the floor and clattered across it.

'Who threw that?' Mrs Wilson demanded.

'I did.'

Mrs Wilson sent me outside to sit in the corridor between the school's two classrooms. I left the room and closed the door.

I sat on one of the wooden benches. I stared across at the empty row of clothes pegs, where coats and scarves were hung in the winter. A cool breeze flowed through the corridor. The doors at both ends were wide open.

I thought about Mister Pig. Did pigs wear clothes in winter?

I didn't know.

I thought I might learn how to knit. I would make Mister Pig a nice warm pullover for the winter. He would like that.

Mrs Wilson stepped out of the classroom and closed the door. She sat next to me on the bench.

'I've heard about your mother,' Mrs Wilson said. 'Everyone in town has been talking about her.'

After a moment, she added, 'I hope nothing bad has happened.'

'She never came back,' I reported.

We sat in silence, and I thought about Mrs Brown's glory box.

Glory.

I didn't understand how a simple wooden box at the foot of a bed could be glorious. And I had never seen inside; what did Mrs Brown hide in it? There were many grown-up things I didn't understand yet.

'I didn't see you in church on Sunday,' Mrs Wilson said.

'Mr Brown doesn't care much for church,' I explained. 'He says there are more important things to do.'

'Mercy?'

'Yes?'

'Why do you call your father, Mister?'

'I just do, I suppose.'

There was another long silence, and I had the sense that Mrs Wilson was sitting uncomfortably.

'Mercy?' she finally asked. 'Has Mr Brown ever beat you?'

'No,' I answered. 'Hardly ever.'

Silence.

'I hope your mother is all right,' Mrs Wilson said. Her throat sounded dry like she wanted to cough. 'This is not a good world.'

She clutched at the cross that hung about her neck.

Mr Brown is going to kill Mister Pig.

I had walked home from school in the heat of the afternoon sun. I had just walked along the drive from the road to the yard at the back of our house. Mr Brown had his axe, and he was going to murder Mister Pig.

My blood stopped. 'No,' I yelled.

'Go to your room,' Mr Brown said. He had his hand on the pigsty gate to open it.

'No.' I dropped my school bag. I ran up to the gate and stopped him from unlatching the lock and opening it.

'Go to your room,' he yelled. There was beer on his breath, sweat on his face. 'You're too young to see this.'

You're not going to kill him,' I yelled.

'That's what the pig is for. It's for our table.'

We struggled. Mr Brown tried to unlatch the lock. I fought his hands so that he couldn't.

'Go to your damn room.'

'No,' I screamed.

He shoved me away.

I came back and kicked his leg above his foot. I kicked as hard as I could – the toe of my uncomfortable school shoe bit into him.

Mr Brown yelped. He dropped the axe, hunched down, and grabbed his shin.

I picked up the axe and stepped back away from him.

He raised his head and looked up at me with hooded eyes and a face I had never seen before. 'You damn little horror,' he growled. 'Give me the damn axe.'

He struggled to get back onto his feet.

I took the axe and ran into the house.

I ran into my room and locked the door.

Seconds later, the door handle shook.

'Open the door,' Mr Brown yelled from out in the hallway.

I went to my window and unlatched it.

The door shuddered. Mr Brown had thrown himself against it.

I slid the window up.

Mr Brown threw himself against the door again, and the lock broke. The door spat open and almost broke free from its hinges.

Mr Brown lunged across the room.

I climbed out the window.

He grabbed his axe, yanking it from my hand.

Outside, I ran around the house to the rear yard.

I ran to the pigsty. I had to free Mister Pig.

Mr Brown came out the back door of the house like thunder. 'Come here,' he barked at me. He held his axe with two hands, ready to strike.

I stepped away from the pigsty.

Mr Brown changed direction.

I kept moving away.

Mr Brown kept coming for me.

I kicked off my uncomfortable school shoes, turned, and ran.

I ran along the dirt trail and up the hill.

When I got to the top, I looked back.

Mr Brown was following up after me. He was marching fast, carrying his axe; its blade shone in the afternoon sun. He was no longer interested in murdering Mister Pig.

I ran along the top of the hill. The dirt trail led to the river. I could swim to the other side and then run across the farmlands and into the far-off distance.

I ran down the hill.

All I could hear was my breath and my bare feet on the dry dirt. The land was as quiet as the clear sky.

I ran past the cows and the one that looked like Reverend Salt.

I stopped and looked back.

Mr Brown was coming down the hill, moving faster down the dirt trail. He yelled at me. I couldn't understand the words, only the anger.

I changed direction. I headed across the sheep paddock in the direction of the old well at the back of the farm.

The old well lay next to the fallen shed in a forgotten part of the farm, near the swampy ground where the river took a bend. The shed was a collapsed stone building with a rotted roof. The well was a dark, dried-up hole 20 feet deep.

I looked back.

Mr Brown followed. He was coming closer.

I kept running.

The sheep in the paddock kept away.

I ran up to the old well. Its mouth was an old, crumbling circular wall of mossy stone and mortar standing three feet high. It was covered by an old, rotting wooden lid.

I went to the other side of the well and dragged off the lid.

I didn't look down at Miss Prudence. I looked across at Mr Brown. He yelled dreadful things at me as he came up to the well.

The rusty shovel with the broken handle still lay on the ground where I had dropped it a week earlier. I picked it up.

Mr Brown's eyes were hatred.

He wasn't expecting me to move so quickly, to come around behind him as fast as I did. And I hit him in the back of the head with the shovel.

He stumbled forward. He dropped the axe.

I hit him again. Harder.

He tripped over the well's mouth and fell into it.

He grabbed the side.

He hung for a moment and then lost his grip and dropped.

I found another heavy, loose stone from the collapsed shed and took it to the well. I dropped it down onto Mr Brown's head. He never saw it coming. He had been surprised to find Mrs Brown at the bottom of the well with him. She hadn't seen her stone coming, either.

I replaced the well's lid and walked back to the house.

I invited Mister Pig inside.

I made sandwiches.

OBSERVATIONS ON A TRAGEDY
ACT THREE: DENOUEMENT

NARRELLE M. HARRIS

Art and life mimic each other constantly, drawing on each other for inspiration, for comprehension, for embellishment.

The *Monarch Theatre* was a perfect microcosm of this balance, one day after Brady Templar's final bow.

Brady's friends, family, colleagues had gathered at the place of his last performance, ignoring the police tape that cordoned off the lonely alley where he'd died. Ignoring, too, the stairs leading to the balcony seats, and to the cold little stairway that led to the rooftop – with its cupolas and iron lace detail, with its marble frieze of the Muses in the gable underneath the neon theatre sign, and the gold-painted statues of Apollo and Dionysus with their hips cocked, their beautiful faces serene as they gazed down upon the tram tracks.

Tee Mahoney entered quietly, holding her breath against the cloying scent of all the cut flowers lying four-deep along the *Monarch's* façade, most especially against the giant image of Brady as the Heroic Lead. Even as a picture he was vivid, arresting.

Once inside, Tee was jarred by the unreality of the theatre's foyer in daylight. This was meant to be a liminal zone, the point where life was lifted from one's shoulders, hung in the cloakroom to allow another reality to fill the space that existed beyond the ornate doors.

Instead, raw humanity and the masters of pretend mingled. If not all the tears were real, the masters at least pretended hard enough to suspend their own disbelief for the duration.

Naomi Temple's tears were real, a mother grieving for her son. Abigail Temple's too, full of a sister's grief, the Viola to his Sebastian, though no miracle rediscovery awaited her. Brady had changed his name for gallant flourish, but he was still their own dear boy, a shining star before a portion of his self had been given into public ownership.

His manager and publicist cried for real and true. His school friends, his theatre friends, his movie friends. Even one or two entertainment journalists, the critics. He'd been popular. Kind and thoughtful, or a good facsimile thereof.

Tee folded her arms, tamping down the cynicism. Actors were Real People too, as fine and as flawed as the rest. Writers were no better. She was no better. They all cannibalised their lives in pursuit of the perfect art-life blend.

The strobing imagery of the alley – Brady's skin so pale and hair so dark; his broken head and arms and leg; his blood black in shadow, red in the light; the elegant curl of his graceful hand – flashed through her mind, against her eyelids.

Tee took a breath and opened them on the tableau. The Gathering of the Suspects. Theatre intruding on life, and the other way around, again, and it was time for her to move between worlds.

Gracie was sitting on the carpeted stair, weeping, inconsolable, her flawless cream skin blotchy. She had not learned how to cry prettily, or she was so sunk in grief that pretty didn't matter. The young woman with her held Gracie's trembling fingers in her own darker hand; she kissed Gracie's hair and absorbed the noisy, snotty grief in the shoulder of her cotton blouse. That was an intimacy not to be disturbed just yet.

Brady hadn't yet said who might take Gracie's place on his arm at the upcoming film premiere. A man very conscious of how he presented might have taken Naomi or Abigail, but she'd never seen either on his arm at events or in the photographs of events. Tee had never seen him at any public function alone.

By the bar, Max sat on a stool in shell-shocked silence, in his white-knuckled hand a glass of scotch.

Tee asked him right out. 'Why are *you* so sad? Everyone knows you had a voodoo doll.'

Max choked on a laugh. 'Wish he'd never given me the bloody thing. Was meant to be a joke, and now I… I…' Scrunched his eyes shut. 'Did I kill him, sticking pins in that thing before every audition?'

Even for a theatre professional, this was superstition beyond compare. 'You were rivals.'

'Since drama school,' Max agreed. 'He had a doll of me too, but he just drew a moustache on it. I was never a threat to him. But he made me work harder. He made me better than I was. Who's going to do that for me now?'

Well, that was actorly enough. The star of their own show, always, even in grief.

Tee noticed a man noticing her. Too sturdy, too unaffected to be part of the theatre crowd. The police were here, observers in the crowd. Looking for clues, no doubt. Nothing was ever so real that observers weren't part of the mix. *All the world's a stage*.

Gracie was alone again, head leaning against the banister. The absorbent friend was not at the bar. In the bathroom, de-snotting her blouse maybe?

'I'm so sorry for your loss,' said Tee.

Gracie's diffuse gaze slowly focused on Tee's face.

'You found him.'

'Yes.'

'What did he–? Did he–? Was–?'

'Don't. Don't ask. It was awful.'

Gracie flinched. Tee watched her fingers tremble.

'Remember Brady as Brady,' suggested Tee, wishing she could.

'He was my best friend.'

'I thought he was your ex.'

'He's… was, he…' Gracie hiccupped. 'Oh god. I told him last week I was going to be brave. I was going to be me, all me, and take whatever that meant.'

'What did it mean?' Tee hated herself for asking, but would have hated herself more for silence.

'Brady said he'd be my beard for as long as I needed. Well, you know.

Lesbian *beard*. My *skirt*. But Lou and I had enough, and I didn't want to pretend next week for the red carpet. No more fake dates.'

For such a queer industry, too much fakery still went on, thought Tee. Being out with your girlfriend shouldn't have been such a brave choice. And perfect bloody Brady Templar was there, being a shield for Gracie Gilbert.

'So you didn't fight.'

'Not really.'

'Not really?'

'He wanted to wait until after the premiere. One last red carpet together.'

'But you didn't want to?'

'We'd waited long enough.' Gracie sniffed. 'Lou had waited long enough.' Gracie dabbed the back of her hand under her wet eyes. 'Have you seen Lou? Dark curly hair, olive skin, blue top. She was just here.'

'Sorry, no.'

Distracted, Gracie looked about the room, lips trembling. 'She said she wouldn't be long.' Her voice seized, strangled by her closing throat.

Too real for Tee. All of it.

Gracie hadn't killed him. Max hadn't killed him. Tee, whose whole job was to absorb, perceive, analyse fictions, was as sure of those truths as she could be.

So what had happened to topple Brady from the *Monarch* roof?

Tee withdrew, walking alone up the stairs. On the balcony level she paused at the empty bar area and looked down at the grieving throng. Some there to commune. Some to be seen. A reality show that nobody wanted to be in.

Tee turned her back on it all, and saw the plain wooden door that led to the roof had been left ajar.

Something wicked this way went?

She entered the cool narrow space, the unadorned steps and walls with cracking plaster. No need to dress up this behind-the-scenes passage with glitz and a lick of paint.

The sun shone down on the rooftop, throwing shadows that grew shorter as the sun rose high. On the far side, behind the unlit *Monarch Theatre* sign, sat a curly-haired woman in a damp blue blouse, drawing deep on cigarette.

Gracie's Lou had come up for smoko, a hip hitched on a ledge, a curlicue of iron lace between her and the fall.

'Hello,' said Tee cautiously.

Lou breathed out a plume of smoke. She offered Tee the pack.

'No thanks,' said Tee. 'Gracie Gilbert's looking for you.'

Lou sighed. 'I needed a minute.'

'You've worked at this theatre,' noted Tee.

'Front of house to start with. Then I used to check the actors in and out of rehearsals and performances.'

'You knew Brady.'

'Yeah,' said Lou, toneless. 'I knew Brady. Such a good guy.'

Still toneless. A voice quite dead.

'You didn't like him.'

'No. He wanted Gracie to keep going with the whole charade. Until after the red carpet, anyway.'

'Gracie said.'

'She was going to give in, do him one last favour. After he'd been so supportive.' Lou stubbed the cigarette out on the wall, dropped the butt at her feet, with the others. 'Selfish prick. He said he didn't have time to find another date, and reckoned he couldn't get a good dress in time for his mum or his sister. Vain bastard. So cocky. He always got his own way.'

Lou trembled, head to foot. Her breath hitched and choked. Lou's gaze flicked to the wall diagonally opposite.

Oh. Oh, *here* was truth.

No iron-lace barrier, however inadequate, stood there like it did on the façade. That part of the rooftop wasn't visible from the street. No need to gussie it up to create a fairy tale illusion. Just a blank wall and a sheer drop where bright and fearless fools liked to sit and dangle their feet storeys above the earth.

Tee was used to reading between the lines. 'What happened?' she asked.

'An accident,' said Lou. 'He was sitting on the edge. Like he always did. Like it made him braver than me, or smarter. Luckier. Told him it was dangerous. Told him he could slip. He laughed.'

Lou inhaled slowly. Shakily. 'I told him to leave my girl alone. To let her be brave with me.'

The crackle of the tobacco burning at the tip of her cigarette. The exhale of smoke twisting up to the sky.

'How did it happen?' Tee prompted.

'He smiled. You know that smile of his. Boyish. So charming. Such a bloody show. Never fooled me for a minute.'

'And?'

'I told him to be careful. One day someone would see what a selfish prick he really was. How up himself he could be. And I flicked my cigarette butt at him.'

Eyes closed. No tears. Just that dead voice. 'Hit him in the face first. He... jerked away from it. It fell down his shirt front. He tried to get up, shake it out from under and it burned his sleeve and then...' A little gasp. 'I tried to grab him. I did. But he'd already slipped. He didn't even cry out.' A tiny smile, rueful, full of horror. 'He looked so surprised.'

Lou took another drag of her cigarette. Burned out, she dropped it at her feet. Stubbed it out with a twist of her shoe. She stared at her feet.

'Do you want me to tell the cops?' Tee asked.

Lou sighed. 'I suppose I'd better do it. Be brave.' A wrenching sob cracked across the rooftop. 'She won't ever forgive me.'

Tee wasn't sure about that. Only fiction tied up in a cohesive narrative. It was written to have meaning. Life only happened, and meaning gleaned after the fact. That's how you knew it was real.

'Want me to come down with you?' she offered.

'Would you?'

'Sure.'

Tee held Lou's hand, and guided her down the ugly stairs, across the empty second floor bar, down the grand staircase.

And as Lou brokenly confessed to Gracie, as Gracie screamed, as someone went to one of the plain-faced, plain-clothed police at the periphery of the wake, Tee began to put the words together.

> *Shakespeare tells us that all that lives must die, passing through nature to eternity, and so passes Brady Templar – son, brother, friend, a flawed human, as are we all, and, as one of the finest actors of his generation, mirror to our souls, and while his brief candle is out, eternity is in our memories.*

She made meaning after the fact.

THE COMPANY OF RATS
SULARI GENTILL

The ratcatchers' ship had come in. Years ago.

It brought prosperity to all the ratters in Sydney, though no one could be sure exactly which vessel had borne the stricken rodents to the new Commonwealth. A medieval death slipped ashore, crept into shadows and dispersed. The world went to war and limped home, the Spanish Flu killed millions, but the bubonic threat lingered, lurking and persistent.

Every few years a new ship docking in the harbour city would refresh the contagion, begin a new outbreak and remind the good citizens of Sydney that the ratcatchers were all that stood between them and disaster.

The wharves, warehouses, and factories were baited and hunted with the help of the public purse – a price on every tail and incinerators to deal with the spoils. In the inner city the ratters with their billy cans and dogs became a familiar sight. Once in a while, they would be called to one of the grand houses of Woollahra. On those occasions, the ratcatchers would conduct their business discreetly.

When Mary Brown, his housekeeper, mentioned that the ratters would be coming to *Woodlands House*, Wilfred Sinclair did not question the need. He'd lived with rats in the trenches, seen them devouring the last dignity of fallen men. While Wilfred was not generally given to romantic notions, rats were clearly creatures of the Devil and he was content to return them to their master.

Apparently, Mary had learned that *Rosemont House* across the road have been overrun. 'And poor Mrs Carrington-Onslow was widowed only this past August,' she said shaking her head at what some were asked to be bear. Even so, the housekeeper was adamant that the ratter would find nothing in *Woodlands*. Rosemont's misfortune was surely due to the paucity of staff in its employ.

'Mrs Carrington-Onslow makes do with only a girl to cook and clean and a man to tend the garden,' Mary sighed, an expression of compassion which betrayed just a hint self-satisfaction. *Woodlands* employed a dozen maids, cooks and gardeners. It was well defended against any uninvited guest. But Mary was a god-fearing woman who knew pride goeth before a fall, and so she declared she would hear the ratcatcher out.

'Thank you, Mary. I'm sure you have it all in hand.' Wilfred took his bowler from the stand in the vestibule, pausing before the mirror to sit it straight on his head. The rakish angle he'd favoured since returning would not do for the next week. He'd informed the fellows that he would not be attending any parties or like entertainments. Not while he had charge of the enfant terrible.

His younger brother, Rowland, was, according their father, a delinquent, intent on ruining the good name of Sinclair. Wilfred was inclined to believe that Henry Sinclair's assessment was a little unreasonable, but perhaps the boy had run wild since his brothers had gone to war. Whatever the case, a decent fraternal example would not hurt. It would, after all, only be a week before Rowland went home to the family property near Yass for the summer.

Wilfred stepped out when he heard the Rolls Royce Silver Ghost turn into the long driveway. He smiled faintly, imagining Rowland's reaction when the new motorcar had collected him from the station. Wilfred planned to phase out all his father's horse-drawn carriages, to modernise. At the very least, transforming the livery stables would assist with any potential rat problem.

Rowland climbed out without waiting for the chauffeur to open the door. Wilfred braced himself. His youngest brother was, at 14, tall for his age, and looked out at the world with the dark blue eyes that seemed common to all the Sinclair men. Otherwise, he bore little resemblance to Wilfred but he was fast becoming the image of Aubrey Sinclair, who had been born in the years between them and had fallen in France. Wilfred was unsure if Rowland was aware of the fact that he was a living ghost of their late brother, a visual reminder of what was lost. He tried not to have his thoughts stray to Aubrey every time he looked at Rowland, but it was a conscious effort.

Rowland ran up the stairs two at a time, loosening his King's School tie as he did so. 'Hello Wil.'

Wilfred shook his hand. 'Rowly! You look well. What say you about the new motor?'

'She's smashing!' Rowland returned his gaze to the Silver Ghost. 'Why don't we take her out ourselves. I could drive—'

'Steady on, Sport. We have a chauffeur, and you don't know how to drive!'

'How hard could it be?'

Wilfred inhaled. God, it was like talking to Aubrey again. 'I expect you're hungry,' he said firmly. I was always famished when I was your age.'

Franklin Rupert Oldfield might have been any man of means and enterprise. The creases in his suit were sharp, freshly pressed. A gold fob chain and gleaming pocket watch adorned his waistcoat and he wore spats over the polished patent of his shoes. It was only the dogs – fox terriers of varying pedigree – that gave any indication of his business.

Even so, Wilfred Sinclair would normally have left any conversation with the man to the housekeeper – it was certainly not his custom to deal directly with tradesmen – but for the fact that Rowland was already patting the dogs and talking to the urchin who had arrived with the ratter.

He made a mental note to speak to his brother about overfamiliarity, and, because there seemed no other way to extract the boy politely, he introduced himself.

Oldfield was well spoken, though he formed his words slowly with cautious enunciation, in what Wilfred suspected was an attempt to sound refined. Still, one couldn't fault the man for speaking the King's English.

The ratter's boy was thin – nearly as tall as Rowland but there was barely any breadth to him. He wore no coat and in the sunlight the bruises and welts on his back were visible through the threadbare cloth of his shirt. Even so, he smiled broadly, clearly delighted by Rowland's admiration of his dogs.

Wilfred informed Oldfield that his housekeeper had seen no evidence of rats at *Woodlands*.

'Of course not, sir. They're devious creatures. Infiltrators. By the time you know they're here, it's too late – they have the house!' The ratter inclined his head. 'If I might demonstrate?'

'I don't know that that's necessary—'

But Oldfield had already signalled. The boy whistled. A terrier bolted for the kitchen door and scurried inside the house. Screams as the staff was startled by the intrusion.

'Now look here!' Wilfred began angrily.

The screams grew louder, more shocked, and the terrier ran out with a live rat squirming in its mouth. The boy whistled the dog back and put the rat in a large billy can.

For a moment no one said anything; the only sound was the distressed exclamation of the maids and the hollow scratching of the rat in the tin.

'Very well,' Wilfred said. 'You better talk to Miss Brown about checking the house.'

Oldfield nodded. 'I reckon you'll find it a prudent investment, sir.'

Wilfred glanced at the boy with the billy can. He was skin and bone. 'If you call in at the kitchen before you begin, Mary will give you breakfast.'

Oldfield's smile was strained. 'Thank you, sir.'

'The rat is trained,' Rowland said quietly.

'What?' Wilfred murmured as he contemplated the billiard table. Rowland was proving surprisingly competent with a cue.

'The rat Hector put in the billy. It's trained.'

Wilfred reached for the chalk. 'Hector? Oh, you mean the ratter's boy. Really, Rowly, you cannot befriend—'

'I saw him feed the rat.'

'You don't have to train an animal to eat, Sport.'

'Hector was talking to it. I think its name is Vernon.'

Wilfred looked sharply at his brother. The ratters had spent half the morning surveying the house, methodically tapping on walls, checking for droppings and so forth. He'd been busy dealing with some business for the King and Empire Alliance, but Rowland had seemed fascinated by the machinations of trapping rats and spent the day following them around *Woodlands House*.

'The rat's trained, Wil. They brought it with them.'

'For pity's sake Rowly – why the Dickens didn't you tell me? The devil only knows what they've managed to pilfer already!'

Rowland hesitated. 'Did you see– I didn't want Oldfield to take it out on Hector.' He frowned. 'Mary was keeping an eye on them and the silverware, in any case. I suspect they're only after a fee for ridding *Woodlands* of imaginary rats.'

Wilfred cursed. He would not be played for a fool and he did not like looking one in front of his brother. 'Well, we'll see about that.'

Rowland put down his cue and leaned back on the table. 'He wouldn't let Hector eat anything; even what Mary gave them for breakfast. Something about Hector getting too fat to fit into the walls. The old bastard–'

'Language!' Wilfred warned. He sighed. The ratter's boy had been very thin. 'Look, Rowly, Oldfield is his father. There's not a lot we can do.'

'We could–'

'The law does not interfere with how a man deals with his sons. Or allow anyone else to do so. Short of shooting Oldfield there is nothing we can do.'

'But–'

Wilfred pressed his brother's shoulder. Rowland was the youngest by many years. He expected their mother had molly-coddled him somewhat. It was not surprising that he was a little soft. Thank God the War had come and gone before Rowland was old enough to serve. If he'd survived, it would have broken him anyway.

'The ratters will be back tomorrow,' Wilfred said finally. 'I'll have a word with Oldfield. Perhaps the prospect of arrest for fraud, might have some effect.'

Rowland said nothing. Wilfred tried to cheer him up. 'I expect you're looking forward to getting home to *Oaklea*. No doubt Mother and Father will be glad to see you.'

Rowland was non-committal. Wilfred nudged him. 'I hear you've caught the eye of a certain Miss Jemima Roche'

'Did Father—' Rowland began clearly alarmed.

'No. I have my own sources. You forget I grew up in Yass.' He laughed. 'I expect Father is displeased.'

'Father is often displeased.'

With that. Wilfred could not argue. Instead, he suggested they go into the city and see a show so that Rowland would have more about which to tell his sweetheart than trained rats.

Oldfield did not return to *Woodlands*. He might have done so if he had not died across the road. Initially it was feared that the ratter had died of Bubonic Plague as did many in his profession, but after making a few discreet enquiries, Wilfred learned that a razor had done the job. Again, that was not particularly unusual — razors had become the weapon of choice among the criminal classes of late — so it was also not accidental.

'What about Hector?' Rowland asked, gazing out of the drawing-room window towards Rosemont. 'Is he all right?'

Wilfred shook his head. 'The police didn't find him. They have collected Oldfield's animals. I expect someone will take the dogs. I don't particularly like the rat's chances.'

'We could take the dogs, and the rat — keep them for Hector.'

'Rowly, I'm not going to adopt half-a-dozen fleabitten terriers — let alone a flaming rat!'

'Hector will need them,' Rowland persisted.

'For pity's sake, Rowly. You are at school with the sons of the best families — surely you don't need to become chums with the ratter's boy?'

Rowland stared at him wordlessly. Inwardly, Wilfred cursed. Aubrey used to do that.

'I doubt he'll be back, in any case,' he said wearily. 'The police suspect it was the boy who cut Oldfield's throat.'

Rowland started to say something, and then he stopped. 'Why?'

'I'd say it was obvious.' Wilfred sighed. 'Lady Carrington told the police that Oldfield was cruel to the boy, starved and beat him.'

'Can you ask about the dogs? Please. It took him years to train them. He'll want them back.'

Wilfred groaned. 'I suppose it's not their fault that they belong to felons but honestly Rowly, what the devil are we supposed to do with half a dozen ratting dogs.'

'Hector will come back. He wouldn't abandon his dogs.'

If anyone of less impeccable reputation than Wilfred Sinclair, DSO, had requested the ratter's dogs, he might have not have been successful. The terriers were after all found at the scene of a murder. But since there was no suggestion that the hounds were involved in the murder, and Sinclair seemed to be acting out of concern for the animals' welfare, the Police Commissioner agreed to release the animals into his care, at least until some other claimant came forward.

The rat had not been recovered.

Wilfred's custody of the dogs was, however, shortlived. The terriers had no sooner been released onto the lawns of *Woodlands House*, when they bolted, slipping through the iron bars of the entrance gates and across the road to *Rosemont*. Wilfred cursed, first at the dogs and then Rowland, who had talked him into taking charge of the mongrels. Rowland sprinted after the terriers and, afraid that his brother would somehow make matters worse, Wilfred ran after him.

By the time he caught up, the ratter's dogs had slipped through the gates of *Rosemont* and were scratching at its front door. Rowland jumped the fence before his brother could stop him. Wilfred had little choice but to follow.

On the besieged landing, he grabbed one dog by the scruff of the neck and shouted at Rowland to control the others, while he knocked on the door to apologise.

The housekeeper opened it only a crack but that was enough for the terriers who pushed and wriggled through the space despite the servant's attempts to shut it again. Wilfred winced as they heard something crash and shatter inside. The housekeeper left the door to attend to the growing havoc, and Wilfred stepped in so that he and Rowland could help put things right.

The dog Wilfred had by the scruff now twisted out of his grasp and joined its packmates running headlong through the house. The housekeeper was frantic, and then Mrs Carrington-Onslow herself emerged. Wilfred offered apologies and barked at Rowland to grab the dogs, which considering their number, might have been an unreasonable demand. The terriers had converged upon a spot at the end of the hallway and were jumping towards the ceiling. Rowland stood in the midst of them, just staring up.

'Rowly, what are you doing?' Wilfred demanded convinced now there was something wrong with his brother.

Rowland pointed above him. 'There's something up there, Wil. The dogs can smell it.'

'I demand you gentlemen leave my house forthwith!'

Despite her age and diminutive appearance Mrs. Carrington-Onslow had a large voice.

Wilfred grabbed a dog in each hand, clamping one under his arm so he could seize a third. He ordered Rowland to do likewise. But Rowland didn't move, standing with his head cocked towards the ceiling.

'Rowly!'

'I heard a whistle,' Rowland said. 'Hector's up there. He's whistling his dogs.'

The housekeeper paled and crossed herself.

'A whistle. He whistled? That's not possible. Madam—'

'Dear Lord, he's alive,' Mrs. Carrington-Onslow gasped. 'Freddie will kill him!'

Wilfred dropped his dogs. He had no idea what the women were talking about, but he decided he should have a look. 'How do I get up there?'

'There's a ladder in the kitchen,' the housekeeper said. 'Oh dear, oh dear, oh dear.'

'I'll get it,' Rowland volunteered as the housekeeper disintegrated.

'Who's Freddie?' Wilfred asked as Rowland dashed off.

'My boy, poor dear Frederick.' Mrs. Carrington-Onslow was barely audible.

'I thought he fell in France.'

'No, he left.' She whispered now, leaning close. 'He was always sensitive; he couldn't bear it.'

'And he's been hiding in your attic? All these years?'

'He's not well. Only I could calm him. but now...'

Rowland returned with the ladder and held it as Wilfred climbed up. Wilfred pushed the manhole cover away and hoisted himself through.

The attic space was dim but not dark, small-curtained dormer windows letting in just enough light. The stench was almost physical in its force. He saw the ratter's boy first, lying beneath one of the windows. His forehead was bloody and he seemed only partially conscious, turning his head from side to side and whistling in delirium. Wilfred called down to the housekeeper to send for a doctor and find some brandy. And then he saw the Fredrick Carrington-Onslow, whom he had known before the war, but who was much changed. Although he could not have been more than 30, Carrington-Onslow's hair was white as was the unshaved stubble on his face. His ankles were shackled and chained to the iron frame of the bed on which he sat. He rocked in place, shivering, and when he doubled over coughing, Wilfred glimpsed the egg-sized lumps on his neck.

Wilfred could hear Mrs Carrington-Onslow sobbing below. He cursed. What the hell had gone on here?

Wilfred stood slowly and sidled towards the ratter's boy. Carrington-Onslow screamed, pulling the chain taut as he lunged for Wilfred.

'Freddie, it's Wilfred Sinclair. Calm down, old chap. I just want to get this boy to a doctor.'

Carrington-Onslow squatted on the spot and waited, trembling uncontrollably, his breathing laboured. Wilfred pulled out a handkerchief and held it over his nose and mouth.

Rowland came through the manhole. He glanced at Carrington-Onslow before he turned to Wilfred and Hector. 'Is he alive?'

'It seems they both are,' Wilfred said. 'Cover your face, Rowly, and go back down. I fear Freddie may have plague.'

Rowland covered his face, but he didn't retreat, instead climbing into the attic and to his brother's side.

'Let's hope that Mrs Carrington-Onslow and the housekeeper don't take away the ladder and trap us up here,' Wilfred said exasperated that Rowland had not thought of that distinct possibility.

'They won't,' Rowland replied confidently.

'They were just trying to save Freddie. I think he must have killed Mr Oldfield,' he whispered. 'They thought he'd killed Hector too. And so, they left Hector's body up here so that they could blame him for his father's murder.'

Rowland helped Wilfred pull Hector onto his feet between them. 'They didn't know he was still alive.'

Wilfred shook his head as he regarded the broken, sick man chained like a dog a few feet away. A deserter and a murderer and quite possibly a madman. Had the war done this – or was it the shame, and guilt that followed, the life in hiding and disease?

Or just the company of rats.

Voices from below now rose above the unabated barking of the ratter's dogs. Wilfred exhaled. Help had arrived, finally. He shouted down a warning that Carrington-Onslow had the plague before he and Rowland lowered Hector down.

Freddie Carrington-Onslow sat by the bed, inconsolable now. 'Vernon,' he sobbed. 'Where are you, Vernon?'

TOP DOG

VANDA SYMON

THE CACOPHONY OF BARKING THREW ME STRAIGHT BACK INTO FOND memories of life on the farm. I don't know who was more excited to see who – me or the dogs. All of these critters at the Dunedin SPCA were in need of a new home, and I was having to work hard to resist succumbing to their charms. I pulled my eyes away from the gregarious liver-and-gold bitzer who was almost turning somersaults to get my attention, and centred them on the pink-haired young woman with the jaunty chiffon scarf before me.

'When was the last time you saw Melanie Everett?' I asked.

She crouched down and scratched the chin of a Bichon Frise whose face poked expectantly through the bars. Her pastel-blue painted fingernails contrasted nicely with the white of the little scruff's fur. 'It would have been when she left here on Monday afternoon. She finished at her usual time around four.'

'So, you called the police and reported her missing on Tuesday morning; yesterday. That's not a lot of time since you saw her. Why were you so quick to get us involved?'

Issy stood back up. The Bichon Frise wasn't too pleased to have her pat flunky stop paying attention so reached her paw through the bars and proceeded to have a go at some ankle tapping.

'Mel was supposed to be on shift with me again at eight in the morning. When she hadn't turned up by 8.30am I started to get worried because she was never late, especially for the breakfast run. She knew all of the animals would be waiting for us. She was very dedicated, so it felt really out of character.'

She shuffled a little further forward to get out of the range of the pooch. 'I didn't ring the police straight away, though. I tried texting Mel first and when I didn't get a reply I rang Elaine George, who's the Area Manager.'

She moved along to the next cell and bent down to pat the head of a morose looking whippet. It epitomised the term hangdog, even with the attention. 'I hope it doesn't sound weird, but I just had a bad feeling, you know?'

It didn't sound weird to me; bad feelings weren't to be under-rated. I joined in trying to cheer up the whippet. Even with the double attention he still looked miserable.

'What did Elaine say?'

'She was concerned as well, because she knows what Mel's like, so she said she'd give her a ring and get back to me.'

'And she couldn't get hold of her?'

'No, so I suggested she pop around to Mel's house on her way into work, just in case she was sick or something. It's kind of on her way, she lives out at Port Chalmers and Mel's in Ravensbourne.'

'Did Melanie live alone?' I asked. The dog's tail started to give a slight wag. It made me feel immensely better.

'Not strictly alone, she had two cats. They'd been rescue cats. Occupational hazard of working here.' She laughed. I could certainly see the inherent risk.

'I take it from the laugh that you've succumbed?'

'Oh yes, along with everyone else who works here.'

I wondered how my flatmate Maggie would feel about adopting a whippet in need of cheering up? I gave it one more tickle under the chin and we moved along to a rather rotund chocolate Labrador that was busy labradoring a chunk of bone.

'So, at what point did you call the police?'

'Well, Elaine arrived at work and said she'd stopped by at Mel's house. Said her car was in the driveway, but when she knocked on the door no one answered.'

We continued walking along to the exit and ventured outdoors into the rather fresh spring air. 'I asked her then if we should call the police in case Mel had had an accident or something, but Elaine thought that was over-reacting.' She paused and looked at me. 'But I rang you guys anyway, because, well, you know, something didn't feel right. Was I overreacting?'

As it turned out. No.

I shook my head. 'It doesn't hurt to be cautious.' We crunched along the gravel path towards an older chap decked out in coveralls and a sun hat, who was leaning on a rake. He had been busy gathering up the carpet of fallen magnolia flowers that were covering the path. The tree shedding them was glorious. It seemed such a pity to sweep them away.

'Ladies.' He greeted us.

'Gordon, this is Detective Shephard, she's here enquiring about Mel.'

'Ah yes, Steph said something about that. We've got a meeting about it soon?'

'Yes,' I said, 'up in the education room.' I looked to Issy. 'Do you mind if I meet you up there, I want to have a word to Gordon.'

'Sure, no problem,' she said, and continued up the path.

'I take it you're the gardener here' I asked.

'What gave it away?' he said with a wink.

'The fact you were leaning on the rake pretending to do something.'

He gave a hearty laugh. It was contagious. You couldn't help but like Gordon.

'How long have you worked here?'

'Well, I've been volunteering here for over 10 years now. As you can see,' he said, spreading his arm, 'it's a tough gig.'

Tough indeed. The Dunedin SPCA sat on the hill at Opoho, just along from the upper Botanic Gardens, one of my favourite escapes, especially at this time of year. The expansive grounds here were gorgeous with plentiful established trees, and along with the magnolia there were a number of rhododendrons coming into bloom. It was a riot of colour. Even though we were on the fringe of the city, I felt like I was miles away from anywhere, breathing in the fresh air and sunshine.

'So how much land does the SPCA have here?' I asked.

'Forty-two acres all in all. Quite hilly around here of course, and much of it is just bush.'

That was a lot of terrain to potentially hide a body. We wandered up the path in the direction of the main buildings. 'How well do you know the grounds?'

'Know them like the back of my hand,' he said.

'Haven't seen anything odd in the last day or two, nothing disturbed?' He paused and looked at me sideways.

'Nothing obvious, but I've been concentrating on keeping up with this area around the buildings. I could have a look around later for you, if you want.'

'Might need to get you to do that, take a few officers on a tour.' We approached the main buildings and the scattering of cars. The only blot on the landscape was a ruddy great shipping container parked up on the grass next to a building. There was nothing attractive about those things.

'That's new, by the way.' Gordon said.

'What's new?'

'The shipping container. It must have been dropped off Monday night or Tuesday morning. They're using it for storage while they refurbish the randoms' area.'

'Randoms?'

'You know, guinea pigs, rabbits, chickens, the odd goat.'

Interesting timing. I gave the container a last look as we entered the building.

The group meeting was going about as well as could be expected for one where you were telling people something nasty had likely happened to their co-worker. After the initial shock that we believed Melanie had been the victim of a crime came a barrage of questions for which I had no answers. What could I tell them?

A cursory visit to Mel's home from others in the team had confirmed that her car was indeed in the driveway, but no one answered. After a bit of door knocking in the locality a neighbour had come to light with a spare key to the house. Mrs Jones occasionally fed the cats and watered the pot plants if Mel happened to be away, and vice versa. It was heart-warming to know neighbours could still be neighbourly in this day and age. She hadn't heard anything untoward or seen anything out of the ordinary, so was pretty surprised to see a couple of young constables on her doorstep.

When they'd let themselves into the house there were no obvious signs of struggle or anything out of place, it looked very spick and span. But one of the officers did notice the aroma of *Handy Andy* hanging in the air and she'd noted the attentions of two moggies trying very hard to manoeuvre them in the general direction of their food bowls. What little had remained in their bowls was rather dried and manky looking, like it had been there a while.

All kudos to the officers concerned for taking a more than cursory look because there in the kitchen, on the underside of the breakfast bar they discovered four tiny splashes of what looked like blood. Those four tiny splashes brought in the Scene of Crime Officers. The SOCOs investigations pointed to tell-tale trace evidence of a hell of a lot more than four drops of blood.

Cue me standing here in front of her work colleagues, trying to come up with answers to their inevitable questions, with very little to go on.

'So, you're saying you think she's come to grief, that someone has done her a mischief?' Mona was an elderly and conservative looking woman with a flair for the euphemistic.

'We are very concerned for her safety at this stage. I'm going to talk with you one by one, but I want you all to think about anything she may have said that concerned her, or if she had mentioned any issues with anyone.' A collective murmur started around the room that quickly grew to a roar and I caught snatches of comments and exclamations.

'But everyone loves Mel, she's a gem.'

'No one would hurt her.'

'Maybe she's just had to skip off for an emergency and didn't have time to let anyone know.'

Elaine Wilson was the area manager for the SPCA, and the person now charged with managing her upset staff and volunteer crew, explaining to an impatient public that adopting a pet wasn't going to happen today, and trying to make sure it was business as much as usual for the inmates, whose only concern was when their next meal was coming and would they get pats.

To that end I was talking with Elaine in the cat enclosure, dishing out pats and trying to ignore the imploring big eyes of the felines who had figured out the cutesy look was their best bet for getting out of here. The three high tiers of cages were half occupied with a vast array of fluffiness ranging from the pedigreed to those whose Mum had clearly been out for a good time and wasn't that fussy. As much as I appreciated a good moggie, I was rather taken with a ginormous bundle of fluffy white fur whose snooty face made it look like she was used to being Queen of the show.

'Why is this one here?' I asked. It seemed odd that someone would give up or dump what was probably quite a valuable cat.

'Ahh, Victoria's owner had to go into care, and none of her family was able to take her. She's been difficult to find a home for because she needs daily medicine and its a bit pricey. Shame really, because she's a real sweetie.'

I wondered how well a whippet and a Persian would get on? I popped my fingers through the cage, and she gave them an immediate chinny win. Her magnificence seemed so out of place in this soulless grey prison. An odd flash of colour caught my attention as I looked down at her paws. I took a second look. It triggered a question I'd been meaning to ask earlier when I was with the group.

'So, what's with the blue nails? I mean claws, and nails – everyone of your staff had blue nails.' Even the blokes had blue nails.

Elaine laughed. 'Oh that. It's Blue September – you know, Prostate Awareness Month. We decided to have a work fundraiser for it, so we all painted our nails blue and hosted a morning tea.'

I'd heard of SPCA cupcake day, and they were always fundraising for the good work they did. I wondered if there was anything significant about doing something for prostate instead? 'Any reason in particular for this cause?'

'Actually, you met the gardener, Gordon? He had prostate cancer last year, beat it, thank heavens, so it was his idea for us to do something. We were all very happy to hop on board.'

'Was it his idea to paint the cat's claws? And who was brave person that tackled that?'

Bet they had the scars to prove it. Damned if I'd known any cat who'd submit to that kind of attention without putting up a multi-pronged defence and a hasty scratchy retreat. Certainly not our farm cats. It was bad enough trying to get a worm tablet into the fierce little bastards, let alone giving them a pedicure.

'No, no, no. It was Mel's idea, actually. She thought it would be great to put on our social media, you know draw attention to prostate cancer and maybe even find Victoria a home. Gordon thought we should do a social media campaign with the title 'give prostate cancer the finger,' along with the appropriate blue fingernailed gesture. That wasn't going to fly.'

Having encountered Gordon's sense of humour, I could just imagine. He went up even more in my estimation.

'So Melanie painted Victoria's claws? Or did one of the others do it?' I could picture Issy of the pink hair and chiffon scarf having a bit of fun with the nail enamel.

'No, it was Mel. And the cat was surprisingly good about it. Long haired cats tend to be quite tolerant seeing as they're brushed and handled so often. I think she's led a pretty pampered life up until now, with only the best of everything. Lord knows how often she turns her nose up at the food around here.'

She did look like the poster child for every posh cat food commercial under the sun.

'It was funny though, not everyone was impressed about it.'

'How so?'

'Well Issy and Mona thought it was a bit cruel painting the cat's claws; that it was exploiting her.'

OK, so maybe I was wrong about Issy seeing it as some fun. 'And what about your resident vegan? Did Austin have issues with it too?'

'Well, not at first. He thought it was funny, but then when Issy and Mona made a bit of a fuss, he said it probably wasn't a good idea. Issy's a vegan too, by the way. Mona was a full-blown animal rights activist in her day. She once bucketed pig shit onto the steps of Parliament in a protest about the crating of sows.'

I could tell by the look on Elaine's face that she had huge admiration for the old gal. I think I was a fan now too.

'They had quite a discussion about it.'

'And Mel painted them anyway?'

'Yup. She could be quite pig-headed when she wanted to be.'

So, all was not sweetness and light in animal lover's paradise.

The hot Milo was hitting the spot nicely, but I hadn't reached my Toffee Pop satiation quotient yet. I reached across and grabbed another from the packet.

'So, it's the case of a suspicious state of affairs at the SPCA.'

Apart from her appalling tendency to alliteration, my flatmate Maggie was clearly concerned she was falling behind on the biscuit stakes as she dived in for another, thought better of it and grabbed two. PJs, fluffy slippers and a chocolate overload – it had been quite a day and the evening wind-down and debrief was just what I needed. As well as a flatmate and confidant, Maggs had a level head and often brought a fresh perspective to my musings.

'Oh yes. And when it finally filtered through and they realised that they were all being regarded as potential suspects you should have seen it. They turned on each other faster than two feral cats with a full food bowl.' Two could play the alliteration game.

'It was all: *Gerty was too ambitious, Elliott wanted us to go completely vegan, Diedre was a fruit loop, Maisie always hogged the best pets for herself.*' I flipped out the pseudonymous examples with the appropriate silly voices.

'Well, it is a dog-eat-dog world,' Maggie quipped.

'Too true, too true.' I couldn't help but laugh at her choice of words.

'Oh, and you know the dog mantra, don't you?'

'I'm guessing you're going to enlighten me.'

'Seeing as you asked. It especially applies to Labradors. When in doubt eat it. If it isn't food, you can always throw it up later.'

'Ewwww.' My body gave an involuntary shudder. 'Now that you mention it there was quite a lovely chocolate lab there, a bit porky, would need a lot of exercise. But I was more taken with this whippet. He was so sad, looked like he needed some loving. And his name was Bruce. How cute is that? Can you imagine standing out at the park calling for Bruce? Bruuuuce.'

'Nope. Don't even go there. No way. I know you and your bleeding heart – just no.'

Maggs could be a cow when she wanted to be. She was right, of course.

'Meh, you're no fun. Anyway, back to the humans. The hard case thing is, for a group of do-gooder volunteers and idealists, they all had motive in their own way.'

'So not benign do-gooder volunteers and idealists?'

'Not so much. Who knew that a place like the SPCA could such be a hot-bed of passive aggressive egos, discontent, and intrigue?'

'I think you'd be surprised at how many well-meaning organisations attract border-line weirdos. Well, actually, you probably wouldn't, given your line of work. So, your focus is on this group?'

'Mine is. Smithy is following up with her family who likewise haven't heard from her for the last few days, and had no cause for concern. But for the most part, it would appear that she didn't have much of a life outside of her job at the SPCA. She lived and breathed it. Belonged to the usual environmental and animal protection groups you'd expect, Forest & Bird, SAFE, but she wasn't what you'd call an active member. Didn't piss anyone off by chaining herself to a fence. The universal opinion seems to be she was a stellar human being, and everyone loved her.'

'Well, someone clearly didn't. Doesn't give you much to go on then.'

'Not really. And we can't even say if she's dead or alive. No body, no certainty.'

'But I take it by the way you're referring to her as "was", you're thinking homicide?'

'Yeah." I downed the last of my Milo and looked at the seriously depleted biscuit packet. My fingers started reaching across. 'We really do need to find her. I've got a hunch so we're going to be doing a bit of serious lifting in the morning.'

There was always something exciting about watching a shipping container being hoisted onto the back of a truck. There was that delicious tension between will it tip the truck? Will they accidentally hit something? And, I kind of hope something goes wrong because that would be cool. I must have watched way too many seconds from disaster programmes in my youth. Today's hoist had the additional anticipation of what lurked beneath, or more to the point, who lurked beneath?

A small crowd of invested onlookers waited in anticipation as the chains took the strain and the recently arrived container at the SPCA began to inch off the ground. If my suspicions were on the money, then there would be more than grass and the occasional daisy pushing up under there.

We had a team of SOCOs on hand, ready to deal with whatever we might find, as well as fellow detective Otto, and a couple of constables. The morning crew from the SPCA were hovering in the background: Elaine, along with Gordon, Issy the pink, and the young chap Austin who was videoing proceedings on his phone.

The chains creaked and groaned as the container shuddered into the air. Patience was never my strong point and I just had to squat down and peer beneath the rising hulk of metal. Waiting that extra 20 seconds was going to kill me.

Shit.

Shit, shit, shit and bugger.

The container lifted and shadows retreated to reveal grass. Pristine, undisturbed grass.

'Do you mind if we take this lot through to look at all the cats? You never know, they might fall in love and want to take home a furry friend.'

Part of me felt bad for having wasted the SOCOs time, but we had to check the container out, and if my suspicions were correct and Melanie had been hastily buried and been given a two-tonne headstone, then we would have needed their expertise immediately.

Three of them were dead keen for a guided tour. It would also give me the chance to have another chat with Elaine, and a surreptitious pat session with Queen Victoria. Would it be pushing my luck to take them to see the whippet? What ulterior motive could I come up with?

Elaine seemed more than happy to indulge us. 'Course I can, come down this way.'

It was evident from the look of glee on the faces of the SOCOs that there could very well be some new fur-baby family members coming out of this case. As soon as we got to the enclosure they oohed and ahhhed and spread out to take in the array of cats that suddenly appeared at the front of their cages, craving affection. I suspected I'd been forgiven for dragging the team out early to a job that turned out to be a big ole dead end.

I stood off to the side with Elaine and enjoyed watching the mutual love fest.

'When we were talking yesterday, I asked you if anyone had anything to gain from Melanie not being here, or if anyone had recently had any issue with her. Have you had any further thoughts on that?'

Sometimes a good night's sleep, or in her case probably a bad night's sleep, sparked the subconscious to re-examine events, see situations or conversations through a slightly different lens.

'I have been thinking about it, but everything seems very minor. Nothing worth hurting someone over.'

'Try me,' I said. One person's minor incident could be someone else's catastrophe.

'Well, you did ask who would stand to benefit if Mel was no longer here, and both Issy and Austin often expressed interest in paid employment. They're both currently volunteers and put in a lot of hours.'

During yesterday's unseemly descent into finger pointing and throwing under the bus I recalled a few accusations flying about ambition, and Austin accusing Issy of wanting to take over. There was just as vehement a counter claim from her.

'Did they both get on with Melanie?'

'Yes. Everyone here gets on with everyone else. After yesterday you probably don't think that, but everyone was just upset and a bit stressed out by it all and they didn't react very well. I don't think for a minute any of them would hurt a fly.'

That mirrored an exclamation from yesterday in my interview with Austin where he had declared 'I'm vegan, I wouldn't hurt a fly.' I'd jailed a few vegans who had hurt way bigger and more complicated critters than that.

'What else had you been thinking about?' I asked. I noticed that the crew had moved away from Queen V's cage, so I started manoeuvring us in that general direction.

'Not everyone saw eye to eye on some of Mel's initiatives. For example, she wanted to reduce the amount of vetting we do when we are finding homes for dogs. She said it make people more likely to adopt them. Some were concerned that not all of the adoptees would be suitable.'

I tended to side with the concerned crew on that one. I'd seen too many examples of neglected dogs, and dogs that were just the wrong match for their families, to the heartbreak of all concerned. We'd reached her Royal Highness's cage and she'd already started purring in anticipation of some chin rubs. It would have been rude of me not to oblige.

'And of course there was the nail enamel thing,' Elaine said popping her finger under Victoria's paw and giving her a wee tickle between the beans. The cat immediately obliged with a cute claw stretch, beautifully showing off her blue manicure. The contrast against her white fur was quite striking. I was intrigued to know how much her daily medication would cost and what kind of vet bills she'd rack up? Also, if she had been as pampered as much as suggested her food bill would probably be a bit steep. Budget tins of jelly meat wouldn't cut it for Her Royal Fluffiness. Was she a bit out of my league? Still, it was tempting.

I looked over to her food bowl in the corner to see if she'd bothered with the fare served up in her one-star establishment this morning and my eyes fixated on something very out of place. I blinked, shook my head, and stuck my face right up against the cage, to get as close a look as I could. Queen Vic took this as an opportunity to spin around and give me an almighty great head-butt smooch across the kisser. I brushed the long white fur away from my eyes and stood up out of snuggle range, more intent on the incongruous, and now nausea-inducing sight in her food bowl.

There, sticking out of her barely touched meat was what looked like a mangled, pastel blue fingernail.

I stood up very slowly and took a step back from the cage.

'Um, Elaine,' I asked, eyes still fixated on the bowl. 'Where exactly do you get your fresh meat from?' My mind was racing back to yesterday, to the array of felines tucking into their dinner, to the memory of the Labrador chomping away merrily on his chunk of bone, and now back to that tell-tale shade of blue.

'A few different sources. We sometimes get excess supplies donated from pet food factories, cancelled export orders, that kind of thing.' I was guessing this wasn't the case. 'We also get donations of carcasses from farms where cattle or sheep have had to be put down, because they've injured themselves, broken a leg and can't go to the freezing works. They need to be processed first though. We can't do that here.'

'And where do you get that done?' I asked. I closed my eyes and took a few deep breaths, trying to supress the urge to vomit.

'We've got a butcher down in North East Valley that does it for us. Minces everything up, packages it. Makes it nice and easy." I was sure it did. "Actually, Issy's Dad owns the shop, so he doesn't even charge us for it. Does it for love."'

And there it was.

'When did this lot arrive?' I asked, indicating the cages before us.

'I think Issy brought a batch in yesterday morning. We must have had a farm donation. I'd have to look in the freezer – we date all of the bags.'

Farm donation? Or not quite. I looked over to the SOCOs merrily patting up a storm with their appreciative audience. It wasn't going to be a wasted trip after all.

I thought back to yesterday and that young woman with her pink hair and jaunty scarf. I thought back to yesterday and Issy happily introducing me to the dogs. Dogs with bowls licked clean of food, and bones. The bones. That was beyond brazen. But why? What on earth would possess her to kill Melanie? To get her job? To claw her way up, to be top dog? To avenge the exploitation of a cat? I guessed we'd find out in due course.

But for now it was the perfect gut-turning irony, our innocuous, warm fuzzy, animal loving young vegan feeding the body of her victim to the pets she cared for so much. Who would ever suspect? The perfect way to dispose of the evidence right under everyone's noses.

Well almost.

The perfect crime undone by a right royally fussy cat.

THE AUTHORS

ALAN CARTER

Alan was born in Sunderland, UK, and immigrated Down Under in 1991. Since then he's lived in Perth, the Marlborough Sounds, and now Hobart. He sometimes works as a TV documentary director, loves to plunge into the icy Tasmanian waters for fun, and is the author of seven crime novels.

Alan was shortlisted for the CWA Daggers and won a Ned Kelly Award for Prime Cut, the first in his five-book series starring Chinese-Australian detective Cato Kwong; and won the 2018 Ngaio Marsh Award for Best Novel for *Marlborough Man*, his first Nick Chester book.

'Takin Out the Trash' is a Nick Chester story.

AOIFE CLIFFORD

Born in London of Irish parents, Aoife grew up in New South Wales, studied Law & Arts at the Australian National University in Canberra, and now lives in Melbourne.

She is the bestselling author of literary crime novels *All These Perfect Strangers, Second Sight*, and *When We Fall*. Aoife's novels have been shortlisted for the CWA Debut Dagger and Davitt Awards and long listed for the ABIA General Fiction Book of the Year and Voss Literary Prize. Her short fiction has won the SD Harvey Award from the Australian Crime Writers Association and the Scarlett Stiletto Award from Sisters in Crime Australia.

Her story in our book, 'Summer of the Seventeen Poll', won Aoife the SD Harvey Award.

DAN RABARTS & LEE MURRAY

Dan (Ngāti Porou) and Lee are award-winning writer-editors from Aotearoa New Zealand, winners of multiple Sir Julius Vogel, Australian Shadows, and Bram Stoker Awards, and a Shirley Jackson Award.

They co-authored the Path of Ra supernatural forensic crime thriller series (*Hounds of the Underworld*, *Teeth of the Wolf*, *Blood of the Sun*), and co-edited the horror anthologies *Baby Teeth: Bite-sized Tales of Terror* and *At the Edge*.

Lee is a Bay of Plenty storyteller whose solo work includes horror-thrillers, the Taine McKenna Adventures, and the fiction collection *Grotesque: Monster Stories*. Wellington-based Dan is also the author of steampunk-grimdark-comic fantasy series Children of Bane.

'Rock-a-bye Baby' is a Path of Ra story, featuring brother and sister sleuths Penny and Matiu Yee.

DAVID WHISH-WILSON

The author of eight novels and three creative non-fiction books, David was born in Newcastle, NSW and grew up in Singapore, Victoria, and Western Australia. He spent his late teens and 20s in Europe, Africa, and Asia in a smorgasbord of jobs including barman, actor, petty criminal, exterminator, factory worker, gardener, travel agent, teacher, and drug trial guinea pig.

Now an author and creative writing teacher at Curtin University, David lives in Fremantle, WA. His crime novels *Line of Sight* and *True West* have been shortlisted for the Ned Kelly Awards, and his non-fiction for the Western Australian Premier's Book Awards.

His story in our book, 'The Cook', was originally published in 2014 in *Westerly*, the literary magazine of the University of Western Australia. It became the first crime story to ever win the Patricia Hackett Prize.

DINUKA MCKENZIE

Dinuka is an Australian writer. Her debut crime novel, *The Torrent*, introduced her heroine Detective Sergeant Kate Miles. It won the 2020 Banjo Prize for an unpublished work of commercial fiction, and was then published by HarperCollins Australia in February 2022. Dinuka's manuscript, *Taken*, the second novel featuring DS Kate Miles, was longlisted for the 2020 Richell Prize and will be published in 2023.

When not writing, Dinuka works in the environmental sector and volunteers as part of the team behind the Writers Unleashed Festival. She lives in Southern Sydney with her husband, two kids and their pet chicken. She is currently working on her third Kate Miles novel.

In 'Skin Deep', Dinuka has given us Kate's origin story.

FIONA SUSSMAN

Fiona grew up in a publisher's home in Apartheid South Africa before immigrating to New Zealand in 1989, where she completed a medical degree then worked as a family doctor. After she hung up her stethoscope to pursue her writing dream, Fiona's second novel *The Last Time We Spoke* won the Kobo/NZSA Publishing Prize and the Ngaio Marsh Award for Best Crime Novel.

Fiona was overall winner of the *Sunday Star-Times* Short Story Awards in 2018, and her novel *Addressed to Greta* won the NZ Booklovers Award for Best Adult Fiction in 2021. Her 2022 fourth novel, *The Doctor's Wife*, is a domestic thriller.

Fiona mentors creative writing students and, along with her husband, was involved in establishing a charity hospital in Auckland.

GARRY DISHER

Garry has published more than 50 books ranging from crime and literary fiction to short story collections, YA/kids novels, and writers' handbooks. Born in South Australia, where he grew up on his parents' farm, Garry now lives on the Mornington Peninsula in Victoria.

His three crime series starring Melbourne professional thief Wyatt, Peninsula detectives Hal Challis and Ellen Destry, and rural cop Paul 'Hirsch' Hirschhausen have each won the Ned Kelly Award for Best Crime Fiction. Garry is also a four-time winner of the Deutscher Krimi Preis, Germany's oldest and most prestigious literary prize for crime fiction. In 2018 he received the Ned Kelly Lifetime Achievement Award.

'Sinner Man' is a new Hirsch story.

HELEN VIVIENNE FLETCHER

Helen is a children's and YA author, playwright, spoken word poet, and a creative writing teacher living in Wellington. She discovered her passion for writing for children while working as a mental health phone counsellor. This inspired her dark psychological YA thriller, *Broken Silence*, which was a finalist for the 2018 Ngaio Marsh Award for Best First Novel.

Helen's writing – which now includes picture books, plays, a short story collection and several YA thriller, fantasy, and middle-grade novels – has also seen her shortlisted for the Joy Cowley Award and named Outstanding New Playwright at the Wellington Theatre Awards.

KATHERINE KOVACIC

Katherine is a former veterinarian turned art historian and author. In her spare time, when she's not dancing or teaching other people's dogs to ride skateboards, she writes short stories, true crime, and crime novels.

The Portrait of Molly Dean, the first of three books in her Alex Clayton art mystery series, was shortlisted in the 2019 Ned Kelly Awards for Best First Fiction. Katherine's latest books include *The Schoolgirl Strangler*, which examines a real-life crime in 1930s Melbourne, and *Just Murdered*, the first novel starring Phryne Fisher's niece Ms Peregrine Fisher (as seen on the hit TV series *Ms Fisher's Modern Murder Mysteries*).

Her story in our book, 'Water Damage' features Alex Clayton.

KERRY GREENWOOD

Kerry Greenwood OAM is one of Australia's most prolific and successful writers. A lawyer and author from Footscray, she has written more than 50 novels, six non-fiction works, YA books, and several plays. She is best known for creating the fearless and glamorous 1920s sleuth Phryne Fisher, who stars in 21 novels (so far); and a hit TV show and movie which aired in 172 territories worldwide.

Kerry's love of ancient history features in four books published with

Clan Destine Press, the Delphic Women trilogy: *Medea, Cassandra* and *Electra*; and *Out of the Black Land*, set in Ancient Egypt.

Kerry also writes the popular baker-sleuth Corinna Chapman series, and has won numerous awards including the inaugural Sisters in Crime Lifetime Achievement Award and the Ned Kelly Lifetime Achievement Award. In 2020, Kerry received the Order of Australia Medal for services to literature.

'The Rooming House', herein, features Corinna Chapman.

LISA FULLER

Lisa is an award-winning writer and Wuilli Wuilli woman from Eidsvold, Queensland, who has lived on Ngunnawal and Ngambri lands (Canberra) since 2006. She is completing a PhD in Creative Writing at the University of Canberra, and works as a sessional academic, editor, and publishing consultant. Lisa won the 2017 David Unaipon Award for an Unpublished Indigenous Writer.

Her first thriller, *Ghost Bird*, won the Young Adult Book Award in the 2020 Queensland Literary Awards, the Norma K Hemming Award, the Readings Young Adult Prize, and the 2020 Act Book of the Year Award. Lisa has previously published poetry and short fiction, and is passionate about culturally appropriate writing and publishing.

NARRELLE M. HARRIS

Narrelle is a Melbourne writer of crime, horror, fantasy, romance, and erotica. She has published more than 40 works of fiction, including 11 novels, ranging from traditional Holmesian mysteries and queer paranormal romantic thrillers to vampire novels, erotic spy adventures, het and queer romance, and rock n roll urban fantasy.

Her novels include *Ravenfall, Kitty and Cadaver* and, in late 2022, *The She-Wolf of Baker Street*.

Narrelle's novels and short stories have been shortlisted for the Ned Kelly Award for Best First Crime Novel, the Davitt Awards, George Turner Prize, Aurealis Awards, and Chronos Awards.

Narrelle won the Atheneum Library's 'Body in the Library' prize at the 2017 Scarlet Stiletto Awards for her ghostly crime story 'Jane'.

NIKKI CRUTCHLEY

Nikki is a novelist, short fiction writer, and copy editor who lives in the bucolic Waikato town of Cambridge in New Zealand. Before she began focusing on writing Nikki worked as a librarian, including a stint in the UK and Ireland. Her flash fiction has been published in several journals and Nikki is a two-time regional winner of National Flash Fiction Day.

Her first three novels were small-town mysteries set in rural New Zealand; *Nothing Bad Happens Here* and *The Murder Club* were shortlisted for the Ngaio Marsh Awards. *To The Sea* the first in a series of psychological thrillers, was published in late 2021.

RENÉE

Renée ONZM (Ngāti Kahungunu) is one of Aotearoa New Zealand's storytelling rangatira, a lesbian feminist, dramatist, poet, and author who lives in Ōtaki. She left school aged 12 to work in Hawke's Bay wool mills and the printing factory. She wrote her first play at age 50, kickstarting four decades of storytelling on stage and page that featured women in leading roles and humanised the working class.

Renée was a keynote speaker at the First International Women Playwrights Conference in New York in 1988. In recent years, she received the Prime Minister's Award for Literary Achievement, the Playmarket Award for significant artistic contribution to New Zealand theatre.

Renée published her first crime novel, *The Wild Card*, in 2019 – at the age of 89.

R.W.R. MCDONALD

Rob is an award-winning author who grew up on a sheep and deer farm in South Otago and now lives in Melbourne with his two daughters and one HarryCat. He also tutors at the Faber Academy, where as a creative writing student he wrote the first draft of a novel which introduced unlikely mystery solving trio Tippy Chan, Uncle Pike, and Devon.

The Nancys was Highly Commended for the 2017 Victorian Premier's

Unpublished Manuscript Award, then after publication went on to be shortlisted for the 2020 Ned Kelly Awards and win the Ngaio Marsh for Best First Novel. A sequel, *Nancy Business*, was published lin 2021. Rob is working on a third Nancys novel.

Rob's story for our book, 'Nancys Undercover', features Tippy and her gay uncles, Pike and Devon.

SHANE MALONEY

Shane is a Melbourne author who was born in smalltown Victoria, graduated from the Australian National University, and booked rock bands and ran the Melbourne Comedy Festival among other gigs before becoming a writer.

Shane is most notorious for being the creator of Murray Whelan, a political functionary who finds himself investigating crimes linked to his job, in an outstanding series of novels published from 1994-2007. The six Murray Whelan books made Shane one of Australia's most popular crime writers. *The Brush-Off* won the Ned Kelly Award for Crime Fiction. In 2004 *Stiff* and *The Brush-Off* were made into telemovies, starring David Wenham as Murray Whelan. In 2009 Shane was presented with the Ned Kelly Lifetime Achievement Award.

'The Lost Murray Whelan', featured herein, is the draft first chapter of the never-finished and totally abandoned seventh Murray Whelan novel.

STEPHEN ROSS

Stephen is an award-winning Auckland writer who's been crafting stories for 20 years, from auteur-ing short films to penning jokes for TV to creating songs for his own bands and scores for theatre productions. His short stories have been published in Alfred Hitchcock Mystery Magazine, Ellery Queen Mystery Magazine, and Mystery Writers of America anthologies. His work has been shortlisted for an Edgar Award, a Derringer Award, and a Thriller Award.

Stephen also won the Rose Trophy for Best Crime/Mystery Short Story, and was a contributor to the Agatha Award-winning non-fiction book *How To Write a Mystery*, edited by Lee Child with Laurie R. King.

SULARI GENTILL

Sulari is an award-winning crime writer who lives on a small farm in the Snowy Mountains of New South Wales. She was born in Sri Lanka, learned to speak English in Zambia, and grew up in Brisbane before heading to university to study astrophysics; instead graduating as a lawyer.

Sulari is the author of the bestselling, Davitt Award-winning historical mystery series starring Rowly Sinclair, a gentleman artist who solves crimes in 1930s Australia and overseas. The series has also been shortlisted for the Ned Kelly Awards, ABIA Awards, and the Commonwealth Writers Prize.

Sulari's standalone thriller *Crossing the Lines* won the 2018 Ned Kelly Award for Best Crime Novel; and a second standalone mystery *The Woman in the Library*, released in 2022, was a *New York Times* 'Best Book of Summer', a *USA Today* bestseller; and the *Apple* 'Best Book of June'.

Her Dark Deeds Down Under story, 'The Company of Rats', is a young Rowly Sinclair story, originally published in the Spring 2021 issue of *Openbook*, the quarterly magazine of the New South Wales State Library, and republished here with permission.

VANDA SYMON

Vanda is a crime writer, health researcher, and radio host of Fijian/European descent who lives on a hill overlooking Otago Harbour. A former pharmacist, Vanda's bestselling series starring spirited young Detective Sam Shephard has been shortlisted for the Ngaio Marsh Awards, the CWA Daggers in the UK, and the Barry Awards in the United States.

Her standalone thriller *Faceless* was also shortlisted for the Ngaio Marsh Awards. In recent years, Vanda completed a PhD on the communication of science in crime fiction; and now juggles writing with her work at the Va'a o Tautai Centre for Pacific Health at the University of Otago.

She is currently writing her fifth Sam Shephard novel and has given her Kiwi detective a run here too, in 'Top Dog'.

OUR ARTISTS & ARTWORK

SEANTELLE WALSH

Seantelle Walsh is a contemporary Noongar artist, born and raised in Boorloo (Perth), Whadjuk Country. The eldest of six children, she loves creating work that showcases the energy and essence of culture and exploring these connections through creative storytelling. Under her trade name Kardy Kreations she's worked across Western Australia, creating bespoke and commissioned pieces in a diverse practice that includes studio-based paintings, digital work, murals and public art. She also delivers painting workshops to various schools and organisations, encouraging cultural diversity with a contemporary perspective on Aboriginal art and culture. She draws inspiration from what she sees and feels around her through her spirituality and her connection to Boodja (Country).

Seantelle designed the First Nations jersey for the Wallaroos – the national women's Rugby Union team of Australia – which depicts the connection between women and their spirit, as well as the connection with the Dreamtime and overcoming barriers.

For *Dark Deeds Down Under*, Seantelle has created an original platypus design.

MĀHINA ROSE HOLLAND BENNETT

Māhina is an exciting young Māori (Te Arawa, Ngāti Pikiao, Ngāti Whakaue) multimedia visual artist and creative who lives in Tāmaki Makaurau (Auckland). Her pratice includes solo and collaborative pieces. She crafts silk visual artworks with her siblings, poet Matariki and composer Tihema, for the Auckland Pride Festival. She also works in the Costume Department for television series and film, and creates original book cover artwork inspired by traditional Māori art and patterns.

For *Dark Deeds Down Under*, Māhina's original design incorporates the endangered Kiwi, New Zealand's national bird, with several traditional patterns. The koru design running up the Kiwi's legs and through the centre of its body represents growth and community. The Mangopare (hammerhead) and Te Mako patterns signify strength and fighting spirit. The koiri pattern running from the Kiwi's head to its back represents self-reflection and nurturing.

ACKNOWLEDGEMENTS

Whenever you dive into a book that has one name on the cover, you're reading something that may have come from the mind of one person but has been helped along the way by a whole community. So this section is a chance to say 'thanks mate' to the publishing industry professionals, friends, family, teachers, mentors, research experts, and supporters of all kinds. And that's just with one name on the cover; you can imagine how expansive that support network gets with an anthology like *Dark Deeds Down Under*.

First up, it's thanks mate to the brilliant Lindy Cameron, publisher at Clan Destine Press who asked me to to be Commissioning Editor. What a gift.

Lindy is a tireless supporter of local storytellers and a fine crime writer herself. She is also a founding member and long-time National Co-Convenor of Sisters in Crime Australia. Over the past 30 years, Sisters in Crime has played a key role in the domestic and global growth and popularity of Australian crime writing.

A huge kia ora rawa atu (thanks heaps) to all the wonderful storytellers in this first volume of *Dark Deeds Down Under*. I'm a huge fan of Alan, Aoife, Dan and Lee, David, Dinuka, Fiona, Garry, Helen, Katherine, Lisa, Kerry, Narrelle, Nikki, Renée, Rob, Shane, Stephen, Sulari, and Vanda. I'm a huge fan of each of you.

Thanks all for delivering fantastic tales to kickstart this unique series. You rock.

Thank you to Seantelle and Māhina, brilliant young First Nations artists who've blessed us with beautiful artworks created especially for *Dark Deeds Down Under*.

Cheers mates to the wider Aussie and Kiwi writing communities who continue to inspire and make it super easy for this kid from Aotearoa to shout loudly all over the world, on page, stage, and airwaves, about the wonderful storytellers we have. A treasure trove.

The international crime and thriller writing community, a terrific tribe, has been so welcoming. Kia ora.

To the family, friends, and supporters of all our contributors, thank you.

My love of stories was started by my parents and stoked by librarians and teachers. Kia ora to Mrs Gately, Mr Joyce, Mrs Sivak, Mr Ledingham, Mrs Hall, and Mrs Clouston.

I read long ago that you can judge a man's worth by his friends. Thank you to all my amazing, crazy, cool mates spread across the world who've made my life infinitely better.

Finally, to my family. There aren't enough words to do you justice. Mum, Dad, and Claire, for loving me, challenging me, and supporting me through everything, over all my decades.

To Helen and Madi, the two girls who've changed my life in adulthood. Arohanui ahau ki a koe.

Lightning Source UK Ltd.
Milton Keynes UK
UKHW012152030722
405254UK00004B/291